NEVER FAR GONE

KELVIN URENA

Printed by Ingram Spark, Inc., in the United States of America.
First printing edition 2024.

Literary Elite LLC
2807 N. Parham Rd, Ste 320
Henrico, VA 23294
www.neverfargone.com

To my daughter, Ari, whom I would go to any
length to give a better life than any parent could
want for their most precious treasure.

CONTENTS

PROLOGUE

> **Control** (*noun*): "The power to influence or direct people's
> behavior or the course of events" (*Oxford Languages*)

"MOVE! MOVE!" I HEAR A distorted voice blaring over the radio as my hand ushers the men to move forward. With the inferno from various points throughout the outpost illuminating the night sky above, I have no trouble focusing on a familiar-looking building. My stomach turns as I recall meeting *him*, yet I don't let the thought cloud my judgment. We're here with one objective, and I'll be damned if anyone tries to stop us from achieving it.

"Let's get it done…" I whisper to *JB* as I chamber a round into the rifle I'm holding. With nearly 80 men at my disposal, some of whom were already well beyond the walls of the outpost, I stand and begin descending the hill, overlooking the chaos unfolding nearly a quarter mile in front of us. With the rain having made our approach effortless, I do my best not to slip on the muddy ground it has created.

"You heard the boss, form up!" I hear *JB* shout from behind me as a plethora of muffled footsteps emerges from the top of the hill. As we approach the gates of the compound, which are now merely piles of metal and rubble following the explosion, the sounds of gunfire serve to announce our arrival like a horn before battle. Men and women of all ages drop like flies as we collectively enter the foreign structure. I lift my rifle and aim at any person I recognize as being one of *his: Being a threat*. With little hesitation, I feel the trigger retracting with each swift pull.

Bang. Bang. Bang. Bang.

The smell of ash, gunpowder, and smoke fills the air, as does the distant gunfire from around the town, and my team begins to push towards the Admin Building. The closer we get, the clearer I see the dreadful floor-to-ceiling windows overlooking the front of the three-story structure. Approaching the rear of the building, I embrace the hardened rain falling all around me. The smell of wet grass in the distance comforts me as we come to an abrupt halt near the rear exit. As *Jawbreaker* and his squad of about half a dozen cut in front of me and prepare to breach, I give them a nod as I position the butt of the rifle against my shoulder.

"*One. Two. Go…*" I hear one of the *Thrivers* say before the pry bar is set between the door and the lock is blown off with little force. JB charges into the building while his squad closely follows suit as the bar falls to the ground with an audible *clink*, which is also muffled due to the puddles below our feet. My squad does the same as I enter the structure, checking each corner as we collectively clear each room. I hear multiple shots being fired throughout each floor as we slowly ascend the Admin Building.

"Two down…" Corver mutters over the radio before continuing his search. "Cells clear. Moving to the upper level," he says as the receiver in my ear dies down once he ceases communication. With the barrel of the rifle pointed ahead, I quickly peer around the doorway leading into the all-too-familiar room hosting the floor-to-ceiling windows and granite pillars. A disheveled-looking woman, wearing a sloppy bun that was undoubtedly put together in a hurry following the sudden attack on the outpost, glances towards the entrance to the room. Her face is filled with panic as she attempts to raise her shotgun in my direction. She doesn't get the chance before I put three rounds through her upper torso.

Bang. Bang. Bang.

Even in such an opulent room of this magnitude, the echo of gunfire indoors seems to radiate off the walls, creating a ringing in my ears that only increases my heart rate. While cautiously moving toward the assailant, I notice that the previously pristine marble floor - *still letting off a strong smell of bleach* - is now tainted with blood. As she struggles to catch her breath, no doubt from a punctured lung, one of the *Thrivers* behind me raises his rifle to the woman's forehead and pulls the trigger.

"One down in the Grand Office. Moving up..." I hear someone from my squad radio in. The proximity between their broadcast and mine causes a brief screeching in my ear that subsides almost instantly as we collectively turn to exit the room. I take one final glance at the single metal chair in the middle of the room, the one facing the Executive Desk now missing the ceremonial piece I had noticed during my previous visit, and clench my fist as I gaze forward and push ahead.

"*TID 001*, moving into position…" I whisper over the comms as we reach the Top Suite. I can hear multiple voices from behind the closed wooden door and look around as my squad, featuring half a dozen men and women, gives me separate nods to indicate they are ready for what's next. As Luca Silvio crouches beside the door and places a small mirror underneath to better assess how many threats are within the room, he takes a few seconds before bringing up his other hand and throwing up four fingers.

Four hostiles, check.

"*Tall, white man. Mid-to-late forties. Fresh cut and a suit. Sound like your man, Miles?*" Luca whispers as his gaze reverts to me. I crouch down on the other side of the door and give him a slight nod of affirmation.

"*Yeah, that sounds about right…*" I whisper back as I glance over to the rest of the squad. I nod to the woman farthest away, and she gives me a thumbs up as she turns to call in the discovery.

"*TID 042. We've got four Ravelers in the Upper Suite of the Admin Building. Target identified. How copy? Over.*" I hear over the earpiece. It doesn't take long to get a response.

"TID 004. We've regrouped with Delta and are positioned at the other entrance. Awaiting orders…" I hear Corver say in a low tone over the radio. I partially retract the rifle's charging handle to ensure it is loaded before releasing my grip and positioning it towards the door as I stand on my feet. I reach for the bronze knob on the door and twist it slowly to see if the room is unlocked: *it is.*

"Breaching in Three. Two. One. Mark…" I say over the comms as the door flies open with enough force to startle everyone in the room. Without much delay, I can see *JB* and Corver burst into the room with their respective squads. They barge in with as much ferocity as I would expect from some of our most well-trained allies. The gunfire is deafening, yet nearly all of the armed combatants in the room are put down with little effort. The man in the suit makes a break for one of the windows before hurdling his entire body at it. The sound of shattering glass fills the air as my rifle lets out a round in his direction.

Bang.

I hear a low-pitched grunt as the round pierces what I can only assume is his cheek. As the group around me moves in on the three incapacitated assailants strewn throughout the room, I rush over to the shattered window and position my rifle out of it and towards the ground floor, careful not to let the broken glass cut my arms in the process. I expected to see his corpse plastered along the concrete, yet what I see is a car door being shut as a convoy of about three SUVs steps on the gas once the injured man is dragged inside. I flip the rifle to *Auto* as I let out an exhale and hold my breath before squeezing the trigger. It doesn't take long before the magazine in the gun runs dry.

The awkward stance, as well as the speed of the vehicles, makes it nearly impossible to aim at any of the drivers below, so the best I can do is pull back as the convoy peels away through the front gates. They steer right past a sizable horde of *Spectrals* sprinting into the outpost. *Their horrid groans are echoing throughout the streets of the town.* All I can do is watch helplessly as I realize this mission is a partial failure.

Fuck…

"Yo, Miles, looks like Silvio missed this one," I hear *JB* yell out humorously as he points toward one of the injured men on the ground. *JB's* goatee is still covered with a light coat of ash from the explosion outside. With his rifle slung over his back, Luca extends his arms to his side as he takes a few steps forward.

"No, see, I don't miss…" Luca says with a slight sense of hubris. His buzzcut seems to fit perfectly with his military background, as do his impeccable results from our Marksmanship Training over the past couple of months. He stops on the other side of the injured *Raveler,* who is letting out a few pain-ridden moans while attempting to sit upright before continuing to address my close associate. "I only fire at those who pose a *threat*, and he was unarmed," Luca admits as he places his boot on the shoulder of the man on the ground. The bullet wound projecting from the same shoulder Luca is applying pressure on causes the man to let out a shout of agony instinctively.

"Enough! Step back…" I order as I drop the empty rifle on the ground and slowly walk towards the trio. Luca and *JB* both take a few paces backward as I come to a halt over the *Raveler* before me and tower over him. I grab a handful of his hair and forcefully prop him against the bullet-ridden brown sofa sitting alongside the wall of the suite. His yelling and pleas for help are pointless, and they only serve to agitate me further, so I bring my fist down onto his nose. With the blood flowing from it, I can only assume that it is broken, yet his screaming seems to subside as his upper body is forcefully thrown against the front of the sofa. "Where is Damien going?" I ask with little patience.

"W- why don't you go ask h- him? Looks like you just- just missed him th- though…" the man lets out in between breaths. His grunting makes it evident that he is in pain, yet he's trying to conceal that fact by raising his head and acting resilient. His futile acts of courage, mixed with my lack of patience given Damien's escape, drive me over the edge. I pull the Kimber 1911 from its holster and align the iron sights with the man's left thigh before pulling the trigger. His bloodcurdling screams are short-lived once I kneel and wrap my hand around his throat before proceeding to talk.

"*Where. Is. He. Going?*" I whisper into the man's ear in a tone that exhibits both anger and indifference. I place the smoking barrel of the .45 caliber handgun against his right thigh as I pause and wait for an answer.

"Ugh… I- I- don't-" he says before a subsequent round pierces his right thigh. The spatter of blood covers my dark olive plate carrier like a child wielding a paintbrush at a blank canvas. As his mouth opens to let out another scream, I place the 5-inch barrel into it before smacking the side of his face to regain his attention. The incessant radio chatter from the other squads throughout the outpost causes me to abruptly yank the small receiver from my ear and refocus on the task at hand.

"Look at me. The third time's a charm, *right?* Because there will *not* be a fourth…" I say as the man begins to faze in and out of consciousness. "Look at *me!*" I bark out in a monotone voice after smacking him a little harder. The adrenaline rushing through his body seems to cause him to jolt back to reality as if he were hit with a defibrillator.

"I- I don't know! I don't know!" the man says as my eyes bore into him. The fear radiating from beyond his pupils tells me he's most likely telling the truth - *I mean, what else does he have to lose, right?* - so I remain crouched in front of him for a little while longer before retracting the barrel from his mouth and standing up. I let out a sigh of disappointment as *JB* takes a step forward to address me.

"Boss, we've got reports of *Specs* heading towards the Admin Building. We need to leave-" Corver says before stopping his suggestion in its tracks as I stare at him with malice. He refrains from talking further and uses the silence - *apart from the inaudible radio traffic, distant gunfire, and frequent screams* - to retract his advance. I look up at the ceiling before shaking my head slightly at the sheer thought of losing the one person I had come all this way for.

"All of *this*…" I say as I circle my pointing finger in the air. "And for what? Y'know, I was just thinking that this night would go down as one of my biggest failures. Yet, come to think of it, my men and I just achieved our greatest success… We got to rid the world of your *twisted* and *demented* tribe of savages," I say as I begin to kneel down in front of the bleeding man.

"You're m- men? You… You're him. Y- you're Miles Gether…" the man lets out as his breathing slows due to the excessive blood loss. His hands effortlessly fall to the ground below as his weakened state worsens with every passing second. His words seem to resonate with me, even as I grab his chin and force his drooping head upright to look at me.

"And you want to know how I got that name to spread like wildfire? It's because I…" I say before placing the barrel of my handgun against the side of his head, "I am one of the few who does what everyone else is unwilling to do." I hear some of my guys closing in from behind me while others make their way toward the exit for our departure. The man holds up his palm to my chest in an attempt to push me away from him. *To no avail.*

"W- wait…" the man mumbles with difficulty.

"Tonight is no exception," I say before standing and bringing the gun up to the upper portion of the man's head. He musters every ounce of energy in his being to bring his palm in front of his face as much as possible.

"Wait!" the man shouts as best as he can before a round being fired rips through the cold air above.

Bang.

PART ONE

THE RISE

CHAPTER 1

INSIGHT

One year earlier

"WAIT! NO RUNNING IN THE hallway!" I holler out as students of varying ages flood the halls. It's dismissal time. Arguably, it is the most crucial time of the day for any student looking to catch a break from their incredibly mundane courses.

There's some difficulty in choosing a career outside of the Armed Forces, no matter what you may have planned before your contract expires. Maybe that's why some reenlist? I wouldn't know because that was the *last* thing I would do after Pendleton. I couldn't have done so if I wanted to since it was a medical separation. I don't have much time to ponder the thought of a pair of sixth graders in a physical altercation in the lobby.

As a 36-year-old, 6'1", half-Hispanic, half-White male who's only been out of the military for two months, I am already employed at one of the most dangerous jobs in the civilian workforce: *an elementary school security guard in the Bronx.* I walk towards the students in a deliberate, militaristic stroll that can only be described as *dramatic* to separate the two from each other. A small crowd of about 20 sixth graders surround the duo, instigating the fight to continue.

"Alright, kiddos, that's enough!" I say as I slightly squat in between them due to their shorter height. Both of the students are Hispanic; I can tell from the Spanish profanities being thrown around at one another as the argument seems to get increasingly heated with every word that fills the air. However, one is about 4" taller than his "opponent," *if you will*. I have a slightly bigger-than-average body figure due to the consistent physical training engraved into my lifestyle. While it's nothing to brag about at Thanksgiving dinner, I have discovered that most of the students fear that. "Alright, I won't ask what it's about, but unless you want your parents in, this fight ends now. And they *will win*. Trust me," I say as the crowd quickly disperses in different directions around the school's first floor.

One kid, who looks like he's been recording the altercation on his severely outdated smartphone, seems to practically fall onto the slowly growing pile of slush and light snow outside as he sprints away from the crime scene through the blue double doors at the front entrance.

Yeah… that's what I thought.

The two kids I dealt with are going their separate ways, though the disheveled murmuring under their breaths as they walk away is still audible to me, even as their distance increases.

The job's not *that bad,* though. Bullshit pay and benefits aside, it's something I don't mind. I enjoy the hours away from home. That's why I chose the longer hours. I can't stand to be home for too long at a time. With no kids and no wife - or even a pet fish - one can only imagine how mundane a life in isolation can become. The kids at school aren't too bad to deal with, either. Walking the building, especially during the opening shift, keeps my mind busy and alert. Being alert of your surroundings is one of my most valued skills, courtesy of the United States Military.

The school has five stories and is just a quarter mile from the Jerome Park Reservoir. The colossal structure is surrounded by other schools in its direct vicinity, as well as many residential buildings and the occasional townhouse. Yet, it's also not too far from the infamous Kingsbridge Station of the Metro Transit System, nearly two blocks away from the rear of the building. Any true New Yorker can tell you how *lovely* the MTA Trains can be, with the excessive homelessness, seemingly illegal MetroCard fares, and inability to clean trains or stations thoroughly.

That is precisely why I drive…

The first floor is accessed through one of the five entrances surrounding the building, some designed for safety while the others merely make the students' dismissal less chaotic. The front entrance has two blue metal doors that lead into this small corridor, which can best be described as a 15-square-foot foyer. Only when passing the next set of wooden double doors will you be greeted by the front lobby, followed by the most handsome security guard in the borough.

The first floor also hosts the cafeteria for the children on the east and the auditorium, filled with a few hundred brown extendable chairs, bolted onto the poorly painted dark blue floor on the west. The auditorium's stage, surrounded by a 30-foot musky drape that hasn't been washed since the school was built, can only be described as impressive, given its size.

The second floor is easily accessible via the two extremely conspicuous flights of stairs in the school's lobby and the other stairwells throughout the building. One with the slightest notion of common sense would understand that one flight of stairs - *the right* - is meant for ascension to the second floor, while the other staircase is for those descending back into the lobby.

Ironically enough, it's usually the parents who come to pick up their "sick" children from the Principal's office on the second floor that would get this simple notion twisted.

There is also a sizable library on the west side of the second floor. That's my favorite place in the building to check in the morning, considering it smells like a newly renovated bookstore. It's usually quiet throughout the day, even with the substantial number of elementary school students inconsiderably speaking above the noise level for such an environment.

The third floor consists of the typical classrooms one would expect to see in an elementary school, yet between the second and third floors sits a 1,200-square-foot gymnasium engulfed by a light, oak wood floor that seems to get shinier as each day progresses.

Hats off to the janitor, Ramon. What a great guy…

The fourth and fifth floors are also filled with classrooms, but the latter has a smaller gym, probably around 500 square feet, on the east wing of the building. The gym has a mahogany wood floor with the same amount of gloss as its predecessor. Both gyms feature a small equipment room, separated from the rest of the gym by a dark brown 1950s-style door with a padlock. The closet contains all the equipment and toys the students use throughout their gym periods.

The padlock was my idea, as equipment always went missing from the gyms seemingly overnight.

The most important thing to remember about this building is that the elevator connecting all floors is located at the back of the cafeteria on the east side of the school. I volunteered for longer shifts, and that includes the After-school Program that the school offered to parents who were working later shifts and couldn't pick up their children until eighteen hundred hours - that's 6 PM for those who can't read Military Time - which is when we begin closing shop.

Once the last student is picked up and all of the faculty leaves, I do my final sweep of the building for squatters before closing the place myself. Or, at the very least, that *was* the plan until the State of Emergency was levied on the City of New York.

"Gether, the Governor called it in your county, too," is what I hear from one of the only other security guards working the shift with me—a short Honduran fellow named Armando Flores. We all call each other by our last names, which I had already become accustomed to in the service.

"You live near Scarsdale, no?" Armando asks me as I approach the muted TV mounted a few feet over the foyer in the lobby. The question is passed down to me in that all too familiar Hispanic accent that only seems to be infused with the indistinguishable accent of a native New Yorker.

"Yeah, did they say *why* yet?" I asked, slightly unconcerned yet still annoyed at the possibility of driving in the snow on my way home. With a heavy foot, the mere thought of tolerating the cars piling up along the highway makes me nauseous. As the hasty foot traffic around me continues to sway in and out of the building, I continuously glance towards the main entrance whenever a parent or guardian barges in to pick up their child from the Afterschool Program. The time is 5:33 PM.

"Uh, no, not yet," he says while glued to the TV. After a brief moment of staring at Armando, trying to read his facial expression, I can see his eyes constantly diverting away from the TV when a creak from the wooden doors leading into the foyer fills the air.

Good to see he's doing his job.

As my eyes scan the room, I notice something I have never seen before: *faculty scurrying home early;* it's not the *"It's Friday, and I wanna get home to my leftover Chicken Alfredo and watch porn all night"* scurrying. A noticeable concern is on their faces as they pass the double doors into the now dark and slightly windy winter night. Then there's the *parents*. The group of remaining children begins to diminish as their respective parents pick them up; some carry their children as they brush past anyone in their way. When it comes to the moderately crumpled paper in front of me on the security desk that reads *"**Sign-Out Sheet**"* in bold font and all caps, most of the adults are putting little to no effort into their signatures. Others, especially those who arrived closer to the 6 o'clock mark, ignore the sheet altogether, not even pausing to acknowledge us or the questions coming from their children.

"Take over the desk. I'll be right back," I mumble to Flores as I begin stumbling up the staircase in the lobby towards the Principal's office to get confirmation as to our next steps following the State of Emergency, almost tripping in the process of going upwards. I'm assuming the snowstorm coming to the area is directly responsible for the declaration, as New York is notorious for closing their schools for even the most minuscule snowfall.

Now, I own a cabin just West of Millinocket Lake in Maine for unrelated reasons, yet with this pivotal piece of information, it should be made clear that I am *no stranger* to cold weather. So, calling a State of Emergency due to light snow - *which is said to not be more than five inches of snow by morning* - is nothing more than an eye-roller for me. I make it up to the office to see the school principal; the poor bastard goes by Principal Lofter. A*nd here you are, thinking my name is messed up.* He's bundled up lightly but hurrying as if in a rush like everyone else.

"Mr. Gether, I need you to do me a favor…" the old man, who seems to be in his mid-to-late 50s, says out of breath. All I know about the man is that he's from one of the southern states, which is why he has difficulty pronouncing my last name, yet I never over-think it since he seems like the type to hate being corrected.

"Yes, sir," I say, slightly out of breath from skipping steps on the staircase in the lobby.

"I need you to stay in the school if you can, just to see how bad things get by the morning. Ramon left midday without saying a *goddamn* word…" Mr. Lofter says as he extends his slightly shriveled, tanned right hand towards me while using his left to cover his mouth as he begins to cough. I can smell the alcohol from here, albeit faintly. "Nevertheless…" he continues, seemingly annoyed, "We can't rely on him assisting us tomorrow if things get terrible here. The young lad lives in Brooklyn. I can leave you the keys to my office, and you can rest here if need be. I'll pay you overtime as well, of course. I really need you, sport," he says, with his last sentence sounding more like a question than a statement.

"Sure thing, boss, but what about Armando? And do you have any idea what the staff and parents are so shaken up about-" I manage to get out before my last question is rudely cut off by the old man standing before me.

"Son, Armando can go home. He's been working with us lon-ger, yet somehow, I trust you more…" he admits as his disgruntled laugh causes the smell of alcohol to be more present in my vicinity than before. As he pushes away from his wooden desk and begins to stand from his seemingly comfortable rolling chair, he glances at me sincerely before placing a hand on my shoulder and continuing to speak. "This place won't stand without you," he says as his hand slides off of my shoulder and grabs the handle of his ancient-looking satchel.

"I- I can do that, sir. Thank you," I whisper as my tone transitions to concern rather than appreciation for the opportunity to work overtime. He gives me a nod of approval before breaking his gaze and ushering past me. He grabs his windbreaker from the coat rack near the office entrance before storming out of the room as quickly as I had entered.

Great...

As the sounds associated with a chaotic dismissal - *kids hollering, parents scolding, teachers instructing, and so forth* - seem to evaporate in nearly an hour, I find myself standing alone in the desolate building I was hired to protect. Typically, such isolation would console me, yet I can't help but feel a sense of dread looming over me as the various sounds of sirens and honking from around the neighborhood fill the air. With each minute that passes, that dread only seems to worsen. As I scan each floor and find that each classroom is visually cleared, the commotion from outside the walls seems to elevate as time progresses, turning my dread into paranoia.

I can't do this...

The thought of remaining in the dark about what is going on beyond these walls is almost too much to bear. I'd compare the feeling to being ten times worse than a sudden cliffhanger in a TV show, yet I don't think that would do it enough justice. With my uniform still on, I descend the West Stairwell until I reach the first floor of the building. One by one, I verify that each exit is locked before going to the security desk and grabbing my beige jacket and black book bag.

The bag is quite heavy, yet I barely acknowledge the weight as it is flung over my jacket with ease. With the keys in hand that Principal Lofter had given me before his departure, I make my way out of the East Exit before locking the door behind me and heading for my truck in the rear courtyard.

Damn, it's freezing out here…

With each exhale I take, revealing itself in a white cloud that can only be done in the cold, I put my hands in my pockets as I approach the newly released 2014 Toyota Tundra I spent every penny in my savings account to finance. Given my frequent commutes up North, it seemed more like a necessity than a desire. The snow falling on the ground around me only defends my argument. I unlock the black truck, its factory paint still radiating in the night sky as specks of snowflakes accumulate on the hood, and practically throw myself into the driver's seat as the vehicle roars to life. With my bag being swung onto the passenger seat, I crank the heat up before giving the truck a few moments to warm up.

As the frost on the windshield begins to dissipate, I can't help but notice how vulnerable I feel given the lack of information I am met with. Even as I flip through the various radio stations, I see no mention of a State of Emergency. Not once. After a few minutes of trying and failing to scour any news outlet for something that could help me better understand what is happening, I glance up and notice a few people running in the same direction on the street. Even with a couple of inches of snow on the ground, there is little in the way to stop those people from running towards, or *away*, from something that only they can see. Even after a moment of hesitation, I have enough of a reason to justify my desertion. Next stop: *Home*.

* * *

With the windshield wipers on full blast, it is surprising that the roads are emptier than I had expected. A few cars are passing me on the opposite lane of the Bronx River Parkway at a speed that is undoubtedly faster than the limit, but the lack of visibility ahead makes that fact irrelevant in my mind. Instead, I attempt to focus on not hitting anything, *or anyone*, directly in front of me. Even with a truck well-suited for this type of weather, the sporadic and unpredictable behavior of the drivers around me makes it all the more difficult to stay in my lane. I guess the size of the Tundra isn't enough to deter an older compact car from cutting me off so they don't miss their exit.

Dude… watch it!

As I pull off the Parkway and approach a smaller two-lane road leading toward my house, I'm met with the sight of the pavement that has not yet been cleared of snow, causing the truck tires to spin slightly as I turn onto the narrow street. With only one lane for oncoming traffic, I do my best to stay in my lane, given that there are little to no visible markings on the ground. As I begin to close the distance between myself and the house, *which is a few more miles north*, the ever-worsening glow of high beams from the oncoming lane seems to disorient me as a vehicle approaches.

What the hell is-

As the vehicle approaches my position, I slow down to around 30 mph before being met with a sight that serves as every driver's worst nightmare: *a head-on collision.* In a panicked yet slightly collected manner, I softly tap on the brake as I turn the vehicle to the left to bypass the approaching vehicle. Within milliseconds, I can tell that the other driver is going nearly double my speed. As I turn the truck away from the crimson sedan, I slam on the brakes once the other driver flies past me and runs into a metal railing. The sound makes me wince as the impact seems fatal from the start. That hypothesis only seems more credible as the truck rolls over twice before forcefully throwing itself upright on its wheels violently.

I- I can't… what the fu- oh my god… wha-

With both hands on the steering wheel, I can hear my heart beating out of my chest, even over the small amounts of static protruding from the radio. My breaths start to slow, yet my composure is short-lived once I pull myself together. After a moment of recovery, I finally realize the gravity of my situation. Turning in my seat to face the SUV nearly 50 yards behind me, I can see little to no commotion from within the vehicle. I sit upright and turn the steering wheel in the direction of the crash site as best as I can, and the truck begins to slowly advance towards what I only assumed to be the start of a very long night.

As I hastily park the truck about 20 feet behind the sedan, I contemplate whether I should run out to help or call the authorities. The thumping in my skull isn't helping me to decide on the matter, so I fumble for the door handle to my truck. As my quivering hand makes contact with the handle, I find myself instinctively jolting as the driver's door to the SUV in front of me creaks open. After a moment of silence, *apart from the rumbling of my truck and the steam radiating from the front of the crashed vehicle*, a younger woman, probably no older than 30, falls to the wet ground in agony as a bone protrudes from her elbow. The white spattered around the floor is tainted with a dark red as blood seeps from her wounds. Anyone can tell that the pain she's feeling is immeasurable, yet there isn't so much as a grunt from the woman to show for it. I open the door and grab the overhead handlebar to prop my upper body over the open door.

"Are you alright, miss?" I holler over the sounds of a ferocious flurry effortlessly making its way through the neighborhood. There is a cold that follows suit, and it's enough to make all of the hairs on my body stand up. The thought of asking a question I already know the answer to makes me feel like I am wasting my breath. She doesn't respond. Without much hesitation, I sit back down and begin scrambling through the center console to find my phone as the blinding LED headlights place the now motionless woman in the center of attention as if she were the key actress in a play.

I need to call the police…

As I struggle to dial 911 and put the phone on speaker, the sound of a busy line fills the air. As an MP during my time in the military, we worked closely with local law enforcement for domestic issues and the like; even then, I have *never* experienced a busy line when it came to emergency services. I bring the phone to my ear as I redial, only to be met with temporary paralysis as the injured woman nearly two dozen feet in front of me begins to stand. Her rise from the ground is calm and nonchalant, as if she had tripped while going up the stairs. Even though I'm not the one who sustained the injuries, I know that is *impossible* given her current state. No amount of adrenaline in the world could conceal the pain that she must feel as she rises onto her feet with ease.

How the fuck-

Before I can say or do anything, something I wasn't anticipating happens: she begins running toward me. The phone I am carrying in my left-hand slips from my grasp and onto the snow below, yet I pay it no mind as I pull the driver-side door shut just as the woman throws herself against the driver-side of my truck. She must be around 5'6," yet the Tundra vibrates like she has been playing offense for the Giants. Out of instinct, I reach into the book bag on the passenger seat before fumbling for the Glock 26 inside. As I chamber a round, I aim the small handgun at the window and towards the woman.

"I'm armed! Stop!" I shout as my attempts to de-escalate the situation prove pointless. As the streetlights highlight every feature of the woman before me, I can see that her face is covered in blood and lacerations. The crash is worse than I thought, yet here is a woman with more energy than I could ever hope to possess, even on my best days. She hurls a fist at the window that seems to crack it, a feat that would prove challenging even for someone with my build, and I reposition my aim with both hands. They're shaking, yet I hold my ground. "I said stop!" I holler, but to no avail. One second passes. Then three. After a while, I inevitably lose count. I am brought back to my senses once two rounds are fired as small pieces of glass simultaneously fill the cabin of the truck.

My heart is probably ready to pierce my chest from how fast it is beating, and my ears begin to ring as the woman falls back to the ground below. A small pool of blood starts to gather around her body, and the dark substance begins to expel from the two bullet wounds covering her chest and neck. The smoke radiating from the barrel of the handgun makes me nauseous, and I throw the door open before jumping onto the ground and running a few paces away from the truck. I hurl myself onto a small pile of snow as I begin to puke.

Wha- what did I do?

I take a few deep breaths before slowly glancing at the motionless woman a few feet to my right. The pool around her has doubled in radius since I saw her moments ago. The gurgling sounds she is making seem only to heighten my paranoia. I peer up and down the road, secretly awaiting a passerby to assist, but this road looks as deserted as one would expect, given the weather. The same thing goes for the neighbors. Not a single person in sight. Doing my best to remain calm, I keep my head high before walking over to the phone on the ground and redialing 911. As my finger hovers above the *Call button*, I find myself battling with my own thoughts regarding whether I am about to do the right thing.

Of course, I am doing the moral thing, right? Will they even answer? But what if the neighbors saw me? I can't just leave this girl here... right?

Amid all the chaos, I let my instincts take the wheel, *literally*, as I throw my phone into the truck and climb back into the driver seat before placing the car in *Drive*. Every ounce of being in my body is telling me to get out of there. With my foot still on the brake, I glance at the woman one more time, who's presumably struggling to breathe due to the blood in her lungs, before pushing down on the pedal and leaving her behind to face the unforgiving winter storm, *dying and alone*.

As I pull into my driveway, I park the truck and stare down at the handgun leaning against the center console before slamming my palms down on the top of the steering wheel in anger. I let out a scream that seems to radiate off the walls of the truck cabin and through the broken window to my left. Words aren't enough to emphasize what I am feeling: *Anger. Shame. Regret.* We were trained to be courageous and uphold a certain level of honor, so what the *fuck* was that?

The sound of a door slamming shut behind me brings me back to reality as I quickly glance at my rearview mirror to see my neighbors ushering their two younger kids, the twins Melanie and Deborah, both around ten years old, into their older Volvo. The Gleeson Family has always been good to me since I moved in before joining the service, so I feel obligated to check on them to see if they need my help. If they need me. I can't tell if it is out of selflessness or an attempt to right my recent indiscretions. Either way, I open the door to the truck and holler out to the family as my feet touch the ground below.

"Mr. Gleeson, are you guys alright?" I ask while slowly approaching him and his wife. As the two girls are quickly placed into the backseat, their father hastily slams the door shut and rushes to close the trunk, which contains countless items and perishables, before addressing me. As I cross the short pavement separating my house from theirs and slowly approach their vehicle, Mrs. Gleeson scurries around the front of the car and into the passenger seat.

"Ah, Mr. Gether... N- now's not a good time, y'see? I'll chat with you soon, my dear boy..." the older man says as he fumbles for the door handle. Due to his age, 74, as of last month, if I remember correctly, I took half a step forward to help him get into his vehicle, only to be met with verbal resistance that I would've never expected given our cordial relationship. "N- No, don't touch me! Don't touch me!" he shouts as I retract my arm and take a step back.

"I'm sorry, I... I only wanted to help-" I say before Mr. Gleeson lifts a finger to cut me off. He points at me as if his finger alone would deter me from taking another step before beginning to speak.

His cheeks are red from the cold, and I can see his breath as his words fill the air.

"If you know any better, you'll leave New York… Right now. Do you understand me, my dear boy?" he whispers before turning and ducking his head as he lowers himself into his car and slowly closes the door behind him. The thud of the closing door, albeit weak given his age, makes me shutter as I attempt to ponder what he just told me.

Without much thought, the Volvo's reverse lights reflect off my truck's rear bumper across the street, which soon dissipates once the vehicle pulls forward and out of view. One minute, the Gleeson Family was one of the only comforts in the entire neighborhood, the people I could look forward to seeing every time I walked outside. The next, they're gone, and I have a feeling I won't be seeing them again.

As I push against the front door to the house once it's unlocked, I leave it open as I rush to my bedroom and fling open the closet to reveal a safe I had bolted to the floor. Whether due to the hastiness of the situation or the stress, I cannot tell; I enter the code wrong a few times before finally managing to get the safe open. With the door retracted, I pull out a Kimber 1911 I had purchased before the company relocated from New York. It is a Custom TLE/RL II, otherwise known as their Tactical Law Enforcement model, which features a threaded barrel, skeletonized hammer, Picatinny rail, and a few 8-round magazines from Wilson Combat designed to host .45 ACP Rounds. It's truly a magnificent firearm and one that has proven to be incredibly reliable over the years.

Alright, alright, here we go…

I stand up and pull down a black duffle bag lying on top of the closet before placing it at my feet and kneeling back down as I open it. I put a few sets of clothing into the bag before stowing the Kimber, a few boxes of .45 ACP ammunition, the magazines accompanying the firearm, two boxes of 9mm Hollow Points, and my 4-inch Smith and Wesson 686. After grabbing a few .357 rounds from a half-empty box in the safe, I load the cylinder with all six rounds before shutting it and placing it alongside the Kimber before zipping up the duffle bag.

I leave a spare handgun in the safe before grabbing the all-black 6-inch Benchmade that I had carried with me during my time in the service. I never brought it with me on duty since we weren't allowed to take any gear that wasn't explicitly issued to us, yet it was always nearby. As I place its sheathe behind my belt, I stand and hurl the duffle over my shoulder as I make my way to the car. I guess Mr. Gleeson was right: I can't stay here after everything that happened tonight. I need to disappear, and what better place to do so than Maine?

* * *

As regret courses throughout my veins, I make what is arguably the dumbest decision I can before my departure; I begin driving toward the scene of the crime. As the LED headlights pave the way for the Tundra on the road, I expect to see half a dozen police cars waiting to greet me as I pull back on that fateful road, with their flashing lights illuminating every crevice in the area. Maybe an onlooker or two who would at least attempt to resuscitate the helpless woman. When I approach the crash site, though, it is as if I hadn't left the scene to begin with.

No passerby. No cops. Not even a set of fresh tire tracks in the snow. What the hell?

That startles me more than the thought of getting arrested for leaving the crime scene, yet that seems to be overwritten when I notice it: *The woman is gone.* There is a thick blood trail leading from the pool that had grown around her fallen body and towards the cul-de-sac near where the crashed sedan is still faintly rumbling as it was nearly an hour prior. All I can do is stare.

"*I can't run…*" I whisper to myself as my breaths can be seen in the cold air with each exhale. The thought of this woman telling the world about what had happened is too much to bear. Even with the heat on full blast and my hands on the steering wheel, I can't bring myself to peel away. If something was going to happen, I would face the repercussions. It takes a while to get my mind back on track, but I know what I have to do.

Without so much as another thought, I slowly put the truck back into *Drive* and veer off of that fateful road. If I'm going to wait for what darkness lies ahead for me in my life, I'm going to do it in a place I feel comfortable. I am going back to school.

* * *

As I enter the back of the cafeteria from the rear courtyard, I hastily shut the door behind me as the cold air is instantaneously cut off. At last, I have some *genuine* warmth. Although it should be comforting, the gravity of the situation makes my heartfelt appreciation for the heat short-lived. As I glance up at the stairwell near the elevator, I reach out towards the railing and ascend toward the second floor.

I make my way through the doors separating the rear-east stairwell and the second floor before being met with darkness that fills the halls. Even though I am used to the morning shift, I don't think anyone can get over how eerie this building is when drenched in such an everlasting gloom. With my duffle bag slung and my hand resting along the grip of the Kimber sitting idly in its holster, I take small steps as I approach the library. The smell of books becomes more present the closer I get to the room.

Pulling open one of the doors leading inside the room I had once considered my haven, I peer around to ensure the room is clear. Seeing as though I am one of the few with a set of keys and the fact that I had personally walked the building before my departure a few hours ago, I know I am being paranoid, yet it keeps my mind off of the more pressing matter at hand. I place the bag on one of the tables and put both hands on my head as I peer out of the large, gated window facing the seemingly endless stream of flashing red and blue lights.

What have I done?

CHAPTER 2

TIME IS UP

I can't stop pacing around… I can't believe I did that. What am I doing? Did I just kill that woman?

I KEEP STARING AT THE getaway bag, wondering if I should use it in the way it was intended. A part of me wants to, yet I can't get rid of the guilt. I find myself shaking as I begin jotting down the incident on the piece of paper labeled "Daily Activity Report," which is meant for security guards like myself to record any discrepancies we see throughout our shifts. I don't even recognize my handwriting anymore.

The commotion outside, the cars, the people running to get ahead of the snowstorm, and the sirens are making me more anxious than I have ever felt. I finish the letter with the legibility of the elementary kids I see daily and leave it on the main desk of the library.

I need to sit down…

Head in hand, I can't devise a good enough alibi to tell the authorities when they arrive. Was it self-defense? I can hear knocking on the front entrance of the building, yet I don't dare to answer it. With all the sirens illuminating all the apartment buildings outside of the ceiling and high gated windows in the library, I do not doubt in my mind those sirens are for me.

How did they catch on to me so quickly? With the lights off, maybe they'll leave me with a few more minutes to clear my head before I have the balls to speak with 'em?

I can feel my legs quiver slightly as I extend my right hand toward the table next to me and begin to stand up. If I am going to face this like a man, I have to be unarmed and accept the consequences of my actions. I take the Kimber from my holster and proceed to eject the magazine and throw it into the black Faraday bag I have propped upright on the table, then empty the chamber by racking the slide to the rear. Still shaking slightly, I surprise myself by being able to catch the ejected round with my hand before putting it in my pocket. With a slight hesitation, I take off the holster and put the weapon on the table, then proceed to walk downstairs and towards the main foyer.

I can't hear myself think. I think I am going to throw up.

I am not regretful about what I did. I was just protecting myself and took every step to de-escalate the situation. I am petrified of what the consequences of my actions will look like because of *how* I handled it, and every step I take down the staircase in the lobby and towards the front entrance makes that more apparent to me. I don't even make it to the door of the foyer before I have to rush to the garbage can near the front desk for another puking session, with the taste of the previous one still fresh on my tastebuds. Although I felt like shit, this allows me to glance at the authorities standing outside of the school's main entrance. Yet it wasn't the authorities nor emergency services like I initially anticipated due to all the sirens.

What the fuck...

It is a woman and a child. I recognize them, too. The kid goes to school here, and the woman is always the last one to pick up her son due to "the trains running late."

The trains are bad but not THAT bad!

She seems to be shaking while she glances through one of the windows on the side of the main doors. One of her Christmas-themed mittens begins frantically shaking in the air as she notices me. Her incessant knocking transitions into a seemingly endless banging filled with desperation.

"Hey! Excuse me! Sir? We need to get out of the street..." she says as her volume increases. To my surprise, I make it to the foyer doors without puking again but I freeze as my hands touch the cold wood, which I can undoubtedly attribute to the freezing weather nearly three feet away.

The authorities will be coming any minute, right? I don't want this woman and her son to see that. I don't want news of tonight getting out to more people than it needs to.

With some hesitation and overwhelming regret, I slowly back off the doors without revealing myself in the windows again; my hands begin to slowly come back to my sides with each step back that I take. I can't bear the thought of leaving a family in desperation, especially on top of the remorse I already feel after what happened in Scarsdale. I turn around and nearly bump into one of the two doors that lead into the first-floor hallway before I hurry my way through without looking back, her pleas of desperation fading as the door slowly shuts without so much as a creak.

She'll be fine... They'll be alright... This just isn't the night.

For the second time in less than ten minutes, my head is in my hands as I convince myself I am the worst human being in the city. As I make my way toward one of the stairways to head back to the library on the second floor, I hear thuds coming from behind the cafeteria. They aren't excessive and hasty but rather slow and methodical.

This can't be the same person. There's no way she made it to behind the school that fast, let alone with a child. I even locked the parking lot, so how the hell...

The concern I felt a moment ago transpires into slight aggravation. I take advantage of the siren lights seeping in through the gated windows along the front of the building to traverse the hallway and head toward the cafeteria. Since there are smaller window panes within the six wooden doors that make up the lunchroom's entrance, there is less light inside than there is in the main hallway, but I am still able to make up the silhouette of the room. On the wall of the cafeteria lies a magnetic flashlight that I stored on top of a vending machine that I can barely make out in the near pitch-black darkness. The flashlight, which emits a slightly annoying hum when it's running, was placed on top of the vending machine near the middle of the cafeteria to deter the kids from taking it for *shits n' giggles* in the event of a blackout.

I kinda thought one of the little ones would've found this up here already - guess things are kind of working out.

Once I get the flashlight off the vending machine and wipe the dust off my fingers, I use the illumination coming from the bright LED bulbs to quickly deal with the person trespassing on the premises. *Let's be honest, though: am I really one to be concerned with breaking the law right now?* As I simultaneously open the door to exit and step one foot outside, the blue metal door slams on my forehead with incredible force, as if the person is throwing themselves at it. They must also be oblivious to the fact that the door is *one-way*, as the exit is missing door handles from the outside. I only get a good look at who is standing outside once I manage to get the light up with my right hand as I use my left to rub my semi-large and potentially swollen forehead.

Cmon man, what the… fuck…

Once the light reaches their eyes, I'm not even able to back up before I find myself being nearly tackled by the person who caused my head so much pain. Although the pain from the front of my head seems to dissipate almost instantly, it is replaced with a sharp sensation I feel when the man pushes me against the wall near the staircase, only about two feet away from the exit. Instinctively, I use the light to hit him in the head hard, knocking him over but not down. *With this thing weighing a ton and seeing what I would only assume to be blood on the end of the light diminishing its illumination, I can't even tell whose head hurts more now.* It is only now I get a better look at who is kneeling in front of me.

It isn't an officer. They don't attack on-site without reason or without verbally attempting to de-escalate the situation first. It isn't the woman who was nearly ready to break through the metal doors in the front of the building just a few moments ago. Her slim demeanor couldn't possibly produce this much force. It isn't even a man *at all*. He looks like one and is even dressed like one, yet he doesn't walk like one; he doesn't act like one, either. Hell, he didn't even grunt as an undoubtedly painful swing of a stainless steel flashlight came into contact with his head. I don't know what this is, but I don't care enough to get any closer.

"Fuck… fuck, you stay there, sir! Stop! Stop!" I stammer as I take a step back.

The echo coming from the enclosed stairwell is making my already throbbing head feel that much worse. I almost trip over my foot as I attempt to back up to the staircase behind me, all without taking my eyes off of whoever is in front of me. When I see the aggression and pure hatred in their face as they charge at me, fight or flight kicks in almost instinctively, and I don't wait around to see how good my fighting might be. I drop the flashlight in the stairwell as soon as I turn around and grab the handrail to propel me upstairs faster. I notice they are now shuffling up the stairs toward me rather than chasing me.

Is this piece of shit toying with me?! I gotta- I gotta go…

I stumble into the second-floor hallway nearest to the elevator and bolt directly toward the library. I can tell the man pushed the *correct* door this time because I hear it creak behind me as I am holding my hand to my head, looking for blood from the prior impact. Since the wooden doors to the library are already propped open, I make my way to the black bag I had partially opened on the table near the Help Desk without a second thought. The lamps that I once found to be comforting seemed to worsen my headache tenfold. My right ankle gives out as my left-hand slides over the top handle of the bag, knocking it over and spilling the contents small enough to fit through the half-zipped opening. *Of course.* This also causes my stomach to come into contact with the sharp end of the table.

As if I'm not in enough pain…

I ignore the wheezing that comes from the collision with the table and start fumbling for the magazine I had previously ejected from the Kimber. While kneeling and shuffling through the small articles of clothing, magazines, and what appears to be .357 rounds spurred all over the library floor, I feel the cold barrel of the Kimber with the hand supporting my balance on the table. I pick it up but am unable to find a magazine that is compatible with it.

C'mon. C'mon…

I start fumbling in my pockets, remembering I had ejected the round in the chamber but unable to recall whether I had it on me or put it in the bag. *I can't think straight! I can't think!* I back away from the propped double doors and begin limping toward the large windows still illuminated by the sirens.

Got it! Got it!

I use my left hand to pull the .45 caliber cartridge as the man steps into the room. Now I can see he's bleeding from his head, yet I can't even process what to say before he goes into a full-on sprint toward me, ignoring the chairs and tables in our path. *I* have *never* seen such ferocity. The guy practically sends my already knocked-over items flying across the floor as my trembling hands make it seemingly impossible to get the loose round in the chamber.

Let's go, Miles, let's go…

I had never felt more relief than when the round properly sat in the chamber, and I heard the all-so-familiar sound of the slide being successfully released. I aim the handgun right at the man and, without trying to make the same mistake twice today, attempt to walk through the steps to calm him down before resorting to Deadly Force.

"Sir, I have a firearm! You need to calm down. Sir! Stop! Moving! Sir!!" I shout as loud as I can. I feel my throat begin to burn from the excessive yelling. He continues to breeze through the obstacles as though they aren't even there to begin with. I can't hear myself think, *especially* when the round is fired.

Bang.

"Goddamit!" I say as the realization hits me harder than the bullet would've: *I missed*. Instead, I hit the lamp directly behind him, creating an ever-familiar blue and red ambiance within the library. I don't even notice I dropped the gun as I begin to hop around the man, who attempts to grab me by extending his arm over a table he has not yet knocked over. The attempt is fruitless, especially since it lacks the same hostility as was seen when he first entered the room. *What the fuck is wrong with this guy?!*

I practically slide onto the ground directly in front of my bag, which is now a few feet away from where it had fallen since he had kicked it. I can feel slight discomfort in my knees as they are pressed directly on bullet cartridges that have spilled onto the floor. I fumble in the darkness as I feel the cold frame of the Smith & Wesson I had packed when I left Scarsdale and, without thinking this time, throw myself on my back and, with the revolver still inside the bag, fire four rounds in the direction of the man who is now walking just a few feet away from me. The bullets effortlessly pierce the bottom of the bag as I hold it up in front of me. I don't know where most of the rounds land, but I know one hit him in the head, judging by how his silhouette fell backward. I can't hear myself think because of the adrenaline and the ringing in my ears.

Oh my god… Oh my god… Oh my… I can't breathe… Fuck, I can't breathe…

Am I empty? Do I still have rounds? I don't care. I'm not taking that chance. With my hands now shaking again, I am barely able to expel the casings from the cylinder as I reach out to the floor to grab some of the new rounds I was kneeling on seconds prior. I am barely able to get them seated properly before I slam the cylinder shut and cautiously approach the man with the hammer pulled back on the revolver.

What did I do…? Oh my god, what did I do…?

I can barely make out the blood running from his body, seen only because of the dim illumination coming from the windows, which I can distinctively see stained with spots of red. For the second time in a single night, regardless of self-defense or not, I have taken another life. As the sound of blood steadily dripping onto the dirty beige carpet below our feet fills the void of silence overtaking the room, I waste no time throwing up again. I know one thing for a fact: *my life of freedom is over.*

CHAPTER 3

IN THIS NEW WORLD

I DON'T EVEN GET TO take a breath before I remember something that throws me into a frenzy: the woman and the kid are still outside. For all my time employed here, I have seen kids practically skipping down these steps when dismissal is in effect or parents running upstairs to the main office on the second floor to pick up their children because they have an appointment to catch, but these pale in comparison to how fast I hop down those steps. As I do, I can't help but feel like a grown man playing hopscotch since I am relying on my left leg to hold my weight.

"Ma'am?! … Ma'am, are you still there? Kid?" I shout as my voice echoes off the cold, barren walls.

I guess they must have heard the gunshots because they are crouched behind one of the main doors, just barely visible from the window on the right side of the foyer. Judging by how she's frantically looking around while her son's head remains tucked in between her arms, I can tell the woman is contemplating whether she should stay put with the boy or run away with him.

Just as I notice them, I tuck the revolver I was holding moments ago behind my belt near the back of my jeans. My right hand is visibly red, even in the darkness, from how tight I was gripping it. I jolt through the main lobby as I swing open the foyer doors and see the woman and child in an all-out sprint towards the sidewalk as I open the main right door. I must have spooked them with the way I suddenly barged through the foyer.

"It's okay, it's okay. I understand you're afraid right now…" I say to comfort the now paranoid woman as my hands are in the air, and I take one slow but methodical step toward them at a time. "Someone forced their way into the school and attacked me. I handled it, yet you guys shouldn't be out here. Please, come inside where it's warm. If you'd like, we can-" I plead before she interrupts me.

"No! No, no, you stay right there!" she screams at the top of her lungs in what I would only assume is an attempt to get the attention of a passerby to help her deal with the situation. *No one stops*. The traffic keeps flowing as people on the sidewalks keep running as fast as they can given the snow underneath their feet; the woman's cries for help go seemingly unheard by everyone nearby.

"Ma'am, you know me… Look at me, alright? Take a look at my face," I say in a near whisper as a seemingly spooked male in a thin black North Face nearly topples the duo over while proceeding to speed walk past them. Amidst the chaos unfolding all around us, I also decide to stop taking steps forward to ease her mind. "Alright…? Now, you see me every day when you come to pick up your son. Your name, is Renata, right?" I ask as she hesitantly inches her way in my direction with her son now behind her right arm. I vaguely recall seeing the name on the sheet labeled "Checkout" for the Afterschool Program her son attends, yet I was not one hundred percent confident it belonged to her specifically.

"Y… yeah… Yeah, that… that's me," she whimpers as she now pushes her son completely behind her entire body and out of sight except for his bright Yellow Nikes. She almost sounds like she's ready to cry, yet I dismiss it as my imagination since the ringing in my ears from the gunshots is still evident. The woman remains firm and holds her ground.

"Okay now Renata, I need you to come inside with me where it is safe, alright? You and your son *will not* be safe out here in this cold. Do you think you can do that?" I ask in a firm yet relatively quiet tone. The snowfall is making it difficult to see her facial expressions.

She waits a moment before looking around her and grabbing her son's hand as she leads them directly through the main door I have half-propped open with a rock. The two usher past me without another word, and I kick the rock away before looking around the eerie white landscape and yanking the door shut behind me.

* * *

Feeling the wind being instantly cut off as the door slams shut is one of the best feelings I have felt all night. The comforting sensation as my cheeks begin to warm up almost makes me forget that there was a dead body upstairs; what snaps me back to reality are a possibly twisted ankle, a near-frantic family in front of me, and an illegal gun in my waistband.

"I'm sorry if I scared you," I say truthfully as I discreetly pull my stained black shirt over my belt in an attempt to conceal my firearm. I can't see the stains, yet I can faintly smell the metallic and indistinguishable scent of blood radiating off it.

"Are you hungry? I didn't check yet, but I know we have some snacks in the Cafeteria for us," is all I'm able to mutter out as I try to think of a way to console my new guests. "Huh? Whaddya say?" I ask as I place my hands on my hips in an awkward but friendly manner.

"No, I think we'll be fine," Renata says in what sounds like an annoyed but appreciative tone, visibly shaking either from the cold or from being scared - or both. *I know that feeling well.* Her son voices his disagreement with her, though.

"Can I get some of the animal crackers, please?" the boy pleads before his mother intervenes.

"Vito, I *said* we're good," Renata says out loud. Now I can *definitely* tell she's annoyed, although her tremble seemed to worsen after she said it.

"It's no worries, I'll go see what I can find. Can I show you to a warmer room in the meantime?" I ask intending to lead them to the second-floor Maintenance Room sitting right above the chandelier currently hanging over our heads here in the lobby. As the boy's mother hesitantly nods in agreement, I begin to lead the way up the right staircase closest to the front desk - which is meant for ascension, while the opposite staircase was designed for the opposite. We reach the top of the stairs and I turn left to open the Maintenance Room that sits flush in between the top of both staircases that lead back down to the Lobby.

"Here we go," I mutter as the gray metal door creaks open slightly, and a gust of warm air brushes past me and out of the room while I step in with my good foot. "There is a window straight ahead," I say as I point to the large window directly to the opposite side of the room, which would sit directly above the foyer downstairs. "You can open it and step out onto a balcony, but there are heat pipes in here so you'll be warmer inside," I blurt out confidently.

It's only when Renata and her son usher past me that I realize how pretty this woman is. Her dirty blonde hair is polluted with small, melted snowflakes and an intoxicating yet subtle perfume that provides me with just as much comfort as the heat in the room does. "Thank you," she mutters politely as she turns her head slightly while still keeping her body facing the window and hazel eyes on the ground beside her. She's probably no taller than 5'7" so she's right up to my chin.

I turn to my right to flip up the light switch positioned against the wall and try to guess the woman's country of origin as her light skin complexion glistens in the now-illuminated room. *Italian, maybe?*

"You're welcome. I'll be back in a few, alright, guys? I'll see if I can find us some snacks downstairs. Do you have anybody you want to call in the meantime? I mean… there is a phone in the Main Office just outside of this room and to the right, if you need to use it," I say now trying to impress the woman in front of me.

"Yeah… Yeah, ok. I can try to get a hold of my husband and see if he's still home so he can pick us up," she says hastily.

Well, there goes that idea…

"Alright well, I'll be back in a few," I say as I begin to quietly close the door behind me. As I turn left and grab the guardrail on the staircase,

I stop and slowly look straight ahead to see the now-dark Library - *the dim light from the sirens had disappeared.*

Remembering what had occurred just minutes ago, I take my right hand off the rail and begin to walk around the staircase and towards the library, passing the navy-blue double doors that separate the hallway leading to the west wing of the building and the area surrounding the Main Office. As I step into complete darkness, I turn around to ensure the woman hasn't followed suit behind me and begin to reach for my Smith & Wesson, keeping it concealed, but ready.

* * *

I enter the room and begin looking for any signs of movement as my eyes adjust to the dark. With my right hand gripping the revolver, I use my left hand to fumble for the light switch leaning against the left wall of the library's entrance. Struggling, I get a sense of paranoia washing over me and pull the hammer back with my right thumb - *still keeping the gun holstered but, again, ready.* I manage to get the light on and give out a sigh of relief as I notice no one else is in there with me, *alive* that is, but that relief is quickly overwritten by the smell of blood and gunpowder, which is similar to what my nose picked up from my shirt in the lobby just much, much stronger.

Ugh… What the fuck…

I try my best to avoid the smell by only breathing through my nose. As I decock the hammer of the .357 magnum, I notice the man had not moved since I was last up here which confirms that this nightmare is, indeed, real. With the pool of blood seeping from his body having spread slowly across the floor, covering some of the casings on the floor I had ejected earlier, I begin kneeling with my injured leg to pick up the cartridges that are still intact.

Piling them into the charred-smelling black bag which has seen so much in just a few short hours, I begin to take off my shirt and replace it with a clean, white, and black shirt with the famous two-toned logo of Tony Montana from *Scarface* and a phrase *"The World is Yours"* spread across the bottom of the picture. I throw the other shirt into the cheap plastic trash can sitting behind the library's Help Desk.

Great… I loved that shirt.

I take a step back and begin to fumble in the bag for the holster that was compatible with my Smith & Wesson. Awkwardly enough, it is a concealable holster that was meant for lefties, even though I'm a righty yet, I usually have it positioned at the 5 o'clock position on my belt so it can be concealed and still accessible without needing to cross-draw. Instead, I pull out a loaded stainless steel .45 caliber magazine compatible with the Kimber TLE I had dropped a few feet from the window. After making my way to the handgun resting on the floor, which has its slide locked back from running out of ammunition, I insert the magazine and release the slide before placing the handgun into the bag.

As my hand reaches down to grab the stainless Model 686 tucked behind my waistband, I open the cylinder to verify how many rounds are in it. As it turns out, I was only able to load four rounds in my panicked state, and not even in the same order; without much thought, I dig through the bag to grab two more loose rounds before loading them into the cylinder and and snuggly wedging the now-loaded weapon into its respective holster. *Perfect fit.*

"Alright. I'll deal with you later," I say in a tone fit for a library as I give the corpse just feet away from me a once-over. I turn off the light, close the doors that were propped open, & start limping down the hall I had been chased from not even an hour ago, before heading down the staircase and coming to a stop a foot away from the flashlight I had dropped. The light, which is still on, was slightly faded due to the blood at the end of it.

"What the *hell* are you…" I whisper faintly as my eyes remain fixated on the small bloodstain and I am flooded with flashbacks from the encounter. Hesitant to pick it up, I do so and latch it to my belt without wiping it off - *I just got a new shirt and I refuse to dirty this one.* I head through the small doorway at the bottom of the stairwell that leads into the cafeteria and begin rumbling through the drawers and boxes looking for something to eat.

Oh, cmon. Where the hell would I find animal crackers?

Amid my frustration, I realize how much my ankle has swollen, so I give up and dig into the fridge sitting against the gated fence near the window, which is meant to act as a deterrence against the kids and staff from getting near the hot pipes sitting behind it.

"Alright, this could do some justice," as I take out a bag of baby carrots which I use to prop against my ankle.

Wow, this feels good.

I lean my back against the stainless steel fridge, with my left leg on top of my right knee, and let out a sigh of relief as I can feel the cold wash away the swelling from my ankle. When I get tired of standing, I make my way to sit down on one of the dark ebony wood lunch tables nearest to the kitchen and proceed to place the cold bag against the back of my head. Although this, too, feels amazing, the disinfectant from the tables being wiped down by the cleaning staff yesterday evening is still too strong to give me any real satisfaction.

Sigh… what a night. Where the hell would I find anim- wait…

Looking out at the street facing the opposite side of the school, I can make out cars moving faster than they should in a school zone, let alone when there's snow and slush on the ground. *Something isn't right…* I see some people being assaulted physically against the poorly black-painted metal fence that surrounds the exterior of the building. But it's not one person, hell, it's not even a small group of people; *everyone is being attacked.*

The sound of shouting sends chills down my spine, colder than that of the "ice pack" I wasn't able to fully take advantage of, and sends all of the hairs on my arms flying upright. It's not because of the screams themselves, but rather because those screams are coming from inside this building.

Crap, that's the lobby. Oh my god…

I drop the now semi-cold bag of carrots on the floor as I ignore the pain now coming from my left ankle again. Without so much as another thought, I bolt it as fast as I can through the cafeteria entrance and towards the main lobby.

As I get closer, I pull the .357 out of its dark black leather holster and pull back the hammer while I lean against the door leading into the lobby. I bring my left hand up to support the grip of the firearm as I slowly peek through the small, faded window on the door to see Renata yelling at a small group of people, maybe five or six people who somehow made their way into the building, from the same staircase we took to head upstairs. She has her arms extended, obviously signaling someone to stay back. Peeking out further, I notice a man slowly making his way up the first three steps, clearly ignoring her commands.

I burst through the door and startle everyone in the area, including Renata, while immediately attempting to address the man ascending the staircase. I can see he's carrying a blood-stained sledge-hammer. Before lifting my weapon, a slim Hispanic male, probably boasting a similar build as me, just without the height to accompany it, attempts to grab the revolver from my hands. Just as his friends take a step forward to assist, I forcefully retract both of my hands and swing the stainless steel frame at the man's jaw as hard as I can. A small amount of blood lands on my face, yet I don't wait another second before bringing the barrel of the weapon to the group in front of me.

"Get the fuck back, now!" is all I manage to command before the man backs up in fear. He instantly raises his right hand, yet his left is rubbing his jaw in what I can only assume is an attempt to soothe the pain from my swing. I keep the weapon pointed at the group as nearly all of their hands go up in front of them.

"Stay back! All of you!" I bark out as I see two women in the group jolt at the suddenness of the command. My heart is racing faster than ever before.

Control these people, Miles.

Now that I have a better look, I can see there are three men and two women in the lobby, as well as the guy I halted on the staircase. They're all bundled up except for the latter, who is wearing a stained beige windbreaker, yet all of them are raising their hands in fear. I can't make out any firearms, but with the help of the light coming from the second-floor Maintenance Room, I get a better visual of the stained sledgehammer that guy with the windbreaker is carrying, slowly dripping with… *something*. Given how quiet the room is now, that dripping is the only audible thing any of us hear.

Control these people…

"You!" I shout as I return the barrel of the revolver toward the man in question and transition from a yell to a firm and authoritative tone, "I don't care what you're carrying, but you'd best drop it where you stand or I'll send two through your forehead, you hear me?" I shout out as my tone makes the man take another step backward. The man obliges without hesitation.

Control…

"How did you get in here?" I let out with a slight crack in my voice. I don't want them to see that as a weakness, so I shut that idea down before they even have time to react. "How did you get *in here?!*" I ask again in a louder tone, obviously losing patience. The painstaking quiet transforms into echoing shutters of fear and heavy breathing.

One of the women in the group, clearly startled, is the first to answer the question even though I am speaking directly to the man on the stairs. "W- we saw the door was open, s… so we came through an… and…I don't know… we came in…" Anyone with a brain and a little bit of empathy can see she was scared, but that observation is immediately cut off when the man on the stairs, *whom my weapon is still pointed at*, begins to speak.

"Hey, listen, man… we didn't mean to barge in here. We only saw one light on, so we couldn't tell if it was occupied. The front door was open, so we let ourselves in because-" the man says as a shot impacts the wall a few feet over his head. The gunshot is so loud that everyone jolts this time, *myself included*. This time, however, my hands and body are as stable as can be.

"Do *not* bullshit me, son! Do *not* lie to me again! I locked the doors myself." As the tension continues to rise, I can't help but wonder if I really *did* lock the doors, but I continue to hold my ground. "I am the *only* one with a key to this building right now, so I will ask you again," I can barely hear myself talk as the only two things I hear in the room are the cocking of the hammer again and the constant ringing in my ears, "How the *fuck* did you get in here?!"

That I can hear clearly.

The sound of the revolver's hammer locking to the rear seems to startle those who know what it means, including the younger Hispanic man I had struck just moments ago.

Please don't turn me into a murderer, kid… Just answer the question.

"Alright!" shouts one of the men in front of me. In all honesty, the sudden holler brought my goosebumps back as it caught me off guard. The woman in the group who was previously attempting to defuse the situation is now hiding behind the man who has stepped forward to speak.

"Look outside, brother… Look! People are being killed and gunshots going off everywhere! Look for yourself!" he lets out in a confident stance, yet I can hear his voice cracking just like mine did. "We were chased and closed the front gate before breaking the lock to the door. I'm sorry, alright?! But we don't know what the hell people are doing out there! Okay?"

Gunshots? Liar. I would've heard 'em… Is he referring to me? I…

"What about the cops? I heard the sirens. Hell, I *saw the sirens*! If people are being hurt and you're being chased, why wouldn't you call the cops-" I inquire before being interrupted.

"Who the fuck do you think was chasing us?!" the man lets out. His dark complexion seems to radiate some steam from the sudden warmth in the building as tears flow down his face. Another man, obviously the youngest of the group judging by the razor stubble under his chin, puts his hand on the man's shoulder in a futile attempt to calm him down; his hand is thrown off as the African-American man violently shrugs his shoulders in aggravation.

"I…" is all that comes out of my mouth. Instinctively, my mind begins to flood with the recent images of the people on the street being mauled and assaulted; at the same time, I begin to wonder if the chaos beyond these walls is why my distress calls were being dropped. I can't help but feel dread looming over me once again as my gaze shifts between the strangers in front of me. I begin to regain my composure as my breaths begin to shutter.

Control…

"I want all of you against the wall, now!" I command as my heart is racing again. I can see Vito quietly sobbing near the top of the stairwell and Renata attempting to comfort him as I address the group. "Drop all of your stuff against that wall and move to the other side over there with your coats raised above your waist," I instruct as I point to the wall under the opposite staircase where they are placing their belongings. I can't trust these people unless I know I can turn my back on them, and I can't do that if they're armed.

The second woman in the group, who is standing at around the same height as Renata, seems to be the one to break the silence and verbally address her disapproval. "C'mon man, what are you doing?" she asks as one of the other men in the group softly pushes her shoulder so she can face the wall. I guess he doesn't want to see me yell again.

"I am not going to hurt you, but I need to make sure you guys won't hurt us either. We have a kid upstairs," I say as some of them shoot their glances at Vito, who seems to be calmer now. I turn to the man acting as the spokesperson for the group. "What's your name?" I ask while looking into his watery eyes from afar so as not to get close enough to these people in case they suddenly decide to retaliate.

"My name is Derrick. Derrick Simmons," he says confidently again, this time without a deviation in his tone of voice.

"Alright, Mr. Simmons," I say as I de-cock the hammer on the Smith & Wesson and lower the gun so everyone can feel at ease. "Can you please take the reigns on your friends? These nice people don't know me, but they seem like they'll listen to you. Think we can all get along here?" I ask as I keep my eyes trained on the hands and waists of everyone near the wall.

"Yeah… sure thing," Derrick says before hesitantly giving his companions instructions to spin around so I can verify no one was concealing a weapon like I was.

"Thank you, Derrick," I say with a sigh of relief. "I'm sorry for the dramatic performance. We're all a little paranoid. In all honesty, I actually- I had to…" I stutter while pausing to verify whether or not Vito is listening in on our conversation; he's too focused on his mother to bother.

"I was attacked twice tonight. Both people came at me. Both tried to kill me. Both of them lost." My right-hand starts to tremble at the thought of what I've been through, but I do my best to control it. "It was self-defense," I mutter while my right hand comes to a halt as I reassure myself that my actions tonight were justified. "I am sorry if I scared the shit out of you, but I need to ask you all some questions. As it stands right now, I do *not* trust you, but I'd like to," I admit as I put the gun away and extend my hand to Derrick.

"The name is Miles Gether. Would you all please follow me?" I calmly ask intending to use the fifth-floor gym on the west side of the building for the questioning. As my hand is extended, Derrick's demeanor transitions from that of paranoia to moderate tranquility. I immediately notice his willingness to cooperate, even with his semi-stoic facial expressions. He takes two small steps forward and shakes my hand in a manner that is less firm than I expected from someone who is considerably more muscular than I am.

"Guys," he says quietly as he turns his head slightly to his friends, who are now standing behind him, without breaking eye contact with me. "Let's do as the man says. We're in his house, so we'll play along with his rules, alright?" he asks without any verbal rebuttals from his companions.

As I usher the group to head upstairs, I extend my right arm directly in front of the Hispanic guy whom I punched in the jaw earlier. He stops abruptly before glaring directly at me, and I use the silence as an opportunity to speak. "What's your name, kid?" I ask in an increasingly inquisitive manner. It doesn't take him long to respond to my question.

"Pancho," the guy says before I continue.

"You got a last name, Pancho?" I ask as I slowly lower my arm back to my side.

"Ruiz. Pancho Ruiz, sir," he says with more confidence than before as he stands up straight, now fixated on my shirt - *no doubt looking at Tony Montana*. I extend my hand toward him and thank him for his honesty.

"Thank you for being honest with me, *Pancho Ruiz*. Bullshit aside, you've got a hell of a jaw for being able to take a swing like that. You mind if I call you *Jawbreaker*? Sounds more badass, doesn't it?" I ask with a slight chuckle, immediately causing my vocals to hurt again. Pancho seems to notice the pain, as he takes a second to let out a chuckle of his own after processing what I had asked him. I extend my left hand out towards the staircase and proceed to hand him the flashlight I had picked up earlier as he ushers past me.

"Lead the way, *JB*," I mutter as I guide the group towards the fifth floor. Even with the amicability between myself and the group, I couldn't help but notice that my hand was instinctively resting on the grip of the gun.

CHAPTER 4

SURVIVE

<u>Ledger</u>
Vito Caruso - (Mental State: Bored)
Renata Caruso - (Mental State: Anxious)
Hope Starcov - (Mental State: Appreciative)
Charlotte Kennedy - (Mental State: Frightened)
Pancho Ruiz - (Mental State: Stable)
Simon Adams - (Mental State: <u>Unstable</u>)
Derrick Simmons - (Mental State: Stable)
Jayden Walker - (Mental State: Impatient)

Journal Entry: With all of the shit I've been through after the Military accident, I didn't think I would ever put myself in such a dangerous situation again. I was wrong. Last night, I took the lives of two people within a 6-hour time frame, yet I feel calmer now, knowing that my life could've ended if I hadn't done what I did. I met some people – 8 to be exact (see "Ledger" above) – and I vetted every single one of them. I have a gut feeling that I can trust most of those people, yet my instincts have let me down before...

I'll be watching them closely, but I think there is a bond to be made here. I can feel it...

WITH THE INEVITABLE SUNRISE IN the distance, it's easier to write the names of our new, great, big family as I am desperately craving some sleep. I don't remember the last time I got any. I take a good, long look at the slightly mutilated bag I had picked up from the library once I was done showing everyone to the cafeteria. I know they're all preoccupied downstairs with figuring out how to make their goddamn breakfast, yet I can't take the chance that one of them will wander into the library out of curiosity.

Everyone's alibi seems to check out. As much as I want to get some rest, I *need* to take care of the front door first. I reckon no one here wants to experience another incident in the main lobby, and I won't feel at ease unless that's taken care of.

After slamming the journal closed and placing it back into the bag, I throw one of the straps over my right shoulder and make my way into Principal Lofter's office. I can still smell the subtle booze in the air from our conversation yesterday as I place my bag on the coat rack near the window facing the front of the school. Glancing outside, I can see that all the commotion last night seemed to disappear as quickly as it appeared.

It's so quiet… And how the hell does an alcoholic become an elementary school principal anyway?

I take a step back as the sun, which is just barely starting to make its way over the rooftop of the apartment building across the street from the front of the school, abruptly blinds me. "Okay, time to get this over with," I whisper to myself as I take the hooded jacket I had brought with me from the library as well and begin heading to the maintenance closet where Vito and Renata had previously been occupying - *their belongings still spread along the wall of the room.*

I begin searching for something I can use to secure the door and find a drill, which seems to have a relatively low battery, as well as some long screws, a handful of zip-ties, & a randomized box of half-used nails.

Great... what a start...

Disappointed by my lack of resources, I hold what I can in my hands as I begin making my way downstairs to get some help with the project.

I make my way down the staircase in the main lobby and pass through the door I nearly displaced my shoulder with last night before stopping to catch a drink from the water fountain near the entrance of the east stairwell. I can't remember the last time I ate or drank anything either. After a revitalizing sip of water, I continue with my stroll and pass through the cafeteria entrance.

The first thing I expect is to walk into the comforting smell of delicious food being prepared, yet I notice that most of the group is eating snacks or meals that don't require cooking. There's one thing, however, that catches my attention: *everyone in the room is either smiling or laughing.*

This feels good.

I make my way to one of the tables nearest to the kitchen and settle down on the edge, the smell of disinfectant having dissipated, but the bag of baby carrots still on the floor where I had dropped it. I look at Derrick, who seems to be the first person to finish his Cheerios and faded carton of chocolate milk before anyone has a chance to finish their food. It also looks as though Vito got his Animal Crackers after all.

Where the hell did they find those?

"Derrick, I may need your help fixing up that broken door out front. Do you mind giving me a hand?" He nods rather than giving me verbal affirmation. I can see he's still chewing his last bite of cereal. "Alright, cool," I say, feeling triumphant in my *negotiation* as I begin to get up. He starts to do the same while grabbing his trash. My good foot doesn't even hit the ground before Vito nearly drops his Animal Crackers in excitement.

"Miles can I come and help, too?!" he asks in a hyper tone that emerges out of thin air. I'm not even able to respond before his mother practically spits out the apple slice she was eating to shut down the request.

"Absolutely not. Did you not see how crazy it was out there? You don't even have snow boots anyway." She has a good point.

"Hey, Renata, it's alright. I didn't see any commotion a few minutes ago when I looked out there. Besides, we're only going to be at the front door."

Renata looks at me with a dark red glow in her cheeks that contrasts her natural skin tone, as if I had said something she did not want to hear. "I said no," she barks back as she moves her hand to cover her mouth from spitting out the last remnants of the apple slice she was previously consuming, "I don't want him to catch a cold, either. I can feel the cold from here."

I take a brief look at the kitchen window I was glancing out last night near the fridge and notice it is cracked open. I didn't even know those windows could *be* opened.

Derrick intervenes in the conversation as he discards his breakfast into the gray mobile trashcan near one of the six stone rectangular pillars holding up the cafeteria ceiling. "Hey, it's cool. We wouldn't let him freeze out there. How about we fetch his coat and have him inside the whole time while we work outside? Does that sound fair?" he asks as I can see the unmistakable look of disapproval written all over Vito's face. *The kid wants to help.*

"Fine," Renata mutters under her breath as she transitions to address her son directly, "you stay close to him, alright?" she lets out as more of a command than a suggestion as she points to me. "And make sure you have your hat, alright? Don't step outside and get your socks wet from the snow, you hear me?" I can tell that even though we've only had a few interactions, she trusts me.

Is it because I protected her and her son?

"C'mon, kiddo," I whisper to Vito as I usher him towards Derrick before quietly asking if he can bring Vito upstairs to get his stuff.

"The kid will guide you to where it is," I whisper before getting a nod of approval from the man as the two begin making their way toward the main entrance of the cafeteria from where I had entered. As the two step off, I slowly turn to sit about a foot next to Renata, my back against the table and my body facing the opposite side she is facing.

"Any word from your husband? Did you try calling to see where he is?" I ask with concern in a tone low enough for only me and her to hear. I don't want the others to know her business.

"I uh- I tried using one of the phones in the Main Office, but there was no tone," she says as her voice begins to crack and her eyes start to water. "I went to all of the phones, and none of them are working, so…" she mutters under her breath just as she had done when she consented to her son coming with us moments ago.

Maybe that's how she knew someone had entered the lobby last night. Did she see them as she came back from the office?

"Alright, well, he knows you were coming here, right? We will keep an eye out for him, alright?" I ask in an attempt to reassure her, but it only seems to make her more upset as she places one of her hands under her chin and proceeds to fetch another apple slice from her tray without making eye contact with me.

I put one hand on the back of her shoulder before getting up and following Derrick and Vito, who were just passing the doors leading to the main hallway.

* * *

I can see the light seeping through the hole where the exterior door handle *used* to be as I push the right door open just enough to get a peek outside. *Nothing.* I can see that the front gate of the school is being held in place with the doorstoppers on the bottom of it, which are planted firmly into their respective slots in the ground. On the ground, directly on the other side of the gate, I can make out the metal chain and the now-busted padlock I had previously used to lock the gate behind me when I first returned to the school last night.

Ah c'mon! I just bought that lock…

As I continue to push against the door and step outside, hearing the grinding of the broken handle as it scrapes against the concrete in the process, I can't help but notice the various patches of frozen but distinguishable blood spatter lying on the thin sheet of snow on the ground below.

This is probably from Derrick's sledgehammer…

"Alright, what the hell do we have here?" I quietly ask myself as I cautiously kneel to grab the detached door handle while still scanning the streets for movement. It looks like some of the screws that are still attached to the door are intact as I examine it further. I can hear the foyer doors swing open and get up so as not to get hit by the door when Derrick steps outside.

"Hey… there we go," I say in a joyful tone as I put my hand in the air for a high-five from Vito for his hasty effort to bundle up. Without hesitation, yet with a little bit more force than I expected from a child, Vito happily claps his hand with mine, causing a muffled but audible "*poof*" as our cloves collide. I can see Derrick is coming out with a coat of his own. I had the group move their stuff to the only classroom on the first floor, which sits directly in front of the double doors in the lobby leading to the main hallway. I didn't want anyone else breaking into the school and stealing their stuff.

"Glad you can make it. Come, join me. We've got some fine-ass beach weather," I let out alongside a slight chuckle. This time, my vocals aren't in pain when I do so, which I chalk up to the cold water from the fountain. Derrick's smile and genuine laugh of approval make me feel like I'm funnier than I give myself credit for.

"I don't know what beaches you go to, but if you say so, man," he exclaims. Hearing his authentic laugh made me calm in an extremely tense situation. I have Derrick hold the lock against the door as I begin seeing if the long screws I picked up from upstairs are suitable to replace the bent ones laying on the snow.

"Guess we're in luck. Vito, see if you can hold these," I blurt out as I hand him a bunch of zip-ties without looking his way, *too focused on the task at hand,* and continue to align the lock with the interior of the door.

"Alright, now to hold it in place while I get the drill to… *What the hell…*" I say while glancing behind Derrick, who is kneeling in front of the door while holding the handle up in its correct place. I didn't have to voice my concern before his head turned to face the direction I was now looking at. There was movement, but it was near the reservoir, roughly a quarter mile away from the building.

"Did you see that?" I ask as I begin to stand up. He continues to hold the handle in place as the silhouette in the distance staggers out of sight. I could've sworn I heard some type of disgruntled shriek as they bolted behind a building blocking our view, but Derrick denies hearing it at all once I bring it up.

About half a block away from the main gate, which is around five to six cars away from where we're now standing, I can see what looks to be two uniformed corpses lying lifeless on the concrete which I hadn't noticed before. Even at such a relatively close distance, I can barely make out the bodies as they are covered under a thin sheet of snow that came from the blizzard overnight.

I guess they were telling the truth. Fuck…

"Derrick, come with me for a second?" I ask in a low tone that resembles a command rather than a question as I see him subtly dropping the lock on the ground without diverting his eyes from the building where the figure disappears behind. I turn my head to Vito, who looks confused in the comfortable, warm foyer he's standing in. "Do me a favor, kiddo, and wait here, yeah? You take those and put them together right *here* when we leave, alright?" I ask, pointing at the zip ties in his hand, followed by the door handles inside the lobby. His nervous nod of approval is enough to convince me he'll get the job done.

As Derrick and I head toward the gate, I hastily pull the .357 from its holster. As one can imagine, it is more difficult to grab the gun with thick winter gloves compared to when they're inside, but I somehow manage as we position ourselves beside the entrance to the courtyard. "Alright, go," I whisper before Derrick lifts the doorstopper previously securing the gate in place. Holding the gun with both hands, I rush around the corner and onto the sidewalk, facing the direction of the uniformed corpses.

In the cold, I can see a fresh gust of cold air being expelled with every breath I take. The closer I get to the bodies, the more I see them.

"Keep an eye out behind us, alright? I doubt anyone can run in this snow, but you never know," I say to Derrick, who's following about two feet behind my right shoulder. His breath seems to be more controlled than my own, either because he is calmer or because he is wearing thicker apparel than I am.

Surprisingly, the snow around us is sitting at what I can only assume to be around two to three inches, which isn't a lot for New York's standards and is a lot less than I anticipated to be left following a blizzard.

Fuck... this is bad...

We manage to reach the bodies, and to my surprise, they look exactly how I imagined from how *Jawbreaker* told his story. One is on his stomach with his face - *or what is left of it* - spilling over the curb near the rear passenger wheel well of the white truck, he mentioned. The truck in question is spattered with blood. I can't recognize the facial features of the second officer at all.

Oh my god... I think I am going to be sick again...

The cold isn't doing anything to mask the stench of decay and iron in the vicinity, yet I practice breathing through my mouth as I had done in the library the last two times I was there. I can see there is a single fifth-generation Glock 17 handgun secured on each of the duty belts the officers have attached to their respective bodies.

How has no one confiscated these?

I start to reach down, trying my hardest not to look at the faces of these men as I attempt to pull their service weapons from their holsters. As I struggle to get one of them loose, I briefly realize that everything on their duty belt is intact - *the pepper spray, the radios, the handcuffs... hell, even their tasers are there, just like Pancho mentioned.* To make my life easier, I unclip their belts entirely and remove one of the Glock 17s before I drop the belt on the snow and partially pull the slide back to see if the weapon has a round in the chamber - *it does.*

I stand up and turn to Derrick, who has his head turned towards the apartment complex across the street from the school, scanning for any potential threats. Grabbing the slide of the Glock, I turn the handgun around in my right hand before placing my left on Derrick's shoulder to get his attention.

"It's time for you to prove to me you're as trustworthy as I believe you are. I just hope you know how to use it," I confess in a low tone before extending the pistol to him. His facial expression unmistakably displays bewilderment but gradually fades into that of sincere appreciation and gratitude. As he slowly takes the weapon from my hand, I give him a nod of approval and turn my back to him as I kneel to recover the duty belt I had dropped.

Feeling my dark jeans becoming increasingly damp with every knee I take in the snow just makes me want to get out of the cold quicker, but I press on. I extend the belt to Derrick, and he takes it with his free hand before throwing it over his shoulder.

As I move toward the second corpse near the truck and start working to remove his duty belt, I hear the same muffled shriek I had heard earlier. This time, however, I can see Derrick's already white face becoming slightly more pale. I initially take it as a confirmation that he heard the disgruntled noise as well. But as I glance over my shoulder to face the direction he's looking toward, I finally understand why he looks the way he does.

What the hell are you looking at... Oh my god.

There is not one figure as I had previously assumed: *there are dozens of them, and every single one of them is charging at us from about two blocks away near where I had heard the shriek initially.* My mind is flooded with images of how fast the corpse in the library had run at me. This is *no different.* I wasn't even able to break out of my trance. I'll tell you what did work though: *The gunshot.*

"Oh fuck... Fuc- those aren't people! Fuck!" I hear Derrick shout as our adventure transitions from a recovery mission to an escape. It takes everything I have to peel my eyes off the group and focus on the belt I am working on. I drop the revolver and throw off my gloves for better friction on the clasp securing the belt.

"C'mon goddammit, c'mon... C'mon!" I shout at the buckle as though it will somehow affect the speed at which it'll come undone. "Vito! You stay in there and go get everybody else!" I shout, slightly turning my head so my words are more clear but without diverting my eyes away from the belt clip. I can't tell if he can hear me. Hell, I can't tell if *anyone* can hear me besides Derrick because I can't even hear *myself* with the 9-millimeter consistently going off only a few feet behind me.

Stop shooting!

Derrick desperately attempts to get my attention. "Miles, we gotta go... get the fuck up, man, we can't stay here!" *To no avail.* "Miles!" he screams as he puts his free hand on the hood of my jacket. My anxiety and aggravation are through the roof as I can hear my heartbeat more audibly than my own thoughts.

"Gimme a second..." I calmly but impatiently mutter back as I finally manage to get it undone and practically flip the corpse over as I yank the belt from under it. Having my head straight now, I can see they are already on the street - *not even 50 feet away from us* - and I throw my hand on the floor to grab the revolver before nearly tripping as we simultaneously turn around and bolt for the front gate of the school.

Fuck! I can't run in the snow with this ankle!

As painful as it is for me, Derrick and I make it back into the front courtyard. We simultaneously throw our respective duty belts to the side of the large metal gates, which we immediately attempt to close with as much speed as we can muster given our fatigued states. Derrick slides on the snow below as he attempts to press his body weight against the door but still manages to recover in time to shut it.

We each turn the handle on the bottom of the gate to lock it in place. The doorstoppers fall into their respective slots just as the seemingly impenetrable 12-foot metal gate is met with unimaginable force. The "people" who had previously been chasing us are practically throwing themselves at the gate. *There is no hesitation, no regret, and no fucks to give*. The way they are doing so would be painful for *any* normal human to endure. It isn't calculated. It isn't methodical. It isn't remotely close to what any sane person would categorize as normal. Rather, it's *instinctive, primitive, and barbaric*.

What the hell are you...?

With all of the chaos unfolding around us, I barely even notice our allies trying to force the door open from within after I had instructed Vito to tie it shut. I look at Derrick as he's now fumbling for another magazine in one of the duty belts for the Glock 17 he had dropped in front of where he had slipped a few seconds ago. My hands are shaking, no doubt a mix from both the cold and absolute terror, but I do the only thing I think is rational; I pick up the revolver I had dropped to lock the gate, and I open fire.

This isn't enough... fuck, this isn't enough!

I lose track of the number of shots I let off before finally hearing the dreadful *click* serving as an indicator that I have run out of bullets. Given the heartbreaking realization, I still managed to stop three of them in their tracks. With Derrick struggling to put the magazine into the pistol, I practically throw my Smith & Wesson onto a small pile of snow as I start fumbling for a duty belt myself. It is only a couple of feet away, but it doesn't seem to matter. The unmistakable sound of a hinge breaking off is what immediately causes me to pin myself against the gate to prevent it from coming down entirely.

Oh no…No. No. No!

As my back is against the gate, I can feel the amount of pressure these things are exerting on it - *that doesn't seem possible.* There are less than a dozen of these *things* on the gate itself while the rest are throwing themselves against the 10-foot high exterior metal fence surrounding the gate on both sides. My thoughts are interrupted as I hear Derrick discharging his handgun into the crowd directly behind me. One of the hot pieces of brass lands on my hand as I prop myself up against the gate, instinctively causing me to jolt it away in pain.

"Take your shots carefully!" I yell out as my voice cracks slightly. I simultaneously see a small group of our group barge through the already broken door at the entrance of the building as they all seem to flinch with every shot being fired in front of them. One thing is certain: *I will never forget how petrified they looked when they realized what was going on.*

"Help!" I scream out as loud as I can so they can hear the command over the gunfire. Of the three men who stepped outside, only two came to assist, with Simon being the only one who was frozen in his tracks - *useless motherfucker.* Both *JB* and Jayden push up against the gate with me as I instruct them to hold it while throwing myself at the handgun still lodged in the holster on the duty belt.

Got it!

I turn and pull the trigger once my iron sights are aligned with the head of one of the assailants pushed up against the gate, just for my already deaf ears to be met with a *click* instead of a gunshot.

Oh, for fucks sake! C'mon…

I rack the slide and realign my sights before pulling the trigger and seeing one of the bodies against the other side of the metal gate fall to the ground. Then another. Then another. The standard police-issued Glock 17 has 17 rounds, yet some of them either hit parts of the body that were seemingly ineffective at stopping them or just missed entirely. As I run to get another magazine, I throw the last one from Derrick's duty belt over to him, which he surprisingly catches even in a panicked state. As I kneel to grab the last magazine in the duty belt that I have recovered, I shoot Simon a look and bark at him to help his friends as he is now backed up and against the functional entrance door. There's a look of *pure terror* in his eyes.

I'm not even able to retrieve the magazine before the lower hinge of the right gate snaps off, nearly crushing Pancho in the process but ultimately pinning down Jayden with unimaginable force.

Oh my god.

I will *never* forget the scream Jayden had let out as his body was pummeled with the sheer weight of the steel gate now on his body, mixed with the weight of those *things* that jumped on top of him as he cried out for help.

They waste no time bolting into the courtyard, and we waste no time bolting back to the main entrance either. I was able to count nine of them before I, too, turn around and haul my ass out of that courtyard. The broken door starts to close prematurely after Simon bolts through it, merely seconds before we're given a chance to turn around. Pancho and Derrick practically shove each other as they enter the foyer and I attempt to swing the door shut with my left hand as I bolt my way through.

"Everybody back! Now!" I scream at the small audience of people who are standing around in the main lobby as the three of us close the wooden doors to the foyer. I have the Glock, but no magazine. "*D*! How many rounds do you have left?", I shout as Derrick and I lean against the doors, hoping the hinges won't come off like our previous line of defense. I can see him hesitating to eject the magazine with such danger over our heads. *Literally.*

"I got… uh- I got five rounds… No! Five, plus one in the chamber."

That's not enough…

As I'm struggling to think, I glance at Vito, who seems to be one of the only few in the room not balling his eyes out as the world seems to be crumbling around us.

"Vito! Kiddo, I- I need you to go to Principal Lofter's office, alright?" I say with a slight stutter. I'm not afraid to admit to myself that I was now more scared than ever before. "You know where that is, right? You've been to the main office a thousand times," I exclaim, feeling my wet feet slipping from under me, even while they're against the worn-out wool rug on the floor. "Inside the office, there's a book bag on the coatrack… you need to get me that bag, kiddo. Do you think you can do that for me?" I ask, praying he knows exactly what I'm talking about.

Renata, in her concerned state, holds her son tight, as the disapproval in her face becomes more obvious with each passing second, but concern turns to panic as her son breaks from her grasp and starts running up the stairs toward the second floor. I can hear her yelling for her son to return, but my attention is immediately rerouted to the cracking coming from the two 4-foot tall windowpanes surrounding the foyer on both sides. They're about to break through the doors *and* the windows.

We can do this… c'mon, Miles… we can do this.

The sound of glass cracking becomes more audible with every thud I hear. The doors are becoming increasingly heavy as time progresses, yet time only seems to slow in my eyes as I take a deep breath.

Control these people, Miles… Control the situation… Control…

"Hope, Renata. Get that desk on my right up against the window! Pancho, help them get it up and hold it when they do!" I bark while I drop the empty Glock so I can point at the desk with a free hand. I can feel the pressure on my shoulders becoming nearly unbearable as *Jawbreaker* gets up from against the door to assist the girls.

Control...

I shift my attention to the remaining two in the lobby. "Charlotte, help Simon wheel the desk right there over to this window on my left - your right - quickly," I instruct firmly as the glass seems to become weaker and the sound of cracking becomes unbearable. I see Simon is in shock again.

"Simon! Help Charlotte!" I holler at the top of my lungs as Charlotte also begins pleading with him to help her wheel the desk. My vocals feel like they're bleeding, just as my legs begin to slip a little more.

Derrick fires his Glock 17 near Simon's right arm in an attempt to break him from his state of paralysis - *it worked*. Hesitantly, he begins pushing the desk to one side as Charlotte continues pulling from the other, and the duo manages to flip it over just as relatively large chunks of glass are propelled from that same windowpane. One of the glass shards ricochets off the desk and lodges into my left forearm.

Just as I pull the quarter-sized shard of glass out of my forearm without trying to let out a whimper, I see Vito nearly fall as he slides out of the office and holds a black bag in the air. He's looking directly at me so I can verify if it's the right one. *It is.*

"Throw it, kiddo! Throw it and stay up there..." is all I manage to get out before he flings the bag over the rail with as much effort as an elementary student can. With a loud thud, it lands about eight feet in front of me. I can both hear and see some loose rounds in the bag fumbling out of the small hole on the bottom as it hits the ground.

I can do it...

"Derrick, as soon as I say so, I need you to hold both doors, alright?" I mutter out as I turn my instructions to the rest of the crew while struggling to hold the door as my back is beginning to slide closer to the floor. "The same goes for all of you! Hold your position until I say break, then run to the stairs with everything you got, understood?! Derrick, you'll cover everyone from the right staircase, and I'll go left…" I order while better positioning myself to make a run for the half-opened bag.

"Alright. Derrick, go!" I yell before getting up and making a sprint for the Kimber. In my hasty effort to do so, I see from my peripherals that someone abandoned their position too early from my left and was making a run up the stairs prematurely. *It's Simon.*

Ugh… this motherfucker!

I practically fling the bag as I manage to pull out the 1911 and a spare, single stacked 7-round magazine I had placed in the water bottle net for easier access before storing it in Lofter's office. *Gotta learn from our mistakes right?* I bolt to about the eighth step on the left staircase and ready my weapon at the door while flicking the safety off.

"Break! Break!" I shout as soon as I hear the safety switch off. The first people to move are Renata - *no doubt to get back to her son* - and Hope, followed by *JB*. Next up is Charlotte, who is squealing as she is barely able to support the weight of the desk herself after Simon ran. I nod at Derrick, whose face is turning red as he continues to withstand the immense pressure from behind him while waiting for my signal. I nod, and he gives off a sigh of relief as he sprints for the staircase. *Then they come…*

The wooden doors of the Foyer fly open with so much force that I half expect them to drop off the hinges right then and there. The glass surrounding the exterior of the now crowded foyer shatters as some of those *things* clumsily fall through each of the windows, only to be illuminated by the dim light seeping through the two much larger, gated windows in the main lobby.

"Fire!" is all I hear Derrick shout as best as he can from across the room before his firearm starts to go off. I follow suit as soon as the first gunshot rips through the air. I can see some of the bodies dropping as the faint sunlight and our muzzle flashes are the only things providing us with any source of light in the near pitch-black structure. These things seem to now be stumbling toward us and slowly climbing the stairs, just as the 2nd guy who attacked me did when I ran up the southeast stairwell.

What the hell...?

As the magazine runs dry, I quickly insert the second magazine I have in my pocket before releasing the slide and shooting one of the things above its right eye, causing its now lifeless body to fall down the stairs and trip the last two on my stairwell as one was ascending the right staircase. I can just barely make out the slide of Derrick's Glock being locked to the rear - *he's empty*. I quickly turn my dimly lit tritium iron sights to the one in front of him as best as I can in the dark before briefly witnessing the aforementioned silhouette collapse just a few steps from where Derrick is standing on the stairwell.

Now backing up myself, I return my focus to the two in front of me and, as they are steadily ascending the staircase one step at a time, I manage to pull the trigger as both of their heads line up for what feels like less than a millisecond. *Bang*.

Is- is that... is that it?

Silence. Even with the all-too-familiar ringing in my ears having returned and now at full throttle, I can still feel the uneasy silence in the room. Even out of breath, I turn my eyes toward the top of the stairwell behind me while still keeping my firearm pointed toward the Lobby. I can see Renata embracing her son as she's on both knees while Hope is doing her best to console Charlotte, who has her arms around Hope's neck. She's trying, but failing, not to cry out loud. Pancho is checking to see if his friend, Derrick, is alright while I make my way upstairs once I give the Lobby a final look over. *Silence*.

I check to see how many rounds I have left in Kimber's worn-out, single-stacked magazine as I eject it from the handgun while turning to walk up the stairwell. *Four rounds*. I can hear the audible *click* from inside the grip of the 1911, indicating the magazine is locked in place as I slam it back in before putting it in my waistband and setting my eyes on Simon Adams. He's leaning against the closed door to the classroom directly in front of the Main Office's entrance while adjusting his glasses, or so he was before I got to him.

All the pain I have experienced throughout the past twenty-four hours pales in comparison to how my knuckles feel once they connect with Simon's chin. He stumbles over as my fist makes its way back around. Even though his nearly transparent glasses fall to the ground after the impact, I don't even give him a chance to recover before grabbing him by the collar of his dark red polo shirt and pinning him against the closed door with both of my hands.

"You piece of shit… You *left us*!" I scream only inches away from his face. As I glare directly into his eyes, I can hear everyone else stumbling their way over to us in a concerted manner. *So much for the peace and quiet.* I can hear someone calling my name from my side, yet I pay no attention to it as my mind is elsewhere.

"Charlotte almost *died* because of you," I growl as my tone becomes deeper than it has been in months. I ignore the pain in my knuckles as my hands are getting tighter around his throat. I start to lower my voice as my face gets closer to his. "Jayden *did die* because of you…" I whisper loud enough for only him to hear. He looks *terrified*.

"Miles, stop!" I hear in a voice that no doubt belongs to someone going through the stages of puberty. *To no avail.*

This man is a coward…

Now *everyone* is screaming my name as Simon's white complexion is being polluted with dark shades of red and blue. *To no avail.*

This man is dangerous…

I slam Adam's head against the window of the classroom door by pushing his throat with my left hand as my right pulls out the Kimber and brings it up under his bruised, and possibly dislocated, chin. The small audience of people around me seems to all take a step back simultaneously.

This man should not be with us…

The shouting around me seems to supersede the ringing in my ears as I start to anticipate it will be drowned out by another gunshot momentarily. They're taking steps closer. They're telling me to stop. My heart rate is out of control, but my mind is clear. I know what needs to be done. Then I hear it. The sound of metallic scraping emanating from outside the main entrance. It sounds louder than all of the gunshots and shouting combined, yet it's nothing when compared to the excruciating slam that follows shortly thereafter.

There can't be more… No… I thought we-

I can hear Simon practically wheezing for fresh air from behind my shoulder as I withdraw my hand and lean my triceps along the railing of the staircase where the kid threw the bag over. I position my sights toward the broken foyer doors below as something enters through the partially open, busted blue door in the main entrance. Now my mind *was* racing, but it went absolutely quiet once I saw what came through. *Or who…*

But…

I can hear nothing but *hysteria* from one of the girls behind me as every single one of us sets our eyes on the familiar dark-skinned man whose complexion seems to be radiating in the dim sunlight. My head turns slightly to reveal a severely distraught Charlotte falling to the ground as Hope and Derrick do their best to prevent her from running downstairs. As my eyes revert forward, I can see Jayden as clear as day. His body is disheveled, with blood oozing from the various bite marks and chunks of missing tissue covering his upper torso. Even as he stands nearly forty feet away, I can tell one of his legs is broken, yet that doesn't seem to phase Jayden in the slightest as remains standing while sporadically scanning the room and letting out an agonizing groan. I found myself shuttering, no doubt a mix of disbelief and fear, right alongside those around me.

The sounds of trembling breaths and the occasional gasps must have caught his attention because Jayden shoots us a slow, yet steady, glance from the lobby and nearly trips over one of the decaying corpses on the floor as he stumbles toward us from the stairs. I can see parts of his previously cream, cashmere turtleneck are missing and, instead, are replaced with dark red patches of blood. His eyes look almost translucent in the darkness.

I won't…

Charlotte's screaming becomes almost intolerable as Jayden shambles his way upstairs in a clumsy manner. I can see Derrick continue to hold her arms in an attempt to keep her away from her boyfriend. *Jawbreaker* puts his arm in front of me. In his own way, he's telling me to get back.

I can't.

I brush *JB's* arm to the side as he retrieves a now broken, yet sharp, wooden mop handle that I can only assume he brought as an improvised weapon. Even with all the commotion unfolding around me, my eyes are still fixated on Jayden. His groans of agony slowly turn into a nearly inaudible growl, which seems to get louder with every step he takes. Despite Pancho's pleas of concern to stay back, I step onto the top of the landing and look at my seemingly deceased acquaintance. My right hand, still holding the handgun, drops to my side.

I- I have to…

A single second passes. Then two. If I'm being honest, I can't tell you how much time it takes. Yet, as hard of a decision as it is to make, I have no other choice. I begin to raise the gun as my hand begins to tremble. It feels heavier with each passing second. As Jayden continues to close the distance between the two of us, I take what has to be the deepest inhale I have ever taken. With my right hand stabilizing,

I let out a long exhale as I glance at the man one last time. I'm alive because of him. We *all* are. With the gun now motionless in the air, I wait until Jayden's head is positioned mere inches away from the barrel before pulling the trigger once the sights are aligned with the top of his head.

Thank you. Bang.

Jayden's body falls down the stairs with a loud thud with every cobblestone step his corpse hits along the way. When it finally stops at the bottom of the stairwell, I can hear the sound of liquid dripping onto the floor of the main lobby. I can't even tell if Charlotte is screaming anymore. My mind is so clouded that the only thing I can hear is my own heart nearly pounding out of my chest. I don't know how long I was standing on that landing, yet it wasn't until Renata grabbed me by the hand that I turned around.

I... what did I do?

I can see tears in Renata's eyes as I glance over to see half of the group consoling Charlotte while the other half, including Vito, is checking to make sure Simon is breathing. I don't know what is happening in the world. I don't even know what's happening in this city. Hell, I don't even know what change is occurring in our own backyard. I do know one thing, though: *Something in here has got to change, too.*

CHAPTER 5

YIELD TO THE NEW ORDER

Ledger

Vito Caruso	Renata Caruso
Hope Starcov	Charlotte Kennedy
Pancho Ruiz	Simon Adams
Derrick Simmons	~~Jayden Walker~~

(There are 18 additional names on the list)

Journal Entry: I can't get over the kid. We got him killed because of negligence. Fucking stupid! I know it's been a few weeks, yet every time I see Charlotte, I get flooded with guilt. ~~How the hell was I supposed to know they were engaged?~~ On the bright side, we were able to bring in a few more people over the last couple of days. I had Derrick and ~~Pancho~~ JB help me with security as we started bringing more eyes to the school. I can't do everything by myself.

We were barely able to fix the broken doors and windows with the shit we got around the place, yet I know we need to be doing more here. We've rounded up some small weapons from those who we brought in, yet our food is my primary concern. What we've got left will only last for so long.

We need more...

I SLAM MY BOOK CLOSED in aggravation, probably stemming from the guilt I feel around Jayden and how it could've been avoided, as I can hear a handful of kids laughing in the third-floor gym. That's the perk of bringing in families with children. Having worked security here, I would normally shutter at the idea of living with kids, yet their authentic giggles seem to shed some much-needed light on an otherwise dark situation.

At least Vito can make a friend or two, I suppose.

I begin to rise from the chair in Principal Lofter's Office when I'm met with a faint thud under the desk in front of me. The Kimber I have sitting in my hard shell thigh holster, collided with the bottom of the mahogany wood desk as I stood up. This gun stays on me at all times now. I'm not taking any chances. I shift around to clear the obstacle and close the window on my right to cut off the cold breeze. *It's snowing again.* I put the journal on the desk and make my way out of the office before closing the door behind me and walking towards the classroom that I almost killed Simon in front of.

I can still feel my knuckles hurting from that day, yet they're healing up quite nicely.

When I peer into the classroom, I can see the sleeping bags of the people we have brought in so far. There's only a couple and their daughter in the room, who all appear to be focused on their seemingly tense match of *tic-tac-toe* being played on the dirty chalkboard near the wall. *Killing time perhaps?* I turn around to head down to the cafeteria. I think it's lunchtime.

I walk down the hallway of the second floor as I pass the library on my way to the rear staircase near the elevator. Instinctively, I immediately recall my second encounter with these *things* before averting my eyes toward the hall and proceeding onwards.

I'm glad that horrid smell faded with time after we carried him out to the back. I thought it would never leave…

As I head down the stairs and walk into the Cafeteria, the smell of food being cooked in the kitchen starting to make me hungry, I see both familiar and not-so-familiar faces strewn around the room, sitting at different tables. The first person I notice on my right near the old vending machine is Charlotte, using her plastic spork to toss some vegetables around in her small styrofoam cup. Anyone with a brain and functioning eyes can tell she's heartbroken just by looking at her. *Poor thing.*

Here comes the guilt again…

A few tables down, I see Hope talking with a newer member of our little family. *I think his name's Jack. John? No, David.* From what I remember from his interview, he's a little younger than Hope, but his deep voice seems to contradict that fact. Nonetheless, I make my way to the left of the room to get in line with the rest of those waiting for food. I can see Vito, who I could've sworn I heard playing upstairs, volunteering to give food out with his mother and a few other guys whose faces I can't yet put names to. He's barely able to reach over the small glass panel separating the line from the kitchen.

"You work so damn hard; I didn't think I'd see you awake until the evening if I'm being honest" I hear with a chuckle as footsteps approach me from behind. It's Derrick, walking up to me with a plastic tray in his hand as his other is on his hip. His Glock 17 is visible inside his belt.

How the fuck did he get a tray before I did?

"Ah hey, partner," I say with a chuckle of my own, although mine is more tiresome compared to his. "This kid is my role model," I say truthfully as I point toward Vito, who notices me with my finger in the air as he hands a cup of warm baby carrots to a person twice his size, nearly two feet in front of him. He waved to me with so much enthusiasm that I thought he was going to accidentally sprain his wrist.

"That kid is going to outlive us all, I'm sure of it," I say to Derrick with a sharp pain in my side as I let out a laugh that was louder than the previous one. *I need some water.*

When the person in front of me steps off, I pick up one of the beige plastic trays on the right near the thick green gate blocking the window. When I step in front of one of the men helping with the food, I wish him good morning before placing my tray above the glass, only to be met with a small amount of pasta in return.

Did I just say good morning when it's the afternoon? Great job, Miles.

As I shuffle to the left, I find myself in front of Renata, who shoots me a smile and greets me before I am even able to open my mouth to do the same.

"Hi, Miles," she says in a cute but non-flirtatious manner that fills my stomach with butterflies nevertheless as she puts a portion of freshly cooked white rice on an empty section of my tray.

"Good morning," I say enthusiastically.

Nice...

Her subtle laugh makes me freeze in place as I attempt to analyze her body language to see whether she is laughing *with me* or *at me*. I can't figure it out before I'm nudged in my arm by the left elbow of the armed and muscular man standing on my right. "Alright, alright, I'm going," I let out playfully to Derrick as he chuckles again. He can probably sense my embarrassment.

I shuffle a few more paces to the left until I am directly in front of Vito, who is reaching out with a half-filled cup of baby carrots, probably the same bag of baby carrots I had dropped weeks earlier, yet my cup seems to have nearly half the amount of carrots than the person who came before me.

I feel cheated here.

"Hi, Miles!" Vito lets out with invigorating energy. I almost feel fully awake just hearing him. "It's my birthday today!" he shouts out as he stomps in place in a jovial manner.

"Hey, that's fantastic! Happy birthday, kiddo. So, how old are you now?" I ask with a friendly tone as I take the small styrofoam cup from his hand. He takes his other hand to extend something else to me before whispering to me from behind the glass.

"Thirteen. And *here*. Don't tell the others," he says as he backs away from the glass but leaves a small area of fog on it in his attempt to remain quiet. *I'm sure the others near us still heard him, anyway.*

"Animal crackers?" I ask in a confused yet appreciative tone as he places his pointing finger over his mouth - *sign language to keep my mouth shut* - before he begins to fill up Derrick's cup of baby carrots.

This boy is going places.

I take a seat at a table near the end of the cafeteria, close to the three sets of wooden double doors acting as the main entrance for the room. Derrick takes a seat across from me about a minute or so after he has gotten his food from Vito. Again, I can see his cup of baby carrots exceeds my own.

Ain't this some shit…

I sit up as I take one of his mozzarella sticks and exchange it for my carton of chocolate milk that I grabbed on my way over here. His face says it all: *disappointed but content*. He then starts to peel the carton open as he begins talking in a serious yet still energetic tone. "Alright, Miles. What's the plan today?" he asks as his eyebrows raise when he takes a sip of the moderately cold milk.

"I think we should start checking out apartments and stores nearby for food. We have some for now, but with every other person we bring in, our time cuts down substantially," I say as I take a bite of the mozzarella stick. *It's cold.*

Son of a bitch…

He nods in agreement as he is chewing on his rice with his mouth closed. From how he's bobbing his head up and down slowly, I can tell he's enjoying his food. *That's one of us…*

"You want me to take the lead on this?" he asks as he finishes chewing. "I mean… we have a few more guns. Why don't I take *JB* out with a few of these newer guys and check out the buildings across the street? There's even a supermarket down the block, next to the train," he informs me, not knowing I've worked here long enough to know what's around the area.

"Nah, man. Most of the guns should stay here. I have *JB* watching the kids upstairs in the gym since he's the only other one with a gun right now besides us," I say before I take a bite of the pasta. *Surprisingly, there's nothing off about the pasta.* I manage to finish chewing before he can, so I continue chatting.

"The supermarket is probably cleaned out, but you and I can probably check-", I say before being cut off abruptly by the sound of distant gunfire. It's not in the school, yet it sounds close nonetheless. We stand up, and I ask Derrick if he can hear it as he starts to put his hand on the pistol.

Looking around, I notice some of the people in the room begin to look slightly spooked and frightened, so I slowly take my right hand off my Kimber as I put my left hand on the one Derrick is gripping his pistol with. "*Let it go. The last thing we want in here is to start a panic,*" I whisper as he slowly puts his hand back at his side. I use my hands to motion to everyone looking in my direction to sit back down. Many obliged as the gunfire stopped.

"We need to check that out," I say intently as I take one spoonful of rice, then give my tray to someone sitting behind me.

"But… can I at least finish the food?", he asks while trying to imitate the look a puppy gives you when you yell at it.

"Motherfucker…" I say in a whisper - *so nearby kids wouldn't hear me* - before letting out a sigh. "Fine, but be dressed by the time I come down. It's going to be cold out there," I instruct as I point to the white tank top that looks too tight for his muscular figure. "And who the hell wears a tank top in the winter, anyway?" I ask as I retract my finger.

"Who the hell thinks *Jawbreaker* is a cool name?" he retaliates with a slight attitude that is met with a heartfelt cackle.

Fair enough.

As I start to pull open one of the six doors to the cafeteria entrance, I can see Simon ready to open the same door from the opposite side. I glance at him and catch myself rolling my eyes as I use another door to exit the room, without saying so much as a word when I pass him. I begin to make my way down towards the main hallway as I try not to give it another thought.

Prick.

* * *

As I make my way to the Westside Stairwell on the first floor, closest to the auditorium, I position my body toward the water fountain to grab a much-needed drink of water since I had surrendered my only beverage for a stale mozzarella stick. Before I can reach it, I pass the open classroom that sits directly in front of the two wooden doors that lead into the main lobby, which still smells like iron, and stop in my tracks as I notice supplies strewn all across the floor from the desk that formerly belonged to one of the teachers here. Since it's in the same direction, I glance outside one of the windows facing the rear courtyard and freeze.

Oh, fuck! Fuck!

I unholster my Kimber and sprint to the exit leading into the rear courtyard at the end of the westside stairwell. As I approach the door, I can see there is a pencil sharpener holding it open slightly.

What the-?

Without so much as a second thought, I forcefully make my way through the partially opened metal door as I lay my eyes on them. Seeing four well-bundled men, two of whom are carrying what appear to be bolt-action rifles, I plant my two feet perfectly in the light snow as soon as I clear the doorway leading outside. Their presence doesn't concern me; what does is the fact that they are peering into the cafeteria from nearly 20 feet away. Seeing this, I fire a round into the air as a warning shot, then proceed to aim at the men with both hands on my weapon.

"Everybody get down!" I shout at the top of my lungs. The sudden gunshot and command aren't meant for the men; it is meant to alert those inside of the building. I can tell from how the men nearly slid on the black ice below that they were all caught off guard. The men who were armed had raised their weapons in my direction once they managed to catch their balance. From my peripherals, I can see movement on my left, confirming that my warning shot had worked to get everybody who was inside away from the windows. I briefly avert my attention to the third-floor windows on my right to see *JB* bolt away once I catch a glimpse of him.

Did he see me?

"Don't you fucking move!" I bark at the guys standing about fifteen yards in front of me. At this range, I can hit them with ease, but that goes both ways. One of the armed strangers, who seems to be limping, has the look of fear all over his face. As luck would have it, the harsh snowfall hitting my face doesn't make it any easier for my eyes to stay on target. "We don't want to hurt you, and we don't plan on it, yet what happens next depends on you," I exclaim before the door leading to the east stairwell on my left is flung open. Derrick fixes his eyes on the threat as he aligns his now-drawn pistol in their direction.

"Do as the man says!" Derrick hollers at the men standing motionless in front of us. My hands are shaking in the cold, yet not enough to disorient my aim. I can see both of the rifles are still pointed at me. Before anyone can say anything, I hear the door directly behind me being pushed open from the inside with great force. The recognizable voice calms me down a little.

"Well, ain't this a motherfuckin' pickle we got ourselves into, huh boys?" I hear Pancho say as his monotone laugh seems to anger one of the unarmed men. I can hear the same unarmed men shout something in Spanish to one of the other guys holding a rifle and see *JB* take a step forward to interrupt them, his grip on the second Glock 17 recovered from the deceased police officer weeks earlier transitions from one hand to two. I don't know what the guy said, but it wasn't something Pancho wanted to hear.

Control the situation, Miles.

"Tell these guys to drop their rifles. Either they give 'em up or we put 'em down…" I direct to *Jawbreaker* without letting my eyes off the group. I can see Derrick is beginning to flank them slowly on the left. Even in the cold with a tank top, his grip on the handgun is not faltering. "We all have people to look after, so let's make sure we keep it that way, yeah?" I let out with a confident posture so as not to show any signs of fear or weakness.

Don't do it, guys. Please, don't do it.

My head is pounding but I remain calm nonetheless. As does Derrick. As does *JB*. We wait. And we wait. Then it happens.

"Ok!" I hear one of the armed Spanish men shout in broken English as he drops the weapon. It makes a muffled *thud* as it hits the snow below him. He throws his arms in the air with little effort as he backhands his seemingly injured friend on the right firmly in the arm, signaling him to drop the rifle. *He does.* As I size up our most recent acquaintances, my eyes stop once they notice a tightly wrapped strand of fabric around the limping man's right ankle. By the looks of it, there's dried blood that has seeped through the make-shift bandage. Although the urge to ask about it begins to surface in my mind, I ultimately bury the inquiry as I gain a better grip on my handgun.

My saviors and I begin closing in on the small group without lowering our guard. We don't know these people. We've brought in armed people before, but *not* like this. Not a great start to a friendship, I'll admit. I keep my weapon trained on the group as their now discarded weapons are confiscated by my security, yet I start to lower it once I see Derrick and *JB* have cleared a considerable amount of space between themselves and the men.

"Ask them to lift their jackets and show me their waistline," I command over to Pancho as he pauses for a moment and, after realizing what I am doing, he begins to translate. They all do as they're told, albeit with a little hesitation, even as I circle my finger in the air, signaling them to spin around. I don't see anyone concealing anything under their clothes, yet I guess my companions don't either because they give me a quick nod once I give them a brief once-over.

With the weapon being placed into my retention holster with an audible *click,* I proceed to offer an apology to the guys and offer them some food for their troubles. Although I'm still on high alert, I do my best to show what civility I can given the barbarity we've all faced over the past few weeks.

"I am sorry about all of this," I say with both authenticity and a slight shiver in my voice. I place my hands in my pockets for some semblance of warmth as my eyes instinctively continue to size up the group. I can see the guys to my side lowering their handguns as well when *JB* starts speaking to the men in Spanish. From the words I can make out, I can tell he's repeating what I said so they can understand me. He then gives me a nod before I turn back to the men and proceed.

"We have a lot to talk about, yet how about we get some chow and calm ourselves first, huh?" I ask as my question is subsequently translated. I can see their nods of acceptance and start making my way to the door I had previously come through before knocking on it with some effort. Thankfully, it's one-way, so it has to be opened from within. Once we're let in by a short, middle-aged woman with red hair who I recognize as the mother of one of the kids we took in, I thank her and take the lead to show the men the cafeteria as my guys follow closely behind them. I can hear the sound of distant groaning echoing through the air as the doors shut close.

As we enter the cafeteria, I reassure those who are still taking cover under the tables and behind the pillars. "It's alright, everyone. There's no harm done here. These men were just looking to join us for a meal, that's all. They just lost the entrance," I shout out with an awkward laugh as I can see people hesitantly resuming their previous activities with inaudible murmurs under their breaths.

Tough crowd.

I turn around and use my hand as a signal for the men to wait as I begin walking to the back of the group and toward Pancho. I can see he is a little uneasy, yet he's still maintaining his composure even after all of the stress.

"How are you doing, *JB*?" I ask with concern but in a mellow tone. I notice him shifting around in place as he readjusts the holster on his duty belt. Unlike Derrick, *Jawbreaker* just took the whole belt for himself following the incident with Jayden.

"I'm good, yeah. Heard the shot, so I left the kids upstairs and ran out to help, y'know?" he says, crossing his arms in a way that suggests he's waiting for me to scold him about leaving the kids.

I put one of my arms over his neck as I lightly pound his chest with my fist like King Kong would then proceed to slowly grab the rifle he had picked up from outside. "Nah, man. You did great, you hear me?" I reassure him as his look of concern fades away. "You looked out for me when I needed you, and I won't forget that," I say in a low tone so others won't ease their way into the conversation. I can see people glaring at the men with distrust and skepticism.

"Why don't you show these guys where they can get some food, yeah? When *that one* is done, see if you can escort him to the Nurse's office on the second floor, alright?" I ask after briefly pointing at the man with the bleeding ankle wound before nudging *JB* forward a little on his back with my free hand. He agrees and begins speaking Spanish while leading the way to the cafeteria line. I shoot a quick look at Renata and Vito. Their demeanors changed from that of joy to that resembling discomfort.

I take a few steps back, rifle pointed downwards with my right hand, and toward the entrance of the cafeteria as Derrick, with the second bolt-action rifle leaning against his thigh, starts rubbing his biceps to create a little bit of heat.

I guess that tank top isn't as warm as I thought it was.

"*Keep an eye on 'em…*" I instruct with a whisper as I glare over at the men, who are now grabbing trays from the short stack I had gotten mine from earlier. With my eyes remaining glued to them, I continue speaking to Derrick discreetly. "I'm going to drop this rifle off in the office, then check on the other kids, hold the fort while I'm gone, yeah?" I ask as I break my glance away to look at Derrick. He nods before walking toward the group without so much as a word; his own newly acquired rifle is resting in his arms. I glance over to Simon, who's sitting near where Charlotte had been sitting earlier this morning. He keeps giving a side eye to our newest arrivals. Not wanting to take another look at Simon, I turn around and exit the cafeteria before making my way outside to the hallway.

* * *

After propping the rifle against the mahogany desk in the Principal's office - *the same room I am discreetly storing all of the other recently confiscated weapons* - and closing the door behind me, I head up the west stairwell and swing open the heavy oak wood door leading into the third-floor gym. The first thing I notice is the five kids playing dodgeball with one of the balls taken from inside the storage closet. I can see Hope and David watching the kids together while sitting against the gates designed to block the windows from the children's access, so I start making my way over to them.

I try to avoid the balls as I jog past the kids playing in their respective, *but uneven* teams, yet one of them beams a slightly deflated blue ball at my head and giggles as he runs away, leaving me with a headache that is now worse than the one I had just seconds ago.

This is why I can't have kids…

"Hey, guys," I mutter as I continue rubbing my head with my right hand. "How long have you guys been here?"

"Oh, howdy Miles," I hear Hope say with an adorable jitter, accompanied by a little bit of concern trailing in her voice. "We came up together after we heard a gunshot a few minutes ago, but… is- is everything okay? I mean, we didn't know what to do or where to go and-" she says before I cut her off. I don't want her or any of the kids to worry.

"Yeah, no, we're alright. No need to worry," I reassure Hope as I can hear her take a long exhale through her nose. I can see David is a little uncomfortable.

Am I third-wheeling?

"There were some men who were lost. We brought them in, at least for now, so I have Derrick and Pancho watching them in the cafeteria until they're ready to talk with us," I say as I put my hands on my hips. "Just wanted to make sure everyone was okay, that's all," I say as I voice my concern.

"Awe, well, we're alright," she says in a Southern accent as she tucks a small strand of blonde hair behind her ear. With every word she says, I can tell she's not from around here. "I'm just looking after the babies," she declares in a friendly manner as she looks at the kids, who are now arguing about who gets who while they begin to switch teams.

I give her a side grin as I reach behind me after a long pause. "I… uh, I want you to have this," I say as I unclip and turn over the .357 Smith & Wesson I had been carrying in my rear holster. At first, she looks bewildered, but as I kneel in front of her, I can see her face turning a little red.

"But… I- I've never shot a gun before," she admits as she looks back up at me, awaiting a response.

A Southerner who doesn't know how to shoot? That doesn't seem right.

"I promise I'll teach you once we have a little more time, alright? For now, I don't trust anyone else to look out for these kids as much as you," I say as I recall Hope consoling Charlotte and Vito after what happened with Jayden. I extend the weapon out to her while it's still in the holster and can see David turning his face away as I do so. I guess I was right about him feeling uncomfortable. I usher her a slight nod of approval as she looks up at me. She slowly grabs it with both hands; the weight undoubtedly catches her by surprise as her eyes nearly pop out of her head once she has a good grip on the stainless steel revolver.

"Now, it's a *little* heavy for someone who's never held one, but you pull this thing back and then pull the trigger when you're ready to fire," I explain as I point to the hammer followed by the trigger. I can see her nodding as I explain it to her. "My one rule though: *Never* point this at anyone you don't want to hurt, alright?" I ask in a serious tone while I look into her eyes for confirmation that she has registered what I said.

"I won't let you down," she says as she places the holstered firearm in her lap and shoots me a smile. Her blonde hair seems to glisten in the sunlight, and I notice a faint smell of perfume as I begin to stand up.

"I wouldn't be here if I thought you would. Thank you, Hope," I say as I give another glance at David, who seems preoccupied with his fingernails, then glance at the kids before making my way down the rear staircase and back to the cafeteria.

I land on the first floor and make my way through the westside stairwell before I hear the distant but unmistakable sound of arguing. Coming out of the stairwell through a poorly painted wooden white door, I see Derrick pointing the Remington bolt-action rifle at one of the men whom we had brought inside no more than twenty minutes ago. The man in question has his arm around someone's neck.

Oh shit... shit, shit...

My foot is almost caught on the doorframe as I begin running down the hallway, unholstering my Kimber in the process. I can see a large group of people around the man, which blocks my view of who they are holding.

"Get back!" I yell to the crowd as many are caught off guard by my sudden appearance. The crowd begins to disperse as the shouting gets louder, and the previously inaudible dialogue from the onlookers becomes clear. I keep my handgun pointed toward the ground as the people around me continue to clear a path. It doesn't take long before I have a clear visual of what's going on.

To my dismay, I can see one of the previously unarmed men we had encountered earlier is now shielding his body behind Pancho, his attacker holding a Glock 17 to his head which was undoubtedly stolen from *JB's* duty belt when he was grabbed.

"Let him go!" I command as I begin to align the sights of my handgun with the attacker's head and flip off the safety. I can't get a clear shot with Pancho in the way. Derrick doesn't seem to react to my arrival at all, but the hostage taker gets startled when he sees I'm armed.

Crap, there's kids here...

As I constantly flick my eyes back and forth between the assailant and the crowd surrounding us, I notice Renata standing directly behind Derrick as she covers her son from harm.

"Renata, take the kids out of here!" I bark without any hesitation or deviation in my tone of voice. I meant what I said. I can see her grabbing her son and another little girl nearby, probably a few years younger than Vito, before she makes her way behind me and pushes through the door leading into the closest stairwell.

With the children gone, my focus is immediately back on the assailant about twelve feet in front of me as I repeat my instructions to the remainder of the crowd. Some flee due to being overcome with fear, while the brave ones do their best to take cover behind anything they can find nearby that would allow them to continue their observations out of harm's way. I can only make out a few words from the older, ragged-looking Spanish man holding Pancho as he starts to speak the same broken English his friend had earlier.

"*Propano y la comida. F- Food. Need food…*" the man says in broken English that was accompanied by a minor stutter. I guess he senses my confusion, so he stops his attempt to communicate in English altogether and begins talking in what I can only imagine is his native language. "*Y también quiero todas las pistolas,*" the man declares in a very ferocious manner as he seems to press the stolen firearm more firmly against Pancho's right temple. I can see Pancho desperately attempting to pull the man's arms away from his throat to catch his breath. It doesn't seem to be working too well.

"*JB…* tell him I'll have his rifles returned to him with a little food as long as he lets you go. Tell him they can keep the pistol, too. But we gotta see him lower it," I command, knowing it's merely a bluff. This man *is not* walking out of here with *anything*. The petrified look of the man in question, as well as the impatient yet uneasy facial expressions coming from his associates pacing back-and-forth on the side of him, tells me they don't believe they're walking out of here, either.

I can vaguely make out Pancho's attempt to translate as the man interrupts him. He is now speaking Spanish again as he turns his head to communicate with Pancho directly, struggling to hold him upright in the process.

I need to get that gun away from his head…

"What is he saying?" I shout out as I discreetly approach the stone pillar a few feet on my left for cover. I can see Derrick from the side of my eye doing the same as he notices me cautiously walking. He positions his body and rifle behind one of the other gray stone pillars in the large, open area near the cafeteria entrance.

"He… he doesn't want just the rifles," he manages to mutter out with a harsh cough, no doubt from his consistent asphyxiation, before attempting to speak again. "These *putos*… want all nine guns we have in your office-" he cries out before being hit on his head with the bottom of the gun. I assume the disheveled man holding him wasn't a fan of what he was called.

How did they know about the-?

"Alright! Alright. I can- I can do that!" I shout out as my stomach turns inside out. I feel sick. As much as I want to throw up at the thought of these men knowing our business, I maintain my composure and keep my aim steady. "But he needs to listen to me if he wants his shit," I shout directly at Pancho knowing he'll translate my instructions. "He needs to trust me." I see the man shutter with every word Pancho struggles to let out with his constricted vocals.

He doesn't believe me… think, Miles.

"Hey! Look at me when I'm talking to you, asshole!" I shout out louder than anything else I've said in the past few minutes, only this time, the words are being directed at the disheveled man, himself. It seems to garner his attention as he suddenly trains his eyes on me once his words to Pancho are rudely interrupted. As the sudden command fills the air, some of the onlookers, including the hostile men within their group, jump as the words echo throughout the room.

Yeah, motherfucker… look at me…

"You hear me talking to you, right? So you fuckin' look at *me*!" I exclaim with a now serious, but firm tone. All of the worry in my voice previously seems to vaporize into thin air as the man's prior look of worry and mistrust turns into anger. His eyebrows are flared and I can feel him staring *through* me as if I am now an immediate threat.

"You want your shit? Then how about you act like a man instead of being such a little *bitch*," I annunciate as best as I can over all the chatter filling the air. The man is furious, which is evident from how he grabs Pancho by the neck and hastily forces his body to the side as the man raises his gun in my direction.

Bang.

My heart feels like it's in my throat as the gunshot echoes throughout the open space. I can see *JB* losing his balance as the man is still gripping his neck while he falls back. The wooden doors directly behind where the man was standing, the ones leading outside to the East parking lot, are now dripping with blood. I can see white smoke exiting from the barrel of my Kimber as the now-deceased attacker drops the Glock 17 he was holding with an audible rattle. Some of the onlookers begin running away, while everyone else in the room is looking at me in shock, including Derrick.

Before anyone else can move, the Spanish man who had been limping around his now-deceased buddy begins to stumble for the handgun lying idly on the ground. Even with his ever-worsening ankle making his steps toward the pistol look sloppy and sporadic, the man seems to ignore the pain as he reaches down to grab the weapon. I step out of cover and begin walking toward the group as the remainder of the onlookers begin to bolt away from the commotion.

Bang. Bang.

The man, who is mere inches away from reaching the polymer pistol, topples over as both rounds I had fired go through his torso, spattering the walls with dark shades of red. His agonizing shrieks of pain come to an abrupt stop once I'm about a foot away from him. In an attempt to stop the bleeding, the incapacitated man is desperately clutching his torso with both hands. Without another second to waste, I bring my weapon up to his forehead before swiftly pulling the trigger.

Bang. Silence.

The blowback from the execution forces me to blink as a wet substance splashes over many parts of my face. In no time, the familiar smell of iron hits my nose harder than it had ever done before. The two remaining men were crying out in anguish as they had just witnessed the death of their two colleagues. One of them nearly pisses himself as I make eye contact with him before I hesitantly put my gun in the holster and make my way to him.

Derrick runs past me to check on Pancho, who is still violently coughing on his knees to catch his breath. The gust of warm air that brushes past me as Derrick does seems to spread the blood I feel on my face, yet I pay no mind to it. I grab one of the guys with both of my hands and prop him up against the cold stone wall on the side of the male bathroom facing the pillar I had previously positioned myself behind.

"Where?" I demand in a tone so deep that the familiar taste of blood seems to reach my throat again. "Where did you hear about the guns?" I call out as I pull out my firearm from the holster and place it inside his mouth. I will never forget the look on this man's face; he was petrified. I can hear him trying to speak, yet the only thing that comes out is inaudible gargling. I take the gun out and place the warm barrel against the man's temple.

"Anteojos!" the man repeatedly screams out in fear as he begins to cry. I can't make out what else he's saying, but he seems to be rambling to me. The incessant dialogue is starting to agitate me more than I already am, yet I hear *JB* attempt to speak in between his coughing fits.

"He… he said, gl- glasses," *JB* mutters before he pukes on the floor directly between his hands. I take a step back and start to process what I was just told as I bring the handgun to my side. After what seems like an eternity, I turn back to the man in front of me as he begins to clamp his hands together. I can tell he's begging for mercy. I don't need to understand what he saying to see that.

Control...

I abruptly raise the .45 caliber handgun to the man's head but before I can do anything else, I hear Derrick shout my name to the right of me. He tackles the fourth Spanish man to the ground as he attempts to fumble for the 9mm pistol that his former associate was reaching for. As my head turns, the crying man before me is now attempting to strike me as I interrupt his swing mid-air. We stumble to the ground, causing my handgun to slide a few feet away from us after suddenly being slapped out of my right hand.

Ugh... you- motherfuck-

I can see Derrick pinning the other man to the ground while the man's futile attempt to pull Derrick off using his tank top was failing. Derrick was too big for this scrawny kid to handle alone. *JB*, who was now wiping his mouth with the back of his fist as he starts to get up, stumbles back down as the pinned man manages to kick Pancho's knee while he attempts to grab Derrick's recently dropped rifle.

My attacker punches me in the abdomen before positioning himself on top of me. Every punch to the face is blocked with my forearms, yet I can feel pain shooting up my whole body as he jabs my lower back. One punch. Then another. Then another. Each one sends more pain to my lower back than the last. I grab the back of his neck with both hands as he begins to wind for another blow, then pull his head towards me as I push mine towards him with as much force as I can muster from the ground. I can see some of the blood on my face transferring to his forehead upon impact.

Ah, crap... my head.

With the throbbing inside my skull becoming increasingly audible as time progresses, I push the man off me as I turn on my stomach and start crawling to the gated windows facing the street in front of the building. Just as I grab the Kimber and throw myself onto my back, I see the man start to lunge toward me with both of his arms extended. Then I hear it…

Bang.

It doesn't take me long to realize that I had not fired, yet the man in front of me falls to my left as I immediately aim my sights to the right of the hallway where the shot rang from. As my eyes transition, I can see a tall, young white male with dark brown hair holding a bolt-action rifle. By the looks of it, the dude couldn't be older than thirty. He was wearing a flannel long-sleeve shirt with faded, dark blue jeans. I don't immediately recognize him, but I soon recall him having been one of the first people we had recruited a few weeks back. Come to think of it, he was also the first to arrive with a loaded weapon, so I guess that explains how he knew his way around the rifle. He gives me a slight nod as the ringing in my ears gets worse from the shot the rifle had let out.

Is that the rifle I put against my desk?

When I see him lower his weapon, I start to lower mine as I begin standing and walk to the man who Derrick and Pancho now had on his knees. I glance at my previous attacker as he's lying on the ground, attempting to stop the blood seeping from the side of his stomach, and continue my way over to where my guys are standing. The kneeling man's face lacks any sort of remorse, as Pancho spits in his face as a *"fuck you"* for having almost kicked his knee in. When I stop in front of him, I hear the echo of another gunshot ringing out from behind me.

I turn my head while keeping my body positioned toward the kneeling man to see my *knight in shining armor* standing over the corpse of my previous attacker. Smoke is emanating from his 22-inch barrel as he lowers it to his side. I glance at Derrick and point my thumb at the man standing behind me, signaling him to go retrieve the rifle. As he nods and makes his way past me, I turn my attention back to the sole survivor of the group, who now has his hands at his side as his knees become soaked in the pool of red coming from the corpses of his former associates. *Jawbreaker*, who is now standing about a foot to my left, mutters a few profanities under his breath as he stares at the man kneeling before us.

"Y'see, now why did you make us do that?" I ask with more curiosity than sarcasm in a tone just loud enough for only us three to hear. I'm still trying to catch my breath from my most recent scuffle. I continue to grip the Kimber in my right hand, before glaring over at Pancho. To him, I know one thing is certain; this attack felt personal. I didn't want to kill these men, but they had stripped us of a choice. That is a choice I intend to give back.

I wrap my hand around the slide of the Kimber as I turn it around and face its textured grip toward *JB*. As he's standing on my left, I can see him turn to look me in the eyes with a bit of confusion. "These men threatened us. They threatened the security of everyone who lives here, including the kids. They took your freedom away, and this is me giving it back to you," I mutter to *Jawbreaker* without deviating my eyes away from his as I further extend the handgun in his direction.

Pancho pauses for a moment, then proceeds to grab the weapon with his left hand before partially pulling the slide back to verify if there is a round in the chamber. He places the gun to his side as his gaze transitions back to the man kneeling in front of him. The man looks at Pancho as I see him battling in his mind with how to proceed. The disgruntled man says something to him in Spanish that I can't make out, yet I know it isn't a good thing because he concludes his sentence by arching over and spitting in *Jawbreaker's* direction. The man isn't even given a chance to reset his body before *JB* brings the pistol up to his head and pulls the trigger.

Bang.

I look over to see Pancho's eyes beginning to water slightly, yet he's trying to hold his composure after what he just did. I slowly reach out for the handgun that is now resting against his side, as I use my left hand to grab his shoulder. "It's okay… you're alright, kid," I say in a near whisper as he gasps slightly once my hand connects with his shoulder. It seems to bring him back to reality as his facial expressions tell me he's battling his own internal conflicts. "It's alright… these were dangerous people, you hear me?" I ask as I slowly pull the weapon out of his hand. He nods as he catches his breath, then immediately ushers past me and inside the cafeteria to throw up in one of the mobile trash bins lying around.

I insert the Kimber in its holster as I make my way towards Derrick, who is now holding a rifle in each hand, and the man who had saved my life. I want to shake his hand and thank him, yet I only have one thought that keeps making its way to the front of my mind. I stop in front of the duo as they both turn their heads toward me. The man puts his hands in his front jeans pockets as I set my eyes on his.

"How did you know where to find this?" I ask while pointing down toward one of the rifles in Derrick's hands. The man looks at the rifle before looking back up at me with slight discomfort that's visible in his body language.

"The guy said the weapons are in your office, so I ran upstairs to find one. I wanted to help," he says as he gestures towards the now deceased man who had been holding *Jawbreaker*. I know he's telling the truth. Partially because he barely stutters when he says it, but also because I recall seeing him in the crowd of people who had been gathered around the hallway when I first arrived.

"We'll need to find a better place for these things," Derrick says as he interjects his way into the conversation, all while placing the rifle in his left hand over his shoulder. *He's right.*

"We will figure that out later," I say after giving him a quick look. "For now, we need to get everybody in order." I look at the man again and extend my hand out to him, my face changing from that of hostility and mistrust to that of appreciation and gratitude. "Thank you for saving my life. What's your name, kid?" I ask assertively as he squeezes my hand with more force than Derrick had weeks ago.

"You're welcome," he says as he gives me a grin and retracts his hand. "And it's Corver. Corver Whitlock. And, uh- sorry for going into your office. I'm just not the type of person to stand around while shit falls apart around him, y'know what I mean?" the man asks with sincerity as he glances over at the man he had saved me from.

I give him back the same nod he had given me when I was on the ground, to which he grins. "First order of business, we need to get the place under control," I admit to the men as *JB* walks up to us while wiping his mouth for the second time today. After a brief moment of silence, I walk over to the Glock belonging to *Jawbreaker*, which was still on the floor beside the trio of corpses lying just a few feet apart from one another, and kneel to pick it up before the growing pool of blood submerges the weapon. As I walk back to the group, I hand Pancho his gun back, which he hesitantly grabs. His face tells me he is still slightly embarrassed from having it stolen, but he takes it anyway before checking the magazine and tucking it behind his belt.

"I need you two to wait for me in the Auditorium. I'm going to get everyone to meet us there, yet I want you to hold down the fort as people come in. Don't let *anybody* leave," I instruct directly to Derrick and Pancho as I transition my eyes back toward Corver once I get verbal confirmation from the other two regarding my orders. I extend my hand while glancing at one of the rifles Derrick is holding. He places one of the rifles in my hand before using both of his hands to get a better grip on the other one.

I retract the bolt until I see a round sitting in the chamber before slamming it closed and locking it in place. I point the barrel towards the floor as I extend the butt of the rifle over to Corver. He glances at me with what I can only assume is disbelief plastered all over his face. I guess he wasn't expecting to have the rifle returned to him after I just had it confiscated.

"Go help them. You're probably a better shot with this thing than I am anyway," I say as my chuckle quickly turns into a groan once my bruised lower back reminds me of the pain I had endured just moments ago. Corver takes the rifle and flips the safety on, before thanking me.

"I want each of you covering a different exit. Now go. I'll meet you guys down there," I say as I point in the direction of the Auditorium. The men start jogging over toward the doorway leading to the Auditorium as I make my way up the east stairwell and to the Main Office.

***

As I stumble into the Main Office, nearly falling over as I position my lower arm against the sleek wooden Assistance Desk for support, I start walking to the Public Announcement System that was frequently used to call for students who were getting dismissed from school early. The PA system was linked to various speakers placed throughout the entire building.

This should get everybody's attention.

As I make my way over to the small table where the PA Microphone is sitting, I position myself against the table before holding the button and tapping the end of it. The amplified thuds coming from one of the speakers above the entrance of the Main Office sound slightly muffled to me due to the recent gunfight that undoubtedly impaired my hearing.

"Everybody, this is Miles. Miles Gethe-" I say as I instinctively release the button while I turn my head to let out a grunt from the pain I'm experiencing as I arch over to speak. I continue once the pain subsides. "We're safe now. I need to see everyone in the Auditorium located on the west side of the first floor. Hope, if you can hear me, I want you to stay with the kids where you are," I instruct in a calm and methodical tone. I still don't want her or the kids to be worried.

"I say again, everyone else please make your way to the Auditorium on the first floor," I instruct before releasing the four-inch beige button on the bottom of the microphone labeled *"Speak."* I stand up, feeling a little bit of relief as I pull out my Kimber from the holster and eject the magazine.

Two rounds in the magazine, with one in the chamber.

Magazine in hand, I start limping toward the Principal's office now standing with its dark wooden door wide open. Once inside, I set down the handgun before reaching into the drawer to fill up the stainless steel magazine with some .45 ACP rounds I have in a half-opened box. Once full, I pick up the 1911 with my right hand before sliding the replenished magazine into it with an audible *click* as it locks into place, then I flip the safety off and pull back the hammer before placing it in the holster.

Let's get this over with.

* * *

I follow the small line of people heading into the auditorium before giving a nod of appreciation to Derrick, who is standing near the main entrance of the auditorium with his rifle under his arm, as I make my way past him. I can see people already positioning themselves sporadically in one of the 500 or so creaking wooden foldable seats lined up into rows of twenty. I gently push past a few people as I make my way down the middle of the aisle of the 40-foot ceiling resting over our heads with a chandelier dangling in the middle.

I glance over at Corver as he props himself against the wall near the exit on the right of the twenty-foot wide stage at the other side of the Auditorium, which ultimately leads to the southwest staircase of the building. *JB, with his handgun resting on his knee,* is sitting on the steps leading up to the stage to the left. Both men notice me. Both men give me a nod.

As I continue to walk down the middle aisle, I can hear gasps as people look at me. With all the commotion, I had forgotten that there was still blood on my face. I continue walking and prop my sore lower back against the edge of the stage as soon as I make it to the bottom of the slope. I turn to face the rest of the group as more people make their way inside the room. Crossing my arms, I can see familiar faces making their way into the Auditorium, including that of Renata and her son, Vito. With my eyes remaining fixated on the two of them, I slowly push myself away from the stage before looking at Derrick and shaking my head. It takes him a second, yet after looking at Renata and Vito as they venture further into the Auditorium, he finally understands what I'm trying to tell him.

I don't want them here for this.

Derrick places the butt of his rifle on the wall behind him before calling the two back over to where he was. I can see the visible confusion on Vito's face as Derrick directs his attention to his mother. Seeing as they're on the opposite side of the room, I can't hear what they're saying but I can barely make out the three fingers Derrick is making with his right hand as he points to the ceiling above us. He's ushering them to the gym where the kids are.

There we go…

I can see Renata turning her head while keeping her body in place to scan the room, locking eyes with me once she sees I'm at the end of the middle aisle she's standing in. She gives me a look of confusion as I break eye contact with her and avert my gaze to the floor in front of me. *I don't want her to see the dried blood covering my face.* After a moment passes, I see the silhouettes of Renata and her son disappearing from view as they are ushered past the entrance from which they had initially come.

When I pick up my head, I start counting the number of people in the room. When I realize everyone is here, except for those upstairs, I swing my right hand at Derrick as he closes the doors behind him. I look at Corver and nod as he does the same. When people realize what's happening around them, the Auditorium starts to fill with incomprehensible dialogue. I turn around and lift myself over the three-foot wall separating the stage from the ground. When everyone looks back at me, I begin to do what I came here to do: *I start speaking.*

"Today, we met a small group of men who were graciously offered some food and a warm place to stay," I begin as my voice begins to bounce off the walls of the Auditorium. I know everyone can hear me.

"These men were invited into our home, and what did we do? We *fed* them, with the hope that they could eventually become one of us. But what did *they* do?" I ask out loud as my tone gains more volume with every sentence. "These men *threaten* us. They hold a weapon to the head of one of our most loyal members. They try to shoot at us. They try to shoot at *me*! And for what?!" I scream out. I can see people in the crowd shivering as they begin to relive the traumatic event. I begin walking back and forth now as I continue, without diverting my eyes from those in front of me.

"I could've been killed. Many- hell, *all* of you could've been killed if these men would have succeeded. But we *stopped* 'em. And I'd do it again and again if it meant we'd be alive to see tomorrow," I say truthfully as I start to hear some in the crowd verbally stating their approval while getting nods from others - *that's when I stop moving*.

"But *someone in this room* had brought them here…" I declare while looking at every face in the room as gasps of disbelief echo off the walls surrounding the stage. "*Someone* had used a pencil sharpener to prop one of the exit doors open so these men would come inside. *Someone* had intentionally told these men who we are. What we have. Probably even where we sleep," I say while standing straight with a confident demeanor.

"The threat did *not* end in that hallway. The threat is *still* here. And I'm looking at him," I say as I set my eyes on one of the men sitting in the back of the room. "Simon Adams!" I yell as I point to the back of the room. I can see many turning around in their seats, while others stood up entirely to face the back of the Auditorium. Once he's called out, Simon nearly trips on the edge of the row he was sitting in as he attempts to make his way toward the exit only a few feet behind him. Derrick shoulders his bolt-action rifle and points the barrel right at Simon's chest, ultimately stopping him in his tracks.

The poor bastard nearly falls on his ass as he abruptly backs up and throws his hands in the air.

Got you, motherfucker…

"*Bring him here…*" I let out before the echoes of anger-filled chants from those in front of me flood the room. As Derrick leverages his rifle to escort Simon down the aisle, I can see some of the people in the crowd rush to grab Simon, whose arms are still in the air. He flails around in a futile attempt to break free from the mob. With Corver forcefully grabbing Simon's arm as he and Derrick practically drag him to the right side of the stage, Simon is placed in front of me and falls to his knees as Corver slams the butt of his rifle behind his right leg.

With Simon now on his knee, I kneel in front of him right when his glasses begin to fog up from how hard he's breathing. I can see both snot from his runny nose and tears from behind his partially crooked glasses running down his face as my left knee touches the ground. "*I should have killed you when you let Jayden die, you piece of shit,*" I whisper near Simon's ear in a low-pitched growl. As I turn to walk away, I quickly swing my fist as hard as I can at the upper portion of Simon's face, shattering his glasses once it connects. He stumbles backward and cries in pain as he holds his face in between his hands.

I can hear those on the ground floor roaring as the truth seeps in. I pick up one of the lenses from Simon's shattered glasses and stand up. "This! This is what the attackers said the traitor was wearing. Seeing as though Simon here is the *only* one who wears glasses out of all of us, what does that tell you?" I say as I stand right in front of Simon, who is now on his back with his face still in between his hands while he sobs, and throw the shard at his torso. I continue.

"The pencil sharpener used to prop the door open for the attackers came from the classroom on the first floor. The same classroom where a desk had been ransacked just moments before their arrival. Want to take a *wild guess as to who* occupies that room?" I shout into the crowd as I scan each face for signs of disapproval. I don't see any. There is one person who doesn't seem to be reacting to the events unfolding in front of them though, and she locks eyes with me once I notice her.

Charlotte. Ah, yes…

I break eye contact with her and place my attention on Simon as I grab him with both hands and prop him back on his knees. As he attempts to use the momentum to stand up, he falls back onto his knees as I punch him in his midsection. While Simon clenches his stomach with both of his arms and arches over, I retract the Kimber from its holster with my right hand and aim at the top of Simon's head. The roaring stops almost as abruptly as it started and is replaced, instead, with gasps of shock. This time, though, no one is yelling for me to stop. Simon does his best to look up at me and nearly falls on his back in fear once he does.

Control the situation, Miles…

"We brought you into our home, where there are *kids*, and trusted you to help us make this place safer for *everyone*. But as it turns out, the only threat we have in front of us right now… is *you*," I say loudly enough for everyone in the room to hear. I can make out the chants of approval returning from those standing in front of the stage.

Control…

With the Kimber still in the air, Simon shutters as the thought of dying forces him to close his eyes. As the barrel of the handgun reaches Simon's right eye, I do something no one could've expected; I lower the Kimber back to my side. I can see Corver and *JB* taking a step back after I begin to walk around Simon. While doing so, I lock eyes with Charlotte as I extend my left hand out to her. Some of the people in the audience turn to see who I'm reaching out to. As she's put in the metaphorical spotlight and the peer pressure begins to reach unfathomable heights, Charlotte looks around in fear. She doesn't know what to do, yet she starts inching her way down the left aisle of the Auditorium. When she is next to the stage, Pancho grabs her hand and helps her up the stairs until she is in front of me.

"*This man let Jayden die*," I mutter out to her in a low tone adjusted for only her and me to hear. Simon tries to sit up straight yet grabs his stomach again just as Charlotte covers her mouth with both of her hands and lets out a whimper. "*When Jayden came to help us hold off the attack, this piece of shit stood back and did nothing...*" I say in a growl once I mention Simon. She begins to cry while she falls to her knees, so I kneel to get closer to her while I look at her in her red but watery eyes. She wasn't outside when it happened, so she deserves the truth. She moves some of her dark red, wavy hair to the side to get a better look at me as I gently place the palm of my left hand on her cheek to address her directly.

"Because of *this* man, your fiancé had to endure the weight of a half-ton steel gate on his body as those *things* took chunks out of his flesh," I say without breaking eye contact. I wanted her upset. I wanted her to see the man that she had in front lying of her for the cowardly monstrosity that he truly was. "You want to know what he did when Jayden pleaded for help? He *ran away*, just like he did when he left you to fend for yourself in the lobby. This man is *dangerous*. This man *should not* be with us..." I whisper.

I stand up without diverting my eyes from Charlotte's as I flip the Kimber in my hand, as I had done earlier with *JB*. She grabs it with both of her tear-soaked hands as she rises and I grab her shoulder.

"You see *Jawbreaker* over there?" I ask while pointing at the young, Spanish man on the other side of the stage anxiously fiddling with his handgun while remaining vigilant. "That man *almost* had his life taken today, because his choice of retaliation was taken away from him by those who attacked us. I *gave him* that choice back, just as I'm doing for you now," I say while I release my hand from her shoulder. The water flowing from her eyes seems to have dried up as she looks at me, not knowing how to respond.

"Pancho took his life back. What will *you* do?" I ask before taking a few steps back to leave her in front of Simon, who is now pleading for his life as he tries to wipe the snot from his face. Even with two hands, Charlotte struggles to raise the weapon to Simon's chest. From where I'm standing, I can see her hands are visibly shaking. She begins to let out a whimper as the barrel is barely aligned with Simon's torso. I can hear the chanting from the crowd getting louder.

"Kill that son of a bitch!" a male from the crowd shouts out as the volume in the room becomes deafening. One second. Then two. Then three. Then ten. It's too much to ask of her. I take a step forward and begin to extend my reach for the Kimber as it shakes in Charlotte's hand. I wasn't able to take another before my ears rang again.

Bang.

The entire front of the stage is spattered with blood and I can hear screaming from the crowd as I readjust my eyes following the sudden blink due to the weapon being discharged. Simon has both hands trying to stop the blood from racing out of a sizable entrance wound located where his heart is. He looks down before slowly raising his head back up to look at Charlotte, who is now sobbing quietly as the unmistakable sound of another gunshot rips through the air.

Bang.

As if the first one wasn't already a surprise, the second shot catches me off guard. With the second shot, Simon falls backward as the round perforates his body and becomes embedded near the edge of the stage in front of us. There was *more blood spatter*. He was barely able to groan as his breaths became *slower. It seems like an eternity is passing us by as we all stand in silence. Before long, it became clear to me that Simon had stopped breathing entirely.*

Charlotte drops the gun on the floor, which makes an audible *thud* once it hits the ground, and she puts her face in between my arms as she makes her way to me for an embrace. As I wrap my arms around her, I nod at the men near me to take her from the stage and instruct them to bring her to the Nurse's Station near the Main Office to get her cleaned up. With all the spots of blood covering her face and her bright green turtleneck, she was beginning to look like me. "Get her some food from the Cafeteria, too" I instruct to Corver and Pancho.

"You got it… boss," *Jawbreaker* says with a nod of respect before he and Corver turn to carry Charlotte off stage. As they make their way towards the entrance Derrick is standing by, I begin to address those in front of me.

"This does *not* have to happen!" I exclaim as the silence in the room is deafening. "We are *better* than those just looking to *get by* as the world around them turns to shit! You know what we do when that happens? We make a better fuckin' world!" I holler out as the room starts to become lively again with nods of approval.

"We'll make this place safer than you can imagine, yet that starts with *us! You* think we're going to accept scrapes of garbage as men like *this* help others take what keeps our kids fed? No! You think we're going to let *whatever the fuck* lies beyond these walls stop us from stepping outside? No!" I can hear the chants begin to return louder than ever as the blood from Simon's body starts dripping over the edge of the stage. Even with the echoing chants, I can still hear every drop as it lands on the floor beneath me. "We are not merely *surviving*. We're better than that. No, we're *thriving*."

"We're not survivors…" I shout out as I pick up the now bloody Kimber from the floor and place it back into its holster. "No, we're *Thrivers*."

CHAPTER 6

ONBOARD

Ledger

Vito Caruso	Renata Caruso
Hope Starcov	Charlotte Kennedy
Pancho Ruiz	~~Simon Adams~~
Derrick Simmons	~~Jayden Walker~~

(There are 47 additional names on the list)

Journal Entry: Some look at me like a hero for what I did last month. Those on the other side of that spectrum fear me. I still can't read Charlotte yet, but JB seems to be wrapping his head around that night pretty well. I mean, fuck... he was almost killed for Christ's sake. I didn't know if he'd take the gun when I handed it to him, but I gave him a chance to take back what was taken away from him.

I know one thing for sure: We're better off now than we have ever been. We've got security. We've got the Armory. We've got a small surplus of perishables from the area. We've even got some more firearms, ~~although those are getting hard to come by since we're in city limits~~, mostly from those we've taken in recently.

We've come a long way already, yet I can't help but wonder how far we can go... these people all seem to have something to bring to the table. I can use that.

What a start to the day…

IT'S STILL DARK OUTSIDE, YET I can hear a faint groaning coming from outside the partially opened window on my right. It doesn't sound close enough to be an immediate threat, so I do my best to not pay it much mind. I begin slowly dimming the small metallic lamp sitting on my desk so as to not draw attention from anyone, or *anything*, past our gates. As the unmistakable sounds of anguish fade away into the dark abyss before my eyes, they're replaced by multiple footsteps coming from the hallway on the second floor. *Nocturnal security patrols.*

I close the journal and throw it into the drawer beneath my desk before locking it with a key and picking up the Kimber I had sitting near the lamp. Even in the dark, I feel comfortable when my hand makes out the frame of the pistol. I pull back slightly on the slide using the front serrations on the handgun to ensure there's a round in the chamber before placing it into my holster once the dim illumination from the light reflects off the brass casing and confirms it's ready to go. I grab my *new* bag, referring to a mildly used black assault pack we found in one of the nearby apartments that worked wonders when compared to my bullet-ridden substitute, and turn off the lamp before slinging the bag over my shoulder while I make my way out of the office.

As I step into the hallway, which is lit with small candles strewn about the floors, I walk by a group of three armed *Thrivers* who are all on duty for the night. Given our growing numbers and the bull-shit we've had to deal with so far, having a patrol on each floor at all times seemed like a good idea that everyone was comfortable with. There are two men, both carrying what I can only imagine are the Ruger bolt action rifles from the armory, and one woman carrying a faded .22 caliber rifle walking together towards the library.

"Hey, boss," the girl says to me as the group acknowledges my sudden appearance. It was in a tone I can only describe as drowsy yet forceful. They all look tired, but the sight of me causes them all to straighten their backs in an attempt to conceal their fatigue. The female who had called out to me lowers her head as she and her team continue to stroll toward the library in the same manner an introvert would if called upon to speak in a lecture.

Well, that was awkward...

I tail them a few feet before coming to a stop at the maintenance closet at the top of the staircases leading to and from the main lobby. I can't help but reminisce about when Renata and her son had camped out here when they first arrived. Times were more simple then. Pancho is in front of the steel door, which is now serving as the entrance to the *Armory* we set up after the whole ordeal with Simon. As he begins to straighten his back, the creaking coming from the legs of the dark blue chair that he likely retrieved from one of the classrooms nearby echoes off the walls around us.

I'm almost certain that chair is way too damn small for this man.

"You holding up alright, *JB*?" I ask in a concerned manner. I know he's been watching the door for longer than I had been asleep, so he must be tired.

"I could use a coffee or something, y'know? Fallin' asleep here," he lets out with a scruffy chuckle. He looks like he needs a breather or two.

"Gimme the key and go get some rest. I'll get you when everyone's up for breakfast in a few hours, alright?" I ask as I put out the palm of my hand in anticipation of his approval.

JB hesitates before nodding and throwing me the keys he has in his right pocket. He puts his right hand on my shoulder before slowly brushing past me. The brief gust of cold air as he does so is inviting since the the fire emanating from the lit candles is making the hallway a little warm. He stops a few feet behind me when I call back to him abruptly.

"Hey…" I bark out just low enough so as not to disturb those sleeping in the surrounding classrooms. As he turns around, I throw him the Glock that had been lying on top of the book used for recording authorized *Thrivers* from heading in and out of the Armory. He almost doesn't catch it, yet I blame that on him being tired. "Don't ever leave this behind again," I growl out as he nods and turns to continue down the hallway. I watch him disappear past the blue door leading to the stairwell before proceeding into the Armory.

As I pass the metallic doorway, I can hear faint gusts of wind coming from behind the large sliding window on the other side of the room. There are unloaded firearms propped up on some of the desks we had positioned in here a few weeks back, and I had placed ammunition in some of the heavy footlockers we secured from the third-floor gym.

As I notice my breath becoming visible in the cold, I walk to one of the footlockers and kneel directly in front of it. I open the case with my left hand and can see a single box of .45 ACP ammunition in a half-empty box.

I free my shoulder of the bag I had been carrying and grab the box before sitting on the now-closed footlocker and replenishing two empty magazines for the Kimber. I guess the cold kicked in quicker than I thought because the shivering that accompanies the sudden gust of wind ushering past my body makes it harder to stabilize my hand when loading the rounds. There is just enough in the box to fill both magazines to the brim, so I place the plastic tray that was holding the rounds in place back into the now empty box before throwing it in the trashcan at the corner of the doorway I had entered from moments ago.

Alright, I think I'm done here.

I pick up the open binder sitting on the mahogany desk closest to the window and begin writing on the paper labeled *"Inventory"* with the black pen hanging on the top of the page. *Everything* needs to be accounted for. I can't help but feel dread as I scribble the number zero in the category labeled *".45 ACP"*. The list goes as follows:

Firearms:
     (Handguns) - 7
     (Rifles) - 6
     (Shotguns) - 2

Ammunition:

    .22 LR - ~~117 Rounds~~ 332 Rounds
    9mm - 214 Rounds
    .45 ACP - ~~16 Rounds~~ 0 Rounds
    10mm Rounds - 30 Rounds
    .308 - 59 Rounds
    5.56x45mm - 63 Rounds ("We're lucky we even found these")

Other:

    3 Hand-flares
    ~~49~~ 27 Zip-ties
    2 Collapsible Batons
    (The list goes on)

We've done a good job getting ourselves situated here, yet it's not enough. I've seen just how fast ammunition can disappear even when being conservative. One thing is certain: *We don't have enough*. I slam the book shut in aggravation as I straighten up and glance out the window. The wind seems to be getting stronger as I notice it starting to blow some of the snow off the rails of the second-floor balcony. I throw the pen on the table before turning around and heading to the entrance of the Armory while snatching my bag from against the footlocker.

I open the door to be immediately greeted with the now comforting warmth irradiating from the candles in the hallway. As I shut the door behind me, I see Derrick about 15 feet away, heading toward the office from where the second-floor nocturnal patrol had previously walked toward just minutes ago. He stops when he sees me and begins striding in my direction with a black and white notebook in his hand.

Is he looking for me?

"Boss, I've been looking for you," Derrick says in a hushed manner so as not to wake up those still sleeping throughout the second floor. *Good to see people in this world still have consideration.* I haven't seen him in over a week, so it calms me down when I recognize him from afar. He stops in front of me and begins to flip through the scribbled pages in the book he is carrying as he starts speaking.

"We kept an eye on the bodies of Simon and his "friends" after locking them behind the gates of the fifth-floor gym as you asked. Now, at first, I didn't understand, but now I think I am beginning to," Derrick says as he diverts his gaze back onto the page he had previously been scrolling for. "Look at this," he commands as he picks up one of the candles near his foot and holds it up to the notebook for illumination. His voice begins to crack slightly as he continues, "Me and a few of the others were watching them after what had happened in the auditorium. Even had the stopwatch ready like you said. But around 40 minutes in, just like Jayden, one of these… these *pieces of shit* begin moving… Your suspicions were right, Miles. Only the one who had that mark on his ankle got back up," he says as his eyes wander towards the wall behind me. I can tell he's reminiscing about something in his mind.

"And?" I ask in an attempt to get his attention back on track. It seems to work because the look he gives me is a mix of frustration and fear.

"*And?* All of these motherfuckers have bullet holes spread across their bodies!" he lets out as I cover my lips with one finger to remind him people are still asleep. His demeanor transitions from irritation and confusion to that of a four-year-old child who wants to show off their new toy to their parents. "Any normal person who has a six-inch exit wound to the neck wouldn't even be able to *breathe*, let alone stand up without a hitch. But that's not what I wanted to talk to you about. No, I need to talk to you about this…" he says in a faint whisper as he places the candlelight closer to the book to reveal a well-done illustration of a bent gate as well as a chart with different times below it.

What the hell is this?

"We found that when there was any kind of bright light, this guy didn't act like someone with two six-inch exit wounds along his back. No, he is… aggressive. He *was* aggressive. The only time I have ever seen anything like that was-" he gets out before I cut him off.

"In the courtyard…" I whisper.

Is that why the guy in the library…?

I don't even know what to think, so Derrick takes that opportunity to continue with his dialogue. "Yes, but a few of the other guys and I took the time to cover up the gates using zip ties and a few curtains we found to strip the room of light. When the room was completely dark, there wasn't a fucking sound to be heard besides that fuckin' groaning," he recalls as his finger thumps against a chart in his notebook consisting of various times he recorded over the past couple of weeks.

"You said he *was* aggressive, D. What the hell happened up there?" I ask as I inch closer to him without losing eye contact. He puts his chin up and begins to talk with the same confidence I have always seen in him since I met him months ago.

"You see this picture?" he lets out as he places the faded illustration in the book closer to my face. "*This* is what he did to the gate when we accidentally let the light seep in. When he got aggressive. The gate wasn't going to stand, so I had him put down quietly. I mean… C'mon, you've seen what they can do…" Derrick's tone of voice gets louder and I don't stop him this time.

"Yeah, I have. Most of us have," I say in my regular tone of voice as I hear the unmistakable sound of yawning coming from those waking up in the classrooms nearest to us. "I have little empathy for those assholes upstairs, but I just wish we could have studied them a little longer." After pausing momentarily to digest everything I had just been told, I give Derrick a nod before walking toward the stairwell leading to the main lobby on my left. I descend about three steps before I hear him call out to me.

"There is something else you should know, but you won't hear it from me," he says as he positions himself at the top of the stairwell I am on. "One of the guys upstairs who helped me with my observations has an idea I think you need to hear," he says as he closes his book and places it into his armpit before putting both of his hands into his jacket pockets. One of the *Thrivers* who came out of the classroom near the library passes me on the staircase and ushers me a groggy and faint greeting as I retrain my eyes on Derrick's.

Fine.

"Bring him to the office after breakfast. I'm going to get it started a little early today,", I say before breaking my glance and turning to continue my descent. As I make my way down the staircase, I can feel his eyes on me before he verbally acknowledges my instructions and turns to walk down the hall he had initially come from.

* * *

With a warm styrofoam container in my left hand, I push past the partially opened door leading into my office to see Derrick and another man both sitting in the two swivel chairs in front of my desk. The gentleman sitting beside Derrick is a short and older white fella with a scruffy beard and a disheveled look that tells me he is either in dire need of a shower or has been through hell and back. As the two who were previously chuckling at something I did not hear become aware of my presence, the room begins to fall silent.

Damn, am I that intimidating?

Another *Thriver* named Abdul, a perfect English-speaking non-native who we had recruited a few months back, is leaning against one of the windows with his arms crossed. Given his 17 years of experience in Personal Protection for some of the city's most affluent figures, as well as his intimidating stature and immense gratitude for bringing him in when he had nowhere else to go, Abdul was the perfect candidate for my own Security Detail. I start making my way towards the desk before exchanging a greeting with my new-found company. Just before I sit down, I extend the container in my hand to the tall Afghan standing closest to me.

"Abdul, can you please bring this to Pancho in Room 403? I promised him I'd get him when breakfast was going, yet I'll make things easy for him today," I say as he reaches out to grab the warm container from my hand. It comes out as more of a benevolent instruction than a request.

"Sure thing, boss," he says as he turns his back to me and closes the door as he steps out. With the audible thud coming from the door being shut discreetly echoing throughout the room, I take another step toward the desk and extend my hand to the man in front of me.

"How're you doing this morning, sir?" I ask politely as he struggles to get up to go along with the formalities. I reassure him he can remain seated with a hand gesture before he hesitantly sits back down.

"I am doing alright so far, son. I do appreciate the manners. Much obliged," I hear in what I can only describe as a true New York accent. As the older man lets out a sigh of relief when he lands back onto the cushion of the seat, he repositions his body to face the desk in a manner that's comfortable to him. Before I can respond, he continues. "I know you and your people have brought in a lot of folks like me, so I wouldn't be offended if you had forgotten who I am. My name is Lance Ri-" he says before I cut him off.

"Lance Ridgehall. Yes, sir, I know who you are," I say in a friendly manner.

"That's correct. Well, I wanted to thank you for everything you've done here so far," Lance says as he reaches for what looks to be a scroll of some sort leaning against the front of my desk. "It's my understanding that you want more for everyone in this place. My apologies. What did you call it? he asks. I take no disrespect from it, as I understand he's still relatively new.

"We're *Thrivers*, and we are all sitting in what we collectively refer to as the *Consulate*," I say with confidence as I can vividly recall the chants echoing from those in the auditorium on the day of Simon's execution. Those people wanted change, security, and safety; We've given them that.

"Extraordinary. Nevertheless, I have worked closely with the Transit Authority for over 17 years. What if..." Lance begins as he repositions himself in his chair to get slightly closer to the desk,

"What if I gave you a way to compound that prosperity?" he asks as he lets out a genuine smile. Derrick sits back in his chair as he shoots me a smile himself.

"How so?" I ask with both of my elbows now touching the desk. The older man lets out a cough, probably from the cold, as he struggles to unroll the paper that was previously propped up in front of him. As Derrick begins to stand to assist the older gentleman with his task, I stand and face the partially opened window before closing it. After doing so, I turn back to the men sitting in front of my desk, *who have rearranged some objects on the desk to hold the four corners of the paper still*, and begin to sit as I recognize what's being shown on the paper: *It's the map of the Train Routes that are strewn all across the city.*

Seeing as these maps are common enough, to the point where I'm certain everyone in the *Consulate* has probably seen one before, I can't tell where Lance is going with this. He covers his mouth as he lets out another cough, then clears his throat before speaking clearly.

"Have you ever heard of the *PCC*?" he asks as the smell of food, no doubt from the Cafeteria, fills the air with every word he lets out. He continues once he notices my confusion. "The *PCC* is the *Power Control Center* on 53rd Street in Manhattan. This is arguably one of the most important buildings in all of the city," he declares as he trains his eyes on the desk. From the way he's frantically scanning it, I can only assume he's looking for something to write with, so I open the drawer of the desk with the keys I had sitting in my pocket and hand him the pen next to my journal. After exchanging a nod of appreciation, he continues to scribble on the paper before continuing to speak.

"Now, I used to commute to the *PCC* every day for work, so I can say with confidence it is right… here," he lets out with a grunt of discomfort as he reaches forward to circle where the building is located on the old map. He then begins dragging his fingers towards the Bronx. "We… we are right here," Lance mutters as he circles the train station sitting about a block away from the Consulate: *Kingsbridge Road.*

What are you getting at, old man?

"I don't mean to sound disrespectful, but I'm not following what you're-" I exclaim with a little bit of confusion in my voice just as Lance lifts his hand to cut me off.

"The *PCC* is where all of the trains in the city are controlled and rerouted. Now, each train needs an operator to physically move them along, but with the *PCC*, you can decide what trains go where and when," he says with a sense of pride. "With control of the *PCC*, you control the *entire* metro system in New York City," Lance lets out before proceeding to cough once more into his arm.

The entire metro system…

"Think about what we can do with that," Derrick interjects as he begins to lean forward in his chair. "We could do anything, go anywhere. On foot, in cars, or even on bikes, if we found them, we'd only get so far with people like Simon out there, but with this…" he says as a slight creaking becomes audible once he starts to sit back in the swivel chair. I position my elbows back on the desk as I clamp my hands together and take a few seconds to examine the map further.

Brilliant… This could work.

"How far is the *PCC* from where we are?" I ask Lance. I can see him looking at the map and assessing the distance based on his experience with the Transit Authority. He looks back up and ushers me a number.

"It's about 10 miles straight, but depending on the city blocks and other obstacles in the way, it could easily end up being more," Lance says as he hands the pen back to me. I take a second to process the distance before grabbing the pen and standing up.

"We wouldn't even need the entire metro. If we can get access to the 4 Train, we'd have access to all of Lexington Avenue. That would give us the ability to transport things from the city safely to the *Consulate* under everybody's nose. Hell… food, building materials, weapons, and even people," I declare as I position myself against the desk and place the ballpoint of the pen on the paper. "And who said anything about traversing the city blocks?" I ask as my hand begins moving. I draw a line alongside the Green Route, which the 4 Train takes to and from the Bronx.

"From Kingsbridge, we can walk along the tracks toward the 59th Street Station and cut across the N, R, and W Line to 49th Street on the West side. From there, we can walk up the next few blocks to get to the *PCC* without having to go through too much of a hassle," I say as the men in front of me nod in agreement. I can tell Derrick is proud of himself for referring this plan to me in the first place, yet he looks more proud of me for helping to make the plan a reality. I set my eyes back on Lance. "What do you think?" I ask once I throw the pen back onto the desk. Lance takes a second to think as he continues nodding.

"Well, a walk like that is still going to take about five hours or so, but it's doable for sure," he mutters in a low tone. He coughs again, this time turning his entire body away from us in an attempt to deflect whatever germs are coming out of his mouth. I take a step back and open the ledger sitting inside my desk to verify how many people we have for a task this big; *We have 53 Thrivers altogether.* 11 of them are children, and seven are scouting the predetermined eight-block radius around the *Consulate*. That leaves us with 35 personnel on hand.

"As of right now, we have 35 people who we can choose for this. I want eight people with me on this, including you. We'll use some of our back stock to get it done and can leave at night if everything you said about our little test subjects upstairs was true," I proclaim to Derrick as I begin pushing my chair in from behind. I can see Lance feeling uncomfortable, probably from the sore throat he most likely has now from his excessive coughing fits, yet Derrick looks concerned. "Speak your mind, brother," I say as his eyes meet with mine. He begins to stand himself and starts rubbing both of his arms once they're crossed.

"Boss, we'd be left vulnerable here. I saw the ledger in the Armory this morning. Fitting nine people for a journey like that would probably take around 70% of our inventory," he barks out with more concern in his voice than aggression. I know he's right because I wrote in that very binder this morning. On the one hand, this is a big risk that could easily backfire with negligence leading the wheel. On the other hand, we could see more prosperity than ever before if we see it through completely.

Control...

"You're right," I admit with little to no hesitation. "It would be a mistake to take on such an arduous task and fail. But we'd be in a far worse position if we let it slide. I'll have *JB* prepare the Armory for a withdrawal once he's done with his breakfast, and I'll begin looking for the best people to tag along with us." I can tell Derrick is not ecstatic with the news of us taking such a large portion of our supplies, yet he agrees without any objection. "We can run the plan by everyone who's going with us in case anyone has an idea of how to make the operation easier," I say as I start to make my way over to Lance. He ignores my plea for him to remain seated and gets up anyway. I shake his hand and thank him for bringing the idea to my attention.

"Mr. Ridgehall, if you'd be so kind, I'd like you to stay and give Mr. Simmons here any info you can recall about the Control Center. The key is in the details, so we could *really* use all the information we could get our hands on right now," I implore as he gives me a forced smirk and turns his head to the right to look at Derrick. Simultaneously, I also glance at Derrick and briefly give him a nod before backing away toward the door to the office. "We got a lot of shit to do, brother. Get some sleep before then," I say while swinging the door open and heading toward the Armory.

***

I nearly get my fingers caught in the path of the bolt as I release the charging handle of the Sig M400 we found three weeks ago in the abandoned armory across the street from the West side of the

Consulate. I am not sure how this wasn't stolen before we got to it, yet I am not complaining.

It's been so long since I've held a rifle, but it feels… natural.

I place a spare magazine for the rifle into my back pocket before putting on my bag and recording what I took into the Inventory Binder. *This better be worth it.* I turn to hand the pen to the next person in line: *David Hall.* Given the trust he's earned from me due to his relationship with Hope, as well as his willingness to protect the kids within the group and his impressive results in our newly developed shooting grounds a few miles north of the *Consulate*, he was an ideal choice for our commute to the city. David takes the pen and gives me a stern nod as I pat him on the shoulder and begin making my way out of the room.

As I approach the entrance of the Armory, I notice *Jawbreaker* on the other side of the propped-open steel door, scribbling into the dark green *Personnel Ledger* so everyone is accounted for. My eyes scout the line of people patiently waiting for their turn to enter and stop once they reach an all-too-familiar face: *Corver Whitlock.* I stop in front of both men before proceeding to speak while placing my rifle in between both of my arms.

"Thanks for helping out here, *JB,*" I say. I receive a nod in return as Pancho's eyes remain glued to what he's writing. I turn my attention to Corver to offer the same appreciation. "And you, I appreciate you agreeing to tag along. You've saved my life already, and I haven't forgotten that," I mutter as I turn my body to the right and bring up a curled fist in an attempt to give a fist bump, all while trying to not drop the rifle I am hugging. He gives out a loud chuckle before meeting my fist with his own.

"At this point, I'd do anything not to patrol the fourth floor and hear *this asshole* snoring again," he proclaims as Pancho extends a middle finger at him with the hand he's holding the book up with. That caught me off guard, so I can't help but laugh at *JB* either, causing him to turn his finger to face me when he hears it.

"If you want to cuddle up, all you gotta do is ask," Pancho whispers sarcastically just low enough to make us laugh even harder. "*Mira*. You're up, *Pendejo*," Pancho says as he picks his head up from his book and rests the pen in the middle of it. Corver simmers down his laughter before giving him a nod and ushering his way into the Armory to prepare for the trip. Once my laughter subsides, I prop myself up and usher a hand to the next *Thriver* in line so they can halt.

"Have you seen Renata?" I inquire while locking my eyes with Pancho's.

"Yeah, boss. I saw her in the library with the kid when I came down here. She probably left, but you never know," he says before taking a seat in the creaking chair behind him.

That chair is still too damn small for this man.

"Thanks, *JB*. Remind them we leave in seven minutes," I instruct as I put my hand down and wink at the person my hand was previously facing before proceeding past the double doors and toward the library.

The first thing I notice about the library as I approach isn't the dim illumination, *no doubt coming from a candle*, seeping through the small window on both entrance doors, but rather how the smell of blood has faded almost entirely since I've last been in there.

I thought that smell would never leave...

As the right door is pulled toward me and flung open silently, the comforting smell of new books fills my nostrils and almost makes me not want to leave. With both hands on the rifle, I glance over the right bookshelf closest to the door and spot Vito scribbling in one of the books he had found somewhere in this room. Renata is sitting near him in a chair directly in front of one of the wooden tables. She has her head down in her arms. By the looks of it, she's probably asleep.

I quietly prop the rifle against the closest bookshelf before discreetly ushering my way toward the duo. I don't want to frighten her, but I don't want to sneak up on them, either. I was expecting Vito to glance up at me first since he's the only one awake besides me, but Renata lets out a quiet gasp and quickly jolts up as the dark wooden floor beneath the wool carpet I'm standing on alerts her of my presence.

So much for not scaring her...

"Whoa, whoa, whoa… it's okay… it's alright, it's Miles," I exclaim as both of my palms extend forward to show her I'm not here to hurt anybody. I guess she really *was* sleeping before I entered because she pauses for a few seconds, most likely buying her eyes some time to adjust to the dark beyond the candlelight, before sitting back down. In the dim light, I can see Vito's pencil tip had snapped from the sudden commotion. Despite this, he still jumps up and welcomes my sudden arrival.

"Miles! Where've you been?!" the kid yells before running to me and giving me a brief but sincere hug. His arms couldn't even wrap around my waist, even though he was a little taller than most boys his age. I put one hand on his back while reaching for another pencil on the main desk to my left with my other hand. Once he lets go, I give him a replacement pencil to make up for the one he had just broken.

"What's up, kiddo?" I say as I come to the realization that I haven't seen these two in a few days. "I've been all over, and I'll show you everything we've done in the school so far, okay? For now, though, do you mind if I talk to your mom?" I ask before he takes off back toward his book without saying another word.

This kid is going places.

I sit in the chair next to Renata, who is now sliding her hands down her face. She looks at me as she places her chin in between both of her palms. I can smell her perfume battling the strong smell radiating off the books around us in my nostrils. From my calculations, the perfume seems to be winning. I start speaking to her in a light whisper.

"I'm sorry I scared you. I just… I wanted to make sure you guys were alright before I left," I admit before sitting back in my chair. I can see her confusion, so I know she hasn't heard about the trip to Manhattan. Without hesitating, I bring her up to speed. *"I'm going with some of the guys to get a train from the city. It's far, but once we have it, we can use it for anything we need,"* I explain as she places her forearms on the desk and leans closer to me.

"A train? Wha- why would all of this happen now?" she asks in an innocent tone that immediately fills my stomach with butterflies again. *Damn, I missed her voice.*

"This place has grown, but it's *not* enough. If we succeed today, we can grow the *Consulate* to be safer than it is right now," I say with slightly more volume as I begin to lean forward again. I can feel her light, warm breath heating my cheeks, even though the room is slightly cold from the outside temperature. As always, I'm having a tough time reading her body posture, yet I assume she's trying to find reason in the idea that we're leaving for something she doesn't yet understand.

"And, uh… how many of you are there?" she asks quietly.

"There's 9 of us. We're leaving in… four minutes," I say as I check the cheap digital watch I gifted to myself last year for my birthday. I lock my eyes with hers again as I proceed to speak, "I can use these people's help to make this place stronger than it ever was. I mean… I- hell, some of the people here are *all* that I have. If I fail, you guys pay the price and I can't-" I say as Renata nearly falls out of her chair to hug me before I'm even able to finish my sentence.

Out of instinct, I almost throw her off me, yet my arms remain crossed on the table as I sit there with my eyes closed. I bring my left hand up to one of the arms she has around my neck before beginning to stand up as she pulls herself back. I can see Vito still has his attention on the book he's scribbling on, so I know he didn't hear anything I was saying.

She takes a step back before sitting back down and biting her fists as she clenches them together and her elbows rest on the table.

Now, I don't know what's going on in her mind, but I do know that it's almost time for me to go. I walk behind the black and red chair I was sitting in before pushing it in slowly enough so as not to distract Vito from what he's doing. Elbows still on the table, Renata looks up at me and begins speaking in a tone just above the acceptable limits for a library.

"I know you have done some *terrible* things for the people here. For… me. For him…" Renata says as her voice begins to crack slightly and she shoots a glance at her son. "Everything that has happened here dies with you if something bad happens to you. Some of the people here are all that I have left, too," she says as she begins to cry softly. I can see her turn her head away from me as I notice her rolling her wedding band back and forth on her right ring finger. I also notice Vito looking up at us, pencil still in hand. After what seems like an eternal pause, I place my fists on the table in front of me and lean in slightly before I begin to speak in a tone matching hers, *which is just loud enough to piss off any librarian left in the country.*

"If I die, *nothing* changes. Because there are certain people here who have more in them to run things better than I can ever hope to," I say in a determined manner. Renata looks back at me, her cheeks slightly red from the *icy tears slowly making their way down them,* and puts her face back into her hands. I can see Vito turn his attention back to his book, now writhing on the page opposite to where he was previously scribbling. I take a few steps back and nearly bruise my upper leg as it collides with the corner of another wooden table behind me.

"Everything is alright…" I whisper to myself as the two remain fixated on what they're doing - *paying me no mind as I back away from the candlelight and into the darkness once more.* I turn around and snatch the rifle before pushing the double doors open and marching toward the main lobby.

* * *

As I descend the stairs in the main lobby, the first thing that catches my attention is the eyes of about ten or eleven bundled men and women becoming fixated on me as I approach. Most of those in the lobby are carrying larger caliber weapons except two people, including Pancho. When my feet touch the bottom of the staircase, I examine each *Thriver* who was chosen for this commute.

I see one of them holding a Mossberg 590 and grab it from their hands in exchange for my AR-15. As I throw them the spare 30-round magazine I had sitting in my back pocket, I walk towards *Jawbreaker* and hand him the shotgun.

"Don't let them out of your sight," I command as my eyes burn through his. From his nod of approval, I can tell he knows exactly who I'm referring to. He takes the shotgun and positions the muzzle toward the floor.

"You got it," he says as he takes a step back. I turn to face the rest of the group in front of me. I can see David and Derrick are closest to the front doors, while Corver is standing closest to me. I hop onto the desk in the Main Lobby and turn to address the entire group.

"Some of you are too new to have witnessed what happened here just a few months back. Someone we were supposed to call family deceived us. Tried to have us killed. Well, we took care of those people… and in doing so, we had their bodies locked away and examined over a few weeks. What we found was that the corpse of one of the men who had threatened us revitalized in a way I can only hope to one day understand, yet what's important to know is that there are threats out there much more dangerous than we are," I say as I scan the room while speaking. There are mixed emotions spread throughout the lobby; some of disgust and confusion, while others are displaying devotion. I point to the double doors leading to the front courtyard of the *Consulate*.

"Most of you have seen what I'm talking about, yet we've come to understand that these things, these *spectrals*, are only aggressive in the light. That means that we're going to do everything we can to keep them out of it, understand?" I instruct as I rest my arm back to my side. I can hear a few people in the group verbally agreeing while everyone else is nodding.

"There's so much room for greatness in front of us, so let's go fuckin' get it," I mutter as the entirety of the group lets out chants of support while I make my way off the desk and push through the front entrance. The wind is the first thing that I can audibly pick up as the metal doors leading to the front courtyard creep open silently. My cheeks and ears instantly become cold from the exposure to the outside temperature, so I abruptly put my hood on in an attempt to maintain my body heat. As we approach the train station down the block, I keep our objective in the front of my mind.

Next stop: 59th Street

* * *

We've been walking on the Southbound train tracks for a few hours, and we almost had Archer, one of the more arrogant *Thrivers* within the group, slip off the track a few miles back. Seeing as though the tracks we were walking along were above ground, the first half of our commute had been relatively uneventful. My anxiety, however, reached new heights as we collectively entered the dark tunnel leading into the underground portion of the metro line. As my eyes adjusted to the dark, it became clear that luckily for us, the lights within the first few underground stations we passed were out. This made it easier for all of us to sneak past the *spectrals* aimlessly roaming along the platform of the stations, but we *never* let our guards down.

Even in the seemingly eternal darkness that engulfed the group and me, we were still able to see the various silhouettes in the distance following each station we snuck past. The *specs*, still unaware of our presence, were contorting in a manner that one would only see in a dog infected with rabies. This, mixed with their unpredictable movements, only increased my stress. There's one thing I can't get out of my head though: *Their groans*. They sound agonizing.

As the guys and I approach 59th Street on the Lexington Avenue Line, goosebumps cover my arms even in the muggy tunnels. We all hear screaming coming from up ahead that causes me to jolt just like Renata did when I startled her a few hours back. I try to assess the faces of the other men around me as best I can in such darkness, yet the silence that follows is enough to confirm my suspicions: *We're all terrified.* After some hesitation, we continue to traverse the dark tunnels while using the nearby wall for guidance in the darkness, but the Kimber in my hand starts becoming all the more visible with every step I take.

Oh shit...

I extend my arm to the side to stop everybody in their tracks, *no pun intended*, once I notice that the 59th Street Station is brighter than ever. More frightening is the fact that there are more *spectrals* ahead than I want to admit. As my eyes instinctively glance farther down the tunnel, I can't help but notice the various blood stains littering many parts of the station ahead. It's as if a painter dipped their brush in dark red and started swinging it over their head like a lunatic. With all of us standing there in disbelief, it takes me a while before noticing the ever-so-familiar stench of iron filling the air, and I nearly throw up once it hits my nose.

I can hear the inaudible whispers of the others behind me as one of them *actually* throws up; I don't bother turning around to see who it is. For what feels like an eternity, we wait before David steps forward to the front of the line and points down the tunnel.

"Maybe we can shoot out the lights," he suggests in a faint whisper before he places his hand back onto his .22 caliber rifle and looks at me. One of the other *Thrivers* quietly rejects the idea before calling it a waste of ammunition, yet I shut the objection down.

"No, he's right," I say as my gaze transitions to the ceiling of the train station no farther than 200 feet in front of us. "Some of you have .22 caliber rifles, which is what we have the most ammo for. It's a long shot, but it would be more than enough to take the lights out if you can hit 'em." Seeing as though we only secured our Shooting Grounds recently, I can only assume that most of these people don't have much experience using firearms. I'm not in love with the plan, but it's the only one that's been proposed so far. Corver steps forward and abruptly injects himself into the conversation.

"If our experienced shooters can get close enough with the .22s, we can lay out as many lights in the station as possible. That should lower their aggression and make them easier to put down," he suggests. I like it, yet I turn to Derrick for further suggestions. As I do, I briefly wipe the sweat off my forehead. *Whether from the heat or the fear, I can't tell*, but Derrick notices my glance and puts one of his hands in his pocket before quietly speaking.

"I can stay back here with the rifle and put down anyone who comes near us assuming you trust me enough to cover you," he whispers as he takes his hand out of his pocket and wipes off his sweat. "Those who've never fired a weapon should be behind those taking out the lights and preparing to attack when they're finished," he suggests as nods of approval begin to emanate from everyone else in the group. It doesn't take long before he gets my nod of approval, as well.

Alright, let's get it done.

"I'll take the closest position to them as I can," I say with a slight voice crack as I do my best to keep my voice down while remaining comprehendible to those around me. I holster the Kimber and extend my now empty hand towards David, who passes me his rifle without a second of hesitation before unslinging a 12 gauge pump-action shotgun he was carrying on his back. "Whitlock and Simmons will take positions next to me, while Archer will watch over us from there," I say as my finger points to a barely visible ledge standing about four feet high on the side of the tunnel. "David, you have the shotgun, so you and everyone else will stay back here. Remember to take the weapons off *safe* and remain calm no matter what you *hear* or *see*. Just breathe and remember what we've all practiced," I reiterate.

I don't receive any nods, yet I can tell they understand what to do from how they're all looking at each other with worry splattered all over their faces. Derrick and Corver begin to walk behind me and I can hear everyone checking the rounds in their chambers as I begin to do the same. My body turns, and I follow closely behind my two trusted companions.

Here we go…

As the three of us move up to about 50 feet or so away from the station, I usher the guys next to me to spread out, so as not to have anyone deflecting brass at one another when we begin shooting, and take a knee to get a more stable firing position. I look over my left shoulder and barely notice Archer lying prone on the ledge about 100 yards behind us, as well as the rest of the *Thrivers* propping themselves against the walls nearly ten feet behind where I am. All of our muzzles are pointed toward the station.

"Don't fire until we move," I whisper in a nearly inaudible manner to the five *Thrivers* behind us as my attention turns back to the front. "Aim at the lights. I got far right," I whisper as Derrick speaks up immediately after.

"I got closest to the left," he whispers back.

"I guess that leaves me with the light above the track in the middle," Corver lets out in a muffled yet seemingly disappointed tone. I can see from my peripherals that everyone is ready.

"*Four… Three… Two…*" I whisper as my voice gets louder and louder with each subsequent number that is called out. I align the iron sights of the rifle with my chosen target and give the cue that starts it all. "*One.*"

My ears begin ringing almost immediately as the sounds of gunfire bounce off the walls of the tunnel. Even with the minimal power of a .22 caliber round going off, it's still loud enough from such proximity to do some damage. Besides the brief illumination from the muzzle flashes, the first thing I notice is two lights being destroyed almost simultaneously when we fired.

What a shot!

I can see one of the lights on the left is still up and running. Derrick must've missed it. I immediately realign my shot with any other source of illumination I can find at this distance and continue firing. What sends shivers throughout my body is seeing nearly every *spectral* within the train station turning their attention to the dark tunnel we are standing in. One fact is irrefutable: *They are now sprinting.*

Shit…

At this point, I can't tell who's hitting what. I keep shooting as accurately as I can, given the long distance, above the heads of the rapidly approaching abominations that are nearly tripping on the train tracks below their feet to get to us. As the darkness within the tunnel seemingly consumes the bodies of the *specs* that were advancing, their previously distinguishable features become mere body outlines resembling more of an apparition than a person. As they enter the darkness, everyone around me takes a breath once it becomes clear that their aggression is instantaneously suppressed.

It's working…

I take one last shot at the lights in the station before hearing the unmistakable locking of a bolt on the rifle: *I'm empty.* Once the realization hits me, I holler out to the men on my left and right. "I'm out," I shout out as I turn to retreat while keeping my head low, so as not to get in the way of the barrels being pointed over my head from those nearly directly behind us.

"Moving!" I yell out as I turn around. When I hear David shout for me to move, indicating he's covering me, I begin running as fast as I can while attempting to remain crouched. As all three of us fall back, I hastily drop the empty rifle while grabbing the Kimber from my thigh holster. As Derrick, Corver, and I position ourselves behind the five *Thrivers* who are now preparing to take the lead on the assault, I can faintly hear Corver and Derrick beginning to reload their rifle. After double-checking the handgun to ensure it's loaded, I address those in front line.

"Support team, aim above the neck!" I yell out to the *Thrivers* ahead. I pick up the barrel of the handgun and align the glowing iron sights with what I can only assume is the head of one of the *spectrals* now stumbling in the tunnel. With Derrick, Corver, and myself safely behind the firing line, one of the men in front of us fires off a round that ignites a chain reaction of gunfire throughout the tunnel.

Bang. Bang. Bang. Bang.

Seeing as though many of those in the support line have larger caliber weapons, the various sounds of firearms discharging are more deafening than ever before. As the thought of potentially losing my hearing floats around in my mind, I notice the silhouettes of bodies dropping as the seconds pass. Judging by how frequently rounds are ringing out from around me, I can say with certainty that some people are missing their shots, but that doesn't stop anybody from trying to hold the threats back. I begin to fire as well once the apparitions get close enough for me to land accurate shots with a .45 ACP.

Breathe, Miles… Bang!

One falls. Then two. Then three. It doesn't take long for me to lose track of my shots, but I'm fairly certain I am landing every one of the shots I have taken so far. Given the dark environment we were in, apart from the sporadic illumination from the muzzle flashes, my perfect accuracy impressed me more than the 50-yard shot with iron sights I had taken earlier. I feel the slide of the handgun lock back once the magazine runs dry. I take a step back, grabbing another magazine from my pocket in the process, as Derrick and Corver replace my position and begin firing their now replenished .22 caliber rifles.

Two magazines left. I trace my sweaty fingers alongside the magazine well so I can insert it properly without having to see it. Due to my frustration regarding the heat, I yank off my hood before placing a hand on the shoulder of the nearest *Thriver* to me.

"Back up!" I yell out at the top of my lungs, barely able to even hear myself. Simultaneously, everyone apart of the front line begins backing up one step at a time. From nearly 100 yards behind us, Archer's distinctive .308 caliber rifle lets off a round that causes one of the apparitions ahead of me to fall on the tracks below like a falling block of cement. I kneel against the right wall of the tunnel nearest to the group, for stability, before firing off a couple of rounds myself.

Bang. Bang. Bang.

Although I don't pause to get an exact count, there are only a few *specs* left, so I join the rest of the group and take a few more shots before having to reload again. *One magazine left.* As I eject the depleted magazine, I can make out the stainless steel reflecting off of it from the bright red light that suddenly appeared from behind us.

The hell…

In a moment of confusion, I instinctively turn my body to face behind me, only to see Archer cocking his arm back to throw a hand flare he had undoubtedly grabbed from the Armory in the *Consulate*. When he releases it into the air, it travels some distance before landing about halfway between where we are standing and his location.

"Wha- Archer!" I scream as I fumble for another magazine in a frenzy. I'm shaking, both out of fear and anger, so it's not making the reload any easier. The groans of the *specs* now standing about 20 feet in front of us transition into the painful roaring I'd only heard in front of the *Consulate* the day Jayden died.

Oh my god…

I look up, empty pistol in hand, to see the facial features of the things in front of us becoming more visible with each stride they take further into the tunnel. They're running now. I nearly drop the handgun as I get up from my kneeling position and start speed walking backward.

"Run, now!" David yells from beside me as he and some others in the group turn to sprint behind us.

I couldn't agree more.

I grab the magazine in my pocket and use the bright crimson light seeping through the tunnel from behind me to insert it into the handgun with an audible *click* as it locks into place. I send the slide forward using the slide release and look up to see Derrick quickly ushering his way toward the rear of the tunnel. My body kicks in all the adrenaline it possesses when it comes to my attention: Derrick didn't even notice one of the *spectrals* thrashing around nearly four feet behind him as it was attempting to grab his arm.

Crap...

"Move!" I holler out while using all of the force I can muster to throw my body against the disfigured humanoid that is reaching out to grab Derrick. Our bodies fall to the ground as I hear Derrick's footsteps stop abruptly a few feet away. I immediately smell the decay coming from the corpse of this creature in front of me. It is worse than *anything* I have ever smelt before, yet I don't have time to get back on my feet before the creature resumes its attempt to claw at me once it has regained its momentum.

The sheer strength... I... I don't know what to do...

"*Agh...* Fuck!" I shout out at the top of my lungs as the rest of the *specs* approach my helpless position. I don't even know where my gun is. Amidst the chaos unfolding around me, I'm briefly blinded when one of the creatures catches on fire as it comes into contact with the third rail I had warned the others about earlier. The smell of fire and rotting flesh enters my nostrils as I struggle with my ferocious opponent. *Now I have smelt the worst of the worst.* I hear yelling coming from some of the men in the group.

I can't breathe. I can't move. I can't think...

Then my ears ring again. I can feel small particles of a liquid substance land on my face as two .22 caliber rounds are fired into the head of my strong assailant. As the previously aggressive attacks are instantly replaced with the weight of a motionless 200-pound body, I begin to push the corpse off me while fumbling along the ground for my firearm. From my peripherals, I notice Derrick now aiming near the train station and walking toward the remainder of the abominations flooding the tunnel just as Corver grabs my right bicep.

"Are you alright, man?" Corver asks in a concerned tone as he keeps the muzzle of his Ruger 10/22 aimed at the ceiling. I can barely make out his question from all the ringing in my ears. He pulls me up as some of the other men in the group follow Derrick's lead.

As the corpses of all but one of the creatures fall onto the tracks, I see Derrick lift the butt of his rifle before slamming it down on the head of the remaining attacker, whose body is completely engulfed in flames. He knocks it to the ground with as much force as I would come to expect from someone Derrick's size. As the creature attempts to regain his balance, I can see its decaying body fall motionless as David brings the shotgun up to its head before firing. One of the only sounds I can hear as the echo of the shotgun blast starts to disparate is the sound of my heavy breathing.

We're alive… we did it.

Some of the men rush to my side once they realize we are in the clear, yet I wave my hand to signal I don't need anybody's help. Most back off once I do. Trying to catch my breath, I pick up my Kimber and scan the crowd as my eyes begin to adjust to the light again. It doesn't take me long before I lock eyes with exactly who I'm looking for. I aggressively shrug off Corver's hand, which is still on my arm in an attempt to help me catch my balance, and stride closer toward the light separating Archer from the rest of us. Even as his words begin to fill the air, I can barely make out his muffled dialogue.

Control…

"Sorry about that. I couldn't really see where I was aiming. But hey, you see… I knew you could do it-" Archer says as I bring the handgun up to his head once he's about three feet away from me and fire.

Bang! Silence.

The only audible things within the tunnel are as follows: *The sound of the flare, the sound of Archer's body hitting the ground, and the sound of his bolt-action rifle slamming against his body.* The iron smell from the warm blood now sliding down my face overwrote the smell of burning flesh and gunpowder embedded in the walls of the tunnel. After a few seconds of no commotion from anyone, I bring the handgun down to my side and turn around to face those behind me. No one knows what to do or what to say: *so I start talking.*

"He put us in danger," I mutter loud enough until I can hear my own words. "Almost got us killed, for what?!" I yell out rhetorically, not expecting an answer. "Negligence like that gets people killed. It has *already* gotten people killed," I yell out as I aimlessly point the gun back at Archer's corpse lying behind me. "If we die out here, so does our family back home…" I say in a slightly hushed tone that is still audible to those in front of me. *Silence.* After a long pause, David steps forward and begins speaking faintly.

"He's right, we- we have people to take care of," he cries out as he begins to rub the back of his neck without making eye contact with me. I don't hear or see any signs of objection from the other seven men, but I can't tell if it's because they *agree with me* or because they *fear me.* Corver inserts himself into the conversation shortly thereafter.

"He was an asshole anyways. Let's just get this done so we can keep thriving, yeah?" he asks in a joking manner before proceeding to continue down the now-dark 59th Street Station. I can tell by his serious facial expression that Derrick is not too fond of my recent decision, but he breaks his gaze away from me and follows Corver into the station.

"Let's clear the bodies from the track so we can get the train through here once we're done," I firmly but politely instruct the men standing idle. Most of their eyes are still locked on me. I turn to face Archer's corpse as some of the guys step forward to move the bodies, then kneel to grab his rifle.

"There's no room for people like you here," I mutter under my breath so the others won't hear me. I place the rifle against the wall before grabbing the contents of Archer's dark blue book bag and placing it into mine. Once I zip up my bag and place it on my back, letting off small grunts of pain in the process as pressure is applied to the bruises I had endured from being pinned down with such ferocity just moments ago, I roll his corpse off the track as the light from the flare starts to dissipate in front of me.

Time to go…

* * *

With countless rounds of ammunition being spent and an unfathomable amount of commitment and sheer willpower, we finally did it. The sudden warmth that hit my skin once a few of the *Thrivers* and I simultaneously slammed the steel doors leading into the Power Control Center shut made the literal blood, sweat, and tears all worth it. We nearly lost a few people just trying to get out of the train station, yet we weren't accepting another loss today.

We- we made it…

I hesitate for what feels like an eternity before pushing my body off the set of one-way steel doors separating us from the *Specs* pounding on the other side. With my anxiety still through the roof, I can feel my heart rate steadying with every deep exhale I let out. David, Derrick, and I back away from the entrance and venture further toward the dark corridor leading into the building. As we turn around, Derrick proceeds to dig into his book bag for the same black-and-white notebook he had brought to me earlier yesterday morning.

"Alright, Lance helped me draft a schematic of this floor. We came in through the west so we are right… *here,*" Derrick says as he aims his right pointing finger at one of the entrances he drew on paper. I hand him a flashlight I had in my bag, the same one I picked up from the Cafeteria when I first got back from Scarsdale, but retract it before he has a chance to get a good grip on it.

"Turn it off if you hear or see anything that you shouldn't," I mutter as I place the grip of the flashlight in his left hand. He flips the light and turns it on before aiming it at the book and taking a few steps forward.

"Let's go boys," I say to the others as I turn my head to the side without breaking my glance at the dark corridor ahead of us. As we begin to follow Derrick, I eject the magazine from the Kimber to check how many bullets are left: One round, plus one in the chamber.

Great…

I slam the magazine back into the weapon before locking my eyes back onto Derrick and the notebook he's holding. Even with such a detailed account of the PCC's layout, there is no way of truly suppressing our fear of the unknown. We begin to clear each room in pairs. With every corner we peer around, I'm reminded of the possibility of danger.

After a few turns, we make our way into a huge room surrounded by large computer terminals and a plethora of switchboards and desks strewn all across the area. As I scan the room from right to left, I can't help but notice the large wall near the front of the large room consisting of different colored lights. Each light illustrates a different subway line spanning throughout the city. By the looks plastered on the faces of nearly everyone in the group, it becomes clear to me that the tension looming over our heads seemingly evaporates as quickly as it had festered.

Oh my god… this is… incredible…

"Wow…" I can hear one of the men say as we all start to take in the intriguing sophistication that went into designing such an extraordinary piece of technology. One of the lights above us switches on. Followed by another. Then another. Before I know it, the seemingly vacant room is now completely visible. The suddenness of the bright lights being activated causes my eyes to squint slightly, but I don't voice my slight annoyance.

"I need you four to collect as much shit as you can find in this building, *carefully,* that is…" I let out quietly as I point at David and three other *Thrivers* nearest to me. "Y'know the drill. Anything from toilet paper to half-empty bags of chips you find on a desk. Bring it all and we'll figure it out from there," I say.

"You got it, boss," one of the men says as the four look at each other as if trying to decide which direction to go first. They take off in a light jog as they decide which room to search first. I turn my attention to Corver and the female standing immediately on the right. The woman, whose name is Ruby, is the same woman who was part of the *Nocturnal Patrol* I saw on the second floor yesterday morning.

"You guys will take the rest of this floor to make sure we're not alone, yeah?" I ask in a more worried tone.

"We'll uh- we'll fire off a shot if we see anything dangerous," Ruby says as she moves a strand of her dark blonde hair behind her ear before gripping her rifle more firmly. I take the flashlight Derrick had placed on one of the desks nearby and throw it over to Corver. He catches it with his free hand before nodding and turning to lead the way toward the opposite side of the room where the previous four *Thrivers* had wandered off.

Once it's just Derrick and me standing in the heart of the PCC, I turn and start walking to where he is standing just a few feet from me. He grabs one of the rolling chairs idly standing in front of the desk before sitting down and flipping through his notebook.

"What now, D?" I inquire as I roll over a chair sitting near one of the other desks and place it at his side before taking a seat.

"The old man had me writing everything there is to know about this place, so I'm trying to find out how to reroute the Lexington Avenue trains to our advantage," Derrick lets out as he briefly picks his head up from his book before gazing around the room. He notices the brightly lit Terminal against the wall I had noticed earlier before placing his nose back into the notebook. My eyes avert back and forth between all of the exits surrounding the room.

This place can work. Yeah…

Placing my attention back on Derrick, I recall that it was Derrick's idea to bring Archer along for the commute. All of my rage in the tunnel had made me forget that, and I can't help but wonder how that is making him feel. As Derrick continues to silently fumble with the various switches on the Terminal, I step forward to address him.

"Hey, uh… listen, bud. I know you chose Archer to come with us today, so I wanted to-" I say before being hastily cut off.

"Look, man, Archer was a dude who did stupid shit. And that almost cost me my ass in those tunnels, too," he lets out as he nearly knocks one of the pencil holders nearby over onto the floor when he swings his arm behind him in frustration. His gaze is now on me as he continues speaking. "I saw what you did back there. You almost lost your life just to save mine, man. If you had died before I got to you, I would have shot that *piece of shit* myself," he snarls as he starts to rise in his chair in an intimidating manner.

I take a second to process what he said before smiling. A few seconds later, Derrick walks over to his bag and grabs a half-empty water bottle and a semi-clean rag that was tied to one of the carry straps of the bag. After pouring some water on the rag, he extends his hand before silently offering it to me. Sensing my confusion, Derrick circles his pointing finger around the front of his face, reminding me of the dried blood I had felt on mine in the tunnel.

"Sooner or later, that's not going to wash off. Take advantage while it still does," Derrick says quietly while continuing to usher the damp rag in my direction. I wait for a moment before taking it. While nodding at him in an appreciative manner, I extend my hand in his direction. He keeps his eyes trained on mine as he grabs my hand without looking. He breaks his gaze before sitting back down and placing his attention back on the book.

Seeing a mirror in the distance, right above the counter in the break area near the other side of the Terminal room, I make my way over to it and lower my head as I position myself in front of it. It takes me longer than I'd like to admit to muster enough courage to look at myself. As I do, I barely recognize myself as my cheeks and forehead are covered with long strains of dried blood. The dark red substance seems to wipe off with ease as I drag the wet rag down my face.

It takes nearly half a dozen times before I'm able to completely eradicate any evidence of the atrocities I committed from my skin. I wring out the rag in the sink, causing a flow of red to drip into the stainless steel amenity, before turning the valve to wash it away. Although it shouldn't surprise me, no water comes through the idle faucet above, leaving the various streams of trained blood to effortlessly flow toward the middle of the sink. I take one last look at myself before slowly backing away from the mirror and turning to address Derrick, who is glancing at me from his seat nearly 30 feet away.

"Do what you can and shout out if you need my help," I say as I place the rag into my pocket before turning toward the exit of the room. With each step I take toward the exit, I retract the Kimber from its holster and raise it before making my way toward the stairwell to begin my search of the building alongside everyone else. Toward the unexplored areas of the building. Toward the unknown.

* * *

In less than 20 minutes, I make my way back into the Terminal Room and see Derrick still fumbling with some of the controls nearby. I shoot him a thumbs up before placing three garbage bags full of various commodities I managed to find throughout my search onto one of the desks where David and his buddies had piled their loot.

"Not bad for half an hour's worth of effort," Ruby says with a cute laugh that slightly resembles that of Renata's. I feel more at ease as I hear it; the clarity of sound in my ears, albeit still ringing slightly, is returning with each passing minute. Ruby places her rifle against the desk closest to her before grabbing the chair in front of it and letting out an exaggerated sigh of relief as she sits down. Corver gives me a tiresome nod once he takes a seat in a chair of his own. Before I can get comfortable myself, Derrick enthusiastically shouts out.

"Alright, alright! Miles, I think we're up and running," he exclaims with more enthusiasm and joy than I had ever seen from him before. He slams his book closed and tosses it on the floor before examining the lights on the Main Terminal where the Lexington Avenue line is illuminated.

Green. Green. Green. I think we're set…

"Oh my god…" I say as my legs start to give out. I catch myself before I look like an idiot in front of the rest and prop myself against one of the desks in disbelief. I can hear the others cheering behind me, seeing some of them hugging or exchanging high-fives with one another. *I guess no one gives a shit about keeping the noise to a minimum anymore.* In my shell-shocked state, I am almost struck in the face as I narrowly catch the thick paperback book Derrick throws over to me. I recognize the cover: *It's an official train manual for Conductors.*

"We still have to move them, but the closest train we have to the *Consulate* is the abandoned one we passed in the tunnel near 68th Street," he states with certainty as he further examines the location of the trains from the terminal. I flip through the book hastily, slightly intimidated by the sheer amount of information it possesses, before stuffing it into my nearly full black book bag.

"This place is secured enough, so I think it's best if we have some of you stay down here to help with the trains," I advise as I receive looks of uncertainty from some of my peers. "Ruby, do you mind camping out here for a few days while the three of you stay with her?" I ask while also addressing David and a few of the others standing nearby. "Derrick can help since he's the only one who seems to know how to operate this thing," I mutter out to the group.

"Uh, yeah… sure, but what about this stuff?" Ruby asks while ushering her hand toward the variety of stuff on the table near the men. Those around the table back away from it to give me a better view of what's in front of them.

We could use some of this at home.

"We can split it as evenly as we can: Half of it stays here while the rest goes back with us to the *Consulate*," Corver suggests as he nearly falls back from his chair while attempting to throw his feet on one of the desks. I pause for a while and look around for any signs of disapproval, but don't find any. "It's a done deal, then," I say as I signal the men near the goods in question to begin packing half of the contents on the table for our departure. "I'll send word to Hope about you holding this place down for a while when we get back, alright?" I ask while making direct eye contact with David. As I glance over his shoulder, I can see there is a set of communication equipment sitting at the far end of the room.

"Hold on a second…" I mutter under my breath while slowly making my way to the equipment in question. As I begin twisting some of the nobs on the machine, I realize it's a functional UHF Transmitter and Receiver, which was probably used for communication with other stations around the city back when the trains were running. It doesn't take long before my fingers are running up and down the machine in a moment of nostalgia.

"I gained some experience with these in the Military, so if we…" I say while fiddling with some of the switches before nearly jumping out of my seat as a voice abruptly comes out of the speakers. The Volume Nob is turned up so, from my peripherals, I notice those who are closest to the speakers were also startled. Since my eardrums feel like they are going to explode, I quickly turn the dial down as the voice gradually becomes more clear.

As if my headache isn't bad enough.

It's the somewhat distorted voice of a female who sounds as though she's been talking for years straight, judging by how dry her voice is. She has a seemingly determined yet monotone voice as her desperation to connect with anyone over the air becomes more apparent with every word she lets out.

"There's *more*…" I mutter to myself in a nearly inaudible manner. I don't even know what to think. I continue to lower the Volume until her pleas become nothing more than a moderate whisper before standing up straight and turning my attention to the people behind me. "We can *use this*… If there are other places like ours in the city, we can use each other. Hell, we'd be unstoppable…" I spit out without so much as a deviation in tone. In my excitement, I didn't even take a breath between my words.

"You think we'd be ready for something like that? I mean… we barely have our own shit together, boss," Ruby says as she crosses her arms. *She's right.*

Control the situation…

I take a second to look around and scan the faces of the crowd before me. As I pace back and forth while pondering what to do, the idea hits me as hard as the airborne Conductor's Guide did merely moments ago: *We don't need to do everything ourselves.*

"Have you ever heard of the Reciprocity Principle?" I ask the group while coming to a halt in my tracks. I look back at Ruby, who is shaking her head at my question. "You're right. We've barely gotten anywhere alone. But if we look out for others around us, they're more inclined to do the same for us. Picture it: Need food? *Trade for it.* Need propane? *Ask.* Need bullets? *We're covered.* We'll go further running together than we ever would standing alone," I declare as I defend my position on the matter.

Silence.

Some of the men are looking back and forth at each other, while everybody else just has their eyes trained on the muffled speaker resting on the crowded table a few feet behind my left arm. The silence *- which seems to overpower the woman's faint cries on the radio -* is enough to drive anyone insane if it persists for too long.

Before I can utter another word, Derrick breaks the silence as he steps away from the terminal he is leaning against and makes his way past me. The smell of faint smoke, most likely from the burning infected he put down in the tunnels, hits my nose when he does. He walks over to the radio before turning around and looking at me.

"We're not just skating by. If we're going to take over this city, then we're taking *everything*," he says before facing the communication system and picking up the microphone in preparation to speak. I hear the faint static in between the unknown woman's faint yet desperate attempts to reach someone come to an abrupt stop once Derrick hits the "Push to Talk" button on the microphone. As he does, I turn to face the rest of my peers, all of whom are nodding at Derrick's recent declaration. There's not a whisper of opposition within the room. We've been through too much to let an opportunity like this slide. We owe it to ourselves and everyone who has died for less to make something of ourselves. We need this. I need this.

"Good," I say, "then let's get to work."

PART TWO

THE REIGN

CHAPTER 7

UNTAPPED POTENTIAL

<u>Ledger</u>

Vito Caruso	Renata Caruso
Hope Starcov	Charlotte Kennedy
Pancho Ruiz	~~Simon Adams~~
Derrick Simmons	~~Jayden Walker~~

(There are 82 additional names on the list)

Journal Entry: We have 14 areas within our "Network of Traders" (we all agreed on the name). It took us a few weeks to secure the train stations along the Lexington Avenue line, but we've finally managed to barricade them all. It costs us quite a lot via commodities, yet outsourcing most of that labor by paying others in our network saved us a fortune in time. We've even been bringing durable building supplies from the city to the Consulate, making this place one of the most substantial buildings within the entire borough in just a few months.

Even with stricter recruiting standards (thanks, Simon), we're almost a hundred strong in just this building alone! That doesn't include the 14 we have at the PCC. Still, I can't help but feel we are not quite as powerful as we can be. I can't lie down and rest until everyone here is safe. I keep recalling what Renata said: "Everything that has happened here dies if something bad happens to you." She's wrong. We're a force that will never wither. I'll help her see that.

EVEN WITH THE ARMORY WINDOW closed, the sound of drilling and the faint smell of sawdust filling the air is delightful. As I close the journal, which is now sitting idle next to the Armory's Inventory Ledger, I glance outside the window. While my eyes struggle to adjust to the sudden exposure of sunlight beginning to seep in as the sun rises, I notice some of the *not-so-handy Thrivers* perching up thin metal sheets against the gates surrounding the front of the building. It's the same set of materials that David brought back from a construction depot he and his group found near the *PCC*. Meanwhile, the more experienced *Thrivers* are helping them to secure the seven-foot, heavy-looking sheets by welding them in place.

I hope they get this shit finished soon.

Kneeling to pack the journal in the open book bag I have leaning against the mahogany desk in front of me, I briefly glance at some of the numbers on the Inventory Ledger. Some items, such as smaller caliber ammunition and various cans of nonperishable food, have their quantity in the *three and even four digits*. With the decision to establish our Network being relatively fresh, I can't help but feel a sense of pride and security as our numbers continue to grow rapidly. I close the ledger, stand from the seat, and back away from the desk while simultaneously slinging the bag over my right shoulder. I turn around and start to walk out of the Armory, only to find myself nearly tripping on one of the many rifles leaning against the wall. Frustrated, more at the fact that I had knocked over the rifle as opposed to the potential for injury, I bend down to pick up the fallen weapon and prop it back up. Once I stand up, the sound of a brief truck horn coming from the rear courtyard of the *Consulate* overwrites the sound of the construction being wrapped up for the morning.

About damn time. I thought they'd never return.

After locking the Armory door behind me, I begin slowly jogging toward the stairwell and practically glide down the stairs with enthusiasm. As my feet hit the ground, I throw my weight against one of the double doors leading into the rear courtyard and fling myself out into the cold.

In no time, I can see my breath in front of me as plain as day. About 70 feet in front of me, I can see a few *Thrivers* posted outside, running to open the gate on the west side of the building. I run over, trying not to embarrass myself by slipping on the slush built up on the floor. Once we reach the gate, I remove my black wool gloves and shove them into my faded fleece jacket to better grip the metal.

"Alright, go!" I holler out over the rumbling of the idle truck engine to the other *Thrivers* holding the opposite gate. We yank them inwards, with the metal continuously scraping against the wet concrete until we make a big clearing for the truck to pass through. With the truck being only a few feet in front of us as it makes its way into the rear courtyard, the sudden but unnecessary sound coming from the horn startles the *absolute shit* out of me. Even through the slightly frosted window, I can see the men in the truck cabin laughing uncontrollably. Their jovial expressions fade out of view as the truck passes me and is parked near the entrance I had come through just moments ago.

Let's see if they keep laughing tonight when they're posted for patrol.

Before we close the gate behind the transport, I veer my head around it and quickly glance up and down the sidewalk before fixating my eyes on the elevated train tracks down the block. I glance over to Kerrie Mordecai, one of the women who helped me open the gate just seconds ago, before politely addressing her.

"Can I see that, please?" I ask as I point to the bolt action rifle slung behind her. It's nearly half her size, but she handles the rifle like it's weightless as she puts her head through the sling and extends the stock in my direction. "Thank you," I whisper as I rub my hands together and exhale some hot air in between them before grabbing the rifle.

How is it so damn cold in the Spring?

I point the magnified optic down the street to get a better view of the track. As I hold the rifle up with my dominant hand, I use the other to unclip the radio attached to the duty belt Derrick and I retrieved from one of the deceased police officers during the winter. I position the device a few inches away from my mouth before holding the button down to speak.

"You guys see me?" I ask over the radio without clarifying who I'm speaking to. Just as I regain a comfortable grip on the rifle, I see a thumbs-up from one of the men in the train car overlooking the entire street. We call it our *Overwatch Convoy*. Through the scope, I can tell he's struggling to look for a radio as he frantically thrusts around in the train car while attempting to keep his thumb pointed up at me. The two or three guys accompanying the man in the train car laugh at him as he flails around like someone who just woke up six hours late for work. Even in the distance, I can see the profanities expelled from his lips as he attempts to throw something small at his associates.

After a few seconds, the silence that filled the air once the truck's engine ceased behind us was replaced with the words coming from the various voices in the Overwatch Convoy. "We got you, boss." As I place the rifle at my side, I lower the radio's volume slightly before bringing the handheld as close to my mouth as possible without dropping the rifle.

"I'll have someone bring you guys dinner as soon as we're done here," I say enthusiastically before handing the rifle back to the young woman in front of me, who I recognize as one of the few married people in our group.

"Thank you, sweetheart," I say with a genuine smile as Kerrie's husband, standing a few feet away on my left, glares at me. His name is Francis, but we collectively agreed to call him *Igor* due to his gigantic size. With his shoulders alone bearing the resemblance of a Greek mythological being, this guy is by *far* the largest, most intimidating human being I have ever encountered; all I can do is nod and walk away as the thought of getting my head squashed for flirting with this man's wife enters my mind.

Well… that was awkward…

As I make my way around the hood of the white truck, the paint damn well peeling off at every angle, I get a better look at the comedic driver in his entirety as he exits the vehicle and slams the creaking door behind him. The driver is an older Indian male, probably hovering around his late fifties, with more facial hair than I have on my head. He starts to smile once he sees me peer around the corner, but it fades as quickly as it appeared once I tilt my head like a confused canine.

"If I go deaf, I'm gonna blame you…" I declare as I playfully swat his right arm with the wool glove I retrieved from my jacket before putting it back on.

"Yeah, well… This will make you forget all about that," the elderly man lets out with a grunt as he makes his way to the sliding door on the back of the truck. It is the frequent grunts of pain that cause me to realize he has a limp. *I will never know how this man was approved for collection.* We turn the corner, and the older gentleman attempts to bend down to reach for the door handle. I extend my palm in his direction as I take a knee myself. Once my glove touches the metal handlebar, I throw the door above my head as hard as possible.

There she is…

"Did they give you trouble during the exchange?" I ask, still kneeling, now pointing a finger at the older man's co-passenger standing about two feet to my right.

"No, sir… they were very cooperative and wanted us to tell you that they hope this brings you 'many nights of good rest…'" the much younger gentleman says with a slight stutter as I stand. I break my gaze away from the large red and black reloading bench resting against the driver's side of the musty truck and a bunch of other components necessary to reuse spent ammunition. As my eyes reconnect with the younger, red-haired kid who seems to be no older than Corver, he tosses me a bag filled with shiny pieces of brass: *Bullet casings.*

"Jarek ushered that it's a gesture of goodwill and a downpayment for future services," says the older man as he begins to sit on the edge of the truck, the rear of which suddenly sinks due to his weight. As the brass casings jingle with every move I make with my hand, I lift the bag slightly over my head in appreciation before gently casting it inside with the rest of the stuff.

"For twelve guns and half our propane, it better be," I whisper to myself as I usher toward the men coming out of the *Consulate* to assist us.

"Abdul, have your guys bring this up the elevator and to the Armory with the rest of the stuff," I instruct in a manner that is neither rude nor optional. He gives me a pat on the shoulder as he passes me to jump on the truck, the scent of his cologne striking me in the face harder than the wind that follows suit.

"Consider it done," he says with a heavy yet comprehendible accent as he lifts himself inside the truck and begins tossing the smaller items to the other men who followed him outside. Before I turn to leave, Abdul calls me back before passing me the invoice sitting on top of the machine. The details of the transaction are written sloppy but legible by the man who requested the trade in White Plains, thoroughly recounting everything they received from us and what was given. After glancing over the pages briefly, I grab a pen from my pocket and sign the bottom before folding the paper twice and handing it back to Abdul.

"Looks good. Place this in the binder when you get up there," I say as I hold out the folded paper between my fingers. Even with the glove on, I think I got a paper cut from how quickly he grabbed it. "Thanks, buddy, take the night off afterward. When was the last time you even slept?" I ask with sincerity.

"Sleep is overrated, sir," Abdul declares with conviction as he places the hand-written invoice into his dark blue denim jacket pocket. "I'll rest when we're able to do so without needing to keep a gun in sight," he says as he graciously bows his head before turning toward the rear exit of the *Consulate*. With my attention back on the men sent on the collection run, I give them an appreciative nod, nonverbally thanking them for their help, as I follow Abdul's lead and step off toward the office to get some rest myself. However, my desire for relaxation evaporates instantly as I hear it.

Crash.

It's sudden, but it takes me a while to realize what I just heard: *a vehicle collision.* After a second or two, the sound of spinning tires immediately puts everyone who is posted outdoors on alert. Then the radios start going off.

"This is *Overwatch*. We've got vehicular contact approaching the west gate!" is all that is said before my pistol is in hand. In a militaristic manner, Abdul uses one of his hands to grab my shoulder while retracting a handgun from his holster using his other. He swiftly moves in front of me, and we collectively begin inching toward the commotion as the crew assisting with the truckload stops what they are doing before rushing to aid the married couple stationed near the gate. The duo in question are now getting into defensive positions. As we pick up the pace and begin running toward the gate, I use my teeth to pull off my glove again before using my now-exposed fingers to pull the hammer back on the 1911. *What the fuck is going on?*

"Get back!" I bark out loud for everyone inside the building to hear. Given the relatively small size of the rear courtyard and the various vehicles parked throughout it, I hear my command echoing throughout the air as I step closer to the rear gate. Perching my body alongside the southwest exit leading to the auditorium, about seven feet from the gate, I use the staircase railing to steady my aim once I align the iron sights towards the decade-old SUV hastily approaching us. The driver of the vehicle can barely keep a straight line.

15 feet. 10 feet. 5 feet. Boom!

The SUV hits the side of the gate just hard enough to stop the vehicle in its tracks but not hard enough to tear it down. When I think I have heard enough for one day, the horn goes off near the same spot the cargo truck did just minutes prior. There is one significant difference, though: *this one doesn't stop.*

"Move. Move," I hear Abdul instruct as his men and I lead the way toward the gate. The metal panels welded onto the fence obscure our view of the assailant in the vehicle, and I drag it open with one hand as my handgun remains raised in the other. As the group of about four men surround the SUV, I swing around and position myself near the passenger-side headlight of the vehicle. The unnerving sound of the horn continues to pierce my ears with every step I take toward the vehicle.

"Get out! Now!" I yell at the top of my lungs as I faintly hear the unmistakable sound of rounds being chambered into the firearms of the men around me. As the weapons are pointed at the driver, who seems to be slumping over on the horn, I see Corver and David peering around the gate using my peripherals. My left hand goes up, signaling the men to hold their positions as I cautiously step closer. Then another. Once in front of the SUV, I slam the bottom of my fist on the hood to get the driver's attention. It doesn't seem to work.

Come on…

I circle with my pointing finger while those near me rotate around the vehicle and approach the driver-side door. The blood spatter over the rear passenger-side window is obscuring my view of the second occupant. Still, I can faintly make out what appears to be stained blonde strands of hair and the unresponsive silhouette of a female in the backseat as I make my way around the vehicle.

Refocusing my attention to the threat at hand, my sights align with the driver's head as I yank their door open, half expecting it to be locked. Instinctively, those closest to the door take a step back almost immediately. The noise is unbearable and brings much more attention to the area than we need, given that the sun is now out.

It's only when *Igor* calls out to us as he points down the block, closest to the Overwatch Convoy, that I begin to pick up the pace. Ignoring the sporadic group of *Specs* nearly slipping on the slush below as they sprint in our direction, I glare up and nod to Corver as I pull the disheveled and seemingly injured man off the steering wheel he was leaning against.

"Contact rear!" I hear Corver yell out as gunfire begins to over-write the brief silence that followed once the horn stopped. As nearly everyone in the vicinity turns to address the threats approaching the *Consulate*, I see Francis cover Kerrie as she pulls out her radio.

"Overwatch, take 'em!" I hear Kerrie shout into the microphone. Without a moment of hesitation, bright muzzle flashes are coming from the train car overhead as the men in the Overwatch Convoy begin to provide support from above. Some of the *Spectrals* are hitting the floor violently as the street becomes littered with blood, corpses, and bullet casings. Not wanting to waste any more time, I turn my attention back to the unconscious man in the SUV.

Wait a minute…

"Christ, it's Montero…" I hear David let out as he stands directly behind me, his rifle pointed at the floor as he seems to be frozen in shock from what's going on. *He's right.* Jorge Montero is one of the first people we brought in during the winter, and he's sitting before me with blood spilling from multiple gunshot wounds and what appears to be a variety of lacerations.

Are those… cuts?

"Crap! Here, take it!" I holler as I hand David the stainless steel .44 magnum revolver resting on the dashboard. When I feel its wooden grip disappear as the gun is forcefully yanked out of my hand, I holster my weapon and hastily pull the 6-inch Benchmade from its sheath on the side of my belt. I don't even bother attempting to undo the seatbelt that is sloppily twisted along his body, indicating he put it on in a rush. Instead, I cut the restraint entirely before placing the knife back where I retrieved it from and dragging him out of the car.

I got you, buddy…

Seeing me struggle to carry the nearly 200-pound man with a weapon in my hand, I can feel the weight on my shoulders being alleviated as someone grabs his other arm to speed up the rescue.

"Close in! Lock the gate behind us!" I yell as many of the *Thrivers* around me begin backing away from the street and toward the rear courtyard. I nearly twist my ankle as I slip on the slick floor, nearly dropping Montero in the process. As the gunfire dies down, I hear the all-too-familiar metal scraping along the concrete floor, and I slightly turn my head to see three people pushing their bodies along the gate to expedite the process. I guess it works on time because I hear the gate's latch fall into place, followed by what sounds like aggressive pounding on the metal panels that were recently welded onto our perimeter fences.

As Corver runs over and replaces me as Jorge's guide, with my panting becoming more and more apparent with every stride, I swap places with him and snatch the radio hanging on his backpack before issuing a command to the convoy. "Overwatch, let them get through," I say as the sounds of bullets ricocheting nearby echo. The constant thudding coming from the other side of the gate seems to dissipate following every distant gunshot that rings out slowly.

The men carrying Jorge, who are a few paces ahead of me now, lay him down in the back of the open bed of the cargo truck. The previously musty smell in the truck is, instead, replaced with the metallic odor of blood oozing from Jorge's wounds. What's unnerving is that those are only the wounds I could visibly see.

"Find Jonah and have him get the sickbay ready," I instruct to those nearby as I take a knee beside Jorge, referring to one of the only medical professionals residing in the *Consulate*. "I don't give a *fuck* who does it. Just get me a goddamn sleeping bag and an *IFAK*, now!"

I yell out as Corver, and I attempt to stop the bleeding by applying pressure.

The movement of the truck bouncing as a few *Thrivers* abruptly jump from the vehicle to get help only makes my efforts at stopping his blood loss less effective, and I catch myself before I have time to let out any more profanities. With such immense pressure being applied to Jorge's wounds, I can only assume the pain that followed is what throws him into a frenzy of panic and confusion that seems to frighten me more than any of today's most recent events. Without warning, Jorge flings his arms around frantically as he tries to sit up and back away from Corver and me.

"Jesus, wha-! It's alright! It's alright, hey! It's us… you're home… it's us, calm down…" Corver reassures as the man beside us takes more time than he should to situate himself in his new surroundings.

"What the hell happened?" I ask in a manner that resembles an instruction rather than a concerned inquiry. At that moment, I can see the fear in Jorge's eyes, even as he continues to look at my companion kneeling beside me. As Jorge continues to ignore me completely, I glance down to see his fists nearly turning white from how hard he's clenching them. After several seconds of repeatedly calling his name to get his attention, my heart sinks once it hits me.

Jorge was one of eight *Thrivers* who departed from the *Consulate* last night en route to one of the home improvement stores along Route 87 in Yonkers. They were supposed to be back this afternoon with building supplies and equipment so we could continue our fortification of the *Consulate*. They took two vehicles in preparation for a big haul, but the maroon SUV Jorge miraculously drove up in was *not* one of them. Also concerning is that the Armory's Inventory Ledger didn't contain a .44 Magnum like the one he had lying on the vehicle's dashboard, meaning he must have either found it or, worse, taken it from another person.

"Montero, where are the others?" I ask as Corver looks up at me with concern. As my head is gradually filled with more questions than answers, I immediately begin losing patience and grab Jorge's face before forcefully positioning it in front of mine to address him directly. Even with me hovering mere inches from his face, he seems to be looking through me instead of at me, so I smack him in an attempt to break him out of his state of paralysis. "Where *are* they?" I repeat in a louder tone.

"T- They…" is all Jorge manages to get out before he attempts to cover his mouth as he ferociously coughs up blood, some of which got on my shirt and face, but I am too focused on trying to decipher what he's trying to say to care. Corver and I prop him up along the relatively clean reloading bench to ensure he didn't choke on his blood. Jorge spits near some of the equipment on the floor before looking at me and attempting to converse again. I know he's strong, but he's fighting to keep his eyes open in his weakened state.

"They're still at the… at the store," he mutters before violently coughing again.

Oh my god…

"Get me in touch with the 87 crew," I command as I turn to whoever is standing outside the truck behind me. While still kneeling, Montero yanks on the sleeve of my jacket and nearly pulls me to the floor in a desperate attempt to regain my attention. I'll never forget what I saw in his bloodshot eyes as they began watering: *regret*.

"I don't think anyone got out, boss. Hell, I- I'm not even sure I did, either. And Violet…" he whimpers before releasing his grip on my jacket and letting his arm fall to the ground with an audible thud. He begins to cry as he recalls the events in his mind. I realize now who the woman in the back of the car is.

"You need to tell us what the *fuck* happened in Yonkers," I repeat, this time getting agitated from the lack of communication.

"Th- there were other people, and they were waiting for us… I- I don't know who fell first, but… Miles, they were *everywhere*. All I hear is one yelling '*kilogramo*' and another calling out '*cuedra.*' I don't even know what that means," the injured man says in broken Spanish as *blood continues to trickle down his mouth and stain the white goatee he had maintained over the past couple of months.* He doesn't seem to notice or care about his horrifying appearance.

"I'm sorry, man. I know… I know some of those people have little ones in the house-" Jorge says as his voice continues to crack.

"Hey… shh shh shh. We're not going to worry about that right now," I say as the noise of the doors slamming against the wall makes me jump a little in my vulnerable state. The sound of various footsteps approaching the three of us fails to comfort me as I turn around to see a First Aid in the hands of the younger kid who arrived in the truck earlier. I nearly snatch it before dumping the contents on the floor of the truck bed and grabbing as much gauze as I could find. I bring a finger to my lips as I glance back down at Jorge, then show him my palm. *I need him to remain as still as possible.*

I don't know how long it took… ten minutes? Half an hour? Who gives a shit, anyways? When it comes down to it, the military taught me two very important things: how to *take a life* and how to *save one*. After a while, Jorge is as stable as could be given the limited medical resources at our disposal. The seemingly inhuman shouts of agony coming from the man I barely knew in front of me will forever be embedded in my brain, yet he passed out after we sanitized his wounds. Placing my fingers, which are stained with relatively dry blood, along his wrist, I give out a sigh of relief once I feel his faint pulse.

"Let us take him upstairs to Dr. Estevez," I hear one of the men say as the group approaches the truck. I can't get my eyes off of the bloody shirt we cut off of Jorge, lying as lifeless on the floor of the truck bed as the men in Yonkers. *My men.* I suppose Corver gives the *Thrivers* around me a non-verbal command that I cannot see because I know they won't act in this situation without my consent. Yet, they begin laying out the sleeping bag I had requested to carry him to sickbay nevertheless.

One second, he's lying unconscious in front of me. The next, I'm left alone, kneeling in a shapeless pool of red that my nose has no doubt become accustomed to inhaling. I guess I was there for a while because my legs were asleep even as I struggled to stand. As I lower myself out of the truck, trying not to fall, Corver comes to give me a hand. Without much thought, I fling it away out of either guilt or anger; I couldn't differentiate the two right now. Once my feet hit the wet concrete below, Corver grabs my arm as I begin losing my footing.

"Get off of me!" I shout out instinctively as the sudden contact throws my emotions into overdrive. I regret it the moment I say it, realizing he is only trying to help. Rather than apologize, I try changing the subject. "How many people did they get a hold of from the 87 crew?" I murmur loud enough for only him to hear, eyes glued to the floor. Even with my eyes on the ground, I can feel everyone nearby staring at me.

"You don't want to know the answer to that question…" Corver says quietly with some hesitation. The feeling of my right hand becoming increasingly numb as I gradually tighten my grip on the Kimber only serves to heighten my anger with each fleeting second. Without uttering a word, I lift my head high and turn to face the rear of the *Consulate*.

"I'll be back…" I say as I begin heading toward my office. I only make it a few steps before I hear Corver contesting my decision to walk away. As soon as he grabs my shoulder, I find myself forcefully swinging a fist behind me and connecting with the man's chin. I now understand why they call it *blind rage* because I didn't even realize I had a gun pointed at his head until he had his palm positioned in front of my barrel while kneeling on the ground.

Control…

"I… I'm sorry… I- I need to get this done…" I say as every subsequent word becomes quieter than the last. I re-holster the Kimber, the sounds of gasps from the nearby onlookers more evident than the thumping inside my head, and begin slowly backing away before I see Corver's gesture of surrender transition to a single finger, signaling me to wait. Once he regains his balance, he spits before talking.

"My brother. I think my brother is there…" he says.

What? What the fuck are you talking about-

"He mentioned the word *kilogramo*. My older brother's name is Graham. Graham Whitlock," he says as he catches on to my suspicion. "Look, calling it a long shot is an understatement, but I want to head up there," Corver declares as he stands up straight. "My brother used to live upstate as a truck driver so that that bitch could be *anywhere* in the country, but I can't let this chance slide," he says. Deep down, I knew that if he was right, and Corver did have a relative who participated in the massacre of nearly a dozen innocent people, he would ultimately end up grieving for another person today. *Do I want him there for that?*

"If what you're saying is true, and he's there, you may find yourself wishing he wasn't…" I say as my eyes connect with his while I move closer. I can feel the hot air from his nostrils hit my face as I stare at him without so much as a blink. *From the look he's giving me, he knows I'm not bluffing.* Without so much as another word, I begin stepping backward. After a few paces, I pivot around and begin making my way to the PA System in the office.

"Get your shit ready! We're heading out!" I yell out without looking back. At that moment, the last thing he hears is the sound of the metal doors slamming behind me as I enter the *Consulate*.

CHAPTER 8

RUSTY BEGINNINGS

WITH EVERY BUMP THE CAR rolls over, I find the grip on the semi-automatic Sig MPX sitting on my lap tighter. This was a specialty item that I traded for with a few of our traders in Brooklyn, forcing me to sacrifice more medicine than I would like to admit. I haven't been given an opportunity to use it yet, but I pray that changes today.

"Press checks," I whisper to the six other men in the car without averting my eyes away from the two black Ford Raptors about a dozen feet ahead of us on Route 87. Sitting in the passenger seat, I hear the distinct sound of a *push-to-talk* button being held down from one of our radios behind me. My instructions are repeated over the air, causing a slightly painful screeching due to the proximity of all the radios in the car at one time, but I presume the order was for those in the other vehicles. I don't bother checking my firearm; I *know* it's loaded.

As the drivers ahead of us approach the highway exit leading to the home improvement store in question, they pull into the parking lot with caution so as to not damage the vehicles on the slippery surface or hit any of the abandoned cars nearby. The cluster of abandoned passenger vehicles, some vacated with their doors wide open, doesn't make this location any less eerie than it already is without much light to go on with the sun setting overhead.

As we finalize our approach, I adjust the olive green plate carrier I'm wearing for protection. Like the military-issued plate carriers, this vest consists of three placards near the abdomen where spare rifle magazines can be inserted, followed by 2-inch ceramic plates tucked inside the vest to lessen the impact of smaller caliber bullets. It is an impressive invention, but I pay little attention to it as the vehicles before me begin to stop. As the brake lights ahead of us illuminate the cabin of our seemingly newer Cadillac XT6, I tighten the faded black sling attached to my short-barreled rifle before ferociously throwing the door open and stepping out into the now cooler outdoors.

Game time.

Pulling up the iron sights to my dominant eye, I scan a few areas of the parking lot as thuds from the vehicle doors bounce off the second-floor ceiling above us. One of the first things I immediately notice is that the building has no power; I guess we've been spoiled since we're maintaining our own. As we regroup about a hundred feet away from the entrances of the building, Corver uses his finger to single out five random *Thrivers* before pointing to specific spots around the perimeter. *None of those motherfuckers are walking out of here.*

"Eyes open. Each squad will have a light, but use it *sparingly*. Don't give yourself way. With that said, limit radios once we're in, as well. Stay in groups of four at *all* times. Do you understand me?" I ask as I look into the eyes of the men and women around me. *There are 17 of us in total.* With the sounds of sharp winds and pigeons flapping their wings breaking the deafening silence around us, the nods of approval from the audience before me confirmed everyone was on the same page. "If they're still here, these people *will* die. The people they've hurt… they were *our* people, and we have to explain what happened to their families when we get home," I say as my voice begins to crack. I regain my composure before it goes any further. I guess some in the crowd catch it nonetheless, as a few of them wipe away what I can only assume are tears from their faces.

"Damn right," one of the female *Thrivers* says before coughing into her sleeve.

"These *people* will not win," I whisper. "And *we*… we can thrive in a world *without 'em*…" I mutter as my heart beats faster than it has in weeks. With my breathing becoming more concentrated as the wind makes its way through the underpass, small pieces of dead leaves and minor car debris scatter around our feet. I put up two fingers before bringing them down toward the store, causing everyone to break into small groups and realign their weapon sights with the dark corridors ahead.

"Watch yourself… they're not the only things we gotta worry about out here," Derrick mutters to the small group as they get out of whispering range. With a walnut bolt action rifle in hand, he moves closer to me without diverting his eyes from the entrance.

"What are we *really* doing out here, boss?" he asks hesitantly as one foot lands softly before the other.

Silence.

"Just keep your eyes up, *D*…" I whisper after uncomfortably glancing at him for a few seconds. He acknowledges my dismissal of the question and doesn't go any further. After giving me a nod, he walks back over to his group of four, tagging along with David, Pancho, and Igor. Out of curiosity, I turn my head slightly to gauge who's tailing me; the first person I see is Corver, who averts his eyes to the side after briefly looking at me.

As we reach the large silver sliding doors separating the store from the parking lot, a few of the men position themselves along the side of each. With no power in the building, the sliding doors must be pried open manually. Once we all reach the entrance, two men position themselves alongside both doors and grab onto their respective corners before looking up at me, anticipating the command to proceed.

"*Go*…" I whisper as the warmth from inside rushes out when the doors are pried open, inviting us into a potentially hostile environment we've never been in.

* * *

Comforted by the warmth, I can feel my hands a little more, but then the smell hits me. No one mentions it, verbally, at least, but I can tell I'm not the only one to smell the decay we cannot visibly see yet. The smell of gunpowder and metal seems to fill the entire property, and it is a humungous structure. We continue walking collectively to escape the smell, with some *Thrivers* tucking their noses into their shirts or jackets to avoid it, but the farther we walk, the stronger it gets.

This is not good…

Too worried about the scent, I don't even realize I am walking mindlessly. Using my support hand, I turn on the slightly worn flashlight mounted on the left side of the weapon to better orient myself. Not wanting to give my position away to those who may be lurking in the dark, I turn it off once I can pinpoint where we're going.

One aisle. Two aisles. Then three. It doesn't take long for me to lose track of how many aisles we've cleared. The sound of liquid dripping, most likely from a leaking pipe overhead, is unnerving when compounded with our muffled footsteps and the occasional squealing of rats in the distance. While the men and I make our way toward the middle of the store, I notice a faint light at the end of the aisle. Lifting my hand, I signal the men behind me to halt in place. Without averting my gaze from what lies ahead, I silently instruct those behind me to distance themselves from one another to make us less of a target if we're ambushed.

With all four of us now a few feet apart, we continue our descent into the depths of the unknown. The constant sound of dripping gradually gets louder with each step we take toward the end of the aisle, and my anxiety is replaced with agitation as I begin looking around for the source of the noise. Unexpectedly, one of the guys tailing me puts his hand on my shoulder, ushering me to stop. When I do, he points to my right, where the washing machines are located, and I nearly fall to the ground.

Oh my god…

I fail to regain my composure as my eyes remain fixated on the ceiling. One of the men behind me knocks over some of the items on the nearby shelves as they bolt away from the group to puke in isolation. From about ten feet in the air, two lifeless bodies swing back and forth with minimal momentum; their faces are unrecognizable from the dim illumination coming from a flashlight on the ground near them. I now know what the dripping is: *their upper limbs are missing entirely.*

"I…" is the only thing I can let out. It is barely loud enough to even comprehend. After what feels like an eternity, I force my eyes to the ground and continue approaching the corpses.

Cuerda… Rope. Is that why they were asking for it?

Corver's legs begin to quiver as he kneels, grabbing the flashlight while struggling not to step in the blood all over the slick floor. He starts speaking normally while extending the flashlight in my direction, clearly breathing through his mouth to avoid the strong smell of decay. "It's one of the ones they checked out of the Armory," Corver says, now rushing away from the bodies to get a relatively fresh inhale of air. He's right.

Gunshot.

"Motherfucker!" I yell out as all sense of stealth seems to dissipate almost immediately. Bringing up the MPX, I flip the light back on before running in the opposite direction and toward the back of the store.

"Boss, wait!" one of the men shouts behind me as I take off. All of my military instincts kick in. Corners are checked. Footwork is on point as I hastily traverse the aisles. Soon enough, I see flames coming from hand flares tossed overhead a few aisles down where I am now standing. Muzzle flashes help to further guide me toward the position of conflict. I reach the end of the aisle and slowly peer around toward the left.

There you are...

About three aisles to my left, a few *Thrivers* are propping themselves against whatever cover they can find as multiple silhouettes in the distance, more or less twenty feet away from them, are raining down a storm of bullets in their direction. The sounds of various firearm calibers being fired become nearly indistinguishable from one another as the echoes from indoors make the noise sound louder than it should be.

The attackers are standing near an open corridor leading to a truck filled with various materials from this place. Looking back at the group defending themselves, I notice it's Derrick's group. JB is attempting to reload his 9mm handgun while the rest of the group seems to be frantically looking around from behind cover, possibly looking for a way to retreat.

I position myself against the metal shelf and grasp the front of my weapon for stability. As the attackers attempt to retreat toward the idling truck outside, I align the iron sights with anyone I can hit. *Inhale. Exhale.*

Bang.

The recoil is minimal since the MPX is only chambered in 9mm ammunition, yet the stability from my body leaning against the shelf makes it seem immovable. I fire two more rounds before seeing one of the men trip as he turns to run. Without much of a pause, I pivot to realign my sights with another attacker. Like a deer caught in the headlights, another one of the attackers glares directly into the flashlight mounted onto the MPX, and I use that opportunity to take them down with ease.

Inhale. Exhale. Bang. Bang.

Even at a distance of about 35 feet or so, I can tell the first round went through their head judging by how their body fell. The second shot seemed to hit the body, but that's only an assumption at such a range. I let off a few more rounds in their general direction. It's not until my position is immediately exposed by a blinding light coming from the small group of assailants ahead that I truly understand the definition of fear.

Ah... crap.

I nearly throw my weapon as I drop all of my weight to the floor; the sounds of bullets flying over my head make me feel like I'm in a sleeping trance. Ferociously, I begin backpedaling to conceal my entire body behind my metal savior. Judging by the proximity of the gunfire that follows shortly after, I can tell Derrick's group has taken the opportunity to resume their assault. Still on the floor, I turn around to see my group rushing to help me.

"No! Flank them! We can't let 'em leave!" I holler out over the sound of gunfire. It takes them a little while, but my group eventually acknowledges the possibility of their escape and retreats in the other direction to flank the assailants. I regain my surroundings before ejecting the magazine from the gun to verify the ammo count. After reinserting it into the magwell and shouldering the rifle, I take a few rapid breaths in preparation for my advance.

Alright... Alright. Alright!

With my light flipped off to conceal my movement, I kneel and pivot around the same corner, realigning my sights. *They're out of view.* Still crouching, I begin rushing toward the attackers while using any cover I can find nearby. Four figures emerge from the dark as I approach the large service corridor leading to their vehicle. As they gradually distance themselves from the flare during their hasty retreat, the silhouettes of the attackers are becoming more difficult to distinguish. I see one of them get hit in what looks to be their arm by my crew, but I position myself upright in the darkness to finish what they started.

Bang. Bang. Bang. Bang. Bang. Bang. Bang. Bang.

When they hit the ground, I knew one thing with absolute certainty: they we*ren't getting back up*. As I throw my body against the customer service desk about 15 feet away from the assailants, the deafening sound of a shotgun blast causes my ears to ring as small pellets are lodged into the thick wood protecting my head.

"You thought you would get away from us…? Huh?!" I yell out with a laugh that only adds more adrenaline to my body. I can hear one of them screaming back as the sound of gurgling can be heard in between the gunshots.

I guess their buddy is still alive, after all…

"Fuck you!" I hear from what sounds like a female with a heavy Southern accent in their group. "I'll skin your fingers with wire strippers, you cocksucker-" the female says before she collapses. Her body makes an audible thud as it hits the floor next to her seemingly deceased partner in crime. I peer over the right side of the round desk to see Pancho quickly reposition his body behind cover as the same bright light is shunned back at him, followed by subsequent gunfire from the remainder of the hostile group.

Near the wall of the building, I can see my group peering around as quietly as they can be, but that effort is abandoned after Corver abruptly steps out of cover and rushes forward. He throws his weapon to the ground as he runs toward the commotion. Corver doesn't seem to care about the danger even as my men try to stop him.

"Enough! Stop! Stop!" Corver screams out as his hands go up in the air. His entire body is illuminated almost immediately as the beam of light exposes his location to everyone in the vicinity.

What the fuck are you- Ah, shit!

"Hey, hey, hey! Whoa! Easy…" I bark out to the two men standing idle behind the entrance of the service corridor once I push off the desk and begin staggering in their direction with my weapon raised. One of the assailants is holding a handgun in one hand and a flashlight in the other, no doubt the same one that caused me to drop on the ground earlier, while the other is holding what appears to be a pump-action shotgun. My finger has never felt more firm on a trigger than it does right now.

"W- We are *leaving!*" the male with the shotgun says as he constantly transitions his aim between myself and the group of *Thrivers* slowly approaching him. The duo's facial features become apparent as my light remains fixated on them, while the light on Corver doesn't seem to wither. The man waving the shotgun, probably no older than nineteen, looks petrified as he realizes the gravity of the situation he's in.

"You're not going anywhere, kid," Derrick says as the teenager instinctively points the weapon at him once he begins speaking. He seems to panic more as we close in on them.

"You're right. He's not…" the other attacker declares as he brings the barrel of his handgun up to the side of his associate's head before swiftly pulling the trigger in one fell swoop.

Bang.

Even with an immense surge of adrenaline coursing through my veins, I take a step back out of pure instinct. The only two things I can immediately focus on are the pink mist that briefly fills the air, followed by the smoke exiting the barrel of the handgun. My heart is racing as the thought of this kid being mercilessly gunned down by his own teammate keeps bouncing around in my mind.

"Drop it! Drop It!" I shout as I re-shoulder my firearm to get more stability while approaching the nearly six-foot white man in front of me. His bald head seems to reflect the light I am pointing at him, and his alcohol-stained beard indicates he is a heavy drinker. That fact seems to contradict his relatively fit demeanor.

With each step I take in his direction, I come closer to the middle-aged female choking on her blood at the man's feet. The woman is desperately attempting to apply pressure on the gunshot wound protruding from her neck as thick streams of blood continuously seep through the space in between her fingers. As I stand over the bleeding woman on the floor, who extends her left palm up to me, revealing what appears to be some carved symbol in the middle, I bring the MPX up to her forehead before pulling the trigger without any hesitation.

Bang.

The sudden execution seemed to make even the most loyal *Thrivers* jump. I bring the now smoking gun back up to the taller male, who still has his pistol up nearly three feet in front of me. I want him to know that I am not to be tested, but he seems to be sizing me up; his eyes are frequently moving up and down as he examines me from head to toe. *Is he serious right now?* An eternity passes, and with his gun still in hand, I am done waiting. I lean in while lifting my sights to the man's forehead and step forward.

"Miles!" I hear from my left. Finger still on the trigger, I practically freeze in position while hesitantly listening to the companion calling for my attention. *It's Corver.* Without breaking eye contact with the man in front of me, I can see movement from the side of my eye as Corver slowly begins inching towards us, both arms still raised.

"Graham, put it down…" Corver says as he ushers with one of his hands for the man to lower his weapon. *To no avail.* I can barely breathe as I feel the trigger slowly giving way as I pull on it ever so gently. "Graham, these men will *kill* you. Put the fucking gun down!" he screams out in an attempt to break the tension between his brother and myself. After about ten seconds, I guess his older brother realizes he has no choice, as he throws the handgun to the side, which lands on the corpse of one of his dead companions.

I move in with my gun lowered before swinging the stock at the man's cheekbone as hard as I can, nearly twisting my ankle in the process, yet I know his pain is much worse. As the man falls to one knee, I aim the weapon at his head, and Corver rushes over to intervene. *Jawbreaker* stops the attempt in its track as he raises his Glock to Corver with both hands, and I hear him yell out for me to stop.

"You killed my guys…" I say. The sweat is dripping from my eyebrows, but I don't flinch.

"Boss…" Derick mutters out a few feet behind me.

"Some had *kids*… And you butchered them like *animals*…" I say as my weapon's warm barrel is placed against the man's smooth temple, which is tainted with the wet blood of his fallen comrade. His stoic demeanor remains steadfast as his eyes lock in with mine, and I can feel the hatred radiating from them as my grip on the gun gets tighter.

"Boss…" Derrick repeats as he extends his hand toward me, cautiously taking a step forward.

"Don't worry, you've *earned* what's coming to you…" I say.

"Boss!" Derrick yells out, standing straight and tall.

Control… Bang.

The sound of agony fills the seemingly endless room as Graham's right hand is penetrated by a bullet from the MPX. The spatter of blood gushing out of his two-inch wound gets over my face as he attempts to stop the bleeding with pressure from his other hand. For the first time, I notice that the crowd behind me doesn't let out so much as a whimper of remorse. As Corver walks around *JB*, getting inches away from his face as he does in the process, he stops once he's in front of me.

"That's enough," he says in a quiet manner that does nothing but infuriate me more than I already am. As I turn to my left, tossing my weapon over to Pancho, I use both hands to grab Corver by the collar of his denim jacket before pinning him against a vanity nearby that was set up for display. I can feel something dripping down my forehead, but I can't distinguish whether it's sweat or blood.

"He is coming back with us, but let's get something straight… if *anything* happens to my men, it'll be on your hands," I say in a manner that comes out more like a growl. "And I won't hesitate to take 'em from you like I did to him if they're hurt. Do you understand me?" I ask.

He waits a second or two and takes a hard swallow before responding. "Loud and clear," Corver reassures as he attempts to recollect his bearings once I force myself off him. He looks around at the other *Thrivers* nearby, embarrassed but acting as if nothing happened.

"Restrain him. I don't care about his *fucking* hand," I say aloud as those who were in the other two small groups step forward to secure our newest addition to the family. I can see one of them pulling out handcuffs that were checked out of the Armory before we left. I didn't bring mine because I didn't plan on using them.

As I make my way over to Derrick, I glance at Graham, who's slowly rocking himself back and forth on the concrete floor in a desperate attempt to alleviate the pain in his dominant hand. As Graham picks up his head to look at me, he lets out a grunt that sounds like a mix of suppressed agony and aggression. While leaning against the same customer service desk that saved my life earlier, the wood ruined by various minor intrusions along its surface from the shotgun blast, Derrick looks at me without saying a word. I can tell he's holding back the urge to tell me something.

"Spit out what you gotta say," I mutter in annoyance over his previous intervention. I cross my arms and lean against the desk next to him, keeping my eyes fixated on Graham as *Igor* picks him up almost single-handedly.

What the hell does he eat to get that big?

"Dude, you fucked up that guy's hand," Derrick says with a chuckle that seems to brighten up the mood a little bit.

"I should've gotten both…" I mutter out with a forced chuckle. "I've got some questions for him when we get home," I say. As Derrick digests my previous statement, a look of concern spattered across his face; I can't help but notice he's tapping his fingers against the stock of the walnut rifle he has propped up against his chest. He's holding something back from me, but he begins talking once I reposition myself in front of him.

"Look, I- I need you to be careful," he says as he looks around for who's nearby. "You know I'll be by your side until the end, but we've gotta take a step back and think about what we're becoming. I mean, look, I know what they've-" he lets out before I cut him off.

"You have *no idea* what they've done..." I whisper while pointing toward the middle of the store, not wanting to recall the sight I had accidentally stumbled upon just a few minutes ago. I can tell he's not trying to argue, as he doesn't push his point further, yet he continues talking.

"If we don't draw the line, we will *never* know when we've crossed it..." he says without raising his voice to avoid drawing attention from those around us. "I'm not crying for these assholes, but sooner or later, shit like this is going to get all of us killed," he warns as he gets closer to me. His sheer size is intimidating, but I don't move regardless.

Overall, I know that Derrick is a good person, probably one of the most selfless people I've ever met, and I know he wants the best for everyone in the family. As he lays the situation out with complete transparency, I can't help but admire his inclination to prevent future bloodshed. However, I also understand that few within the *Consulate* have what it takes to do what is necessary to get ahead.

"We've done well taking care of each other, but we can only get so far being the nice guys," I whisper as I point a finger at his chest. I can see that this point of view bothers him, but his facial expression tells me he understands it. "Sometimes the nice guys are forced to do bad things," I say before shooting him a genuine smile of appreciation and smacking his shoulder joyfully as I head back toward the vehicles.

"Take point on their truck. We've still got some work to do," I yell out to close the distance between us as I turn and begin walking backward.

"Yes sir..." he mutters under his breath before picking up the deceased group's gear and throwing it into the back of their truck before closing the rear shutter door.

Slam.

CHAPTER 9

TURMOIL

<u>**Ledger**</u>

Vito Caruso	Renata Caruso
Hope Starcov	Charlotte Kennedy
Pancho Ruiz	~~Simon Adams~~
Derrick Simmons	~~Jayden Walker~~

(There are 75 additional names on the list)

Journal Entry: Seven. That's how many people were taken from us yesterday. For what? Some fucking wood and tools? It wasn't the first time I executed someone in cold blood, yet I find it becoming easier the more I'm exposed to the cruelty of the people in this city (and out of it). It's getting harder to look in the mirror whenever I have to shower, as if the blood I'm constantly rinsing off my body is seeping into my pores and tainting who I am inside. I am not a bad guy... right? Derrick is right... no more killing. But first, there is one more thing I need to do.

IT'S STILL DARK OUTSIDE, YET the sky is glowing bright orange as if announcing its inevitable arrival over the city. I throw the pen I'm writing with on the desk and sit back in my office chair, which makes an abrupt creak the farther my body leans back. As my forearms lay on the peeling leather cushions separating my skin from the bare metal beneath, I can't help but reminisce about the horrors I have seen over the past few months.

For what…?

The chair rolls back, nearly hitting the cot behind me as I stand up and grab the 1911 from the duty belt I have propped up on the coat rack near the office door. I check the slightly scuffed stainless steel magazine, which is packed to the brim, before forcefully reinserting it and tucking the weapon into the front of my waistband. With the MPX standing upright on one of the chairs in front of my desk and my scouting backpack sitting against it, I grab a brass key from my pocket to lock the door behind me as I exit.

As I enter the hallway, I nearly bump into Renata, who is attempting to enter the same room I had just left. Her eyes shoot up and connect with mine as she tries to stop mid-step to avoid an accidental collision. Judging from how much stronger it is than I have noticed before, I can tell she just put on a fresh spray of perfume before coming here.

"I- I'm sorry," I say with an embarrassed laugh that seems to make her look down to the floor and smile awkwardly.

"It's quite alright…" Renata says before she wraps her arms around my neck, tippy-toeing in the process. She lays her cheek against mine as she inches closer to my ear. "I'm *so* sorry. I mean, what you saw… I can't-" she says as her voice cracks.

Forced to do…? What did she hear?

Without much context regarding what she knows or, better yet, *how* she knows, I assume that she heard Derrick and me talking with the adult family members of those who were a part of the Route 87 Crew earlier in the auditorium. She can't see my face yet, but I can feel my eyes starting to water: *Guilt.* She pulls herself off of me, to my dismay, and grabs my face with both of her hands. Her lips are slightly apart as she examines me, and I can see a few nearly transparent strands of saliva in between.

"Don't worry about-"I say before looking down to conceal my degrading mental state. I can't seem to understand what the families are going through now that they know where their loved ones are, but I try not to show I am sharing that pain as the urge to cry looms over me. Hearing her sniffling as she turns her head away from me toward the main stairwell seems to make the effort that much more difficult. "I uh- I have something I need to handle," I say as I begin to compose myself by clearing my throat. "Do you want to have dinner with *me*? Later?" I ask.

She looks just as caught off guard as I felt when I asked. I start to feel dumb as I realize no one has even had breakfast yet, let alone that the sun hasn't fully risen either. She folds her hands together and looks down with a more genuine smile than she had just moments ago; something about her body posture tells me she had been expecting that question.

"Only if we're not having the mozzarella sticks," she exclaims with a giggle that nearly wipes my memories of the previous 24 hours.

Funny girl…

"What's wrong with mozzarella sticks?" I ask as I put my hands on my waist, exposing the .45 caliber handgun sitting idly behind the black buckle of my gun belt. Feeling my smile return after dealing with so much turmoil makes me wish I could talk with her forever. I open my arms to provide another warm embrace, with her forehead against my neck as she steps forward. I don't know how long we stood there.

"I'll meet you tonight in the Library whenever you're done with what it is you have to do," Renata says as she remains pressed against me, this time not pulling away so suddenly. As I lift my head and step back, I hear *JB* calling out from behind me as he reaches the bottom of the stairs leading to the third-floor gym.

"Miles, we need you to come with us," he mutters as he and Nicolas, one of the few *Thrivers* accompanying us in Yonkers, stop a few feet from where I am standing with Renata. I quickly glance down and see Pancho attempting to use his left hand to cover up his right; his knuckles are shaded with red, clearly bleeding. After turning around and realizing that Renata hadn't noticed, I nod at the young woman in front of me, her blonde hair glowing even as the sun begins to show its face along the side of the building before slowly backing up toward the men behind me.

"Sundown," I whisper as I give her two thumbs up before watching her turn around and nearly skip toward the library. I look over to the duo standing at my side before giving them a nod. "Let's go," I mutter as we collectively make our way upstairs and toward the fifth-floor gym.

***

As the gym's wooden door swings open with a little force, I embrace the sunlight peering in from behind the gated walls near the sides of the room. I stretch my arms to my side as far as possible and overemphasize my inhale as the cold wind jolts through the partially open windows. It's invigorating, yet I can tell Graham, handcuffed to a metal chair in the middle of the gym, isn't enjoying this as much as I am; his bare body is bruised, and his mouth is covered in blood.

I can only guess who did that to him…

As the men who brought me here usher past me and bring one of the foldable metal chairs leaning against the stone wall near the gym's supply closet, I position it directly in front of Graham and slam it down dramatically to get his attention. With Graham's eyes still glued to the wooden floor below, he *refuses* to acknowledge my presence even as his brother, Corver, is leaning against the wall with his arms crossed only a dozen feet away from him. Corver's slight head shake tells me he disagrees with what we're doing to his brother, but his reluctance to intervene tells me he understands why it's necessary. I turn the seat around so the cushion faces me, and I sit down as I face Graham, with my arms leaning against the metal backrest.

"Good morning, *Mr. Whitlock…*" I mutter sarcastically, clearly displaying my lack of empathy toward the man. *I don't care how shitty his morning is.* "It's come to my attention that you haven't been too cooperative with my men here," I say as I lean further into the chair. Graham's upper body lifts slightly as he lets out a soft chuckle, still looking at the floor.

Does he think I'm joking?

"Let's start with an easy one…" I say as he begins to pick up his head. *The bags under his eyes tell me that last night was not the only hardship he's faced recently.* Without so much as a second thought, I continued speaking. "Who are you?" I ask sternly.

"I'll tell you what, *asshole…* why don't we just skip the dumb-ass questions and get to the real ones, eh?" Graham says aloud for everyone around us to hear. I glare over at Pancho, who takes a step forward but keeps his distance when I abruptly put up my hand for him to stay where he is. Corver rubs his eyebrows with his fingers in such a way that resembles a student who just got back a failing test grade.

I wait a few seconds, analyzing Graham's ragged body posture, before slowly standing up and walking around the chair separating us. I only take a step or two before I swing my right fist into Graham's cheek, causing his chair to stumble slightly. He almost seems unfazed by the impact.

"Wow… you don't do this much, do you-" he asks before I react with another, more violent swing using my non-dominant fist. With blood now on my left knuckles, I casually shake it in the air in an attempt to mitigate the pain I felt after the last strike. He takes a second to realign himself before letting out a laugh. I can't tell whether it's genuine laughter or merely a way for him to preserve his ego, but it throws me over the rail, nevertheless.

Grabbing the bottom of his chair by the small bar welded near his ankles, secured with zip ties to each chair leg, I flip him over onto his back. With Graham landing on his injured hand, he lets out a blood-curdling scream that is quickly overshadowed by the noise being generated from the *Consulate's* ongoing exterior fortifications. As the white cloth around his dominant hand slowly becomes a dark shade of red, I use my fingers to point to the windows around us: *what happens in here stays in here.*

"You must think you have a goddamn choice!" I yell out as I step down on his shoulder, which increases the volume of his screams as the weight of his own body continues to rest on top of his bleeding hand. Derrick, who's staring at me with a blank expression, notices my reluctance to resort to violence immediately and gives me a nod of approval to proceed with the direction I was heading.

"Who are you?!" I shout as my black combat boot presses slightly harder on his shoulder.

"Ah! Fuc- Graham…" he screams out as the handcuffs keeping his hands in place jingle with every movement he makes.

"No! *Who* are you?!" I yell.

"I just fucking told you, you piece of sh-" Graham lets out before I use my other foot to stomp on the middle of his chest, causing him to yelp in agony before I drop down to one knee and ferociously cover his mouth with my hand.

"No. I want to know who you were with… I want to know what group butchered our people like fuckin' livestock?" I ask as Graham's attempts to inhale are restricted by the lack of air traversing from in between my fingers. I let go and stand back up right before he spits to the side and begins coughing up more blood. I take a step or two back to avoid the spatter.

"I've only ever heard them calling themselves *Colonists*," he says as his breathing becomes more concentrated. He begins to cough a little more violently when he accidentally inhales small amounts of blood through his nose, but I move in for confirmation of what he said.

"*Colonists?* You think this a fucking joke?" I ask, acknowledging how repetitive my question sounds.

"Oh, screw you, alright? Believe what you want to believe, you prick," Graham says with frustration as I interrupt him. With his eyebrows furrowed, his bare chest rises as his temperament does the same.

"Alright, I'll bite. Now I want to know where they *are*," I declare as I impatiently pace back and forth in front of him. Graham begins to cough once he moves his head too far to the right in an attempt to follow me with his eyes. Corver, who I can see is no longer leaning against the wall, looks at his brother and begins speaking as Graham regains his composure.

"This is all he wants to know…" says Corver as he puts his hands in his pocket.

"Oh, no, I'm nowhere *near* the end of this conversation…" I say as I bend down to prop Graham in an upright position. Choosing to ignore his hand dripping crimson liquid onto the wood floor below, I can tell Corver isn't happy with my recent declaration.

As I prepare to sit back down in the gray metal chair, I turn it around to sit in a normal position. I move the handgun under my belt to get more comfortable, and I cross my right leg over my left knee to show that I am attempting to transition to a more civilized conversation. He's giving me that look again: *sizing me up*. He spits to the side before addressing me.

"I swear to you that when it's your time to leave this miserable world, I'll be standing right over you…" Graham mutters as he displays a row of bloody teeth to me and the rest of the room. Rather than resort to my previous method of questioning, I ignore his threat entirely and begin speaking normally.

"I need to know where these… *Colonists* are set up," I say as I put my hands together and lay them on my right calve positioned in front of me. I can tell he's hesitant about speaking, so I continue. "This isn't about *retribution*; this is about *avoidance*. I'm not apprehensive about another encounter; I'm more concerned about how many lives I would've been responsible for taking by the time that encounter is over," I confess. Given his limited range of movement, Graham takes a second to position himself upright as best as he can. The look in his eyes tells me he doesn't care about my reasoning, but he confesses anyway.

"We had sentry routes throughout most of the upstate highways. They never came this close to the city because we were pretty fucking certain that *no one* could survive the sheer number of infected this city was about have running through the streets," Graham says as he looks around to those closest to him. "Yet *here you are…*" Graham says, letting out a sly smirk before slowly glancing around the room. I can't tell if that is a statement of the obvious or a concealed threat, but I chose to perceive it as the former.

"You're going to tell us *everything* about these people. You can start with their habits and MO. How do we know if they're around?" I ask as I switch the position of my legs.

"Besides them slashing the tires of every abandoned car on their turf to stop others from taking cover during an ambush? Let me ask you this: have you *ever* seen anyone else hang people like they do? Fucking *animals*… I mean, you can see why I won't shed a tear for those assholes. Still, they took me in regardless of whether or not I hung a few *nobodies* on a string or-" Graham says as the sound of an infuriated Derrick charging toward the restrained man becomes audible from behind where I am sitting.

"You piece of shit-" Derrick yells out as he lunges forward toward the apprehended man I was speaking with. Being one of the largest people in the room, even Igor has difficulty holding him back, given how well-built Derrick has remained over the past couple of seasons.

"Hey, hey! Whoa!" I yell out while springing out of my chair and holding both hands in front of Derrick, easing him to relax. It takes him a second, but he eventually steadies himself and forces everyone's hands off him as he storms out of the room angrily, nearly setting the wood from under his feet ablaze. Once I hear the wooden door slam shut, I turn back around again and sit before addressing our man of the hour.

"Alright, next question…" I say.

* * *

Following Corver's lead, I walk through the same doorway Derrick had stormed through nearly half an hour ago as I hold open the door for whoever is tailing behind me. As I glance over my shoulder, I can see Pancho speed walking to catch the door before it swings shut as *Igor,* unlocking the handcuffs on a weakened Graham, releases him under the supervision of the two other *Thrivers* watching his back.

Placing my hands into my pockets due to the cold gusts of wind circulating throughout the halls of the fifth floor, I stop a few feet away from the gym's entrance. When Pancho catches up to Corver and me in the hallway, I begin addressing them.

Fuck that guy.

"He seems like he doesn't know shit. Either way, I don't trust him. If he's staying with us, he'll be locked up in there and away from the others," I whisper as I point to the gym where we had just come from. "He'd be alone and would have to pass the *Nocturnal Patrols* if he ever got out," I state as Pancho begins to pace around.

"And what of the Armory?" asks *JB*, who glares back up at me when he notices me shift my posture to display concern.

"It's next to me, so I'll hear anything that goes down, but I want two people on it per shift now. I don't care *who*, just as long as he stays away from that room. He's dangerous… I also want him running collection with the next crew we send to the shooting ranges," I say as I recall how a few of the *Thrivers* are supposed to be heading to a shooting range in New Jersey to collect brass casings for our reloading workshop, as well as ammunition and firearms if they can find them. I transition my attention to Corver, who is rubbing his hands together in a desperate attempt to generate some warmth.

"You good?" I ask.

"Yeah… You did what you had to. I know it's for a bigger purpose other than ourselves," Corver admits. I can tell he meant what he said, as Corver has sacrificed more than most to keep us safe over the past few months. From training some of the *Thrivers* in marksmanship to saving my life more than once, my instincts tell me he's someone I can trust.

How can such a loyal kid have such a douchebag sibling?

"Look, we need to learn more about the *Colonists*. They could unravel everything we're building here if their group is big enough. In the meantime, I was hoping you could do me a favor and run down to the cafeteria. Tell the culinary team I said to bring out some of the dark chocolate and biscuit mix from our reserves in the fridge for you guys. You two deserve it," I mutter as I grab both men's shoulders simultaneously. "Just be discreet. I don't want to have to explain to Vito why only the adults can have chocolate today," I say as the two men at my side begin to chuckle.

"Don't tempt us with a good time," *JB* says jokingly. "Just keep us posted about these… *Ravelers*, alright?"

Ravelers, huh? I can work with that.

"Alright. I have to run to the office real quick, then get ready for this evening," I say as the men turn to each other with confused looks, then back to me. Although they don't know about my evening plans with Renata, their facial expressions tell me they're fighting the urge to pry for more information. I let out a sincere laugh I needed right about now before releasing my grip on their shoulders and cutting in between them, grabbing the door handle leading to one of the staircases. I look at the men about ten feet to my right and smile. "Keep your eyes open and ears to the sky. Shit is about to change," I say with intentional ambiguity as I disappear into the stairwell.

* * *

As I fling open the door leading into the main office, I swing my body around the long countertop separating the seating area, where I remember most parents would impatiently wait for their "sick" kids to joyfully run out of class early and the remainder of the faculty's office.

I unlock the wooden door leading into my room and grab the journal still sitting idly on my desk. While I make my way over to the PA system, which hasn't been used since last night, when I rallied the crew for the Yonkers retaliation, I remove the handgun from behind my belt and place it on the desk near the microphone. After taking a deep inhale, I hold the fresh air in my lungs before casually letting out an identical exhale and hitting the transmit button on the microphone.

Here we go.

"Can I have everyone listen up, please?" I ask calmly into the bendable microphone as the speakers begin blaring around the hallways. I guess the speaker in the office had been blown out recently, as no sounds are coming from it, but I ignore this revelation and continue to speak. "This is Miles Gether. I know I look much better than I sound," I say jokingly as I hear muffled laughter coming from the hallway. "But on a serious note, I wanted to let you know firsthand that things are going to be changing around here," I declare as the button below the microphone is released. Inhale. Exhale.

Control the situation, Miles…

"I know we are more than a team or a group around here. We're the closest thing we've got to a *family*. As such, we make decisions *together*. Therefore, a group of our most trusted members will govern the decisions made for the *Thrivers* in good faith of the *Consulate*. This group will be known as the *Delegation*," I say. The previously distinctive laughter transitions into that of confused murmurs in the distance.

"There will be seven people I will be listing. These people have gained my trust, admiration, and utmost respect. I am confident that these people will put their own at stake to ensure we make the Consulate safer than ever been…" I say. The sounds of inaudible dialogue seem to subside in anticipation of the reveal. I take the rooster of names from the personnel ledger in my journal, which I have opened on the table before me.

"Hope Starcov. Pancho *'Jawbreaker'* Ruiz," I say before releasing the button to catch my breath. The mugginess within the office is making me want to crack a window open.

"Lance Ridgeford. Derrick Simons," I let out. I can see some people peering around the doorway leading into the office. They all want to know.

"Corver Whitlock."

"Yours truly is number six… and-" I declare in a friendly way as the group gathering around the office entrance begins to whisper. I catch myself smiling before letting out a small laugh.

"Well, I'll announce number seven later," I say as waves of disappointment flood the halls, even beyond those a few feet away from me. "For now, please enjoy the rest of your morning," I implore as the microphone bends backward once I push it away from my face. A few in the small crowd smile at me; the others, *not so much*. After a few seconds, people within the crowd begin dispersing, and I take the opportunity to head back into the office with my pistol in hand.

Closing the door behind me, I place the firearm on the mahogany nightstand next to the cot at the end of the room, which we picked up from the truck we seized from the *Ravelers* in Yonkers. I flick off the small beige lamp, also found in the truck, that I had accidentally left on when I rushed out of here an hour ago.

I'm so tired.

I lay down in the foldable cot we had retrieved a few months back from the abandoned armory across the street and position myself around until I am comfortable enough to fall asleep. Even as the previously absent sunlight is beaming down into the room, it doesn't take long for me to start dozing off in anticipation of tonight's events.

* * *

Ten feet. Six. Five.

As I approach the double doors separating me from the library, counting each step in my head, I see the dim light radiating from multiple lamps inside. The bookworms in the building could use a dim light source for nighttime reading, so we implemented the remainder of the lamps we got from Yonkers into the library.

Four. Three. Why am I so nervous?

With each hand holding the edge of a warm ceramic plate that we saved for the more festive occasions, I am hit with the smell of freshly cooked canned beans, white rice, canned corn, grilled chicken, canned sweet potatoes, and, of course, an uneven portion of mozzarella sticks that were probably on the brink of expiration.

Just as I extend my hand to reach for the door handle, the intoxicating scent of cologne I had borrowed from Montero, which he lent me after I brought him food in the third-floor sickbay, begins to overpower the comforting smell of food. *Did I put too much?* Nevertheless, I shake my head and nearly stumble backward as Renata smiles through the window positioned on the upper portion of the door, cautiously pushing the right one open from the inside once she sees me struggling to balance the plates.

"Hi there," she says as her dimples show almost immediately, arguably her most distinctive feature. Even as she stands slightly shorter than me, her blonde hair, which she has washed since our last encounter in the morning, flows seamlessly as she extends her left arm out to hold the door open for me. The black sweater she has tied around her waist goes well with her dark red top.

Come on, say something…

"I uh- I got mozzarella," I say.

Dude…

Her soft laughter makes me question whether she is laughing with me or at me. As I make my way into the room, she removes her hand from the door and dances around me before pointing toward one of the tables she has set up near the larger window facing the front courtyard. With the plates set gently on the tabletop, I notice the unmistakable sound of a light draft effortlessly making its way through the small bullet holes created from my first night here.

"I wouldn't have expected anything less," she says with a slight chuckle, no doubt referring to my fumbled remark, as she rubs the front of her legs with her hands before placing them in front of her and toward the table. "Please, sit," Renata says as she bites her lip while simultaneously letting out a beautiful grin.

I reciprocate the smile before gently placing the plates down and removing the tin foil wrapped around them. *I'd hate to bring cold food to a dinner date.* I pull out her chair, which seems to catch her by surprise, and she pauses for a second before placing a hand on the side of my face and taking a seat. The touch of her hand is soothing, and amid my appreciation of her embrace, I stand in front of her awkwardly for a few seconds before quickly remembering to take a seat.

I pull out my chair on the opposite side of the square-shaped oak wood table before sitting down and positioning myself closer to the edge of the table. As I examine the food on the plate, which is letting off a warm steam, I reassure myself that dinner could be much worse than this.

"Who says canned beans can't be sexy?" I blurt out as we begin to pick up the utensils that Renata had already placed on the table prior to my arrival.

Shit, I hadn't thought to bring any utensils…

She lets out another subtle laugh before biting the sweet potatoes. We usually don't eat this good in the *Consulate*, so her face is plastered with satisfaction. It's probably not the most edible food, but it sure as hell beats tree bark and moss. I follow suit shortly thereafter, digging into the chicken before anything else. Before speaking, I finish chewing and wipe my mouth clean, but Renata beats me to the punch before I can move my lips.

"Can I ask you something?" Renata asks as she leans forward and places her exposed elbows on the table.

"Um- yeah- yeah, of course. What's up?" I ask while rubbing my hands together.

How is she not cold?

"I… alright, I really like you. I just want to know something before anything else happens. I want to know, what *really* happened to

Simon in the auditorium that day?" she asks as her eyes seem to pierce through my soul. *She's asking about the truth*. Once my surprise, mostly stemming from the fact that she hadn't heard anything from the other people who witnessed the event, wears off, I reposition myself in the chair I am sitting on.

"I don't-" I mutter out before she cuts off my sentence.

"Nobody let us go back down when the crowd was released. I practically had Hope and her boyfriend holding me at gunpoint with the kids. Then I heard what sounded like a gunshot, and… I- tell me what happened, please…" she quietly implores as she retracts her elbows and places the palm of her hands in between her thighs.

I don't even know where to begin. How do I explain the fact that most of the *Thrivers* haven't seen Simon in months? Or the fact that Hope and David were instructed to keep Renata and her son in the gym until any evidence of foul play in the auditorium was removed? Was I trying to protect *her*? Was I trying to defend *myself*? I don't even know the answer to my *own* questions, let alone hers.

"I uh- I don't think we'll be seeing Simon again. He… he was very dangerous. Not physically, but- look, he was a parasite that I cut from this family," I say in an attempt to justify my reasoning behind the execution of another man whose betrayal she knows little about.

"Cut out with *this*, you mean?" she asks in a frustrated manner, right before she tosses a small metallic projectile onto the table that she retrieved from the pocket of her sweater wrapped around her waist: *It's a .45 caliber bullet casing*. As my hands remain motionless on my knees, I stare at the casing, rolling back and forth on the white tablecloth before coming to a halt. After a few seconds of awkward silence and rising tension filling the room, I glance up at Renata with my head still lowered.

She's good.

I don't know what to say to her. She has the right to know, but I can't predict how she will react. Her stoic demeanor is hard to read.

Maybe she'll be scared of me. Or perhaps she'd leave the *Consulate* for good. Would she accept me for who or *what* I am? Do *I* even know what I am?

"I had him killed…" I whisper with minimal hesitation as my head begins to rise. My eyes don't break away from hers. The sudden revelation of what she already knew to be true makes her sigh, although I can't tell if it is one of relief or disbelief. "He could've helped us save Jayden, but his actions got Jayden killed. Simon was working with that group of people we brought in to take what we had…" I assert. The feeling of temporary regret surrounding the truth about what happened that night subsides with every word mutter.

"W- wha-" she stammers before I interrupt her.

"Charlotte had the right to know what had happened. She also had the right to choose what happened next. I *gave her* that choice… Hell, the truth is that *I* would've done it if she had backed out," I declare as I lean in and place my arms on the table. All sense of joy in the room seems to dissipate almost immediately as the truth about Simon's murder comes out in the open.

"Renata… Simon was a *bad man*. Everyone in that *group* was a bad man. Shit, I am starting to believe that *I* am a bad man, too. But, I'd like to believe that sometimes good people can get away with doing the wrong things so long as they're for the right reasons," I say. I retract my arms from the table and sit back in my seat. Her expression of bewilderment disperses as she nods and stands up.

Shit…

She comes around the table and gently throws her arms around my neck without saying a thing. Her perfume is intoxicating, but it doesn't seem to affect me as much as it typically would since I'm still trying to gather my thoughts. She lets go of me after a few seconds and grabs my face with both hands.

"You are *not* a bad man. You're the man making sure everyone here has a home," she says with a slight crack in her voice as her eyes become reflective from the water building up around them. I feel relieved that she hasn't stormed out in anger or fear.

"Sweetheart, I have done some *terrible* things…" I confess while I begin lifting my hands to grab hers. "When I went upstate, I found…" I say before she removes the hand she's holding against my left cheek and begins caressing my hair, messing up its sleek style while making a *shushing* noise.

"I know," she admits. *Perhaps she overheard people talking about what happened to Archer? Or the Ravelers?* How she knows about my past indiscretions is anyone's guess, but those two little words provide a sense of relief that washes over me the more I ponder what she said. With little to hide, I feel a warm sensation simmering from within, knowing that our trust is gradually becoming stronger.

I begin lowering my head, but she softly picks it back up as her hazel eyes, still watery, feel like a remedy to all of my problems; within a moment's notice, I begin to feel warm and comforted by her presence again. She doesn't say a word as she begins breathing slightly heavier; *she doesn't have to.* As I start to stand, I can see her eyes glance down at my lips as I grab the back of her neck and close in the distance before kissing her. I don't know how long we stand there, but it is rejuvenating. After what feels like a lifetime, I pull back slightly as my hands remain entangled in her wavy, freshly washed blonde hair. As we open our eyes and realign our sights on one another, we both let out a genuine but slightly embarrassed laugh before I place the palm of my hand on her cheek.

"I want you to be the seventh member of the *Delegation*," I say in a slight whisper as she takes a step back, nearly hitting the table as she does. Today seems full of surprises, yet Renata looks more confused than repulsed. "I told you, there are better people who can run this place better than I can. Now, I'll help where and when I can, but I want you to be there with me when I do," I mutter as I place my hand at my side. I remain standing idly in anticipation of a response that seems to take an eternity to arrive. She lifts her head as if asserting dominance in a rap battle and begins to speak as she places both of her hands into the pockets of her tight, dark gray sweatpants.

"Let's do it, then," she says with confidence. I nod before extending my hand, signaling her to sit back down. I push her chair in as she takes a seat and do the same for myself once I get seated thereafter. Realizing how well this evening is going so far, especially after such a colossal derailment, I let out a grin before picking up one of the mozzarella sticks and biting: *it's cold.*

Son of a-

CHAPTER 10

UNDERWHELMED

<u>**Ledger**</u>

Vito Caruso	Renata Caruso
Hope Starcov	Charlotte Kennedy
Pancho Ruiz	~~Simon Adams~~
Derrick Simmons	~~Jayden Walker~~

(There are 94 additional names on the list)

Journal Entry: We finally did it! We've finally gotten the Thrivers to a hundred people. How can something so minuscule feel like such a grand achievement? I've had some of the Thrivers collecting ingredients during their searches ever since David's team at the PCC radioed in for seven new prospects they vetted two months back (~~what would I do without them?~~). Today is the big day. It's about time we get a breather...

We've never thrown a party in the Consulate this big before – those small fires we built outback for the kids to make s'mores (~~w/o the chocolate and fresh marshmallows~~) don't count – but everyone was invited nevertheless. Well, almost everyone. Even with his ass on the fifth floor, I can feel his presence every time I enter the building. I guess he's noticed that because his resentment toward me only seems to increase with every redundant task he's assigned. None of us trust him with the big shit. Still, I can't help but feel like I have to watch my back with him around...

"YOU COMING, BOSS?" I HEAR Derrick yell from the living room after he and Charlotte walk through the front door and into my former residence in Scarsdale. I haven't been in this house since the night I was preparing to run away from the Police. From *all* of this. Still, I can't help but feel a little nostalgia being here.

"Yeah, just finishing up here!" I shout as I close my journal and throw it into the bag against the wall. With the safe wide open, I kneel to grab a few boxes of handgun ammunition and a full-size Beretta that I had left here during my last visit. After replenishing the magazine, I slide it into the Beretta before placing it in the bag and zipping it shut.

Time to go...

As I stand and throw the bag on my back, I make my way out of my former bedroom and into the living room, where Charlotte is sitting on the white couch I picked up about a year ago. Derrick, laughing at something she had clearly said before I arrived, is seated beside her and is the first one to get up once he sees me come out of the room.

"Do you need anything else before we go?" Charlotte asks gently without getting up. She wants me to confirm we're leaving before she depletes her energy to stand. With small strands of sunlight peering in through the window behind her, I can see that her face has more color than I've seen in the past couple of months: *Good for her.*

"No, we're set," I reassure as I hold up a garment bag filled with a few suit jackets for tonight's occasion over my shoulder with two fingers. She exhales before letting out an exaggerated grunt as she propels herself onto her feet, nearly falling back down in the process as she briefly loses her balance and picks up the Sig P229 sitting on the couch's armrest. I give a thumbs up to Derrick with my free hand as he grabs the key fob from his pocket and cuts in front of me to open the front door leading to the front of the house.

As we walk outside, with the humidity hitting me harder than any bullet, the trunk steadily opens with a slightly audible beep from the key Derrick has extended out in front of him. I throw the garment bag into the seemingly empty trunk, followed by my backpack, before hitting the button on the door above my head and letting it close automatically.

Damn, I love technology.

Once Charlotte's rear door slams shut with a muffled thud, I clasp my hands together as my partner in crime throws me the key fob and heads for the passenger seat. Once in, I hit the ignition button with my foot on the brake, and the car shakes slightly as it rumbles to life. Desperate for some fresh air in the cabin, I lower the windows slightly before putting the car in *drive* and rolling out of the driveway.

"I forgot to mention…" says Charlotte from behind Derrick's seat. I look in the rearview mirror to see her struggling to find the buckle for her seatbelt. She glances at me in the mirror once she does and continues speaking. "Some of the guys found something for sale when they met with the Astoria Traders, and I told them to get it for you once they radioed in. I hope the trade was worth it, but I'll let you be the judge. They're in the glovebox," she declares as I keep my eyes on the bright road ahead.

Derrick opens the glovebox and pulls out what looks to be a few 9mm magazines before moving them closer to the passenger side window to get a better look. I request one by sticking my right hand out while constantly transitioning my eyes between the road and the thin, after-market magazine in front of me. As I examine them closely, I realize they're spare magazines for the MPX.

"They should be for that gun you always carry around," says Charlotte.

"Wow. That's a *hell* of a gift. Thank you," I say with more enthusiasm than anticipated as the words leave my mouth. I guess today really *is* a fantastic day. I hand the magazine back to Derrick, who places it with the rest and puts them where he found them before shutting the glovebox. He almost closes it on his finger as we run over a slight bump along Central Park Avenue. I look in the rearview mirror again to see Charlotte grinning at me right before she breaks away and glances outside her window.

"*D*, I don't think I've ever asked; what did you do before?" I ask with genuine curiosity. He wastes no time before giving me an answer.

"I uh… I used to do all sorts of shit, like being a barber part-time, but nothing tops doing comedy at some of the jazz clubs in the West Village," he admits without an ounce of uncertainty.

Well, that explains why his goatee always comes out so clean, but Derrick as a comedian?

"There's no fuckin' way…" I blurt out sarcastically as I get hit on my right shoulder with a soft punch from our female passenger sitting in the second row.

"Be nice…" she says as she begins to chuckle herself. Derrick reinserts himself into the conversation.

"It's true. I used to go home with a different woman *every* night I had a show-" he says as he starts laughing and swats my arm with the back of his hand.

"You're sick," Charlotte says as Derrick's seat swings forward slightly after she kicks the back of it with her left knee. She continues chuckling as she readjusts her position in the seat and lowers the window some more.

"What about you, *Ms. Perfect*? What occupied your time?" Derrick asks while he jolts up slightly, turning his body around as best as possible to get a better look at the passenger behind him. I can almost swear that the weight accompanying his massive size made the car bounce when he did so.

"When I wasn't at college? I was working as a hostess at a bar in Queens that Jayden was a bouncer at. That's how we met… that's also why I asked Miles if I could oversee communication with the traders in Queens. It's my home," she says as the color in her face evaporates with the thought of Jayden entering her mind after so long. I can tell Derrick regrets asking as he slowly turns around in his seat and looks outside of the windshield. As I look back in the mirror, her eyes meet with mine.

"You did good, you hear me?" I ask, subtly referring to how she handled the situation the last night Simon was alive. "Don't worry. He would be proud of you," I mutter over the loud wind seeping through the open windows. She pauses for a second before nodding and placing her hand under her chin as she starts staring back out of the window.

She's come a long way. We all have.

"You know… I was shot once before," I admit as bewilderment seems to flood the interior of the car; both of the other occupants shower me with their undivided attention as their glances seem to pierce my soul. I reposition my eyes on the road before speaking.

"When I was in the military, I was instructed to watch the front gate of the base where I was stationed. It was after hours, and the whole area outside the gates was dark besides the light posts we had over our heads. And this guy…" I say before pausing, taking in as much fresh air as possible before clearing my throat and continuing.

"One of the guys who lived on base showed up at the gate around 1 am and was more drunk than I thought possible, even for a heavyweight. The *cursing*. The *yelling*. The *slurred words*. It was nothing new to me, but I guess I was too worked up to notice the snubnose .38 special revolver in his jacket pocket. I… I tried to draw the handgun I had for duty that night, but instead felt a sharp pain in my side, right under my kevlar, before I was able to pull it out," I say as I recall the events of that night. No one in the car says anything immediately, but Charlotte leans in as best as she can, given the seatbelt holding her back.

"What happened to the guy?" she asks.

"He was court-martialed and given a few felonies for his troubles, so I didn't shed a tear. No… you see, my regret came from my carelessness. It took me a few weeks to recover, but every time I think about this, I can't help but think how things would've been different if I had drawn my gun on time. And that look he had, the hatred in his eyes… I see that same hatred when I look at Graham," I admit.

Silence.

As we approach the *Consulate,* I lower my window down completely and wave my hand so the *Overwatch Convoy* can see us as we begin driving toward the West Gate. I gently press on the brake near the front of the gate and hear Derrick radio in our Entrance ID before the now-reinforced steel gates trail open methodically. We're met with a few *Thrivers* who greet us as we pull into the rear courtyard and park alongside the six other vehicles we had secured over the months.

As we step out of the car, Derrick opens Charlotte's door like the gentleman he is, and I open the trunk and grab all of my stuff. With my hands nearly full, I toss the key fob over to Derrick as he comes around the back of the vehicle and approaches me. He trades me for a handful of magazines he retrieved from the glovebox, and I point my thumb toward my pack so he can throw them in while I grab the rest of my stuff from the car.

"Do me a solid and sign that key back into the Armory, yeah?" I ask while shifting to a more comfortable grip on my garment bag. He gives me a friendly slap on the arm before turning to walk away. *I'll be surprised if it's not bruised at this point.*

"Dress nice, too. Who knows if we'll ever have a party like this again," I say jokingly before making my way toward the office. With the party at sundown, I have a few hours to prepare. Given how much we've sacrificed to make tonight possible, I hope it's perfect.

* * *

Approaching the gym where the party is set to take place, I embrace my attire and feel like a new man. The haircut Derrick gave me a few hours ago only enhances my self-esteem.

I guess he really was a barber.

As I enter the gigantic room, I notice that the ambiance in the gym is more inviting than I could've imagined. Who knew Hope and her band of decorators had such great taste? There are a few long, foldable cafeteria tables, all covered in a gray patterned cloth, sitting against the stone walls of the gym. With ceramic plates, champagne glasses, utensils, and recently lit candles spread methodically on the tables, there is space for everyone in the *Consulate*. The dim lights and low music, so as not to draw too much attention from the outside, coming from the record player near the entrance make this feel more like a cozy home rather than a fortified castle. Deflated balloons in all sorts of colors are floating around the floor covertly.

Not everyone came with nice clothes, but those who lived in the borough or along the Lexington Avenue line could retrieve a presentable outfit for tonight. The indigo shirt I'm wearing feels slightly larger than I remember, and I can't help but wonder if I am losing weight. The black, slim suit jacket I have over the shirt helps conceal that discrepancy. With as much clothing as I have on, I still feel naked without my handgun.

Don't worry, Miles. The Thrivers who volunteered for the Nocturnal Patrol will keep us safe tonight. Just relax… It's a party.

As I continue walking into the room with a large bottle of champagne in hand, I make my way over to Hope, who is joyfully chatting with a few of the other well-dressed *Thrivers*. She looks absolutely stunning in her dark olive dress, which complements her heels. Her smile is one of a kind, and it only seems to get bigger once she notices me.

"Miles!" she yelps as she raises her arms and strolls towards me, trying her best not to fall in her heels.

"Hey, sweetheart," I say as I embrace her. I can smell her deodorant as she wraps her arms around my neck. Her perfume is definitely a competitor against Renata's, but I try not to focus on it too much. David, *dressed in a tucked black shirt with an open collar and black slacks,* follows suit, no pun intended, directly behind her and gives me a fist bump before stepping back.

"You guys look absolutely *beautiful*. This *place* looks absolutely beautiful. It came out better than I could've imagined," I admit as I unintentionally let out a chuckle of satisfaction. She seems to be blushing from the sudden plethora of compliments as she constantly moves her body side-to-side with her hands together in front of her. I politely hand her the bottle of champagne I have in my possession.

"Thanks," Hope says as she tucks a strand of hair behind her ear. "Is she coming?" she asks without clarifying who she is referring to, but I already knew.

I have no idea.

"Yeah, I believe so," I say with slight hesitation. "I asked her to be my date this morning before I went out to Scarsdale. I even asked Vito if he wanted to come, too. Of course, he only wants the cake…" I say while recalling how hard the Culinary team has been working to prepare the food for the party. As Hope lets out an adorable laugh, David also seems amused as he crosses his arms and looks down with a smile. They've always taken care of the children here. I know they'd be outstanding parents.

As if the timing couldn't be better, I turn to see some *Thrivers* from the Culinary Team wheeling in a large, white-layered cake that has taken all day to prepare through the wooden double doors about 15 feet behind me. Standing about three feet tall, with various designs strewn all around it, I can only imagine how well it would compete with a modern-day wedding cake. The small group of four roll the cake into the room on one of the metal carts we had previously been using to bring resources onto the elevator for the roof defenses.

It's stunning…

Turning to continue my conversation with the couple in front of me, I peer over Hope's left shoulder at the rear entrance leading to the stairwell that descends into the auditorium; to my delight, I see Renata ushering her son into the gym's warm atmosphere. Vito wastes no time running over to the cake, which hasn't even been *placed* on the table yet, but a few of the adults nearby intervene before he is given a chance to destroy it.

With her blonde hair in a beautiful braid, Renata pulls down on her dark blue dress without so much as an afterthought. As she turns to make sure the door is shut behind her, I can see the back of her dress is purposely exposed by design; her clear skin radiates in the light provided by the sinking sun above, and the straps above her shoulders contain subtle, colorless gems that seemed to glisten with every step she takes into the room.

I… wow.

I'm shell-shocked, and she *knows it*. She laughs as I involuntarily keep my mouth open to compliment her once she's within speaking distance. She hugs David and Hope before stopping before me and slowly wrapping her arms around my neck. I embrace her with my hands on her lower back so as not to mess up the braid, which she undoubtedly put a lot of time into perfecting.

"Uh… you-" I say before she gently places a finger on my lips. The smell of nail polish, which seems to match the color of her dress, fills my nose in the process.

"You can tell me later. First, you owe me a dance…" she declares with a sexy smirk. Her statement causes those around me to gossip as they turn to each other while snickering at my embarrassment, like high schoolers laughing at a kid who just fell in the hallway. I wanted to eat first, but how can I say no to a woman as tempting as her? Even as she looks up at me, I can't help but feel as though she is the one with the most power over me.

"Allow me," I say, extending my arm to her. She throws her left arm around my right and walks with me slowly as I wink at David and Hope. As we stroll toward the makeshift dance floor, I glance over to see Pancho, *who is wearing a slim, dark blue suit jacket I let him borrow from the variety I brought back this morning*, as he gives me a half-assed salute with two fingers before continuing to flirt with *Igor's* wife, Kerrie, near the supply closet.

Well, that's not going to end well…

Sitting on the opposite side of the table where the Culinary Team is placing the massive cake, I notice Corver holding his stomach with both hands as he rocks back and forth, laughing hysterically at something Derrick had said in confidence.

I guess he really was a comedian, too.

Seeing as though he is the only one to notice Renata and me as we walk past the table, I give Derrick, who's wearing a white button-down with jeans while Corver is sporting a dark red dress shirt with a walnut shoulder holster - a thumbs up with my free hand. The stainless steel Ruger 1911 in Corver's holster seems to comfort me, knowing I don't have a gun of my own. As I turn to face my date for the evening, I grab her waist with one hand once we reach the middle of the room and use the other to raise her hand in the air.

"Let's make this one of the better nights to remember, yeah?" Renata asks seductively as her reflective hazel eyes make me forget all the bad that looms outside this building. Without much thought, Renata and I steadily sway our bodies while making strides with the music filling the room.

As the *80s* music playing in the background begins to quicken its pace, we find ourselves simultaneously laughing as we attempt to remain in sync with the song that doesn't fit the dance style we chose to go along with. After a minute or so, we begin moving to our own fruition as our laughter would make even the most devoted alcoholic think we've had enough champagne for the night.

This is what all of this work is for. This is home.

I nearly trip as I try to pull away, but my companion yanks me back onto the dance floor and almost trips herself in the process. Someone must've noticed how much fun she and I are having because I can feel the vibrations in my chest as the music becomes slightly louder.

Vito begins chanting in support as we miserably fail to demonstrate any fundamental dance skills. After the song ends, my feet feel like they're on fire as Renata leads the way toward the glasses on the table where her son is sitting.

"You need to get better at dancing," Vito says as he glances up at me and places his head against his mother's arm.

Kids...

"Yeah, well... maybe you can show me then, huh?" I let out as I playfully push Vito's head off Renata's arm, to which he retaliates by repeatedly slapping my arm in a jovial but assertive manner.

"Alright. Alright. Go pick up a plate, kiddo. *You*, here..." Renata says as she turns to address me while handing over a full glass of champagne from the table. She picks up another and holds it out in front of her. "Your party, your toast," she says.

"To the continuation of a good thing!" I declare aloud as I slam my glass gently against hers. Some of the *Thrivers* around me who overheard the toast repeat it while raising their glasses as well.

"To the continuation of a good thing!" I hear a few people shout. Many of the adults within the room seem to effortlessly swallow the sparking contents in their glasses without so much as a breath.

I've never understood people's fascination with champagne...

"To the- the continuation... of a *good thing*! Is *that* what this is, Miles Gether? A *good thing*?" I hear Graham asking as he forcefully snatches a nearly empty champagne bottle from Jorge, causing Montero to almost fall to the ground. He is only saved by the table nearby since he's still using a retractable crutch for his recovery. Montero's wife, Destiny, ushers her injured husband to sit down just as he attempts to push himself up and confront the man who was partially responsible for the death of his crew a few months back.

Fuck... is he drunk?

"What are you *doing here*, Whitlock?" I ask as he takes a swig of the glass bottle before dropping it at his feet. *To my surprise, the bottle hits the ground without shattering before rolling underneath one of the tables.* I see a group of men from the *Nocturnal Patrol,* with rifles resting at their sides, hold the door open for one another as they quietly enter the gym a few feet behind Graham so as not to disturb the party. *Too late.*

"What? Was I not invited?" he asks sarcastically as the razor bumps on his face, evident from how poorly he shaved before trotting downstairs, become more visible with every step he takes toward me. Corver and Pancho are the first to stand from the table as I step in front of Renata.

"No, you weren't..." I bark out as my tone deviates from the cheerful tone I had just moments ago. "These men will escort you back upstairs-" I say before he interrupts.

"Wow! *Look. At. You. Mrs. Number Seven.* The *last* of the *Delegation...*" Graham whispers to Renata as he stops a few feet away from us. In my surprise at the fact that he can even pronounce the word "delegation," given his current state of intoxication, I reassert myself in the situation.

"*These men...* will escort you back upstairs," I say in a growl that seems to repel some of the non-confrontational *Thrivers* around us. Pancho and Corver take a step closer while everyone else either remains in their spots or takes a step back. Even as I address him, Graham seems fixated on the woman behind me.

"I don't blame you, y'know... With a girl as fine as that... *Shit...*" says Graham as he attempts to stay in control of the attention. Pancho positions himself an arm's length away on my left while Corver stands at the same distance to my right.

"Oh, you're *asking* for it now," *JB* interjects as his impossibly white teeth become apparent when he threatens Graham. Pancho's fist begins curling up in anticipation of an altercation.

"Your threats don't scare me, boy. Besides, you're not really my type, if you catch my drift. Her on the other hand..." Graham says as he licks his lips at Renata in an attempt to spark a reaction from me. I can feel her hand starting to squeeze mine in discomfort. I glance over to Derrick, who's slowly moving around the table, and his looks say it all: *Don't.*

"*Leave…*" I direct as Graham now transitions his stare to me. His smirk tells me he's not taking me seriously.

"You are going to have to kill me to make that happen," he asserts.

Before I can say another word, Vito gets in front of Graham and me. I take a step back as his sudden appearance catches me off guard. Even as Graham towers over Vito, I can tell the boy's fearlessness is making that fact irrelevant in his mind.

"Vito…" I say as I attempt to keep Renata behind me while she resists my hold. "Vito, get away from him," I instruct with a stern tone of voice. *To no avail.*

"Don't talk about her like that," Vito says as he stares down the man who interrupted our gathering, even as he has to look up at Graham. Judging by how Graham is laughing and the smell of alcohol filling the air with every exhale, he must view Vito's intervention as nothing short of a humorous theatrical stunt.

"Ah, this must be your *mother*…" Graham whispers as the revelation seems to catch him off guard. "Don't worry, I'll be gentle with her," he says before taking another step forward. I think we all step forward simultaneously, but it's only when Vito grabs the gun from Corver's shoulder holster that we all retract our step. Even the armed sentries are caught by surprise, hesitant to aim their rifles at a child. Vito aims the handgun directly at Graham, who jokingly places his hands above his head while laughing.

"Damn! You've got some guts!" Graham proclaims as he begins to lower his hands while still chucking. "There's something you should know, though, kid. You can't fire that gun with the safety on," Graham says before Vito lowers his head to examine the firearm. Just as he does, Graham lunges forward and grabs the slide of the weapon. Before he's given a chance to do anything else, I pin Graham against a stone wall just as the all-black knife attached to my belt is unsheathed and propped against his throat.

Some of the others are appalled by everything that just went down, still trying to process the speed at which it happened, but

Corver runs over to me and his brother while Renata and Pancho run over to check on Vito. Those apart of the *Nocturnal Patrol* run up and point their weapons at the man against the wall. With Graham still gripping the slide of the handgun, I place the blade closer to his throat as I move in to whisper to him.

"Your brother is the *only* reason your lungs are filled with air right now and not blood…" I truthfully confess. Every ounce of reason within my body is telling me to kill this man.

He's dangerous. Why shouldn't I…

"*I knew you lost your way…*" he whispers for only me to hear, but I can tell his words are still audible to those around us. "What happened to the legendary *Leader of the Thrivers?* You're a shell of your former self," he says as he further provokes me.

I should kill him…

"If I kill you, *and God knows I want to*… I would be no better than you," I admit as I maintain the blade's pressure against his windpipe. I can tell the men with the guns are yelling at Graham to drop the .45, but the only things I can hear are the words of the man in front of me and the pounding inside of my own head. The smell of alcohol radiating from his breath is unbearable.

"Someone who executes a group of men trying to keep their families warm and safe with propane? Or shooting one of his own guys just because he disagreed with his method of clearing a train station? How about having an innocent woman brutally murder another person for his own sick fucking agenda? Kid, you *are* me…" Graham asserts as the thud of a fallen gun clears my ears to the sounds around me.

How did he…

"Hands on your head!" the Lead Sentry commands as Graham stumbles once I push myself off him. I back up while the sentries approach, yet Graham's attention immediately shifts to Corver, who walks up to face him directly.

"One of these days, you'll see him for who he *really* is…" Graham whispers with a scowl that seems to only aggravate Corver further. I feel no sympathy as Corver's elbow connects with his brother's cheekbone, forcing Graham to fall to one knee.

The blood trickling down Graham's neck from the pressure of the knife doesn't seem to phase him, even as he's pinned to the ground and handcuffed. As he's picked up and escorted out of the entrance he came through, I grab the Lead Sentry's arm and force him to look at me before addressing him.

"If I see him out here again, *you'll* be in that closet with him," I threaten as he gives me a nod of comprehension. He forcefully shakes his arm to loosen my grip before turning back and signaling his men to proceed upstairs.

Once the doors are closed, my arms go up to reassure everyone in the room that they can continue what they were doing before they were interrupted. I make my way over to Vito and his mother, who are now sitting at one of the tables.

"What the hell was that?" I ask Vito in a tone resembling concern rather than aggression. I can see his mother glance up at me, probably distraught from my seeming lack of empathy toward how traumatized her son probably is. Rather than apologize for his actions or cringe at the fear of punishment, Vito jumps onto his feet and begins to defend himself as his eyes lock with mine.

"He was talking about my mom…" he barks out as his eyes refuse to deviate from mine. I can see the fire in them as he stands up for his loved ones. Even now, with no threat in sight, Vito's inclination to put himself in harm's way to protect his mother is overpowering.

Damn…

I glance over to Corver, pacing around while venting to *Jawbreaker*, and call him over with my hand. Once standing beside me, Corver extends the pistol he had re-holstered just moments ago to me. Without breaking my gaze with Vito, I take the handgun from

Corver's hand and eject the magazine. After grabbing the rear serrations and retracting the slide slightly, I notice the faint glimmer of a brass casing seated in the chamber. Without a second to waste, I release the slide and hand the loaded handgun to Vito. His mother, who seems hesitant to intervene, refrains from doing so as I give her a subtle nod before placing all of my attention on her son.

"Go ahead, pull it down with your thumb. As hard as you can," I direct to Vito while pointing at the safety positioned on the weapon's frame. After a moment of silence, he flicks the safety down with both of his thumbs until we all hear an audible click.

Good…

"Great job, kiddo. Now…" I say as I kneel in an attempt to match his height. "Aim the gun at me," I instruct.

"Boss…" Corver says worryingly.

"He's a grown boy. He can take it," I reassure as I gently nod at Vito, who looks at his mother for affirmation. She seems just as puzzled as Corver is. It takes a few seconds before the stainless steel barrel eventually aligns with my forehead. The gun is a little heavy for him, but he doesn't complain. *Not once.*

"You feel that? That warm feeling in your stomach? If you think you're ready to use it on another person, you'd better get used to that feeling…" I declare as his face tells me he is nervous; his hands, which are slowly starting to shake, seem to confirm my hypothesis. "If you think you're ready, pull it," I say as Corver steps forward.

"Boss!" Corver shouts. I don't even acknowledge his concern as my attention remains fixated on the boy. Even Renata attempts to talk me down, but all the chatter around me flies over my head as I stare at Vito. There is no conflict behind his eyes. It's almost as if he already knows what to do. One second. Then two. Then five. It doesn't take long before Vito lowers his arms and drops the gun, which lands on the wood below with a loud *thud*. Looking into his eyes, I realize that Vito didn't do it out of fear or malice; *he did it to prove a point.*

"No one deserves to die. The people outside are just trying to *stay alive*, just like us. I learned that from you," Vito says as Corver grabs the handgun and inserts the replenished magazine while digesting what the boy had said. Even in my state of paralysis, I can't help but let out a smile.

He's right...

"I wish we were all like you, kid..." I say as I stand and extend a hand to Renata. She grabs it and lifts herself onto her feet. I grab her forearm to better stabilize her before looking down at her. "I'd like to bring him to the shooting grounds tomorrow. I can teach him how to be safe and defend himself. Is that alright?" I ask.

She changes her stance while balancing on her heels, but her nod of approval seems to light up Vito's demeanor. Holding her hand, I accompany Renata to the table littered with freshly cooked food while nudging Vito forward with my left hand. I must admit that Renata was half right, though. *This is definitely a night to remember.*

"I swear if this food is cold..." I mutter under my breath.

* * *

As Renata and I scurry into the office, which is covered by a faint orange radiating from the lamp I had grown to appreciate, we slam the door behind us as she pulls me by my neck and begins kissing me once I'm close enough. With Vito sleeping in his room down the hall, no doubt exhausted from helping the culinary team clean up the gym after the party, there's no better time for Renata and I to be alone.

Making our way past the desk and toward the cot positioned against the wall on the other side of the room, we unintentionally knock over some of the smaller items strewn across the room. Her seductive perfume and body heat are rejuvenating, and it only increases my excitement. As Renata yanks off my blazer, we stumble backward and land on the cushioned bed below, letting out a couple of alcohol-ridden laughs before pressing our lips against one another in an attempt to keep our momentum.

"Maybe," Renata says as she sits on top of me while I begin kissing her neck, "we should've left some wine for the others." She lets out a few moans as I pull back and tuck a strand of hair behind her right ear. She pushes my shoulder until I'm lying down and starts unbuttoning my shirt.

"Where's the fun in that, huh?" I ask while smiling. She giggles and stops abruptly before forcefully yanking my shirt open in an impatient manner. As Renata bends down and kisses my chest, commenting on the smell of my cologne when she does, I erotically pull her braid while lifting my upper body to stay close to hers. She lets out a smirk as her eyes become locked with mine, and I kiss her with ferocity as I slide the straps of her dress off her shoulders.

Renata unravels her braid to get more comfortable as the top portion of her dress begins slipping off. With her long blonde hair now dangling free along her bare skin, she looks more stunning than ever before. As the light from within the room ricochets off the closed beige drapes concealing our presence from the outside world, the color in Renata's face is noticeably pale in comparison to how she normally looks. Her cheeks become stained with discreet shades of red as she smiles and addresses me.

"What, cat got your tongue?" she remarks with a luscious grin as her confidence and self-esteem trump even my own. Somehow, the presence of a woman who carries herself as she does only makes her more attractive to me. As she begins undoing my belt, she freezes in her tracks as her hand hovers a few inches above the hilt of my knife, the same knife I had pulled on Graham a couple of hours ago. As the memory floods into her mind, evident by how she gasps slightly while retracting her hand, I use both of my hands to grab her face in an attempt to avert her attention back to the present moment.

"Hey, you're okay…" I whisper as she looks at me. With my pinkie along her carotid artery, I can feel Renata's pulse stabilize as she takes a few deep breaths. Without warning, Renata pushes me back on the bed while keeping her hand on my pectoral. Her grip is firm enough to keep me pinned down as she remains seated on my pelvis. With her right hand, she grabs the hilt of the knife and retracts it from its sheath before bringing it up in front of her and examining it.

"Who knew such a *small thing* can be so intimidating…" Renata says as she turns the blade around in the air to inspect it closer. Her mouth is agape slightly as she remains invested in the weapon.

"Well, if you consider six inches small, then we may have to have a chat," I say while letting out a cunning chuckle. With the knife still in the air, Renata glances down at me before wrapping her free hand around my throat. Although not incredibly tight, her hold on me is enough to keep me at bay as my eyes connect with hers. There's not an ounce of fear in my body—no worry or feelings of anguish. The only thing I feel as she lowers the knife against my throat is content.

"*Why* did you take us in that night? *Why* did you step in front of me today?" Renata asks as she inches her face closer to mine. Her body heat compliments mine, even as her words bounce around in my head. "*Why me?*" she asks as her eyes scan my face for an answer. She isn't upset or patronized. Nothing about her tone tells me that she's scared or afraid. There's only one thing I see in her eyes: *Confusion.*

"We can't save everyone. But why not try?" I ask as the thought of seeing her for the first time, as well as the memories of all the others who have perished since, enter my mind. With the blade still against my neck, Renata's breaths start to become heavier. After a slight pause, she leans in to kiss me more intensely. I fling the knife out of her hand before grabbing her waist and letting the moment flow. She grabs my face with one hand, causing me to slowly open my eyes, and gently strokes the side of my head.

"I love you, Miles Gether," Renata says as her breath begins to shudder slightly. Even as we lie there, I can't help but feel a sense of comfort washing over me. With her hazel eyes peering into my soul, my affection for her only seems to heighten with every passing second. I use the back of my fingers to caress her warm, reddish cheeks before telling her precisely what every inch of my being is feeling.

"I- I love you, too, Renata Caruso…" I say as she lets out an invigorating smile. "God knows I do." After leaning in to kiss me once more, her cold hands begin to slide down my chest and past my abdomen before fumbling with my belt once more. As we stumble further into the night, everything around us seems to fade into the background. From the distant moans of *Spectrals* wandering aimlessly under the sporadic stars plastered above to the occasional gunshot echoing through the borough, nothing seems to get in the way of our evening. In the way of our moment. In the way of the future.

CHAPTER 11

RENDERED

<u>Ledger</u>

Vito Caruso	**Renata Caruso**
Hope Starcov	**Charlotte Kennedy**
Pancho Ruiz	~~**Simon Adams**~~
Derrick Simmons	~~**Jayden Walker**~~

(There are 96 additional names on the list)

Journal Entry: I'm mediocre at many things, but shooting isn't one of them. I'm sure Vito's results can validate that. Corver has helped with teaching him, too. I can't forget the look on Vito's face when he landed his first shot with the .22. He's getting better as the weeks go by. Still, I can't help but wonder how far this kid will go in life. Either way, he's got a lot to learn.

"I CONCUR..." LANCE DECLARES AS the long wooden conference table vibrates when he abruptly strikes his palm down on it. "If the East Village Group wants to exchange some of their generators for one of our trucks, who are we to deny such a request?" he asks with a mix of enthusiasm and conviction. The other *Delegation* members are spread out, nodding at every word Lance says. I drag my fingers along the page of my open journal to see how many topics we have left for discussion.

"Alright, that settles that then…" I say as I reposition myself in the chair I had pulled out of my office. "Pancho, have the *PCC* radio them in after this. Let them know we'll be ready to make the drop by Friday," I instruct. I see him nod as he begins taking notes on a yellow Post-it, all while using his other hand to bring a half-melted ice pack to his swollen left eye.

"And for God's sake, leave the giant's wife alone," I say as he mumbles under his breath. Some of the people at the table are trying, and failing, to hold back their laughter as the thought of a black eye seems to be some poetic justice for *JB's* flirtatious actions.

"Wasn't worth it, I'll tell ya that much," Pancho retaliates as the room lights up with festive hysteria. Derrick crumbles a sheet of looseleaf paper in front of him and throws the paper ball at Pancho, which bounces off his forehead, increasing the volume of laughter in the room.

"Alright, alright…" I say as I begin chuckling myself. "We've only got one more thing to talk about, and you can all go back to doing whatever the hell you do," I say as I dodge a paper ball Derrick effortlessly throws at me from his seat while booing me. Hope punches him in the shoulder to get him to pay attention, forcing Derrick to rub his arm in exaggeration.

"Last night, we received a call from the *PCC* about a request being made from a group hunkered down in a shooting range near Albany. Now, we've never gone that far, but they're willing to barter with us. Weapons, primers, bullet casings, gunpowder; they've got it all," I state as the playful atmosphere transitions to that of focus.

"Well, what do *they* want?" Renata asks, placing her elbows on the table and her chin between her hands.

"They didn't say much, only that they were interested in developing a friendship with those in the *Consulate*. The woman on the other line said she knew us and mentioned Corver's name specifically," Hope says as she recalls the previous night when she was on duty. As we divert our glances to Corver, we see him look around in confusion.

"I don't know a single person upstate, let alone a female in Albany," Corver admits as he ponders why his name would've been mentioned at all.

"I want to check these people out. As far as Hope has told me, we've got an address. I want to send some of our guys up there to verify who these people are," I announce as I am faced with mixed reactions from those in front of me.

"Miles, you said it yourself; we've never journeyed that far up before," Lance says with a very distinguishable look of concern. "We should stick with the traders we have now in our local network. I mean… the amount of people a commute like that would require, the resources it would deplete…" he projects worryingly.

"Yeah, I don't know. Especially if we're scheduled to give the East Village Group one of our trucks at the end of the week, can we really afford the trip?" Renata asks while some of the people around the table begin nodding.

"We'll be down to six vehicles on Friday, but we only need one. I want to send four people up there so they can take the Escalade," I declare as I start to regret volunteering such a beautiful SUV for the trip. Some people in the room relax when they hear my reassurance.

"I'll take point on the team heading up there," *JB* says as he stands up from his chair.

"Dude, can you even *see* out of your eye well enough to drive?" Hope asks as Derrick nearly falls out of his chair from the sudden and unexpected comment. As he composes himself and his laughter, he begins to roll up another paper ball but is interrupted when Pancho throws his pen at him.

"Enough…" I say as I throw my pen at Pancho. He sits back down, all while using his peripherals to glance in Derrick's direction for any other flying objects. I lean back in my seat.

I live with children.

"David will take point on the team…" I say as Renata shoots me a look of disapproval and objection. I glare at Pancho, who seems disappointed in me for denying him the team leader position. "It'll be me, David, Derrick, and Montero if he's up to it. Pancho, I want you to take point on the Village trade," I declare. Derrick throws down the crumpled ball of paper in his palm and begins to stand in retaliation.

"C'mon, boss. I can take care of the Village trade if you-" he says before I intercept his opposition.

"Truth be told, I love you, brother, but you weren't my first choice. I wanted to bring Corver so they'd see a familiar face, but I think it's best if he stays here in case they have a target on his back. He was the *only* one they knew by name, and we don't know their true intentions," I let out calmly. I can see Derrick's look of opposition subside as the decision becomes more and more logical to him with every passing second.

"If you agree with the plan, make your peace now," I say, lifting my hand to show I'm on board with the commute. "Raised," I say.

The room falls silent as everyone considers whether such a venture should be undertaken. There is a short pause between each response.

"Raised," Pancho says before anyone else. His free hand remains stationary, slightly above his ice pack.

"Raised," says Derrick as he lets out a sigh. I can tell he's not fully vested in the idea, but he doesn't object.

Hope, Lance, Corver, and Renata are all sitting idly in their seats, awkwardly exchanging looks with one another. I don't think any of them agree with what we've got lined up.

We only need one more vote…

"Babe, think this through…" Renata says, leaning forward in her seat a foot away from my left. I notice her look of genuine worry, and it's the same look that Lance has on his face. She doesn't want me to head into such an impulsive situation. I refrain from saying a single word so as not to interrupt the voting process.

Silence.

"Alright, but you all better come home safe…" Hope says as she begins to lift her hand above her head. "Raised." Renata slams both hands on the table while standing up and exiting the conference room in anger. I can see Corver look at me as he reaches for his chair's armrest to stand, but he stops when he sees me look at him and shake my head.

She'll cool off.

"That's that, then," I say as I begin to stand myself. "Against my better judgment, I'm going to speak with Graham. He knows the state better than most, so I need him to chart the best course for us to take for the commute," I hesitantly admit. I don't even want to be in the same room as that *piece of shit*, but I need his help on this one.

"Do you want me to back you up?" Pancho asks as he smiles, presumably at the possibility of getting into another scrap with Corver's brother.

"No, I need to talk with him alone. Plus, I don't think you'd stand to lose another eye," I say jokingly as Derrick tosses another paper ball at Pancho. He lunges at Derrick, causing his chair to tip over and both men to fall to the ground. Amidst their wrestling, I grab my journal from the table.

"Hope, radio in to the *PCC* and tell them to set up the meet with the traders in the Village," I politely command over the sound of Pancho tapping out of Derrick's headlock. "I'll let everyone know when we're ready to head out. *Delegation* dismissed," I declare as I make my way out of the room and into the main office.

* * *

With the door leading into Graham's cell now unlocked and swung open, I can see him on the other side of the closet, sitting on one of the window sills facing the *Overwatch Convoy*. He doesn't turn to face me, even after I begin approaching him. As I'm about three feet away, I toss him a set of handcuffs I checked out of the Armory. He eyes them as they land next to his feet.

"Put them on…" I say in a near whisper. I guess he recognizes my voice because he slumps down to pick them up and addresses me directly. Even as he does so, his eyes never deviate from the stainless steel restraints.

"So, is this how things are going to stay between us, Miles?" Graham asks as he straightens his back and glances at me, the bags under his eyes telling me he isn't as comfortable as I thought he'd be given the isolation, and places the handcuffs in front of him for closer examination.

"That depends on what happens in the next couple of minutes…" I say as I begin unfolding one of the white collapsible table tops leaning against the wall to my right. I extend its gray metallic legs and place the table between Graham and myself. "I need you to guide me on the best route upstate. With your… *history*, before the war and after, I reckon you know the seamless ways to move around without any hiccups," I say as I begin flattening a paper map of the highway routes Lance retrieved from the library.

"A war, huh… Is that what *this* is?" he asks with genuine curiosity and a hint of sarcasm.

"It's taking *everything* I have not to push you through that window, so how about you shut the *fuck up* and do what I say. Cuff your wrist to the radiator over there," I bark out as I extend my finger to the cold radiator near one of the slightly opened windows.

I see him hesitating, but after a brief pause, I hear him click one of the loosened cuffs shut, followed by another click as he attaches the other cuff to the edge of the radiator. Now restrained, he sits in the already-opened metal chair and looks up at me.

"You've got my undivided attention… *boss*," he says sarcastically.

I pull up a foldable chair in front of the map strewn across the table and sit down. Pulling my seat closer to the edge of the table, I position my elbows on the top of the map and examine it closely to find our current location.

"I need to get to Albany. If I'm not mistaken, we're somewhere around… *here*," I say. Seeing as though Graham was brought here blindfolded and against his will, I'm fairly certain he's clueless about our general location. I can see him eyeing different routes on the black-and-white paper. The map takes up the entire table, so every highway in the state is easily identifiable. It takes a minute or so before he begins speaking.

"It might be a little slower, but you can cut across the borough and head up on I-87," Graham says as he follows the route meticulously with his finger. "What part of Albany?" he asks without taking his eye off the map.

"Near Troy," I proclaim as I sit back in my chair and let him map out the details.

"No kidding. Well, you can hop onto I-787 around… *here* once you're near Albany, and it's a straight shot from there," he says as he grabs the yellow highlighter on the table and begins marking the path with his free hand.

"How long should that commute be?" I ask.

"Who the hell knows? Normally, a ride like that would take two to three hours, but I hear the roads are packed these days," Graham asserts in a sarcastic manner that only serves to agitate me. "Could take a day if you're driving carefully," he says. I flip the map around once he retracts his free hand from the table and follow the route with my fingers.

This could work…

"Anything I should know about this route?" I ask as my eyes connect with his. I'm examining his body language to assess whether he's telling me the truth.

"As long as you stay off the Taconic, you should be set," Graham says in an attempt to reassure me. Although taken with a grain of salt and a hint of skepticism, I begin rolling the map while I stand. I dig into my pocket and toss a small set of keys onto the middle of the table.

"I don't think anyone here will *ever* forgive you for the shit you did, but do yourself a favor. Do what good you can with whatever life you have left…" I say as I turn and make my way out of the room, leaving the cell door open behind me. I nod at Luca as he remains standing guard outside of the room; his overgrown, dark brown hair works to conceal his eyes once they meet mine. Luca gives me a subtle nod before breaking his gaze, and I slightly turn my head to the side before addressing Graham.

"You never know what greatness might come of it down the road," I say aloud for Graham to hear as I make my way out of the gym.

* * *

It doesn't take long to get the men ready for the trip. As they pack the back of the Escalade with MREs we secured from the Armory across the street, I readjust my lightweight dark olive plate carrier and ensure all my magazines are accounted for.

Check.

I grab the MPX leaning upright against the rear passenger wheel before tossing it into the back seat. As I shut the door, the sound of which bounces off the walls of the rear courtyard, I turn to see Renata leaning against the cafeteria exit. She's still pissed, but I can't leave without saying goodbye.

I make my way to the driver-side window and lean against it to talk with Derrick while keeping an eye on Renata.

"What's up, *D*?" I ask as he adjusts the mirrors on the car doors. "Before we head out, can you run upstairs and relieve Luca? Tell him to take a break til we get back. I'm sure he's sick of babysitting that motherfucker," I instruct. He finishes adjusting the rearview mirror and shifts his attention to me.

"You got it," he says as he waits for me to stop leaning against the door before opening it. As he heads towards the Southwest exit leading into the back of the auditorium, I go the opposite way toward Renata.

With each step in her direction, I can't help but question whether or not I am making the right decision by having David lead the operation. Although I'll be alongside him, it's still a big step, and I want to make sure he can handle it. I suddenly feel nauseous as Renata's unwavering look of aggravation and concern only worsens the feeling.

As I halt in front of Renata, she crosses her arms and transitions her gaze to the other three *Thrivers,* who are getting the vehicle ready. I can tell what she's thinking, but I want her to be the first to talk. I don't want to say the wrong thing, as if there *is* a right thing to say, so I wait a few seconds while maintaining eye contact with her.

"You're making a mistake," she says without averting her gaze, her arms still crossed and her blonde hair following the breeze.

"If we're right, do you know how influential we could become? We could run a statewide trade network," I declare as I take another step forward. The sudden movement in her direction causes her to look directly at me. As she uncrosses her arms, she also takes a step toward me.

"And if you're wrong?" she interjects.

"We won't be," I say with much less conviction than I would like.

"Let me go with you and Derrick. Leave David here with Hope and the kids or Jorge with his wife. I can sure as shit fend for myself and-" Renata says as she stands tall, no doubt confident in her marksmanship training with her son and me over the past month or so.

"And that is *exactly* why I need you here. What if something happens, and we're both in Troy? Vito is a good shot, but he needs someone to look up to," I retaliate. She can see through my lack of conviction but refrains from objecting further. I grab her waist with both hands gently as she begins to turn and walk toward the doorway she came from. "Hey, hey… It'll be alright," I assure her as she places her arms around my neck. Her soft skin and invigorating aura alone can get me through any obstacle. Why should this be any different?

"We're coming home. We *always* come home. Besides, I know you can't stand to be without my *extravagant* cooking, but I'm sure you can manage," I mutter as she tries her best to hold in a gentle laugh. The feeling of her upper body rising with every breath she takes helps to mitigate my worry.

"Boss, we need to go before the sun rises again!" David shouts from inside the Escalade. I can see Derrick, out of breath, shoot me a wink while opening the driver's door and taking a seat before starting the vehicle. As Renata pulls my face towards hers with both hands, her lips seem to quiver slightly as they rest against mine, yet I don't mention it once we pull away.

"Just come back together," she says in defeat.

"I wouldn't have it any other way," I say while trying to clear my throat. I hold my composure so as not to make the temporary departure more complicated than it needs to be.

I lean in to kiss her briefly again before pulling away and heading toward the SUV. I slam the door shut once I'm sitting in the rear driver-side seat and prop the MPX against my right leg. Derrick looks back at me through the rearview mirror and puts the Escalade in motion once I give him a nod.

Go time.

* * *

The highways aren't as packed as I would've imagined. There's enough space for us to drive without much intervention, and I can't help but feel a sense of comfort from that. We've been on the road for a few hours at this point, passing some wondering *Specs* along the way, yet my heightened sense of vigilance causes me to lose track of time.

"So, what's going on with you exactly, Miles?" Jorge asks with a deep Spanish accent. By looking across at him in the passenger seat, I notice Montero lifting his hand to swallow some pain medication for his surgery, from which he seems to have recovered for the most part, before shifting in his seat to look at me. I can't help but admire his resilience.

"What about me?" I ask, not understanding the question.

"I heard that when you first got to the *Consulate*, everything was about the people," Montero mutters as he motions to everyone in the car. "I am not getting that vibe anymore, hermano," he says. Everyone else in the SUV is silent, but their gazes are shifting back and forth as if they want to say something but are holding back from doing so. I see Derrick lift his finger toward Jorge to speak, but I cut him off before he can do so.

"Everything we do is *for* those people. Why do you think we're out here right now?" I ask as I point out of the front windshield.

"I guess we're going to find out, won't we?" Jorge asks as he turns to shift back in his seat.

"Maybe we should-" David mutters before I extend my right hand in his direction while keeping my eyes on Montero.

"No, no, hold on. If you've got something to say, tell it to me straight," I bark out while raising my voice. He turns back around to address me directly.

"You're becoming soft. I mean, letting Graham walk after what he did to me and my guys? A slap on the wrist for nearly assaulting a kid? Talking shit about your girl, then threatening you? Hell, setting him *free*! What the *fuck* is that about?" he shouts. The slight glare outside his window from the rising sun makes it difficult to maintain eye contact without squinting.

"*Watch. Your. Tone…*" I mutter in a near growl. "If I had killed him, it would make me no better than him," I say as I begin leaning forward to get my words across.

"You're *already* no better than him. If you gave a shit about anyone but yourself, we wouldn't even be in this mess to begin-" Jorge remarks before his flow of words is interrupted as I extend my hand to grab Jorge's throat. The SUV comes to a sudden halt, pushing all of us forward in the process, but I maintain my grip.

"If you want to see the old me, Montero, I'll *show you* the old me…" I whisper. Even in a low tone, the lack of movement in and out of the vehicle makes my words audible to everyone. "But I've got a family to look out for now. Being who I was won't bring them closer. It'll only drive 'em away. What? You think you'd be a better leader? You think you'd do better? Then either kill me where we are now or stay in your *fucking* lane," I say before releasing my hand, causing Jorge to rub his throat and let out a few coughs.

Derrick puts the Escalade in *park* before attempting to comfort Jorge, to which he pushes Derrick off in an attempt to save face, and I turn to look out of my window. So many trees. So many cars. So many… tireless cars. Normally, I wouldn't think twice about a vehicle with a wheel removed, but this is almost every car on the road. Those with tires still attached have been slashed. Suddenly, the aggravation I feel is replaced with unease. As I gaze farther down the road, I can barely make out what looks to be humanoid silhouettes swinging ever so slowly in the air. The feeling of unease turns to extreme paranoia.

"Put the car in *drive…*" I say as I hastily shift in my seat to look behind us - *my eyes averting to every corner surrounding the vehicle.*

"I wouldn't have had to pull over if you weren't so *goddamn* aggressive, Miles," Derrick retaliates as he gives me a side eye while still attempting to comfort Jorge during his coughing fit. My level of discomfort rises with every second we remain idle, and I see David start to look around frantically when he notices me doing the same.

"No, no, you're not listening to me. We need to get out of here, now!" I proclaim as I lift the MPX and check the chamber to ensure a round is loaded: *it is.* Noticing the unmistakable sound of panic in my tone of voice, I see Derrick turn his whole body to look at me. As he does, I kick the seat in front of me and get a good grip on the firearm. "Let's get the fuck out of-" I shout before my words are interrupted by a stray bullet perforating the middle of the windshield.

The sound of broken glass and the bullet ricocheting through the cabin, followed by the subsequent ring of a gunshot, causes all of us to nearly drop to the floor as best as we can, given the fact that some of us still have seatbelts on. As we frantically remove our restraints, another shot rings. Then another. Then another.

"Get out! Get out! Get out!" David hollers over the commotion. He flings the rear passenger door open and uses it as cover as he steps out, extends his AR-15 out of the window, and fires in the direction of the shooters—the sound of the rifle being discharged echoes throughout the cabin, causing my ears to ring. I follow suit, flinging my door open as Derrick and Jorge remain in their seats, and I run over to one of the abandoned vehicles to the left of the Escalade. With his door wide open, I can see Derrick looking at me for an opportunity to run.

"Go!" I yell out as I peer around the trunk of the rusting Toyota Camry I'm kneeling against. The roof of the vehicle barely covers my head, so I bend down a little farther as I bring my weapon around the corner and begin firing at a group of people a few hundred yards down the road. The sudden gunfire from David and I inevitably force them to take cover behind some vehicles, too.

Yeah, how about this motherfuckers…

I briefly lower my weapon long enough for Derrick to run past my line of sight and behind the white Hyundai Elantra in front of me. Once he's there, he practically throws himself and his Remington 590S behind the car before repositioning himself against the trunk and checking if his weapon is loaded. I guess it isn't because he fully racks the pump-action shotgun and peers around the left side of the vehicle to assess how far the attackers are.

"Is Montero good? Montero?!" I shout over the sounds of bullets impacting near my feet. I'm behind the car again, shaking slightly as I attempt to reload the MPX with a spare magazine on my plate carrier.

"Yeah, I'm alright, boss!" I hear Jorge shout, albeit slightly muffled, from the other side of the bullet-ridden Escalade.

We're alive… it's okay, we're fine…

Once I insert the fresh magazine and send the bolt forward, I cautiously peer my head to glance through the unaffected rear windshield of the Camry to get a better look down the road. The windshield doesn't stay unaffected much longer, as I duck down just in time to avoid the three or four rounds that penetrate the glass. One thing is clear: *they're getting closer*.

"They said only the one in green!" I hear a woman shout to one of her companions from down the road.

The one in green…But the only person wearing green is me…

After instinctively glancing down at my dark olive vest while propped up against the car, I turn my head to the left to see David slide behind the Escalade, which is lifted high enough to expose his legs. I can hear stray bullets hitting the front of the Escalade, so I turn my sights to the rear wheels of the SUV and fire.

Pop. Pop.

The SUV seeps down just enough to conceal David better from those firing at us. Judging by the look of confusion and terror plastered all over his face, I can tell that David didn't initially understand what was happening, but he nods at me once he realizes I'm merely helping him. Montero, who was previously using the front-passenger door as cover, slides behind the sunken rear of the SUV and props himself against the trunk as a round penetrates the rear windshield of the Escalade. With the two men desperately trying to stay as low as possible amidst the seemingly endless storm of gunfire, they both look at me with conviction.

"We can't let them get the upper hand! We need to move up on them!" David hollers as he looks at me for approval while Montero, nearly back-to-back with him, begins placing rounds into the empty cylinder of his .44 magnum revolver.

"I agree! Derrick and I will move up, but I need you and Montero to rain down on them while we hop the rail and flank from the oncoming lanes!" I shout just loud enough for the duo to hear. *I don't want the approaching shooters to get wind of our approach.* After a second or two, David gives me a thumbs up before ejecting the depleted magazine from his rifle and inserting a replenished one. As if in sync, Jorge shuts the cylinder of his competition-style Smith and Wesson before placing it into the brown leather holster resting on his belt and picking up the rifle from the ground.

After issuing a subtle nod, the duo simultaneously peer around the rear of the SUV and begin firing at the attackers. I use the opportunity to crouch around the back of the Camry before propping my lower back against the rear driver-side door. While our shoulders are mere inches apart, I lean in to address him directly.

"We can use the brush between the rails and the cars on the other side as concealment. They're closing in, so we need to cut them off before they do," I say as Derrick extends his fist for me to bump.

"Let's go get these *sons of bitches*," he says as I slam my fist against his.

Under the cover of thick brush and friendly gunfire, Derrick and I hop the metallic rail about two feet to our left, careful not to put too much pressure on it so the creaking won't give away our position, and use the abandoned cars sitting idle on the oncoming lanes to move farther up the road. As we crouch and slowly approach the shooters, I see the silhouettes of two attackers pushing ahead in between gunshots.

They don't see us yet…

I look back at Derrick, who is kneeling against a ransacked ambulance, and give him a nod as I turn to walk toward the next car. The rail separating us from them is increasing in height the further up the path we go. With a small, two-foot dirt hill and brush in between us, I stealthily make my way behind the group as they pass us. I extend a hand from behind me to get Derrick to stop in his tracks before peering between the brush to see how many there are.

Five.

I retract my fingers and bring them out one at a time until I reach five. Ducking back down behind the rail, I turn to Derrick, who instinctively issues me a nod, confirming he understands what I'm trying to tell him. Without saying a word, he puts up the number two with his fingers and points to his right. *He wants the two closest to us.* I put up the number three, followed by pointing to the left. After repeatedly pushing my palm toward Derrick, ushering him to spread out, he gives me a light pat on the back before quietly using his concealment to lift the shotgun toward the attackers.

Go.

I lean against the small hill of dirt under the railing as cover. With only my upper body being exposed, I cautiously align my aim with the head of a young, disheveled African American woman who seems to be yelling out profanities as she tries miserably to clear a weapon malfunction from behind cover. Without so much as a second thought, I quietly flick the weapon's safety selector to *Semi* as I let out a long exhale.

Bang.

The hood of the white hatchback she was propped up against is suddenly tainted with an enormous splatter of blood that comes from her head as she falls to the pavement. I transition my aim to one of her companions, an older fellow wearing a tan hoodie covered in what appears to be dried blood, and let off a few more rounds before anyone on the other side of the barrier can react.

Bang. Bang. Bang. Bang.

I keep firing until his body hits the floor. As the other attackers turn to face me, presumably from the gunfire and muzzle flashes that gave away my position, I naturally shutter as the blaring sound of a shotgun blast nearly ten feet to my right seemingly bounces off the vehicles around us. With one of the attackers collapsing near the middle of the road, I stand and turn my sights to an older guy with countless, unkempt strands of white hair. As he continues walking toward the Escalade, oblivious to the chaos unfolding behind him and his friends, I pull the trigger once the MPX aligns with the back of his head.

Bang.

His body falls forward stiffly, like a coyote who was just shot in the heart. I drop to the floor as a bullet ricochets near the ground in front of me, and I throw the MPX to the side before hastily reaching down to retrieve the Kimber from its holster. After a few seconds of heavy breathing, I build the courage to peak over the rail once the attacker's gunfire subsides. However, the sound of another shotgun blast, followed by the all-too-familiar sound of a body hitting the pavement, fills my ears.

It takes me a few seconds to realize that the gunfire has died down. Amidst the tinnitus surely developing in my ears, I can make out the shouts emanating from down the road near where we came.

"You alright?!" I hear Jorge shout in our direction.

"We're good!" Derrick shouts as he keeps his shotgun up and scans the scene to ensure there are no survivors. I do the same with the .45 ACP I'm holding.

"Clear! We're coming out!" I holler as I grab the MPX with my non-dominant hand and hop over the railing. I raise the Kimber in the air for them to see where we are before examining the corpses in front of us. The smell of blood and gunpowder is something I have never gotten used to, and I don't think I ever will.

"Boss, take a look at his hand," Derrick says as I holster my handgun and kneel to lift the left hand of one of the male attackers. "Isn't that the same shit we saw in Yonkers?" he asks as I recall seeing a similar symbol carved onto the palm of the female I had executed in the home improvement store.

These people… they're…

"I- These guys are *Ravel-*" is all I can muster as tree branches snapping echoes from behind the tree line on the side of the highway. I can hear rustling leaves and distant chatter as dozens of people approach the highway from the woods. With such a revelation, I grab Derrick's arm and begin bee-lining it for the other two *Thrivers* walking our way.

"Go back. Go back…" I say in a hushed tone as I wave my palm in their direction, signaling David and Montero to flee in the direction they came from. They seem to catch on as David and Jorge walk, then jog backward. It doesn't take long before we all begin sprinting toward the SUV. As we near the Escalade, which has been rendered immobile by gunfire, I can't help but think the worst.

We're screwed.

I pause briefly before removing my dark olive plate carrier and throwing it onto the ground. Grabbing a rock and tossing it through the driver-side window of the Elantra sitting on the side of our convoy, I immediately fling the door open once it's unlocked from within; the murmurs coming from the tree line seem to come to a halt amidst the sound of glass breaking.

"Boss, what're you-" David nervously asks as he frantically looks back at the other side of the road.

"They recognized me..." I whisper as I reach down to hit the trunk release, half expecting it not to work due to a dead battery, and throw the plate carrier into the cargo area once the trunk is open. I unholster my Kimber and hastily place it into the trunk as well. "We don't have enough to take down the number of people coming through those trees any second now," I say as I throw the MPX in the trunk.

"So what, we're going to surrender?" Derrick asks while leaning toward me.

"That is *exactly* what we're going to do..." I say as I remove the six-inch Benchmade from its sheath on my belt. After a brief pause, I stop and look at the men around me. "God knows what's around us, and we've got no way out of here. We can't lead them back to the *Consulate*," I whisper. As expected, they're terrified, but the men seem to understand our lack of options.

"You're fucking crazy, y'know that?" Jorge asks sarcastically as he throws his stainless steel .44 Magnum into the trunk, which makes an audible thud as it hits the carpeted floor panel, and the rest of the men do the same with their gear.

What other choice do we have?

"They won't shoot us if we're unarmed. They're looking for someone or something, so let's make sure we don't give them a *fucking thing*," I say as I shut the trunk once the last weapon is in.

After a few seconds, we see a seemingly endless group of people, *all different genders, heights, and builds*, come out of the tree line about 200 feet away from us. They let out warning shots that rip through the air as they approach. We slowly back away from the Elantra and raise our hands to show we're not a threat.

"Get the fuck down!" one of the men yells, followed by a large caliber round hitting David in the leg, causing him to fall to the pavement in pain. Hearing David's agonizing shouts as he clutches his leg makes me subconsciously wonder if I made the right decision, but we stand our ground. With our hands still raised, I start to kneel. Derrick and Jorge soon follow suit as the chanting ahead of us becomes more audible with every step they take.

"*Not a fucking thing…*" I mutter under my breath for my companions to hear. They all nod.

As the group of *Ravelers* approaches us, a few *Specs* begin sprinting toward the commotion from the direction we initially drove in from. Within moments, the sounds of gunfire cause all of us to jump as the infected are put down. With David lying about a foot ahead of the rest of us, he's the first one the group approaches as they close in the distance between us and them. His shouts of anguish seem to pierce the constant ringing in my ears, but they're cut short when a double-barrel shotgun is brought up to his head and fired.

Bang!

The sudden execution puts me into a state of paralysis. I don't even understand what has just happened in front of me, even as the blowback seems to cover the entire right portion of my face in warm blood. David's face is unrecognizable, and his body has fallen limp on the ground.

Oh my god… Hope… Oh- oh my god…

I'm not even fully aware to notice Jorge lunge at the old white man holding the side-by-side double barrel shotgun and pin him to the ground. For just having recovered from surgery, Jorge's movements and incredible speed are no doubt fueled by adrenaline and anger. He only gets a few punches in before another *Raveler* hits him with more force than I thought was humanly possible using the butt of his rifle.

Before he can even react, Derrick is pushed to the ground from behind by the boot of another *Raveler* just as a middle-aged female steps in front of me. Even as my head is forcefully flung backward from the impact, it takes me a while to register the fact that I had been struck with immense force. After falling to the ground and beginning to lose consciousness, all I can do is attentively stare at David's corpse as I lay in his ever-growing pool of blood.

Then, suddenly, everything around me fades to black.

CHAPTER 12

NO WAY OUT

THE FIRST THING I NOTICE as my eyes begin to open is the ringing in my ears: *it stopped*. Instead, it is replaced with an eerie muffle that seems to suppress most of the sounds around me. The pain radiating from the front of my head overtakes any other sense in my body as I attempt to sit upright in what looks to be a small, isolated room. The cold, wet floor is covered in a slightly sticky substance that I can only assume is urine, judging from the smell. As I rub my forehead, I stand to glance out of the 2x2 hole facing the rear of a stone building a few yards away, only to notice various screams echoing in the distance. The "window" is reinforced by rebars that were sloppily welded here recently.

I try pulling one of the rebars with both hands to assess its durability; it won't budge. Instead, I transition my gaze to the bottom floor beneath the window. I nearly slip on the liquid under my feet as I retreat once I notice the discarded, mutilated remains strewn around the alley separating the two buildings. The lifeless bodies, barely illuminated by flickering streetlights nearby, are giving off an odor only the Grim Reaper would get off to.

Oh, this place is bad…

It's nighttime, which tells me I've been unconscious for a while. The memories of what happened before I arrived here instantly flood my mind. As much as I try, I can't even remember what David looked like before he was executed. As I frantically reach for the knife usually hanging on my belt, I notice the sheath is still there, albeit the blade itself is missing entirely. Filled with anxiety, I had forgotten we had hidden our weapons near the ambush site. We? In my grief-stricken haze, it takes me a while to realize the rest of the guys are nowhere to be seen.

Fuck...

I hear chanting from behind the steel door, separating me from the rest of the building. It's a sort of maniacal chant that one would expect to hear from a cult performing a ritual, and the muffled screams that follow only serve to heighten my paranoia. With what little light there is seeping into the room from the outside, I begin sifting through whatever I can find. There's not much other than a small yellow chair big enough to fit a child and a stained cot near the window. *I don't know, nor do I want to know, what the stains are.*

As I lift the chair, I can feel one of the metal legs is loose, so I flip it and begin turning the bolt, securing the leg counterclockwise. A washer and a chrome hollow chair leg fall on the floor as I pull the screw out, which emanates a loud clattering sound once it hits the floor. I pause for a brief moment, holding the three-legged toddler chair in the process as I listen for anyone approaching.

Clear.

I prop the small chair against one of the concrete walls nearby, making sure to prop it up correctly so it's not lopsided from the uneven support, and grab the nearly foot-long metal rod rolling around effortlessly on the floor. Choosing not to acknowledge the urine covering the hollow leg, I bring it up to one of the rebars covering the hole and bend the rod back and forth slightly at the edge. I do this until the corner of the leg replicates that of a sharp-edged shiv.

The sound of liquid dripping from the pipes overhead and screaming resonating through the walls is terrifying enough. Still, it's nothing compared to the sudden sound of hasty footsteps approaching my location. I lift the cot and place the makeshift weapon under it before releasing it and putting my back against the other side of the room, farthest away from the door. I half expect to hear the jingling of keys, which will buy me a second or two of extra time to prepare for what's coming. However, the only sound I hear is a sliding bolt from the other side of the door.

The lights above the hallway cause me to squint as my eyes struggle to adjust, and three grown men wearing ragged, torn clothing barge in. One of them is holding what looks to be the bottom portion of a broken pool cue, and the other guys are unarmed. I lunge forward, pushing off the wall for momentum, and duck low enough to feel the pool cue whoosh just above my head as I swing my fist at one of the unarmed guys. It doesn't take long for the other unarmed goon to pull me off of his buddy and pin me against the wall. The Hispanic man I had struck in the mouth, blood protruding from his lower lip, lets out a profanity I can barely understand before grabbing my other arm and holding me against the moist wall.

The taller male with the pool cue towers over me by nearly a foot and turns the cue around before swinging the blunt end at my pelvis, causing my legs to give out and pull my weight from under me. I would've hit the floor if it weren't for the other two lifting me back up just in time for the pool player to get in another pelvic strike.

I can barely breathe as my arms are released, causing me to fall to the ground in agony. The urine on the floor mixed with the smell of decay outside doesn't help me as I curl up and puke. I'm not even granted the pleasure of wiping my mouth before being picked up and dragged through the doorway and into the dirty second-floor corridor.

* * *

The *Ravelers* speak a language I can't understand, but I try to make out certain words as they pull me into a room with floor-to-ceiling windows facing what I can only assume is the front of the building.

There are a variety of single-floor retail stores and residential buildings outside, yet what catches my attention is the room itself: *it's immaculate.*

The marble floors, granite pillars holding the ceiling above us, and recently washed window panes. It takes me a while to realize the smell of bleach; it's strong, almost as if someone has recently mopped the floors. I don't have time to dwell on it before I am forced to sit in a foldable metal chair, similar to the one I had in the gym of the *Consulate,* and restrained. I figure I have lost some blood circulation, given how tight the ropes are around my wrists. Having my hands tied behind me, as well as my legs strapped to the chair itself, gives me a sense of hopelessness, yet I maintain my cool as I'm reminded of one thing: *if they wanted me dead, I wouldn't have woken up.*

As I open my mouth to speak, a white man with a freshly faded haircut and a neatly pressed, three-piece, black-and-blue patterned suit walks into the room. His steps are meticulous. Calculated. It's as if he is revered by God Himself. He's holding a black leather briefcase that he places against the wall, the smell of which reminds me of a new car as he swings it around. The men around me seem to gain a sudden sense of civility once they notice our new guest because they stop talking and stand up straight.

"Leave him," the stranger says in a voice that's nothing short of fitting for his demeanor: *deep and methodical.* The non-native speakers nearly bolt out of the room without so much as another word. Now, it's just me and him.

"Welcome to the *Colony.* I apologize. The theatrics can be a little overwhelming…" the stranger declares as he rests against the charcoal executive desk placed between the three large windows facing outdoors. A sizeable metallic spear, in which portions of the handle are wrapped with what appears to be white cashmere cloths, is neatly sitting on a showcase stand directly in the middle of the desk. The blade itself, which seems more like an art piece than a weapon, features various markings and engravings. I can tell this is an expensive artifact, but I'm not given much time to embrace its beauty before the man continues to speak. "Although… I suspect they were very much a necessity given your antagonistic introduction," he says as his eyes begin scanning me.

He's hoping I'm afraid of him.

"The people on the highway deserved what they got *ten times over*, and so does everyone else. I mean, murdering an innocent man as he-" I say before the man intercepts my statement.

"As he lay on the floor, screaming? Thinking about his loved ones back at home? *Sister*, perhaps? *Wife?*" asks the stranger as he lifts himself from the desk. "Do you want to know how many families *you* shattered?" he asks.

What the hell is he-

"*Marianne Richards*, mother of two boys, both three years of age. Shot in the head with a single 9-millimeter round on *Interstate 87*. Mercilessly. *Oliver Brown*, father to our congregation leader, riddled with four stray bullets, one of which pierced his jugular…" the suited man says as he begins circling my chair in a composed manner.

"That's enough-" I mutter under my breath.

"*Joseph Moore*, husband to our head baker for *forty-two years*. Shot in the back of the head without so much as a chance to defend himself. Or how about *Oscar Perez*? Listen to this: he was shot, ironically, in the cranium with a 12 gauge shotgun… *by one of you*," he says as he comes to a halt in front of me and kneels to look me in the eyes; I keep my head down and continue looking at the floor in front of me.

My hands become white as I grip the back of the chair with as much force as I can muster, given the restraints. My teeth are clenched, and I raise my head slightly to connect my eyes with the man's. His expression isn't that of conceit or arrogance but rather that of a leader who just lost someone he cares about.

"And I'd do it *all over again* if given the chance," I say before turning my head to the left and spitting away from the stranger. The man stands and looks down at me with a grin plastered on his face that seemingly extends from one ear to another. He lets out a small chuckle before composing himself.

"*Wow*… he was right about you, y'know," he declares.

He…?

"Oh, come on, Mr. Gether…" the stranger says as he lifts both arms to his side while walking away. "Let's not be modest in assuming loyalty is unbendable. It only took a few severed limbs and digits… a toe here, an eye there… I'll give him this: Jorge Montero is stronger than most of the others," says the stranger as he senses my discomfort. "Or well, he *was*…" the man mumbles as he reaches into his pocket and tosses me a stained, rolled-up brown napkin that releases a well-preserved eyeball onto the floor.

"You sick *motherfucker!*" I yell out as I yank on the restraints. The ropes are digging into my wrists, and I can feel blood seeping down my fists, but I pay little mind to it. The man practically glides toward me in a satanic yet elegant fashion.

"Well, shall we continue our civil conversation?" asks the stranger, extending his hand outwards as if he were inviting a girl to dance at a spring formal. Wanting to conserve my energy so I can personally rip his own eyes out, I stop fussing around and regain my composure.

I'm going to kill this guy…

"In all the commotion, I forgot my manners. What's your name, exactly?" I ask in a genuinely inquisitive tone. I want to know the name of the man responsible for catering to the needs of the sadistic animals under this roof.

"I'm afraid this isn't going to be that kind of conversation, Miles…" the stranger proclaims in a hushed manner. "As I'm sure you can understand, I'm more interested in hearing about the *Thrivers*," he admits.

"Well, I'm afraid this isn't going to be that kind of conversation," I say while straightening my back and lifting my head to assert a futile sense of superiority. He stares at me for a few seconds. I can't tell what he's thinking, as his stoic demeanor is working to conceal his true intentions. Instead of saying another word, the man smiles and walks methodically toward his briefcase.

"When we spoke to your people over the radio, I was told that the leader was someone who walked and talked as if the world was in his control…" the man says as he begins walking back toward me, all the while digging in his briefcase.

"Is that right?" I ask sarcastically.

"That is correct. In fact, I've come to believe that this person is someone who has very little sense of self-preservation. Someone who *desperately* wants to be in control of every situation they face…" says the stranger as he pulls out an eight-inch metal shiv from inside the briefcase.

Oh no…

"You see, you spend *so much time* thinking about *yourself* that you fail to realize the moral of the story…" the man says as he stops behind my chair. "No one is in control," he says as he swings the blunt side of the hollow shiv at the back of my head. The pain and immediate headache that followed are quickly overwritten as the stranger grabs my uncurled left hand and brings the sharp edge of the shiv down onto the lower portion of my pinkie, severing it *entirely* in one swoop.

I nearly pass out as my screams bounce around the previously spotless room. As my shrieking subsides, the sound of blood spilling on the floor beneath me only serves to increase my level of stress. I attempt to catch a few short breaths as the stranger, now sporting a stained three-piece suit, comes from behind the chair and throws the bloody hollow shiv on the floor. He rolls over a pristine leather chair from behind the desk on the other side of the room and parks it a few feet in front of me before taking a seat.

"For every subsequent question you fail to answer, I'll take something from you," the stranger says as he leans forward.

"What the *fuck* do you-" I holler out before being interrupted again.

"The leader of the *Thrivers* was said to have been wearing a dark green bulletproof vest when he departed from the city, yet none of you fit that description. I suspect it's you, but I want to hear it from your mouth. So I must ask, who is the commander of the *Thrivers?*" the man asks sternly.

He doesn't know...

"You tell me! You're the one who cut out his *fuckin'* eye..." I say in an attempt to deflect any suspicion surrounding me.

"Oh, Mr. Montero was many things, but a *leader?* No, his temperament would be nothing short of detrimental to an organization of any magnitude," says the stranger as he begins bending over to grab the metal shiv from the ground. As he does, the smell of his citrus cologne makes me more nauseous than the smell of the blood pooling around my feet.

"You need to learn that there are *consequences* for every action... and inaction," says the stranger as he circles the chair and grabs my injured hand before bringing the shiv down on my left ring finger. My shouts don't even seem to phase the stranger as he casually sits back down in his chair as if he just returned from a restroom break. I start to feel lightheaded, most likely from the blood loss, and before feeling a few light slaps on my cheek as I begin to doze in and out of consciousness.

"Stay with me now..." the stranger says. "Who is the leader of the *Thrivers?*" he repeats.

"The boss... he- he chose not to come with us," I let out in between breaths.

"You're *lying,*" the man says as he begins to stand again.

"No! No, Montero volunteered to take his place instead. The boss, he... he said he'd use that time to get in touch with different outposts around the city," I falsely confess, hoping the alibi doesn't conflict with anything Jorge told him.

"Give me a *name*…" the stranger growls, clearly losing patience as I deflect his questioning.

"Xavier Stern," I confess. There's no one on the roster by that name, but he doesn't need to know that. The suited man examines my expression intently. Here I am, unable to defend myself, lying to the man whose willingness to kill and dismember should terrify me, but he seems to buy my story as he sits back down in his seat.

"Interestingly enough, all of the supplies mentioned over the air, *none of which* you had when my guys found you, were said to have gone with the group that departed from the… *Consulate*? Yet, miraculously, you were *still* able to wipe out an entire group of armed combatants," says the stranger as he leans his head back slightly. "How is that, exactly?" he asks.

Silence.

After staring me down for a minute, the man stands and unbuttons his stained suit. By the look of satisfaction on his face, I can tell he's had enough. That assumption is confirmed when he begins walking toward the door he had initially come from before turning to face me while grabbing the bronze knob.

"When you return, be sure to tell *Sandman* he's got a deal. I suspect my men will not be returning from this voyage alive, so I leave this message for you," the stranger says as he lets off a sinister smile before walking out of the room and ushering the men waiting outside to head in.

Sandman?

A man I had not seen before enters the room first with a mop and a bucket of liquid that smells like Pine-Sol and bleach. The men that follow, all of whom look and smell nothing like the man I was talking to, pay no mind to the blood they're stepping in as they approach. They cut the restraints at my feet and lift me to my feet with ease, leaving my hands tied in the process. Given my weakened state, I don't resist. They drag me downstairs and through the building until I'm hit by the light outside breeze.

As I'm being dragged to an older Tacoma humming idly on the paved asphalt in front of me, I notice just how massive this area is, with various structures and settlements in every direction, and how many *Ravelers* there really are: *dozens are roaming the streets.* The tormented screams that were slightly muffled before are audible now. I look ahead to the truck and notice Derrick in the backseat, motionless and bleeding. Before I can call out, the rear passenger side door is flung open, and a dirty-smelling nylon bag is placed over my head. Without so much as a warning, I am thrown into the backseat with little care.

With my hands restrained and vision limited, I wiggle my body closer to Derrick's to get in whispering range. I can hear him breathing faintly. As my left arm presses against his body, I can feel his chest rising with every breath he takes.

He's alive.

"D, can you hear me?" I whisper without trying to alert the goons who just entered the vehicle in the front. He groans in pain, but the guards don't acknowledge him. I can feel his body contorting to face my direction.

"Boss…?" he asks in a nearly inaudible tone. I can feel his agony just from the question alone.

"They killed Montero… " I quietly confess as Derrick lets out a small whimper.

"We shouldn't have brought them, Miles," Derrick whispers as he tries to clear his throat discreetly. I try to get a better look at my surroundings through the hood over my head, to no avail, so I shift my attention back to my companion.

"Are you alright?" I ask with concern.

"The asshole in the suit… he shot me in the fuckin' knee just to prove a point. I- I can barely breathe with this thing. These assholes might've broken a rib or two, man," Derrick says in a louder tone than before.

"It'll be alright. We'll get you patched up, don't worry about it…" I reassure as I pause briefly to listen to the guards.

"What the *fuck* are you talking about, prick? Damien said it's in the North Bronx, not South," I hear the man in the passenger seat say to the driver.

Damien? Is that our guy?

The men up front are still arguing about directions, so I lean into Derrick and continue speaking once I notice they're preoccupied.

"What did you give him?" I ask.

"I- I gave him the abandoned armory across the street from the *Consulate*… told him that's where we were holed up. He had a revolver to my head, boss…" he recalls. "I'd never sell out the family," Derrick proclaims.

"I know, buddy. I know…" I whisper as I place my head against the rear passenger window.

This is not good…

* * *

With the sun high in the sky, I can make out bits and pieces of my surroundings through the nylon hood. I also notice that the two men in the front of the vehicle are armed, and one of them keeps shifting his long gun around whenever he squirms in his seat. I also notice that the barrage of green outside the window is starting to simmer down, meaning we're closing in on the city. With each bump the Tacoma rolls over, my anxiety increases ever so slightly. It is only when the car comes to a sudden halt that I fear for the worst.

"Get 'em out the back!" I hear someone yell from outside. It's not a voice I recognize. A strong gust of wind ushers past me as my door flings open, and I can't help but shut my eyes once the hood is pulled off my head. The sun is beaming down on us, and once my eyes adjust to the natural brightness radiating from the horizon, I notice where we are: *we're at the Consulate.*

The woman who pulled me out of the Tacoma came out of a sedan that had been tailing us, presumably from the start. As she extends her hand in my direction, signaling for me to stay put, I notice the same branded symbol carved into her palm as the others: *the letter "C" carved within what I can only assume is the outline of a tent.* I look around discreetly to avoid giving away the position of the *Thrivers* taking their positions in the *Overwatch Convoy* down the block. As the *Ravelers* walk around the vehicle to retrieve Derrick from his seat, I see five goons, most of whom are aiming their rifles at the front entrance of the abandoned armory.

"Stand him up!" the driver of the vehicle we were in shouts as he slams the door behind him after exiting the truck. I can see Derrick react to the sunlight the same way I did once his bag is removed. I didn't even hear them put one on him before we left.

While facing the armory, I turn my body slightly to the right as if to glance up the block and turn my attention to the roof of the *Consulate.* Even at this distance, I can see Corver's distinctive features as he and a few other guys duck behind the roof's edge with rifles in hand.

There we go…

With two of the *Ravelers* moving up toward the entrance of the abandoned armory, it is only a matter of time before one of them collapses after a single shot was fired from the roof of the *Consulate* behind us. I jump at the sound, and the woman who dragged me out of the car grabs me by the collar of my shirt and forcibly turns me around to face the group of *Thrivers* running through the now-opened gate leading into the rear courtyard. The sound of the gate scrapping against the sidewalk as more and more men and women, all of whom are armed, come to our aid is incredibly relieving. That relief, however, is short-lived when the woman brings a handgun up to my right temple.

"Stay the fuck back!" the woman yells as the gun pushes my head sideways slightly. She's standing somewhat taller than me, yet her slimmer demeanor would make me a ferocious adversary if I were to attack her head-on. "Where is Xavier Stern? We will only heed to your commander," she yells out.

The *Thrivers* seem to listen to her initial command, refraining from moving closer but using what obstacles they can as cover. The various looks of confusion displayed on the faces of the men and women before me, no doubt trying to understand the question that the woman had just asked, only enhances the sense of dread lingering in the air. From my peripherals, I notice the *Ravelers* beside me doing the same. I extend my bloodied hands forward in an attempt to maintain a ceasefire.

"Whoa, hey! Stand down… stand down!" I shout as the small group of *Thrivers* in front of me and on the roof, the unease radiating from their faces as they look at Derrick and me with terror, remain idle but alert. Both groups are at a standstill, so I use that as an opportunity to calm things down.

"Everybody-" I say.

"Shut up!" the woman says as she presses the handgun closer to my temple.

Well, so much for that…

With my hands still up, I see Corver push through the small group of about a dozen *Thrivers* and stop about ten yards in front of me. I look up to see Vito peering down from one of the windows in the third-floor gym. He jumps frantically before shouting something I can't hear and disappearing from view.

"I didn't miss the first time, so I sure as hell won't miss the next one…" Corver yells as his walnut .308 rifle remains pointed at the guard standing behind Derrick.

The four remaining *Ravelers* become antsy when they hear the threat, which only makes me more nervous. When Corver notices my severed fingers, his face is filled with red as he transitions his aim toward the female using me as a human shield. I let out a whistle to get Corver's attention, and when he glances at me, rifle still in the air, I use my eyes to signal to my left. At this point, Corver takes a second before realigning his aim with his initial target.

"Think about the families we have waiting for us at home…" I holler as my voice echoes throughout the seemingly desolate street. The woman, albeit shaking slightly, doesn't interrupt me again as I continue speaking. "*This* is our chance to let bygones be bygones. *This* is our chance to put aside our hatred for one another…" I say as I slowly turn my right hand.

"*This*… is for the continuation of a good thing," I say as I swiftly close my right hand and make a fist in the air.

Within a moment's notice, the back of my head is covered in blood as my female captor slumps to my left and drops to the floor. The gunshot emanating from the *Overwatch Convoy* is enough to cause Corver to fire his rifle at the middle-aged man holding a shotgun to Derrick's back. Without acknowledging their presence, I slowly lower my hands as I hear the two male *Ravelers* to my left drop their weapons on the concrete.

The shouting coming from the *Thrivers,* who are all quickly approaching the surrendering duo, seems to become background noise to me as I pick up the handgun from the floor. As the men are pinned to the ground, I don't say a word, even as the *Thrivers* clear a path for me while I approach the duo. I don't say a word as I stand over the two men, who are glancing at me with their faces pinned to the ground. I don't say a word as I bring the handgun up to one of their heads.

"Dad!" I hear someone yell from behind me. With the handgun still extended, I turn my head to see Vito shoving the people trying to hold him back and making a run for it in my direction.

Dad?

"Vito?" the disheveled white man pinned on the ground lets out as his eyes are locked onto Vito. His scruffy beard, tainted with various stands of white hair, is held against the concrete as he resists the pressure on his upper back by Corver. I quickly retract the handgun as Vito nearly throws himself onto the floor to embrace the man I'm standing over.

That's impossible… He-

"It's alright, *baby*. Oh my god, I… oh my god…" the man says as he starts to cry. I look at Corver, who looks just as confused as I am before I hesitantly give him a nod. With that, Corver retracts his knee from the man's lower back and pulls his weight off him; instead, Corver comes around and aims his rifle at the man's chest so as not to hit Vito should he have to fire his weapon. In my state of bewilderment, I don't immediately acknowledge the *Thrivers* coming to check on me, even as they attempt to wipe the blood from my head.

"I'm fine…" I say as I politely usher them off me.

In the heat of the moment, I glance over to see Derrick angrily shuffling toward Corver, as best as he can, given his injured state, before cocking back his fist and swinging it once he's close enough. As he stumbles, Corver doesn't even have time to completely recover before Derrick strikes him again in the mouth. Corver drops his rifle on the ground before lunging at Derrick's lower abdomen, causing the two to get into a messy scrape on the concrete below. Half of the people standing around keep shifting their looks between one another as if debating whether they should intervene.

"You piece of shi-" Derrick lets out, accompanied by a grunt of pain, given the pressure Corver's body weight was putting on his possibly broken ribs. "Fucking traitor!" he yells before grabbing a fistful of Corver's hair and pulling his head as far back as possible in preparation for another swing. This time, Corver uses his forearm to block Derrick's attack, following up with an elbow strike on the latter's forehead. As Derrick remains on the ground, trying to recover from the sudden concussion, Corver throws himself off of the man just as some of the on-lookers attempt to hold him back.

"Are you crazy?!" Corver yells at Derrick, who begins coughing as he lifts himself onto his feet. His knee gives out in the process, forcing him back to the ground. Without hesitation, I start walking to the only other survivor of our northern commute.

"Alight, we're done here-" I say as I extend my uninjured hand to Derrick, who slaps it away as he musters all the strength he can from his upper body to fling him onto his feet.

"You killed David and Jorge! You! How else did they know about us goin' up there, huh? They only knew your name, mother-fucker! You tried to have us killed!" Derrick shouts as he attempts to close the distance between him and Corver.

"I just saved your life!" Corver retaliates as more and more people step forward to hold them back.

"I said we're done! We're done!" I say as I turn and extend my pointing finger in Corver's face. With all the noise accompanying the chaos nearby, including the occasional gunshots let out to suppress the wandering *Specs* and the conversations between the *Thrivers*, Corver doesn't even acknowledge my voice.

"No, fuck that! He put his hands on me!" Corver shouts as his eyes remain on Derrick.

"What goes around, comes around, motherfucker-" Derrick retaliates.

"Shut up!" I declare while simultaneously firing the handgun into the air. Even with all the commotion surrounding us, it becomes quiet enough to hear the ejected brass bounce off the concrete. I step forward and grab Corver's face to address him directly as nearly half a dozen *Thrivers* are holding him back. This time, his eyes are staring into mine with a burning rage that can seemingly melt steel with a single glance. "We're done, you hear me? We'll get to the bottom of it, but right now, I need you to walk it the fuck off, got it?" I ask in a manner that is more of a demand than a suggestion.

"Whatever you say..." Corver says as he shrugs his shoulder hard enough to break free from his concerned companions. He smacks my injured hand away, which causes a jolt of pain to spread throughout my entire arm that I choose not to acknowledge, given my attempt to remain as stoic as possible. "*Boss*..." he says before side-eyeing Derrick and storming toward the rear courtyard.

As my eyes follow Corver, I glance at the entrance to the rear courtyard and see Graham walking out with his arms in the air as if someone had just taken his parking spot. Graham and I had switched roles; I am covered in blood and filth, while he looks cleaner than when I last saw him. To my dismay, Graham walks toward me and the remainder of the ever-growing crowd gathering on the street.

"What the fuck is going on out here? Where's the other two?" Graham hollers out as Corver aggressively brushes past him without acknowledging his presence. After briefly looking back at his brother, Graham comes to a halt next to me, staring indifferently at Derrick, then at our newest arrivals, then at Vito. "The hell is this?" Graham asks as his face contorts once he puts the pieces together. Without paying Graham much mind, I graciously walk back to Vito while placing the pistol behind my belt and kneeling beside him.

"I- I need to talk to your dad, kiddo..." I say as I bring my injured hand up to his shoulder. He retaliates as if I hadn't taken the gun away from his father's head and shoves my hand off, which causes me pain that I don't visibly acknowledge, given the circumstances.

"No, no, you're going to *kill him!*" Vito shouts as he looks up at me. His face is red, and his cheeks are soaked with tears.

"No, I just want to talk with him, that's all. No one deserves to die, *right?*" I ask as I recall what he told me at the party. With that, he looks at me. The hesitation on his face shows he's battling with the idea of whether to trust me, while his father averts his gaze from me and places his forehead on the ground.

"Okay..." Vito says before hugging his father as he's brought to his knees. After the embrace, Vito pulls back and walks over to check on Derrick, who is being lifted onto the makeshift stretcher we brought Jorge when he arrived from Yonkers.

"Get him up," I command as I look down at my hand to assess the damage. A few of the *Thrivers* around me hoist him to his feet and restrain his hands behind his back using their handcuffs. The man stares at me with concern as the restraints let out an audible noise when tightened. I can't say the same for the man's surviving companion, as he's fidgeting around verbally threatening anyone who comes near him.

"What's the next move, boss?" one of the armed *Thrivers* asks as he lowers his shotgun once the men are bound.

"Yeah, *boss*. What are we going to do with these lovely gentle-men here-" Graham says sarcastically. He extends his finger to touch the *Colonist* before me, and I immediately shove him backward.

"Enough, Graham!" I shout out as he nearly stumbles. Seemingly embarrassed by the sudden power play, Graham takes a step forward to get in my face. I stand my ground while looking him directly in the eyes. "You want to be aggressive? Then you're going to go find your brother, head upstairs, and have a little *chat* with our friend over there," I proclaim to Graham as I point to the frantic *Raveler* a few feet away. "These are *your* fucking people, to begin with," I shout as I inch closer to Graham's face. After a second or two of silence, he chuckles before slowly backing away.

"And what about this one?" Graham asks as he points to Vito's father.

"I'll deal with it," I say as I turn my attention to the man, who is visibly uncomfortable in his restraints and constantly looking at his son. I hear Graham scoff at the idea.

"Well, if it's anything like how you tortured me…" Graham jokes. I don't pay him any mind and, instead, look at the *Thriver* who put on the man's restraints.

"Bring him to the maintenance room on the fourth floor. I'll deal with him from there," I command as the man is ushered for-ward. He turns to look at me as he gets within whispering distance and leans toward me as best he can.

"Thank you…" the man says as he disappears from view and gradually fades into my peripherals. I glance into the back of the Tacoma and see a lockbox tipped to the side with various hand tools protruding onto the floor of the truck bed.

Don't thank me yet.

* * *

The maintenance room on the fourth floor is essentially a windowless closet, maybe slightly bigger than an average walk-in closet found in most high-end condos, and I can't help but admire the privacy it offers. There's a single deadbolt on the exterior of the door, which can be locked for extra security, so it's perfect for the conversation I'm about to have with the *Raveler* before me. He's standing with his hands above his head, nearly tippy-toeing, as a long metallic chain hanging from the pipes above our heads is restraining his wrists together.

"Before anything else happens today, I wanted to start with an easy one…" I say as I begin slowly pacing around the dangling man. Even the most inaudible statements are perceivable, with the room being as small as it is. "What's your name?" I ask.

"Why does that matter?" the man retaliates. I walk in front of the man and use both hands to forcefully grab his face and address him directly; this causes him to stop moving as he gazes at the ceiling in an attempt to avoid eye contact with me. The recent flashbacks of Vito embracing this man and calling him "dad" keep coming to mind, and my aggravation starts to build as I realize something: *this just became personal.*

"Because if you are who I *think* you are, then I have no quarrel with you…" I say as I fling myself away from the man. "But I need to know which side you're on. I need to know that you're a straight shooter," I hastily disclose.

"Sergio…" the man says before looking up at the ceiling and letting out a deep sigh.

"Alright, Sergio," I say while approaching the various hand tools I had lying neatly on one of the metal wagons we used to bring the cake to the party a while back. "You, my good sir, are going to tell me *every-fucking-thing*. And you can start by telling me why you, this seemingly healthy individual, left a beautiful, *defenseless woman* and an *innocent child* to fend for themselves for nearly a year…" I let out a growl. He looks back down at me.

"Why do you even care-" Sergio says before stopping abruptly as I grab a pair of wire strippers and insert his bare ring finger into the empty gap of the tool. After looking him in his eyes, which are starting to water, I slowly begin applying pressure to the tool, causing the metal to sink ever-so-slowly into his bare skin.

"That girl is the *only* one who kept me alive on the inside. That *kid* gave me hope for a brighter future. And then, there's *you*," I mutter as Sergio begins breathing heavily. "Did you even *want* to look for them…?" I ask in a whisper.

"You have *no idea*…" Sergio mumbles as he ignores the pain in his finger.

"Speak. Up." My face inches closer to his as my tone becomes deeper.

"I called *endlessly*. I- I stopped by our apartment. I did everything I could to-" Sergio says before being interrupted again.

"It wasn't *enough*. If it were, we wouldn't be having this conversation, now would we?" I ask as I press down on both ends of the tool with slightly more pressure. Sergio lets out a continuous groan before I release the pressure and remove the tool altogether, placing it back on the metal cart. It's difficult, but I put my feelings aside after a brief pause and proceed with my initial questions. "As much as I'd like to continue this heart-to-heart between you and me, there are other more pressing matters at hand…" I say while stopping directly in front of Sergio. "Tell me about *Sandman*," I instruct.

"W- who?" he says with a slight deviation in his tone. Whether intentional or not, I can't tell; what is clear is that I am beginning to lose my patience.

"*Colonist*, huh? You may as well be a fucking owl," I say sarcastically as my now-bandaged hand wraps about the handle of my blade. As the knife, which I was able to recover from a *Raveler* who had taken it off me when I first arrived at the *Colony*, is slowly retracted from its sheathe, the look of worry seems to be steadily increasing on Sergio's face. "Make me ask you again. I dare you," I warn as I begin circling him again.

"Listen, I've never heard of anybody named *Sandman*," Sergio proclaims as his bonded hands clasp together above his head. "I swear to the Lord Himself," he says as I slam the blade onto the metal cart before him. The sudden thud of metal smacking against metal, amplified by the room's tight space, makes him jolt out of fear. I stare into his eyes to assess if he is lying to me. I can't afford to be wrong again, yet my instincts tell me he's too scared to conceal that information from me.

"Then tell me about Damien," I instruct as I lean against the thick wooden door leading to the hallway. I cross my arms and exhale as he begins to speak.

"That sadistic motherfucker? What about him?" Sergio asks as his gaze shoots back up to the ceiling.

"He took something from me. From *all of us...*" I say as I press off the door and approach our uninvited guest of the hour. "Something we can't bring back, but we can take something from him. We can take *everything* from him," I declare. Sergio looks at me with a mix of concern and what I can only assume is relief.

"He-" Sergio says before stopping himself. I can tell he doesn't trust me, yet his expression tells me he knows his options are very limited as of twenty minutes ago. "I know he was an Assistant District Attorney somewhere up North. I know that he used his charm as an ADA to get people to do great things, but he used that same charisma to convince others to do *evil shit*, too..." Sergio recalls.

"What sort of *evil shit*?" I ask with heightened curiosity.

"They-" Sergio says as he starts to break down. "They dismember people because of him... used what was left after a massacre to scare others away. He forces people to shoot, stab, bludgeon, or rape their own families... then kills them all for fun afterward. Does that sound like a place for my family? I mean, *what the fuck!*" Sergio shouts out. His sense of remorse shows me he's serious.

Jesus Christ...

"Sergio, you *need* to tell me where these people are... You participated and witnessed a lot of *wrongs*, yet this is your opportunity to make it *right*," I say as I close the distance between his body and mine. "Don't give them up for me. Give them up for your son. Let me handle the darkness so you can embrace the light," I say in a low and empathetic manner.

His eyes are red and watery, and he looks as though he is fighting a dilemma in his mind, but I can tell he's not a bad person. I know better than most what it's like to be on the other side of the moral compass. Although it's sometimes the kind of person I *have* to be, it's not the type of person I *want* to be. Vito helped me realize that.

"I'll tell you everything you wanna know…" Sergio says as he smiles at me. I give him a nod of appreciation and turn around while rubbing the now bandaged stumps where my fingers once stood. Sergio calls out to me before I get too lost in my own thoughts.

"I meant what I said outside. Thank you for looking out for my babies," Sergio says as his voice begins to crack again. I stand there for a few seconds before knocking on the door so the deadbolt can be released from the outside.

"You're welcome," I say as Abdul opens the door from the other side; the light from the hallway seeps into the room as I step out to retrieve the map found in the Tacoma.

They're my family, too.

* * *

I can't help but feel pity for Sergio, even as I escort him out of the Lobby through the main entrance of the *Consulate* and into the front courtyard. Per my instructions to the group of six preparing to oversee a transaction with the *Van Courtland Traders*, they are to, instead, accompany Sergio to where he claimed the *Colony* was located: under *heavily* armed guard. The group of *Thrivers* has also been instructed to radio in every twenty minutes on their progression back upstate.

The truck they're taking is already parked outside the main gates, and the group of six is checking their gear before their departure. I stop Sergio in front of the double doors and turn him around to tighten his handcuffs.

"If you're right, you'll be one of us when you get back…" I say in a low tone. Without turning to face me, Sergio gives me a nod to show he comprehended what I said. As we start walking down the small group of steps leading towards the main gate, one of the double doors behind Sergio and I are thrown open. I turn my head towards the commotion to see Renata storming out of the building and her son following suit with a look of regret; she's fuming, and I can nearly feel the heat radiating from her cheeks as she attempts to rush toward us.

"You had him here this *whole time?!*" Renata shouts over the sound of various footsteps approaching her. "Get the fuck off of me!" she shouts as a few *Thrivers* attempt to halt her advance. Vito looks at me with remorse, as if he is apologetic for something. I can only assume he was the one who told his mother about his father's return, but I don't ponder it. Instead, I force my attention back to Sergio without looking back.

"It's okay, *amore mio*…" Sergio says to Renata as I nudge him forward. "Everything will fix itself in the end," he says as he turns his head back to the front.

"Miles!" Renata shouts as she's held back by the two muscular *Thrivers* standing duty tonight for the exterior Nocturnal Patrol. "Do you know who I am? Do you know who that is? Get off of me! Miles!" she screams out as the distance between her and me increases.

"As of right now, he's not on our side!" I shout while continuing to look ahead and gently pushing Sergio forward again. "I pray that I'm right about this!" Amidst Renata's excessive pleas for the *Thrivers* to let her through, I hear footsteps approaching from behind me. They sound heavier than Renata's footsteps, so I turn my head to the side before seeing Corver and Graham usher past the *Thrivers* acting as a line of defense between Renata, myself, and her husband.

"Boss, there's something you need to know…" Corver whispers so as not to draw the attention of everyone else around me. As Corver walks alongside Sergio and me, there's a look of concern in his eyes. He has a distinguishable expression of worry, made clear by the lack of color on his face.

"You've only got a minute," I say as the two near the vehicle parked on the sidewalk begin opening the metal gates in front of us. All three of us stop in our tracks while they do so.

"The other guy we talked to, he was mentioning something about a *Sandman.* Said something to my brother that I couldn't hear, so I went to get closer, but-" Corver whispers as the chain holding the gate shut falls onto the concrete below. "M- my brother slit his throat…. I mean, the poor bastard didn't even get a chance to say what he had to say before-" Corver says as a gunshot rings out from behind me.

The chain holding the handcuffs together slips out of my hand as Sergio falls forward and hits the pavement. Blood is sent flying in almost all directions, with some landing on the side of my face and Corver's. Stunned, I look down to see an entry wound protruding from the back of Sergio's head. There was blood all over the clothing of the two *Thrivers* on the other side of the opened gate, with more accumulating on the ground in front of me.

Renata's scream sends chills down my whole body as I try to gain an understanding of what happened, and it's only when I turn around that I find out. A frantic Renata brushes past Graham, standing upright with a smug grin and a smoking handgun idle in the air as he holds it up with his arm fully extended.

"Hard times are just one less tear to shed later," Graham remarks as he lowers his weapon. Some members of the Nocturnal Patrol, the ones who aren't preoccupied with holding Renata back, tackle Graham to the ground, causing the handgun he was holding to slide away on the pavement.

All of the sounds around me are muffled and distorted. As I stand motionless behind Sergio's corpse, I can barely make out Renata's seemingly incomprehensible shouts of hysteria at her deceased husband. *Control the situation, Miles...* I could barely make out the radio chatter from everyone in the vicinity talking over one another in distress. *Control the situation...* I can barely make out Vito sobbing uncontrollably as he holds his hands to his mouth in despair. *Control it...* I can barely make out the shouts of disgust from the *Thrivers* outside the gates as some of them pace back and forth. *Control it all...* I can barely make out the sound of the hammer being pulled back on the handgun tucked behind my belt. The only sound I can hear is the sound of my heartbeat as I bring the firearm up to Graham's head.

Control...

"No!" Corver shouts as he throws his body against mine. The sudden intervention causes me to miss my shot, with the bullet being lodged into the concrete only inches from Graham's head. As Corver wrestles the gun out of my hand on the ground, the barrel of a rifle is pressed up against his back as Abdul calls him by name. Recognizing the voice, Corver turns around to face him before hesitantly putting his hands up, and I use this as an opportunity to stand.

"You motherfuck-" I mumble as I kneel on the ground in front of Graham and start pounding his head with my fists. I don't stop until I'm forcefully pulled off of Graham. Even then, I have to be held back from killing him by multiple people. Even Graham's most revered haters attempted to hold back my insatiable aggression.

"Fuckin' hell, if anything, I just did you a solid…" Graham says as he stands to his feet; as he does, he's quickly dropped to his knees by security as they do their best to contain the situation. My anger is incomprehensible, and everyone knows it. They can sense it.

"This *piece of shit… you piece of shit!* I want him locked up and the key thrown in the goddamn garbage disposal. Do you understand me?!" I shout as my blood begins to boil from the amount of rage that has built up. Within a few seconds, multiple people drag Graham away as he shouts back at me, *to no avail*. Looking back at Renata, I can see her sobbing as she lays her head on the head of her late husband.

My god…

"I- I don't-" I say before Corver pulls me to my feet and away from her. He grabs my shoulders and shakes me in a desperate attempt to regain my attention.

"Listen to me! We'll deal with him later. But what do we do now?" Corver asks as he stares into my eyes. "Boss, they're still out there. Say something, Miles!" he shouts as I throw his arms off me from below.

I glance at the front of the *Consulate*, examining every window and the faces of curious *Thrivers* peering out of them, and pause. I look back down to see Vito staring at me, his face wet from all the tears. Turning to Renata, her head still down as she lets out small whimpers, my purpose is made clear as the chaos around us ignites something dark in me that I do not fully understand. As my objective becomes clear, I snap out of it while turning to Corver.

"When you find him, have *JB* look into *Sandman*. I want Graham vetted first. And call the traders in our Network to get additional hands on deck by nightfall," I instruct Corver as I usher past him and walk towards the entrance of the building. "We're going upstate ourselves," I declare. The thought of surpassing the *Delegation* for a decision of this magnitude was irrelevant to me.

"Wha- how many people?" he asks as he faces me.

"Everyone!" I shout as I turn my head to the side. I yank one of the doors open and forcefully slam it behind me as I go upstairs toward the one place I know will solve all our problems: *the Armory*.

PART THREE

THE FALL

CHAPTER 13

CONCESSIONS

<u>Ledger</u>

Vito Caruso   Renata Caruso

Hope Starcov   Charlotte Kennedy

Pancho Ruiz   ~~Simon Adams~~

Derrick Simmons   ~~Jayden Walker~~

(There are 94 additional names on the list)

Journal Entry: It's done. Damien caught wind of the assault right as we blew through the doors. I managed to put a round through the bastard's cheek as he fled. Lucky asshole. Still, I made sure there was no one left alive in that hellhole. It was nothing short of a brutally efficient altercation. It only took 32 percent of our commodities and a hell of a speech to pull seventy-five extra hands from our Network for the operation, yet it was worth it. Even on my way back home, I can't help but feel as though some-thing has changed... ~~are we doing the right thing anymore?~~ One thing's for sure: We can rest easy tonight, knowing there's less evil in the world than there was yesterday...

WITH DRY BLOOD STAINING MY hands, I do my best to wipe them clean against my dark olive plate carrier before closing my journal and placing it into the black book bag at my feet. The feeling of the

Kimber, which we retrieved alongside the other gear we head stashed on our first run through I-87, being back at my side is comforting, and so are all the other supplies we "acquired" from upstate. Whilst in the passenger seat, I pick up the walkie as the caravan of *Thrivers* approaches the rear courtyard.

"This is *Praying Mantis. TID 001*. Standby for re-entry," I say before throwing the handheld device onto the vehicle's center console. Within a few seconds, the gates open, and we drive in. A row of over half a dozen vehicles, some of which are ours, while the others were borrowed from our network for the assault, enter the rear courtyard in a near single file line. As we halt at the end of the parking lot, the engine is turned off, and I step outside the now idle sedan. With a small notebook in hand, Charlotte comes out of the building and begins approaching me.

"Hey, Miles," Charlotte shouts as she walks toward me. Her wine-red trench coat does wonders for her appearance, as it complements her dark red hair. She tucks a strand behind her ear as she stops nearly a foot in front of me.

"How're you doing, sweetheart?" I ask in a non-flirtatious manner. She glances down at the knife attached to my belt. The sheath and the blade itself are both covered in blood, and I can tell she wants to ask about it, but she refrains from doing so. Instead, she picks her head up and smiles at me before opening her book.

"I'm okay. I'm just glad everyone made it back safe," she says as she places a finger on the page she was looking for. "Pancho is back. I know you were asking for him. He told me to give you that," Charlotte says after she rips a page from her notebook and extends it towards me.

"What's this?" I ask as my hand extends to grab the paper.

"He said these are the names of all the *Thrivers* who could be using the alias *Sandman*. *JB* and I examined the names of everyone on duty for the day you first went upstate, then cross-referenced them with those listed for Checkout on the Armory Log," Charlotte whispers as I scan the paper cautiously. "Listen, I- I know Derrick thinks Corver had something to do with what happened, but he hasn't stepped foot near the Communications Equipment the *entire* time we've had it, and the only weapon Corver checked out of the armory was at the rifle he used for overwatch, not a handgun. Lance was on armory duty that day and he confirmed it," she confesses.

Shit. Back to square one.

"So far, we've come up with six names, yet the weapon we found near Graham when he was apprehended wasn't properly logged out," Charlotte says as I look up at her. She has a look of pride on her face as if she was proud of the names she and *JB* were able to come up with. "We'll keep digging into it. If it really is someone within these walls stabbing us in the back, we need to get ahead of it. The problem with betrayal is that it comes from those you expect the least. Either way, we'll keep looking into it today and keep you posted as soon as we learn more," she says as she reaches into her pocket and grabs a scrunchy to tie her hair.

"Thank you," I mutter while placing the paper into my pocket. "If no one's on patrol, let's get the other *Delegates* rounded up later this evening to discuss how we'll deal with Graham and this *Sandman*. It's about time we start addressing the plague festering within these walls," I say before beginning to walk off.

"Miles…" Charlotte says in a low manner. "You need to talk to her. It's been three days, and she's barely said a word to anybody." The thought of confronting Renata for the first time since Sergio was killed frightens me more than anything I experienced during the trip back North. Still, I turn my head, with my body still facing the rear doors leading into the stairwell, and nod before continuing to walk forward and out of view.

* * *

Even as I reach into my bag for the keys to my office, the thought of having to face Renata makes me anxious. It's not due to a sense of fear, but rather immeasurable regret. *And Vito?* At least I can catch a moment to settle down and drop off my stuff before I talk to them. As I open the door, I notice it is already unlocked.

With sunlight coming in through the windows, I can see Renata as bright as day, *no pun intended*; she's sitting in the chair behind my desk, looking at a pair of handcuffs with dried blood sitting in front of her.

Shit...

"Uh, hi..." I say as I gently place my bag on the floor. "Listen, I... I know we've-" I say before Renata cuts me off.

"Sit down," she says without averting her gaze away from the handcuffs. I stand there for a second, trying to assess her mental state, *to no avail*. I can't tell what she's thinking, so I grab a seat in front of Renata as if the office was hers to begin with.

"Tell me what you're feeling..." I whisper as the sound of *Thrivers* completing the *Consulate's* perimeter defenses trickles in through the windows. She looks up at me, and it is only when she does so that I see the anger reignite in her face. She hastily picks up the metal cuffs and throws them at me before standing up, sending the chair she was sitting in rolling backward as she leans forward to address me.

"Maybe that will give you some notion," Renata says as she points towards the bloodied cuffs I'm holding in my hands. "You *betrayed me*. First, you didn't tell me that my husband was *alive*, and then you had your people hold me back when all I wanted to do was talk!" she shouts as I put my head down in regret.

"I'm sorry-" I mumble before stopping mid-phrase. The tears accumulating in my throat are enough to stop the sentence in its tracks. It is sincere, yet I am too ashamed to voice my regret aloud. Renata reluctantly comes from around the desk and kneels in front of me. She tucks a strand of vibrant blonde hair behind her ear as her eyes connect with mine.

"I- I don't want you to be sorry. I want you to think about what you're becoming..." Renata says as her voice begins to crack. Her eyes are starting to water, and it takes me a second to realize mine are beginning to do the same. "I fell in love with a man who *gave* what he could to the people he cared about, not someone who *takes* from everyone else," she says as she grabs my face.

"I'll be okay. It hurt not knowing what happened to Sergio, but at least now Vito and I have the closure we needed…" she says as she leans closer to me. "But *you* need to remember that there's *no going back* once you're on the other side of the moral compass…" Renata says as she stares at me. I can finally see her genuine emotions radiating from her eyes: *She's trying to save me.*

It takes me a while for her words to resonate with me, yet when they do, I close my eyes and extend my arms to embrace her. Her warm body is soothing, and it is only when I realize that I'm covered in blood that I retract my body from hers.

"I, uh… I'm sorry, I got blood on you," I admit as I stand up from my chair in an attempt to find a cloth to wipe it with. In my frantic search, she extends a hand outwards and grabs the side of my face, *causing me to stop moving almost instantly* as she begins speaking.

"We've all got blood on us, Miles. It's how we carry it that differentiates us from the rest," Renata says.

Before I can fully comprehend her statement, there's a sudden knock on the office door. As I turn to see Corver peering in from behind the doorway with Pancho standing slightly behind him, I quickly clear my throat and fix my clothes before addressing them directly.

"Sorry about that, I- I didn't hear you…" I say to the gentlemen aloud as Renata kisses me before smiling and making her way out of the room.

"Excuse me, boys," Renata mutters as she passes the two guys standing in the doorway. Both of them turn their heads as she walks by, then walk in once she's out and sit in the two chairs in front of my desk. I pull the executive seat back toward the desk and tuck it under before leaning against the back of the chair.

That was awkward…

"Thanks for looking into *Sandman* for me, *JB,*" I say as I take out the paper Charlotte had given me earlier and toss it to Corver for him to read. Pancho leans back in his chair while lowering his head and extending his palm towards me as if to stop my commendation before he opens his mouth to speak.

"I would've done that anyway, bro. Any of us would. I mean, what they did to Hope? To *us*? It's not right. We'll find 'em," Pancho says as he sits up confidently. I see Corver nod at the list before putting it in his pocket.

"If you don't mind, can you buy us a moment alone?" I ask Pancho as I extend my finger toward Corver. He doesn't object as he uses both hands to grab the chair's armrests and lifts himself to his feet. He knocks on the wooden desk in excitement before walking out of the office without another word. I turn my attention to Corver as the door shuts behind him.

"Hey, I, uh… I'm sorry about what happened to David and Montero. No one should have had to see that," Corver says.

"You know, I was thinking about letting Jorge take my spot in the *Delegation* after I step down," I admit as the thought of one of my most trusted people being dismembered for no other than the sick entertainment of a single man eats at me from the inside. "I just couldn't decide between him or David, but I guess neither really matters at this point," I confess.

"Step down?" asks Corver. His face turns slightly as he awaits my response.

"My time is running short here, kid," I say as Renata's words re-enter my mind. "I have a cabin in Maine that I use, well… *used*, when I wanted to get away from everything. And *everyone*. I'm going to leave this behind and put Derrick in charge. I already spoke to him about it fifteen minutes ago in the Infirmary," I admit.

"And what about *her* and the boy?" Corver asks as he points behind him, referring to the woman who just left the room a few minutes prior.

"It's their choice, but I'll ask them if they want to come with me," I say. The thought of possible denial sends chills up my arms, yet I don't dwell on it long. "Thank you. Y'know, for having my back," I say genuinely over the creaking of my chair as I lean back.

"I… I didn't mean to- to get in the way between you and my brother. I'm not trying to interfere, alright? I just…" Corver says before leaning forward and placing both arms against the desk. "*He's my brother,*" he whispers.

I pause for a few seconds while I try to empathize with him. Judging by how conflicted he sounds, I can only assume Corver's compassion for his brother is sincere. With people I care about under the same roof as us, I understand the fear of losing them better than most; hell, we've already lost some. I also know how far one would go to prevent that.

"I want to show you something. I'm going to get washed up before we head out. Go grab some gear, then meet me in the lobby in twenty," I casually instruct as I stand up.

"Where are we goin'?" Corver asks as he retracts his arms from the desk.

"It's not far, so we're not checking out any vehicles. Just trust me, alright?" I ask. His eyes squint while he looks at me attentively as if trying to gauge the surprise from my facial expression, yet he gives up after silence fills the room.

"Alright, you got it," he says as he follows me out of the office and ventures off toward the Armory.

* * *

Distant gun fire. Corpses falling to the ground. Agonizing shouts and pleas for mercy. All these sounds continue to echo in my head even as the constant flow of hot water pours out of the shower head a few feet to my left, causing the room to become foggy and incredibly muggy. Standing directly in front of the sink, I feel my grip on the ceramic vanity tightening as I relive the past 24 hours. So much suffering. So much death and despair. With my breath steadily becoming more rapid, I close my eyes and lean toward the drain before instinctively vomiting. After a second or two, my hand reaches out to one of the crystal nobs behind the faucet and turns the water on as I attempt to catch my breath.

With the shower and the sink running, I take a few controlled breaths and hesitantly pick my head up before glancing into the narrow mirror above the sink. My breathing begins to shudder as I stare at the unrecognizable persona staring back at me. Even during my darkest days, I could've never pictured myself looking like I do right now. My face is littered with blood and ash, adding to the smell of gunpowder and decay permanently instilled in my nostrils. I unclip my Kevlar, causing it to fall to the cold tile floor below as I struggle to pull my shirt over my head. Letting out a few grunts in the process, I gradually remove my black, long-sleeve polyester shirt I had been wearing and drop it onto the ground before glancing back at my shirtless reflection.

What... what are you?

With every forced inhalation, my upper body rises as my eyes remain glued onto the anomaly in the mirror. I lift my right hand and reluctantly begin unraveling the makeshift bandages around my severed fingers. As I raise my hand to the set of lights above the mirror, cautiously examining the amputated stumps, something shifts inside me. It's not fear or alarm. It's not worry or unease. *It's anger.* With the steam beginning to conceal my reflection in the mirror, I place my injured hand on the glass before sliding it across to clear the haze. As my palm rests on the right side of the mirror, my attention reverts to the unrecognizable man before me.

Liar.

I shut my eyes again before punching the mirror with my right hand. Tiny shards of glass become lodged near my knuckles, but I pay it no mind as I lower my hand to my side; small drops of blood fall onto the battle-worn Kevlar and stained shirt by my feet. I can almost feel my fingers wiggling effortlessly in the humid air as if they were still there. Looking between the cracks in the mirror, my once-perfect composure was now a shattered figment of its former self.

Murderer.

Clasping both hands together, I hunch over the sink and grab a handful of water before violently splashing it onto my face repeatedly. After rubbing my eyes and letting them readjust to the faint light above, I noticed very little of it came off. All I can do is stare ahead into the ever-desolate eyes, gazing back at me from behind the broken glass. As Derrick's words in the *PCC* float around in my head, I can't help but let out a deep, seemingly maniacal laugh before ripping the mirror off the wall altogether. The sound of shattering glass fills the air once it hits the ground, followed by the echoes of my internal demons mocking me from within my own mind.

Coward.

After an eternity, I take a few deep breaths and regain control of my breathing. As I unenthusiastically pull myself toward the misty shower, with various cracking sounds echoing throughout the tightly-knit room as my boots step over the shards of glass below, I lower my head before removing the remainder of my clothes. With the scorching water falling overhead, I can't help but think that such a painful shower is deserved following the atrocities I committed. Justified or not, I can't help but feel repelled by who or what I have become. Without another second to waste, I attempt to wash away my thoughts as I slowly step into the drizzling inferno.

* * *

Under the cover of night, the streets seem almost abandoned. This is especially true in the blocks around the *Consulate,* yet my men know not to let the silence lower their guard. *Specs* are still in or near the buildings, so we're always alert. As Corver and I approach the bottom of the Clocktower overlooking Fordham Road, about half a mile from the *Consulate,* we wait until we're both in position next to the door leading inside before he pushes off the wall and moves back to kick the door down.

With the corroded wooden door now forced open, I throw two green glow sticks through the doorway before moving inside; Kimber raised in front of me to clear the interior of any infected. Corver, holding his bolt-action .308, does the same as he follows suit behind me and checks the corners around us before continuing forward.

It's clear.

Corver lowers his rifle and follows me to a set of stairs leading to the upper floors of the Clocktower. After giving me a nod, he follows closely behind as I begin ascending the stairs with the handgun still raised. I half-expect to be out of breath when we reach the top, but our cautious approach upstairs helps me conserve energy. At the end of the stairwell, there's a ladder leading to the top of the Clocktower.

"Ready?" I ask while holstering my weapon and grabbing the metal ladder. As my footsteps echo throughout the room with every passing second, I soon hear the same thing further below as Corver begins climbing, too. I vigilantly push the wooden floorboard above my head to peer into the relatively small room housing the giant, rotating gears controlling the clock's movement outside. I pull myself up once I realize it's clear and grab Corver's rifle as he reaches the top of the ladder.

"Damn," Corver mutters under his breath as I place his rifle against the large window pane overlooking the borough.

"Yeah, I've always wanted to come up here," I admit while sulking in the view. Even in the darkness, you can see the entire borough from here, and I can't help but wonder why no one has occupied this place yet. It would make for one *hell* of a sniper's nest.

Not a bad idea…

"So why now?" Corver asks as he turns to face me. "Why come up here? Why bring me?" he asks as I intercept before he can ask another question.

"You see that?" I ask as I point to the *Consulate*, which would look abandoned to the naked eye. I, however, can make out small lamps and candlelight strewn across various rooms throughout the building. "Come sunrise, the *Consulate's* defenses will be complete. We made one building more secure than any other in the borough," I declare while basking in the pride of our hard work.

"We just did what we had to," Corver says in an attempt to justify the labor.

"No, you see, we didn't just unify a single building or even the people in it…" I say as I lift my arms to my side and glance out of the window. "We united a *city*. We brought people together for a cause more important than just ourselves. We created a permanent fire in the eternal darkness," I proclaim as I point toward the ill-lit metropolis.

"Boss, I get that you want to leave all this behind. Hell, on some levels, I can even *relate*…" Corver confesses as the look of achievement on his face slowly dissipates. "But, none of this was possible without you. It was possible *because* of you," he says.

"That's *exactly* why I need to leave," I say with conviction. "With you guys holding the reigns, that place has a chance. With me at the helm-" I say before being cut off.

"With you at the helm, *we're a family,*" Corver says.

The words hit me like a brick. I've always looked out for the people we've taken in, but I had not thought twice about how they viewed *me*. Amidst all the stress and the seemingly endless loss, those eight words were enough to bring me back to who I am, who I *truly am*, under all the power: *I'm human.*

As I'm staring at Corver, who tries his best to hold back a smile, I notice his face instantaneously becomes all the more visible as a light source radiating from the outside seeps into where we're standing. Just as it does, the sounds of *Spectrals* groaning in the distance put us on high alert. Only when I peer outside the window do I realize where all the light is coming from.

Oh my god…

Without a second thought, Corver and I slide down the ladder as the *Consulate* is engulfed in light. The exterior spotlights illuminating the sidewalk from above light up the entire area like a Christmas tree. All the lights from within the school are simultaneously turned on, and I don't waste a second trying to figure out why, even as we run toward the only place we knew was worth protecting: *Home*.

CHAPTER 14

OVERBOARD

CORVER AND I PRACTICALLY THROW ourselves through the west gate as the sound of rapid gunfire simultaneously fills the rear courtyard. I eject the Kimber's empty magazine before inserting my last one. I half-expect to hear the sound of covering fire raining down from the *Overwatch Convoy*, but the first thing I noticed as I sprinted to the *Consulate* was that the train was missing entirely.

"Where is it?!" I shout out over the *Thrivers* running to secure the metal gates. Judging by how quickly he answered, I could tell Francis knew what I was referring to.

"Don't know, boss. They haven't been answering our transmissions!" *Igor* hollers as *Jawbreaker* grabs my shoulder from behind. As I turn and begin storming toward the *Consulate*, Pancho hands me my MPX before extending a few magazines to me. *He must've gone into the Armory when shit hit the fan.*

"I didn't check them out. I just grabbed what I could and ran," he admits. Once his hands are clear, he grabs the shotgun slung around his back before loading a shell into the chamber. I don't give it much thought, as an incorrect inventory count is currently on the lower end of my priorities.

"Where are the kids?" I shout out with concern as I load the MPX. Even though they are holding, the sound of ferocious banging on the metal sheets that were recently welded onto the exterior gates only makes me more paranoid. Corver, who is slightly out of breath after running half a mile, digs into the pack he brought for our commute to flush out some rounds for his rifle. He and I both transition to stare at Pancho for an answer to the question.

"The girls are getting them together..." *JB* says as he stomps around in place. The anxiety from the chaos around us is undoubtedly getting under his skin. "I think they're bringing them upstairs," he recalls.

"No! We need to get them out of here," I proclaim as I turn to address those outside. "Protect the perimeter! Get half of the vehicles ready for withdrawal!" I shout as some of the *Thrivers*, who were previously helping to hold the infected back, rush to prepare the transports. As I turn to address the two men in front of me, the sounds of gunfire begin to emerge near the front of the *Consulate*.

They're everywhere...

"Use the PA in the main office and have the kids brought to the Main Lobby. Some food and water from the pantry, too. Go!" Corver instructs one of the unarmed *Thrivers*, who takes off running toward the rear of the Cafeteria.

"Follow me," I say to *Corver* and *JB* over the gunfire as we sprint straight for the Power Room.

* * *

The dusty room containing all of the generators and power equipment for the building must be what started the ruckus unfolding outside. The room, usually secured with a 2" padlock, was recently pried open, and one of the generators we had recently brought in had been powered on. While entering the room, using our guns to check every corner as we do, the three of us make our way to the panel where the switches are. All the fuses are turned in the same direction: *On*.

In a desperate attempt to flip one of the switches on the circuit board, I immediately retract my hand as sparks violently fill the air once I do. Someone tampered with the panel once all the lights in the building were turned on. This wasn't an accident. This was intentional.

"Listen up! All juvenile *Thrivers* and their caretakers *must* be brought to the lobby now! I repeat, all kids and their guardians need to be brought to the Lobby now!" I hear a male voice frantically say into the PA system. Judging by how muffled some of the dialogue is, I can tell *JB's* mouth is too close to the microphone. As the rumbling of the large generator overshadows the distant gunfire throughout the building, I turn to face the machine and bring the MPX up before repeatedly squeezing the trigger.

Bang. Bang. Bang. Bang.

With the generator being destroyed, the rumbling subsides almost instantly as the lights above us go out. I can only assume the lights throughout the rest of the building simultaneously do the same, as the sudden shouts emanating in the hallway begin to ring out after our room goes dark.

There we go…

"Corver, head to the sick bay and bring Derrick to the roof with the others to help with the barrels. I can't have him risking another injury by running with his leg," I say, remembering Derrick is in recovery. Without a word, Corver begins to hightail it out of the room before having his arm grabbed by *Jawbreaker*.

"Here, give him this," Pancho says as he tosses his pump-action shotgun to Corver. He nearly fumbles the firearm before getting a better grip and bolting out of the room. I look to my right to face Pancho, who grabs the Glock tucked idly behind his jeans and chambers a round.

"Let's get this done, *JB*," I say before storming out of the room behind Corver. *Jawbreaker* follows right behind me as we traverse the dark, dismal corridors of the *Consulate*.

* * *

"Get back, guys! Get back!" I hear Hope yell as she extends her left arm to protect the children behind her. Even as Pancho and I make our way down the stairs leading to the Main Lobby, I can see the stainless steel revolver quivering in Hope's hand as she keeps the barrel pointed at the front entrance. Some of the armed sentries, nearly all of which are supposed to be patrolling the other floors, also position the barrel of their guns toward the entrance as the ferocious banging continues from outside.

"Check your weapons! I need you all to be ready for what's next!" I instruct as the sounds of slides and bolts being retracted echo throughout the room. Hope nearly drops the revolver as the wooden doors leading into the first-floor hallways swing open behind her with force: *It's Renata and* Graham.

How the fuck...

My eyes don't leave Graham's, even after I am nearly tipped over by Renata throwing her arms around me. I assume *JB* also shares my discomfort, as he inherently raises his weapon toward Graham. As one would typically expect, given his track record for unpredictability, Graham effortlessly throws his hands up to show he isn't a threat. As I wrap my free hand around Renata's neck, I grip the MPX harder with my other hand and usher *Jawbreaker* to keep his attention on the man.

"W-where's Vito?" Renata asks as her voice trembles. The luminescent green radiating from the glow sticks being sporadically tossed onto the floor around the Lobby makes her look of concern readily apparent.

"We haven't seen him," *JB* admits as his attention remains fixated on Graham. After a brief pause, Renata looks down before turning to run up the staircase.

"Wait! Wait!" I say as I sling the MPX over my shoulder and use both hands to prevent her from running into the darkness above.

"No, no, no, no! No. This is my baby boy we're talking about, Miles... I won't-" she shouts as I interrupt.

"Neither will I! Neither will I. But we don't know who's up there! We don't know if any of these things got in. We *will* find him…" I assert with certainty as I hold her face in between my hands. "But I *need* your attention to be on the kids who need you right here," I confess. Her eyes seem to be looking *through me* rather than *at me,* and I can tell she's paralyzed in fear.

"Listen to me! I'll send someone to find him! But the kids need you here, now! Okay?" I shout while shaking Renata's shoulders to break her trance. It seems to work because, after a brief pause, she gradually gazes at Hope and the group of nearly a dozen children crying behind her. Renata's motherly instincts naturally kick into overdrive as she consoles the scared kids.

Fuck, fuck…

Two *Thrivers* who overheard our conversation look at me as if trying to assess what's running through my mind. I point to the ceiling, silently indicating that I want them to search the upper floors for Vito, and one of them gives me a thumbs up before hitting his companion's shoulder with the back of his hand and sprinting upstairs. As more *Thrivers* enter the Lobby, some with guns in their hands while others are holding plastic crates filled with consumables, I turn to address them all.

"I need all of you with food to take the kids to the rear courtyard and prepare the trucks. You're leaving now," I command without any hesitation. Their safety is the most important thing right now. I speed walk over to Hope, still shaking with fear in her eyes while facing the foyer, and embrace her. She puts her forehead into my neck as she lets out a whimper.

"Thank you…" I whisper into her ear. After a few seconds, I hastily pull back and give her a nod. I wait for her to nod back to confirm that she understands the urgency of the situation. She does, then turns around to address the children standing behind her.

"Alright, kiddies… let's go, gimme your hands," Hope says in a tone that I can only describe as forcefully cheerful. She wants the kids to think she isn't scared when, in reality, she's terrified. Hesitantly,

Renata helps her gather the little ones around and ushers them through the door leading to the rear courtyard, toward the vehicles out back, and toward safety.

"You're going with them," I mumble as I focus on Pancho. He constantly shifts his gaze between Graham and me, making it clear he's not fully committed to the idea.

"But boss, I-" Pancho says before being cut off.

"They can take care of themselves, but I want someone I can trust to watch their backs. Take them to the house in Duchess County. We can't trust the *PCC* right now…" I whisper so only he can hear. Even with his handgun still in the air, Pancho's frantic movement in place demonstrates that he's still not sold on the idea of leaving. I take a moment to address his discomfort. "And I wasn't asking, either," I proclaim sternly. His eyes meet with mine before he lowers his gun and tilts his head to the side in defeat.

"Fine," Pancho mumbles. I turn back to Renata, who's still focused on getting the children out of the lobby.

"Baby, you need to go with them, too," I say to her before Graham takes a step forward, lowering his hands in the process.

"What, why?" Graham asks demandingly as I step before him to prevent his sudden advance.

"This does not concern you, old man…" I growl as Pancho realigns the barrel of his handgun with Graham's left temple. He stops moving, but the silence is quickly broken as the metal panels fortifying the large windows near the entrance start giving way to the pressure from outside. Renata uses the diversion to interject into the conversation.

"No, I am not going anywhere without my son," she says matter-of-factly. I can tell she means it, yet there's more at risk if she stays here.

"We don't have a choice! How is he going to live if both of his parents are dead? You- you need to live so he can, too…" I proclaim as her look of concern decreases slightly. "I will protect that boy with my life, so you don't have to," I confess.

Please… just go…

Renata pauses for a few seconds even as the distant sounds of gunfire throughout the *Consulate*, both inside and out, fill the room. She takes a step back for every shot that rings in the distance, *her* shoulders lifting from being startled in the process. As her back is propped up against the door leading into the hallway, I take a few steps forward and grab her face to pull towards mine. The kiss seems to last forever, with her quickened pulse vibrating off my palm resting near her neck before I bring my hand around her lower back and yank the door open using the bronze door handle. She briefly looks behind her before staring back at me.

"Just *protect him*. And come back *safe*... both of you," she says before kissing me and bolting through the doors leading into the rear courtyard. It takes me a while to break my paralysis and return to the mundane situation we are faced with: *we need to defend this place.*

"Go..." I say to *Jawbreaker* as I extend my MPX to him. He hesitates before grabbing it with both hands once I shake it in the air to make him realize time is running out. He tucks the Glock behind his belt before reaching to grab my rifle. I nod once he does while simultaneously lowering my hand to my side. "Make me proud..." I whisper out to him.

"Yes, sir," Pancho says as he gives me a fist bump before running around Graham and following suit behind Renata. Graham's gaze transitions back to me, yet I ignore him; there are bigger problems to deal with. Corver nearly trips as he practically throws himself down the staircase and lands in the main lobby.

"Alright, Derrick is up top with Abdul, and the defenses are primed," Corver says, clearly out of breath as he tosses me a hand-held radio. He doesn't even acknowledge his brother's presence as he stares at me, anticipating our next course of action. "What do we do now?" he asks impatiently as he retrieves a two-tone Beretta from his thigh holster. The sound of metal hitting the concrete outside emanates throughout the building from the large windows in front of us.

They tore down the gates...

"Stand away from the windows!" I yell out as I turn to face the foyer. I take a few steps back as the men around me do the same. "*D*, do you copy?" I call out over the radio. The sounds of the metal doors separating us from the *Spectrals* giving way at the hinges is enough to give anyone nightmares, but I maintain my composure.

"Just give the order, Captain," Derrick blurts out before cutting his transmission. With that, I yell out to the *Thrivers* in the lobby to back up and wait until there is enough space between my guys before bringing the handheld to my mouth and holding down the transmit button.

"Light 'em up!" I holler over the radio. After a few moments, the darkness peering through the exposed gaps in the windows is illuminated with a bright orange, just as a barrel of ignited gasoline is tossed from the rooftop onto the front courtyard.

Boom!

Whatever glass remained on the windows is gone now, and I find myself bringing my arms up to shield me from the shrapnel. The heat from the explosion also makes its way into the Lobby, both through the windows and the now-open entrance. The demoralizing moaning previously echoing from the front of the *Consulate* is reduced almost instantaneously with just the press of a button. Still, I know there are more to come.

"Everyone on the stairs!" I hear Corver shout out as I draw my .45 from its holster. Those still on the main floor begin pushing up the staircases along both sides of the lobby. I bring the radio up again and hold the button once more.

"Don't let up, *D!*" I instruct as various entities, completely engulfed in flames, limp through the main entrance. I imagine the *Specs* feel pain because their agonizing screeches gradually increase as the burns worsen with every fleeting second. One of the *Thrivers* behind me passes me a Riley Defense RAK-47 with three full magazines of 7.62x39mm rounds, and I insert one of them into the rifle before yanking on the charging handle and aiming the iron sights at the *Spectrals* stumbling into the *Consulate*. As soon as another explosion shakes the room, I hear it.

"Fire!" Corver shouts.

The sounds of close gunfire never seem to fail when it comes to making me slightly more deaf after every occasion. The ringing associated with mild tinnitus inevitably creeping in makes it harder to hear the dialogue from those around me, yet I somehow manage. The bodies of the slower *Spectrals* drop to the floor with little effort, but the light emanating off their corpses from the flames seems to make the ones behind them more aggressive.

"They're getting stirred up; check your fire!" I shout, *no pun intended*, as I note how muffled my voice is in my ears. The men around me start letting off shots in the direction of our quicker adversaries as we collectively begin backing up toward the second floor. The recoil from the rifle is significantly more noticeable than the MPX, but I don't let it deter me.

"Prep the chandelier!" I command as Corver pushes past an unarmed Graham and bolts into the Armory where the winch for the Chandelier is sitting in the middle of the room. Another explosion knocks some of the *Specs* in the lobby to the ground from the sheer power of the blast. I usher for the rest of the *Thrivers* on my stairwell to climb to the top and take position over the railing. The *Thrivers* on the other stairwell do the same as they see us climb to the second floor.

As we reach the top, I peek into the Armory to see Corver aiming his bronze Beretta 80x Cheetah at the metal chain holding up the Chandelier while his other hand holds onto a thick paracord line.

"Do it!" I yell before commanding everyone to hit the floor. Corver yanks the paracord, tied to various pins attached to nearly half a dozen m87 hand grenades strapped to the metallic chandelier above the Main Lobby. Without hesitation, he lets off a shot from his pistol that severs the chain holding the chandelier in the air. As the ear-shattering sound of shattered glass echoes off the walls below, the Earth seems to jolt as the grenades downstairs go off simultaneously.

Holy shit!

As if I wasn't deaf enough, the explosion below, mixed with those coming from the barrels being thrown from the roof, only serves to alert the entire city of our presence. *Was it the most brilliant idea for crowd control? Maybe not, but it sure as hell worked.* The previously pristine wood railing and marble walls that make up the staircase are now covered in gunpowder, shrapnel, and unidentifiable body parts. The smell of decay that followed makes the temporary victory feel short-lived.

"Hell yeah!" I hear one of the *Thrivers* behind me yell out as we stand back on our feet. Our celebration is short-lived as I lift my head to see infected coming from near the third-floor gym.

"Contact rear!" I yell out as nearly all of us turn our attention to the imminent threat that followed.

They're already up here.

I grab the RAK-47 from the floor and use my other hand to toss a few glow sticks down the corridor for a better visual of the threat. With more *Specs* entering the Lobby and heading toward the staircase, our attention is now set in two directions. Amid the ensuing mayhem, I glance up at the nearly 300-pound metal desks we had hoisted up on the ceiling above both staircases. Without so much as another thought, I bring the iron sights of the RAK-47 up to the chains holding it overhead and fire until they are severed.

The thud of the desk hitting the top of the stairwell isn't as noticeable as the previous explosions, but it is equally as effective in keeping the *Specs* at bay. As the desks slide down the staircases, all infected who were previously on the stairwell are violently thrown back to the Lobby, buying us more time to hold 'em off. With the desks coming to a halt at the bottom of the landing, trapping a few *Specs* against the wall, a few *Thrivers* around me transition their aim toward the Lobby and resume their previous defenses.

"We need to get to Derrick! We can pick off the rest of them from up top while these guys take care of things here!" I shout over the gunfire to Corver. He nods before leading the way toward the stairwell closest to the Library. The footsteps I hear from behind as Corver and I push up the stairs and to the roof comfort me, knowing we've got support.

* * *

The metal door to the roof creeks opens as Corver pushes through it, exposing us to the seemingly endless sounds of groaning around the building. As I push through the doorway, I see Abdul helping Derrick lift a recently ignited barrel of gasoline over the north railing. They pull back from the edge just in time to avoid the blowback from the explosion that follows once the barrel hits the concrete below.

"Damn, you're a sight for sore eyes, man," Derrick says as I approach him. Given his previous condition, he still seems to be limping with a shotgun in hand, albeit improving substantially faster than I had imagined. "We're running low on-" Derrick says before my face is covered in blood. As I stand there, paralyzed, I look with horror as a bullet pierces his head directly under his right eye, causing his body to collapse suddenly.

W-wha...

In my state of paralysis, I hear another unanticipated shot go off from my left, causing my body to shutter instinctively, followed by another as Abdul's body is riddled with bullets coming from behind me. Without thinking, I grab the Kimber from its holster and bring it up as I turn to my right. Just as the sights are brought up to my eye, there is a sharp pain in my shoulder that causes me to drop my handgun and fall to the floor in distress. Before Corver can react, I pick my head up to see Luca Silvio turn his gun from me and aim it at Corver.

"Move, and you end up just like 'em..." Luca proclaims as Corver instinctively puts his hands out in front of him. With the roof's edge behind him, Corver has nowhere to go, even if he chooses to run. The sounds of vehicles rumbling from the rear courtyard fade as the vehicles peel through the gate and away from the area. Although their escape should comfort me, my current situation suppresses such a feeling of triumph. I grab my shoulder in an attempt to stop the bleeding and can see Graham walking up from nearly two dozen feet behind the three of us. Graham begins to talk as he approaches.

"Looks like you're not the only one with friends, Miles. Albeit, it looks like you're *short* one of those right now," Graham says as he picks up the handgun that Luca had swept away from Abdul's corpse just seconds ago. The pain, mixed with the sight of blood trickling from Derrick's wound, causes me to scream in both agony and anger. With Corver unable to move, I try to pick myself up from the floor. Graham shoots a round near my feet, intentionally missing as if he is ordering me to stay down.

"So much for the *'continuation of a good thing,'* huh…" Graham says as he stops a few feet in front of me and brings the barrel of the handgun up to my head. The sudden fling of the door we all came through not even a minute ago startles me more than the thought of death, and the shouting that follows was overwritten with gunfire as Luca and Graham turn to engage the *Thrivers* that were making their way onto the roof.

As the traitors focus on their aim, I stumble to my feet and move toward the roof's edge just as Graham turns around. The sound of a bullet whizzing slightly overhead makes me stumble faster, forcing me to ignore the pain as I bend down and grab the only rope tied to the railing that we used to hoist the barrels of gasoline from the East Parking Lot. A bullet grazes my calf, and without hesitation, I tackle Corver off of the East side of the roof. I hear him grunt as more shots are fired in our direction.

The rope does little to cushion the fall, but it slows our rapid descent enough not to kill us instantly. As I use every ounce of energy to maintain my grip on the rope, I tighten my injured arm to hold Corver by the waist and prevent him from plummeting to his death. We hit one of the gated windows before bouncing off it and falling to the concrete below. I can barely stay awake after the fall, yet I seem to be doing better than Corver because he isn't conscious at all. Despite my affliction, I grab Corver by the collar of his sweater and pull him under the slab of concrete hanging directly above the East Entrance.

I- I don't think they can see us from up there...

I instinctively raise my left hand as the adrenaline begins to dwindle and finally acknowledge the lingering pain and burning sensation resonating from it; two of my fingers are twisted out of place. With this dismal realization, I hastily cover my mouth before letting out a muffled scream so as not to give away our position to the threats possibly looming above. Looking down with my mouth still covered, I notice Corver's dark blue sweater becoming darker as blood seeps into the fabric from underneath. Without so much as a peep, I take my right hand and lift his clothing to reveal a bullet wound in his lower abdomen.

Fuck...

With limited options, I take off my dark denim jacket, starting with my uninjured arm. As my arm clears the fabric, I stuff the vacant sleeve hanging from the jacket into my mouth. After a few seconds of hesitation, I snap my fingers back into position and bite down as hard as I can onto the jacket's thick material. The pain in my fingers starts to subside after what feels like an eternity and a couple of deep breaths, so I take the opportunity to grab the knife from my belt once I regain movement in my fingers. As the blade clears its sheath, I wrap the sharp end around some of the cloth before cutting a portion off.

The gunfire around the building persists, and I feel my body shaking for the first time since this ordeal started. Countless *Spectrals* are walking on the streets and the sidewalks past the gates, but they haven't spotted Corver and me. Instead, they're collectively inching closer toward the front of the *Consulate*. With my attention back on Corver, I tuck the clean fabric under his sweater and apply pressure to the wound, now spewing blood at a rate quicker than expected, before working to undo my belt.

Cmon… stay with me…

As I yank the belt through the loops on my pants, the Kimber's holster, the Benchmade's sheath, and the empty magazine carriers fastened around my waist drop to the ground with various thuds. Paying it no mind, I wrap my belt around the fabric and tighten it just enough to keep the makeshift bandage in place. I tuck the sheathed knife behind my waistline before picking up Corver's Beretta, *sitting idly in his thigh holster*, and ejecting the magazine to get a count of how many rounds we had.

Eleven… with one in the chamber.

After remembering that the vehicles we had are gone, I glance back up at the street as the gravity of our mundane circumstance causes me to sigh. As hope seems to be fleeting from my grasp, I briefly remember a private, indoor, twenty-car garage two blocks away near the Reservoir; it was built for the residents of a nearby apartment building, but I had stored my own vehicle in there with some commodities from the *Consulate's* reserve shortly after the first wave of *Thrivers* had arrived. While making it two blocks with twelve bullets is well beyond the realm of possibility, I had to try. I'd rather die out there than let Corver die right here.

"C'mon, buddy," I say with a painful grunt as I wrap my good arm around Corver's torso and use whatever energy I can muster to lift him up. "We're getting out of here," I whisper. With Corver staggering on his feet in and out of consciousness, letting out pain-ridden grunts as we push ahead, I hold the Beretta in my other hand and peek around the concrete slab overhead to see whether Luca or Graham are still looking for us.

Clear.

With that, I take a deep breath and begin lugging Corver forward while beginning to limp myself. The graze wasn't enough to immobilize me, but all of the injuries my body has taken are starting to weigh down on my morale. We make our way to the entrance of the parking lot facing the street. I use the darkness to our advantage as the flames from my far left, still radiating from the front courtyard of the *Consulate,* are drawing the attention of the *Specs* outside. I kneel slightly to undo the latch holding the gates secure before yanking on the right metal door and exposing us to the dangers that lie ahead.

I wait nearly ten seconds for a large enough clearing before hoisting Corver over my shoulder and dragging him toward the right of the street. With every step we take away from the *Consulate,* I can't help but feel more and more hopeless. One of the *Spectrals* on the street averts their gaze away from the front courtyard and redirects it toward us. As the sound of its profane shriek echoes throughout the street, the sound of the .380 ACP round being fired from the Beretta serves to do the same merely seconds later.

Bang.

Now that we've got the attention of every *Spectral* in a quarter-mile radius, I start hobbling faster toward the garage. As more infected move in on our location, I fire more rounds. With my injured shoulder absorbing the recoil following every subsequent shot, the pain throughout my body becomes all the more apparent as we stagger on; nevertheless, I continue to push forward with the handgun raised. I align its iron sights as best as possible at the heads of the deteriorating figures around us to conserve ammunition.

Ten rounds. Nine. Eight. Seven… Six. Five.

In the commotion, my leg starts to give in from the weight, but I remain standing on both feet. I let out a scream that temporarily increases my confidence, yet it's quickly overwritten when I subconsciously remind myself how much ammunition is left. As another *Spec* approaches from about ten feet to our right, that overwhelming feeling of hopelessness gnawing at my confidence inevitably intensifies as another round is fired.

Four.

Over the sounds of my tireless huffing and the metallic bullet casing bouncing off the floor below, I can hear groans behind us approaching ever so slowly. I try to focus on the distance we cover, but the sound only gets closer with every passing second. It's as if they're closing in three feet for every 12 inches we push. Corver's feet, dragging along the concrete below, are slowing us down enough to make us an easy target. I stop and attempt to turn around to address the approaching threat, but my leg gives out in the process. Corver falls to the ground first, dragging me down faster in the process, and I practically throw myself on my back while bringing up the handgun as best as I can with both hands.

Bang.

My forearm is naturally brought up to my face as the *Spec* that was tailing us falls forward, covering me in more blood while landing nearly a foot in front of Corver and me after being shot from behind. After wiping the blood from my face, I realign my aim with whoever is now standing behind the fallen infected.

"Vito?" I let out in a raspy manner as the strain in my voice from all the screaming fills the air. He is standing nearly half a dozen feet away with what looks like a stainless Walther PPK/S trembling in his hands. The black backpack he's wearing looks identical to the one I had sitting alongside my desk in the main office. His long, dirty blonde hair obscures his line of sight, yet he can still hit a small, moving target with a single shot from a few yards away.

Wow…

As one of the infected approaches a now idle Vito, Heath, the *Thriver* who had given me the thumbs up in the lobby before looking for Vito, puts it down with a single shot from his pump-action shotgun. The blast is enough to bring Vito and me back to our senses as we close the distance between one another. I kneel briefly in front of him as he lowers his handgun and retracts his finger from inside the trigger guard.

"Thank you," I say before his face lights up in the darkness with joy.

"Boss, we've gotta move…" I hear the *Thriver* say as he racks a new shell into the firearm. With no time to lose, I immediately focus my attention on an unconscious Corver lying face down on the concrete and usher the middle-aged *Thriver* to assist. Heath wraps one of Corver's arms around his neck to maintain a firm, two-handed grip on the shotgun while I position his other arm around my shoulder. With that, we push forward. Together.

"There's a garage not too far from here!" I shout out before a *Spec* is brought down from our left. The ejected shell lands in front of us yet disappears as Corver's feet drag across it. "V, get ready to shoot the lock on the garage door panel, yeah?" I ask aloud to ensure he knows what he has to do.

"Okay, Miles," he says in a lower tone than I had expected, given the deafening commotion around us.

Three rounds. Two.

The pain in my shoulder is unfathomable, and I can feel my aim start to sway tremendously. I place the handgun in the front of my pants in an attempt to save the few rounds I have remaining. With Vito directly in front of the three of us, I use both hands to prop Corver up and close the gap between all of us. With nearly twenty yards to go, I order Heath to go ahead and clear a path for Vito to get the lock. As Corver's weight falls on my shoulders, both in the literal and figurative sense, I hear various shotgun blasts go off a few feet in front of us. As the last *Spec* in our path falls to the ground, I snag the opportunity to get us ahead of the situation.

"Go, V! Go!" I yell as Vito sprints to the brown metal garage door between us and safety. With both hands, Vito aligns the barrel of the PPK/S with the padlock securing the controls to the garage and turns his head away as he fires a shot. The sound of the bullet ricocheting after it destroyed the lock echoes between the multi-story residential buildings, yet Vito wastes no time as he stands on his toes to remove the broken lock.

With infected approaching from behind us, Heath swings the shotgun around as Corver and I pass him; as if things aren't bad enough, Heath starts to panic once he hears the dreadful *click* indicating that the gun is empty. While he fumbles to grab more shells from his pocket, dropping a few on the ground in the process, Heath is forcefully pulled to the ground by multiple infected. The indistinguishable sounds of his flesh being torn from his body are concealed by what had to be the loudest screams I've ever heard from another human being.

As I stand there, trying to understand the agony he must be feeling, I quickly realize what I have to do. Using my free hand, I hastily grab the Beretta from behind my waistline and align the sights with the back of Heath's head before pulling the trigger. His screams stop immediately as his lifeless body slumps over. The thought of killing a loyal comrade for no good reason makes me incredibly nauseous, but I turn away and begin running as best as I can to the garage.

One round left. I'm- I'm so sorry...

"Open the door!" I holler as I close in the distance between us and Vito. I can tell the kid is scared, yet his unwavering bravery forces him to scrabble around with the controls to the garage door. Within seconds, the sound of metal retracting fills the street as the door begins to lift.

Yes, yes, yes...

"Go! Go! Go! Go!" I scream aloud while waving my hand to Vito as he ducks underneath the rising gate. With all the vitality I have left,

I throw Corver into the garage and turn to shut the door behind us manually. With the mechanism still raising the door, my efforts to pull the gate down are fruitless. In an act of desperation, I raise the pistol to the control panel that Vito exposed and fire a round. The combustion that follows interrupts the gate's retracting mechanism, and I take that brief moment to slam the gate down just in time to lock the *Spectrals* outside.

Empty.

* * *

When the banging on the garage door subsides, the *Specs* on the other side begin moving away from the damp garage; I have no doubt their sudden change of behavior is attributed to the noise coming from the *Consulate*, but I let out a sigh of relief before falling to the ground right next to Corver in exhaustion. Vito immediately runs to check on me, yet I usher him to turn around as he approaches. Noticing the multitool hanging on the side pocket of the book bag he's wearing, I am confident it is mine. Vito takes off the bag and places it down beside me. I guess the question I was about to ask is written all over my face, so Vito wastes no time answering.

"I didn't know what to do…" he says as I hoist myself against the nearest vehicle and unzip the bag. With what little strength I have left, my hand reaches down to grab the bottom of the bag and flip it upside down until all the contents within fall to the peeling floor below. "I went to look for you in your office, but you weren't… I- I put a lot of your stuff in there, though," Vito confesses as he points to the empty bag beside me.

"That's when Heath found me, and we-" Vito continues before being interrupted as Corver turns to his side and begins coughing ferociously. Blood is protruding from his mouth and covering the floor beneath him. I begin frantically looking for gauze that I usually keep in my bag, but I can't find it in the pile of items strewn around my feet.

"Crap, help me lift him to the car over there…" I say as I grab the keys lying on the ground. I place my arm behind me and use the vehicle I'm leaning against to carry myself to my feet. With that, I bend down to grab Corver while Vito tries his best to assist me with carrying an adult who is twice his height and weight. We stumble nearly three parking spaces before stopping near the bed of the truck. "Lift his feet," I quietly instruct as I yank the door to the truck bed open.

As Corver is placed into the rear of the Tundra, he exerts a few painful groans while his body begins to contort from the discomfort; not wanting to waste any time, I ask Vito to go to the back seat and grab the plastic crate with various medical items in it. Without stopping to catch a breath, I begin cutting away at Corver's clothing with the knife until his torso is fully exposed. Carefully turning him to his side, I can see the exit wound where the bullet passed through.

Thank god…

As the crate is thrown up on the tailgate of the truck with as much force as Vito can manage, I desperately comb through the items until I find a half-empty bottle of nearly expired Hydrogen Peroxide, a Skin Stapler, Clean Gauze, and a small packet of Pain Medication. I open the bottle of Hydrogen Peroxide and pour some onto my hands before rubbing them together and shaking them dry. The liquid sanitizing the various cuts on my hands from the fall causes me to wince slightly due to the sting that follows.

"Get me a shirt from the duffle over there," I instruct Vito as I point at the black duffle bag on the other side of the opened cabin window leading to the backseat. When he comes back with one of the thin shirts I had packed from Scarsdale all those months ago, I hastily snag it and douse it with Hydrogen Peroxide before turning to Corver and wiping his wound clean. The agonizing screams resulting from the alcohol should've been expected, but I can't risk anyone or *anything* finding us when we're so vulnerable.

"Cover his mouth, Vito," I instruct while turning Corver to his side again to disinfect the exit wound. The truck shakes slightly as Vito lifts himself onto the truck bed and makes his way behind Corver's head. He kneels and uses both of his hands to cover the injured man's mouth as I position him on his back again.

Before closing the bottle, I take a deep breath and pour some of the disinfectant onto my shoulder, which seeps in through the thin shirt I'm wearing, before letting out a muffled scream myself. With the hard part over, I tuck a portion of clean gauze through the neck of my t-shirt and place it over the wound with ease. With little blood seeping through Corver's bullet wound, I wipe off as much excess as possible before grabbing the Skin Stapler.

"Be ready. He won't like this, kid…" I say to Vito as he closes his mouth and nods in acknowledgment. With that, I bring the stapler to the edge of the wound while holding it shut with my other hand and begin stitching it in place. Corver's whole body starts shaking due to the pain, enough for me to have to position myself on top of his legs in a desperate attempt to hold him still, yet Vito is doing a great job at suppressing the sound coming from his mouth. As I finish with the last staple, Corver seems to fall back to his previous state of unconsciousness as his body becomes motionless.

"Good job. Hand me that, will you?" I ask while pointing behind my right foot at the clean gauze pads. With clean gauze in hand, I begin wrapping Corver's abdomen as best as I can before unwrapping the small, first-aid-sized packet of pain medication while reaching over to the backseat to grab a water bottle; the packet only contained two pills, so I lift Corver's head and place one of the pills on his tongue before reaching around and bringing the water bottle up to his lips.

"I need you to drink this…" I whisper as Corver starts sipping on the water while fighting in and out of consciousness. I hear him forcefully swallow the medication before letting out a nasty cough that only serves to get blood on the inside of the cabin's windows. I reach down and use the previously clean t-shirt to wipe the blood from his mouth before pulling the duffle bag through the window and positioning it for Corver to lay his head on as I turn him to his side for rest.

I drag myself out of the truck bed and use one of the blankets I had lying in the backseat from a camping trip I went to in Maine last winter to cover my resting ally as he sleeps. As the blanket is pulled over his body, I move my hand forward to grab the wet and bloodied paper hanging from the seam of Corver's pocket. In doing so, I lean against the back of the truck as I unravel the paper and immediately recognize one of the first names on the list: *Luca Silvio*. The dark, crimson substance on the paper makes it nearly incomprehensible. As I lift myself from against the truck and fall to the ground, I begin to phase in and out of consciousness myself. The room seems to only get darker with every passing moment, and seeing Vito running over to me was the last thing I remember before being surrounded in complete darkness.

CHAPTER 15

REVIVED

WITH EACH BUMP THE TRUCK runs over on the road, it becomes increasingly difficult to rest. The wounds plastered all over my body are causing me a seemingly endless cycle of discomfort. I pull the handle under the passenger seat until my body is reclined as much as possible. Vito grunts as the back of my seat unintentionally collides with his body.

"Sorry, kid…" I let out in a groggy tone. I glance at the center console to determine the time. *It's 12:43 P.M.* Not caring whether the clock was adjusted for *Daylight Savings* or otherwise, I shift my body to get a better look at Corver. His seat is positioned closer to the wheel than usual so as not to stretch too much and possibly reopen his stitches, and I notice his face contort in pain with every bump. He looks at me from his peripherals before refocusing on the semi-open road ahead.

"It's not as bad as it was," Corver says jokingly. His laugh is interrupted by another bump, causing him to reach for his abdomen.

"Who're you telling…" I say before clearing my throat as best as I can. I reach down to the side of the door and grab a half-empty MRE. *It's our last one.* Corver, Vito, and I have been conservative with our food over the last week we've been on the road, but such frugality will only last for so long. I fumble in the bag until I grab a pack of crackers and a packet of cheese spread. After peeling the corner of the cheese spread apart with my teeth, I hand the packet over to Vito. "You need to eat something," I confess as he quickly takes the packet and begins sucking some of the processed cheese through the opening. He hands me the packet back after a few seconds.

"You, too," I say before extending the cheese packet to Corver, who glances down at me a couple of times before hesitantly taking it from my hand. I begin unwrapping the crackers as he places the remainder of the cheese spread upright in the cupholder. I break the crackers into three pieces and hand them out, giving Vito the largest piece before savoring my end. As heavenly as the meal seems, it only lasts a few short minutes before ending abruptly. Corver wastes no time adding to my distress as he points at the fuel gauge.

"We're on less than a quarter," he says.

"Of course we are…" I say while bringing my palm up to rub my forehead. "Look, we're almost there, anyways. Just cut through the woods up here," I instruct while repositioning my seat back up. I point nearly half a mile up the road to a clearing meant for off-road vehicles or hikers. As we approach the clearing, I grab the edge of my seat to hold myself in position as the truck climbs off the asphalt and lands on the soft dirt leading into the visually desolate forest.

"Keep going straight for another two miles or so," I say as I extend my hand behind me. Without a word, Vito hands me the Glock 19 lying on top of the clothing in the duffle bag beside him. I rack the slide and place the loaded handgun on my knee; with Vito following closely, I can hear him doing the same with his PPK/S.

"Look, man, I'm sorry about the rest of the guys… I-" Corver says before I intercept.

"Drop it," I mutter as the inside of the vehicle falls silent. With the sounds of various animals in the forest peering into the cabin through the slightly cracked windows, I can't help but feel a sense of guilt overshadowing every other emotion I'm feeling. The silence doesn't persist for long.

"Miles, what else were we going to do? We waited in Duchess County for days…" Corver says before pausing. He's talking slower than usual, yet I can't tell if it's because he is trying not to upset me or because he's awaiting a response. I see him look into the rearview mirror, presumably at Vito, and then back at me. "Even if they did make it out, we wouldn't be able to-" he whispers before being cut off again.

"What did I *just say?!*" I bark out with a tone that demonstrates a loss of patience. Corver shoots me one more look before gluing his attention back on the dirt road. After a minute or so, I shift in my seat and do my best to determine our location based on the seemingly identical scenery around us. Vito taps me on the shoulder, *breaking my observational trance*, and points to the only structure nearby.

"Is that it?" Vito asks as his finger remains in front of him. Corver, now silent, looks to me for confirmation.

"Yeah, that's it. Stop right here. We can walk the rest just in case there are people nearby," I mutter cautiously as the truck slowly comes to a halt. Corver reaches into the center console to retrieve his Beretta, which we partially replenished with a few extra .380 ACP rounds Vito had for his handgun. After glancing at the seemingly abandoned cabin through the bug-ridden windshield, Corver sighs as he opens his door and steps out onto the dirt below.

As I step out of the vehicle myself, I close the door slowly, careful not to give away our position to anyone potentially lurking nearby. Once I turn to face the two-story cabin nearly a quarter mile away, I'm immediately hit with the smell of fresh grass and feel my chest rise as I take a massive breath of air.

Damn, I missed that... The scent of nature.

With extreme caution and paranoia, I glance at Corver and gesture for him to keep his eyes on the front of the structure. He nods before turning to Vito and signals him to follow me instead. Without any audible communication, Vito turns to me and quietly scurries in my direction in an attempt to stay undetected. Vito and I circle the property as we get closer while Corver remains focused on the front entrance.

I take my support hand from under the Glock and make a hand gesture using my thumb and pointing finger, signaling Vito to draw his weapon. Even as a child, he is much more intelligent than most people would assume, given his small demeanor and age. The stainless steel finish on the PPK/S shines in the sunlight above, even with the shade surrounding us from the 20-foot trees overhead. The back door is under the patio, so Vito and I keep our backs against the cabin's exterior stone wall as we creep closer toward the rear entrance. As Vito and I reach the back door, my weapon remains leveled in front of me.

Showtime.

While we position ourselves beside the doorway leading into the basement, I dig into my pocket to retrieve the key to the door and slowly place it into its dedicated slot. The various pins within the lock begin to wiggle as the key is delicately pushed farther inward. Once the key is in, I turn it slowly to conceal the sound of the metal lock retracting before grabbing the rusty door handle and doing the same. With one fell swoop, I push the door open while simultaneously taking a step inside with my handgun in the air.

Silence.

"Stay behind me…" I whisper to Vito, who is still on the other side of the doorway. My eyes are having a hard time adjusting to the sudden darkness. Still, the natural light from behind us makes it easier to identify the various items placed around the room.

Untouched. Wow… I wasn't expecting that.

Picture frames. The TV. Hell, even the First Aid Box I had against the wall on the other side of the room. Everything is where I had left it all those months ago. As if on cue, Vito and I hear the front door on the floor above fling open as Corver abruptly forces his way inside the cabin through the main entrance.

Subtle.

"Miles?!" I hear him call out as the footsteps overhead echo throughout the basement. They're sporadic yet calculated. Even though we can't see him, I can tell he's checking every corner as he makes his way through the first floor of the musty cabin. Vito and I start making our way toward the staircase leading upstairs.

"We're clear down here!" I holler out and give a thumbs-up to Vito. "Watch yourself!" I yell out as the creaking below my feet emanates throughout the narrow corridor. We reach the top of the stairwell, and I push the door open before peeking around the corner with my handgun drawn. I lower my aim once I see Corver instinctively do the same. I point upstairs, causing him to turn to his right and face the stairwell leading to the upper floor. Without wasting a second, I position my body behind him and place my non-dominant hand on his left shoulder, indicating we're clear to ascend.

One step. Then another. Every corner. Every room. Every closet. Every hallway. We check it all. The entire structure has remained untouched since my last trip here and hasn't hosted a living being for nearly a year. As Corver, Vito, and I meet in the main bedroom, we glance out the window facing Millinocket Lake. I throw the bag slung over my shoulder onto the Queen-sized bed to my right before turning to address my remaining companions.

"Welcome to Maine, boys," I say before placing the handgun in my waistband and turning to walk out of the room.

(Three Months Later)

Even as the heat from the stove continues to provide a comforting sense of warmth amid the cold air outside, I barely enjoy it as my intrusive thoughts overwrite any other emotion. The sporadic sounds coming from the wind chimes we had hung up a few weeks back are supposed to drown out the thoughts in my head, anything to avoid the everlasting quiet that usually accompanies such isolation. However, they merely serve as a reminder of my past indiscretions. The smell of burning snaps me out of my trance before I fumble for the fork and flip the sizable pieces of venison in the pan.

I need more pills…

After pouring some olive oil into the pan, I walk over to the bathroom and grab a nearly empty bottle of Adderall from the Alaskan white vanity. The pills had undoubtedly surpassed their expiration date, but they still seem to be slightly potent, given the fact that they've been helping with my focus over the past few weeks. They were prescribed when I had trouble functioning following the shooting that happened on the base. It seems that was the first time I was ever slow on the draw, and it clearly wasn't my last. The thought of screwing up on the rooftop of the *Consulate* makes my hands quiver as I begin shaking the bottle until two sizable capsules fall onto my palm.

I swallow the pills without so much as a drop of water before hesitantly glancing at my reflection in the mirror ahead. With my hair longer than ever and partially concealing my eyes, my attention falls onto the thick facial hair that has sprung from out of nowhere over the past few months. My once kempt goatee was, instead, a shell of its former self as it is currently overshadowed by matted knots and finger-length strands of dark black hair. After an eternity of staring through my reflection rather than at it, I turn away and stumble toward the kitchen.

After preparing some metal utensils at the dinner table, it hits me. The smell of cooking clings to my nostrils as the steam radiating off the medium-well meat and seasoned beans fills the air. Once all the plates are set at the table, I head to the back door and fling it open to address Corver and Vito; the former is holding his position overlooking the lake while the latter sits alongside him.

"It's ready, c'mon!" I shout out as the two simultaneously turn to look at me. Vito wastes no time jumping up and walking towards the cabin, yet the look of concern on Corver's face tells me precisely what he's thinking. "The chances of you starving are higher than someone showing up. Come get something to eat, kid," I say as my hand ushers for him to come inside. Although the cold air is refreshing to me, even as it climbs up my cardigan and causes a shiver, I reckon the boys are tired of the near-zero-degree temperature after being out there all afternoon. Corver grabs his hunting rifle and uses his other hand to lift himself to his feet before following Vito's tracks.

As the door shuts closed behind my two companions, their cheeks start to turn color as they embrace the warmth. Corver props the hunting rifle up against one of the walls in the dining room before glancing down at the plate. We each take a seat around the table and look at each other before touching the food. I know they're hungry, as am I, so I waste no time before beginning to speak.

"I… uh- this meal was possible because of you two. It was a hell of a haul. I know the hunt wasn't easy, and I- I would've helped if it weren't for… well, y'know…" I say as I lift my hands into the air, which are still trembling in the air from my newfound anxiety, before placing them back on the table. "I'm… I'm fighting every day to get back to who I was," I mutter in embarrassment as my mind starts racing with memories I'd like to forget.

"There's nothing wrong with who you are now, man," Corver says as Vito nods in agreement. I should appreciate the sincere sentiment, but it flies over my head once the faces of those who died because of my negligence flood my thoughts. I try to control the trembling in my hands as Vito begins cutting into the meat on his plate. Corver, on the other hand, can read the unease on my face just as well as I did for him just a few moments ago.

"Boss…" Corver mumbles after a few moments of silence around the table.

"Don't call me that…" I whisper with slight aggravation.

"Hey, I know shit around here has been hard," Corver continues before briefly pausing to apologize to Vito for swearing. He looks back up at me after Vito dismisses his apology. "I'm willing to bet that what's going on out here is *nothing* compared to what's going on up there," he says as he points to my forehead. "Yeah, I've seen the pills. I get it. But it's *done*. Hell, we're feeling what you're feeling, too-" Corver says before being cut off as I slam my fist onto the wooden table top. The sound of ceramic plates slamming against the wood echoes throughout the dining room.

"You have *no idea* what I'm feeling," I whisper as contempt and regret take over.

"This kid just lost his mother…" Corver says assertively as he leans closer to the table and extends a finger at Vito. Memories of

Renata flow into my mind, and the feeling of regret and torment only worsen. "I lost my best friend as he was *mercilessly* gunned down by my own goddamn brother. Someone who bleeds the same blood was willing to take my own, and for what?!" he shouts out.

"I lost *everything! Everybody!* All those *kids*, my *friends*, and my *sanity!*" I holler out as I throw the chair backward and stand on my feet. My hunger is replaced with a variety of emotions, half of which I couldn't even describe, and my vision begins to blur from all the water building up in my eyes.

"*Everybody*, huh? That's great. So what... what are *we* then, huh?" Corver asks as he shifts in his seat and places his hands together. "So what the *fuck* are we doing here, Miles?!" Corver yells out as he throws his plate from the table. Vito, who wasn't anticipating the sudden fit of rage, gets startled and jumps up from his chair.

"Guys, please..." Vito says as he wedges himself between Corver and me. His small arms are extending outwards in an attempt to keep us apart from one another.

"You tell me. What *are* we doing here, kid? Waiting ever so fucking patiently while our food runs dry, huh? Waiting until our ammo gets spent? Tell me, why are we not storming that godforsaken building right now and making things right, huh?" I ask as I get close enough to feel his breath hit my face.

"Look, if this is about the power you had when-" Corver whispers.

"This isn't about *power*, Corver. This is about making amends for all the people we swore to look after with our lives. Our *lives!* By the looks of it, we still have ours while theirs are gone..." I say as I begin to lower my tone. "I *never* want that much control again. It turns even the most benevolent person into someone they never thought they'd see when they look in the mirror. Truth be told, we've all got blood on us, yet there comes a moment when you can no longer wash it off..." I confess as I begin rubbing the stump where my ring finger used to be.

"We haven't crossed that line yet, Miles," Corver says in a tone that tells me he's trying to diffuse the situation.

"Kid, we don't even know where the line *is*," I admit. Corver remains silent as he ponders what that statement means, and I use that silence to gradually back away from the table. Vito lowers his arms as I start doing so.

"Where are you going?" Vito asks with a slight voice crack.

"To draw the line…" I say before using my back to open the basement door and start heading into the darkness below.

* * *

Even as I look into the opened gun safe, I can tell there's not enough ammunition to last for another three months, especially when throwing training and scouting into the mix. Still, I take a visual note of everything we have and begin pulling things out.

All in all, I managed to scrounge up a handheld Streamlight, four magazines for the Glock 19, and a 9mm suppressor with stainless steel baffles that fit snugly on the Glock's threaded barrel. There are also half a dozen .357 magnum Hollow Point rounds lying idle on the ground beside the 4" Ruger Revolver I had pulled out of the safe merely seconds ago; alongside the unloaded six-shooter is a compatible black leather shoulder holster that I had only worn once since I purchased it nearly three years ago. In addition, I also pull out a flare gun Vito had previously found on one of the abandoned boats marooned near the lake and the four cartridges accompanying it. After zipping up my bag and placing it on the floor beside me, I put on the shoulder holster and load the revolver before tucking it away; as I stand there, ready to go, I place my hand into the safe to pull out my beloved rifle: *Falkor Petra 300 Winchester with a 6x24 magnified optic.*

Oh, I missed you, darling…

I inspect the rifle to ensure it is oiled and operable before leaning it against my backpack. While sifting through the only box of ammunition for the rifle, I get a better idea of how many rounds I have left for it: *seventeen rounds.*

This will do.

I place a variety of empty magazines, all of which are of different calibers, onto the workbench sitting on the left side of the gun safe and fill them to the brim with loose rounds I pull from their respective boxes. Judging by how the trembling in my hands has subsided, I guess the Adderall kicked in; the stability in my hands makes it much easier to load the magazines. I place one of the magazines into the Glock before racking the slide to load a round into the chamber. The same can be said for the Falkor before setting it back down against the safe.

As I turn to grab my bag, I notice the slightly creepy mannequin wearing the military-grade gear I had collected over the years. *The familiar-looking dark olive plate carrier. The black ballistic helmet. My monocular night vision module. My duty belt.* Everything I had trained in over the years was staring back at me with a blank, pale expression. I couldn't help but ponder how my life could've been different had I taken the man's life that night I was injured on duty. Either way, I lost a part of me that day that I still can't identify. As I look into the milky, nonexistent eyes of the mannequin, I keep imagining how that would've been me on the inside had I kept down the path I was on just a few months ago.

"I won't go back to who I was if it means I'll lose who I am…" I whisper to the mannequin as if I were talking to myself.

As I hoist the backpack up on my shoulders, I glance above the workbench to see various office supplies covered in dust, including a notepad. I pull them down and swipe the dust from the notepad before grabbing a pen. Even as the black ink pen sits idly in between my fingers, I can't help but ponder what to write. It takes me nearly a minute to finally realize what I should say: *the truth.*

* * *

With the cold coming through the cracks in the windowsill, the cabin feels much colder than it is. I can almost taste the smell of food lingering in the air every time I take a deep breath. Miles has been downstairs for a while, so I wonder what he's doing. The wooden floor over my head creaks as Corver walks around upstairs; as I listen to his footsteps, he seems to be walking in circles.

Why are Miles and Corver mad at each other?

I hear the door leading downstairs slam shut, causing me to run over to the backdoor and tippy-toe for a better look outside. I see Miles for a second before he turns the corner and heads toward the front of the cabin. Without wanting to make too much noise, I drag my feet on the floor until I stop in front of the brown couch by the door. My knees sink into the sofa once I pull myself up and look out the big window facing the woods.

As I look through the window, I can see Miles throw a bag into the trunk of the truck we drove here a while ago. He looks through the bag and grabs a gun I have never seen before tucking it into the front of his belt. The sound of wind outside mutes Miles's already quiet movement.

What is he-

As I move the curtain to the side for a better view of the front, I hear Corver's feet hit the bottom of the stairs. I don't want him to know I was being nosy, so I throw myself to face forward on the couch and pretend like I was watching the dark TV ahead. Corver looks at me before staring out of the partially open window and looking back at me; after letting out a deep sigh, Corver starts walking to the front door.

"Stay here. I won't be long," Corver says as he grabs the now-open door from behind and closes it as he steps out. The fresh air only worsens my need to know what is happening, so I place my knees back on the couch and look out the window again. I can see Miles turning to look at Corver as he makes his way down the wooden steps and toward the truck. I can't hear what Corver is saying, but his arms are to the side. Maybe he's asking him what I'm thinking.

I can see Miles's lips moving as he steps toward Corver before the two stop nearly a foot away from each other. It seems like they're out there forever before I can't take it anymore. Trying to stay hidden, I try to yank the window open for a better listen, but it doesn't budge.

Great.

As I place my elbows on the back of the couch in defeat, I see Corver's hands resting on his waist. He looks like he's shaking his head, but maybe I'm seeing things. I am not a good lip reader, but I think I can make out some of the words Miles says: *Town? City? Some bad words I'm not allowed to say?* I'm not too sure. He puts his hand on Corver's shoulder and leaves it there while he keeps talking. Miles notices me staring from the window and turns his head to the side to hide his words from me. Before anyone can do anything else, Corver wraps his arms around Miles's neck before pushing himself off and nodding at Miles. Just like that, the conversation ends as quickly as it started.

As Corver turns and stares at the ground while walking back to the Cabin, I see Miles turn his eyes back to me. I can't tell if he was mad at me or disappointed. The only thing I can do is stare back at him from the frosted window. All it takes is a single smile to make it clear what's going on through his head: *he's proud.*

"I'll see you soon, kid!" Miles yells as he brings both hands to his mouth like a bullhorn. That's the only thing I hear clearly, even with the windows closed. With that, he gives me a grin before opening the car door and shutting it behind him as he sits in the driver's seat. As Corver opens the cabin door, I hear the truck turn on and sit there for a few seconds before driving into the woods and out of sight.

"Get some rest, kiddo. It's going to be a long night," Corver says as he makes his way past me and toward the staircase leading back upstairs. At that moment, I can't take his advice. All I can do is stare into the never-ending trees ahead, wondering what happens now.

CHAPTER 16

VISIONARY

Journal Entry: Guilt is a funny feeling. It has a way of turning even the most rational being into someone who acts purely on emotion. At least I recognize it, but I don't care. All I know is that I can't let Graham Whitlock live after what he's done. That motherfucker has to die. I couldn't tell the boy. He'd probably sneak into the truck to tag along. There must be more for him than the violence he's seen. And Corver... I need to do this alone. I have to. It's been a hard couple of weeks, yet I'm two and a half hours out from the Consulate (if there's even anything left of it). If that piece of shit is still inside, it's my job to make sure he doesn't ever come out...

DAY 1: HE DID IT... *This piece of shit actually had the gall... the audacity... the balls to make the Consulate his own personal fucking real estate. To the naked eye, the building stands out amongst the others around it due to the grotesque nature surrounding its exterior. Anyone with a sane mind would see this place as the embodiment of hell itself. The best I can do is try to put the repulsive sight into words.*

The first thing I noticed was the mutilated heads of various people hanging from the rooftop (most of which I recognize as Thriver's who were in the Consulate when it was in flames). Piles of bodies lined up along the inside of the fence. I can hear the fucking flies from here. And the scent? Even as I sit across the street in this 500-square-foot apartment

I had cleared last year, in case I needed time to myself, the smell radiating from that courtyard may as well be coming from the hallways in this building. In one of the classrooms, I noticed four guys having too much "fun" with a woman who seemed to be half their age. By the looks of it, the woman in question doesn't seem to reciprocate their excitement, as she's pointlessly flailing to get away from her aggressive suitors. Fucking animals...

No sign of Graham yet. Nor that of Sandman. Just a bunch of guys throughout the building (some I used to serve myself in the Cafeteria), while others I've never seen at all. This is the first time I got a good look at the charred walls at the front of the Consulate from the last night I was here. The place is a mess, yet only a group this fuckin' sick can rest their heads on a pillow and call that home.

I don't care about sleep, and I've got enough food here to last me weeks. Good thing, too. Because I'm not leaving 'til I know these guys like the back of my hand.

Day 2*: How didn't I see it sooner? These heartless sonsabitches. I couldn't even count them all... the people ~~that I~~ that WE used to call family - ~~or what was left of them~~ - had their heads strewn on goddamn ropes over the ledge of the Consulate's rooftop: Herman. Lance. Kimberly. Ervin. Oscar. So many Thrivers... After a while, I stopped counting entirely.*

The taste of vomit is still fresh on my lips even as I write this, but my anger has just reached all-new proportions. There's no doubt about it anymore: These people <u>have</u> to die.

Day 4*: There's been a lot of commotion coming from the rear of the building that I can't see. From what I can tell, it's not just Graham's guys. There've been a few sightings of Ravelers being escorted around the Consulate. I can also hear trucks pulling in and out like clockwork. I've jotted down all the times over the past few days, and the average time there's been massive activity on the road is 7:43 am and 9:37 pm. They've got Vehicular Patrols around the block twice per hour. There have also been two days straight where there hasn't been any activity at around 3 am. Are the guards getting lazy? Maybe I can use this...*

As for the front, I noticed two large school buses with the windows covered in what appears to be a mix of newspaper clippings, clothing, and paint. The groans coming from the inside, mixed with the consistent rocking every so often, tell me that this is some new line of defense this bastard has set up. But why? Parts of me don't want the answer to that question. The lack of sleep is getting to me, but I'll keep an eye out for anything I can find.

[Update @11:29pm] Two guards stumbled into the lobby of the apartment building I'm hiding out in about half an hour ago, yet I took them out before they realized that they weren't alone in the first place. Even with the shots suppressed, I waited a few more minutes while watching the Consulate for activity in case I gave myself away. Nothing. I don't think they were searching for me because there would've been a hell of a lot more than two guys if my position was compromised. Got some good shit in the process, though…

Day 6: I saw these bastards! Fuckers pulled up to the front of the building in a caravan as if they were expecting the red carpet: and they fuckin' got it! A sentry of half a dozen guards with rifles came out of the front and surrounded Graham like he was the Pope. I noticed his beard had grown just as much as mine had, yet even from here, I could tell he'd recently had a fresh haircut. Sandman was right on his heels. The two met with a much older man - no doubt one of the last surviving Colonists - who seemed to have been waiting for their arrival for a while. A few minutes passed, and I saw Sandman scribble something into a large book the older man was carrying before throwing it onto the ground and barking at his men nearby. Even across the street, I could make out what Luca said: "Get him his shit, then get 'em out of here." ~~Arrogant prick.~~

Not even fifteen minutes later, the old geezer hops into a rusty box truck that I can only assume was filled with commodities from the Consulate. I guess I know what deal Damien cooked up with these assholes: My death in exchange for access to the Network. So much for ridding the world of these assholes.

I was also right about the patrols. 3 am seems to be the sweet spot. I'll remember that. The heat was speeding up the decomposition of the two dead pricks lying dead in the stairwell, and the smell was too much to bear, so I dragged them out back where they wouldn't be found should any more curious souls stumble into my newfound home.

Day 8: *The handheld I picked up from my friends out back has proven useful over the past few days. I've come to learn that these assholes call themselves **Lockers** [three question marks back to back alongside the word]. I assume this egotistical fuck made that up using his last name. I can't wait to put this bitch into the ground. I've also recorded every time the patrols have announced their shift changes. The only shift that doesn't rotate is those lying waiting in the Overwatch Convoy, which I used to feel so safe around. As far as I can tell, they go radio silent after 2:20 am every morning. I have a feeling that will come in handy.*

Day 9: ~~Nothing new to report.~~
[Update @1:14pm] I saw him again… This time was different, though. Someone was shot and thrown from the rooftop for reasons I can't comprehend. I could see the glare shining off of Graham's stainless steel handgun as he mercilessly gunned down that poor woman. It looked like the woman I had seen in the window last week, but I don't know why. Quite frankly, I don't want to know why. The sound of the woman hitting the pavement made me wince instantly as I recall the moment I did the same and barely survived: a memory I'd eventually like to forget. I could barely understand what was being said over the radio as the chanting from various people caused me to dial the volume down. These guys are fucking sick.

Day 12: *The food in the apartment is damn well near gone, and the juice in the radio isn't too far behind. I have to be conservative now, but I think I'm coming up on the time to make a move. The dark clouds above tell me it will rain soon, and that may be EXACTLY what I need. I've got all I need about the outside, yet I need to know what's happening behind closed doors… Tomorrow night will be the time to make that happen, and I've got a plan to do just that…*

CHAPTER 17

ENDURE

TO MY SURPRISE, THE STAIRWELLS leading up to the Bedford Park Station are still barricaded from when we had sealed off each entry point all those months ago. Deep down, I didn't think a mix of plywood and two-inch thick metal chains would withstand the threats roaming the streets nowadays, especially when faced with human adversaries, but I had come prepared nevertheless. While positioning my body against the wooden panel, I discretely glance into the station to see if any sentries had been sent up here without my knowledge.

I don't see anybody...

As I set down the half-full green jerry can near my feet, I pull off the bolt cutters hanging from the side of the backpack. Even though the tool is slightly rusted, it cuts through the metal as if the chain were a thin string of rope a boy scout would use to tie knots at summer camp. I quietly drop the bolt cutters alongside the severed chain lying idle on the floor before using both hands to position the pry bar between the wood and the doorframe; once set in place, I pull back on the pry bar with as much force as possible. With just a little effort and time, the sound of wood hitting the ground can be heard echoing from below the train tracks.

We're in.

With the tools being dragged into the station and set to the side of the doorway, I grab the Glock tucked behind my belt and start twisting the suppressor onto the threaded barrel before ensuring a round is loaded into the chamber; after spending a moment listening for any movement around me, I lift the handgun in the air as I venture further into the musty, abandoned train station. As my barrel sweeps every corner of the room, I can't help but reminisce about how crowded these places used to be back in the day. What I used to consider an annoyance is now serving as a sense of comfort as I try to maintain my composure while taking one step at a time into the unknown ahead.

While ascending the stairwell to the platform above, I do my best to stabilize my hand since the sound of the liquid splashing around in the metallic gas may as well be giving away my position to anyone lurking nearby. As my head clears the last step, giving me a clear view of the entire platform, I focus on two *Spectrals* standing idly near the end of the Downtown Platform. They're about forty feet away from me but standing mere inches away from one another.

Shit, that's where I need to go...

Without wanting to make too much noise, I quietly lower the jerry can onto the landing of the stairwell and glance at the other side of the platform behind me to ensure there are no more surprises. *Clear on that end.* I refocus on the *Specs* ahead and start shuffling in their direction. The cover of night helps suppress their speed and aggression, yet I know they can still see, so I do my best to mask my footsteps with the light rain hitting the metal shutters above our heads. They're both turned the other way, so I use their lowered perception as an opportunity to remove my blade from its sheath.

Ten feet... Eight feet... Five...

The sounds of their groans make me quiver slightly as I inch closer, and the cold accompanying the rain isn't helping, either; with a firm understanding of how fast things can turn for the worst, I don't let them out of my sight for a second. When I am about an arm's length away, I lunge forward and forcefully bring the knife down onto the top of the closest *Spec's* skull. It let out a faint grunt as the knife went in, yet it ceased as quickly as it started as the weight of its body dragged itself to the ground. The other *infected anomaly*, which seems to be the deteriorating remains of a middle-aged woman who's about half the size of the *Spectral* now lying at my feet, turns and lets out a shriek that is quickly eradicated with a single 9mm bullet from the suppressed Glock.

Crack.

The sound of the bullet hitting the metal wall behind the *Spec* was louder than the shot itself, so I didn't worry too much about giving my position away to anyone nearby. Within mere seconds after the ordeal starts, I'm left standing alone to embrace the ambiance of raindrops and all the mugginess accompanying it. With the gas can now back in hand, I hoist myself onto the train tracks below and make my way to the next stop: *Kingsbridge Road*.

***

The rain makes it difficult to keep my balance on the wooden portion of the tracks below, but I still manage to get close enough to the *Overwatch Convoy*. I place the gas can on the side of the track before gripping the pistol with both hands and cautiously approaching the idle train cars ahead. With each step I take, I am half expecting to hear chatter from within the Convoy, but it never comes. Without taking my hands off the weapon, I twist my wrist slightly and glance down at the black G-shock attached to my wrist.

2:51 am

With my eyes set on the train, I continue my advance until stopping near the end of the train car. Without lowering my sidearm, I grab the railing at the end of the train to hoist myself onto the ledge leading into the driver's compartment. The distant outlines of four people, nearly two train cars down, can be seen as I glance through the window; they all seem to be sleeping, but I can't verify the number from this distance. Expecting it to be locked, I push on the door and realize my assumption is correct as it fails to budge even slightly.

Well, shit…

I use the same railing to hoist me back onto the tracks and stealthily walk around the train, staying well below the windows. As I start pushing past the train car with the *Lockers,* I keep my body positioned against its naked aluminum walls with every step I take. Once I'm past them, I use both hands to propel myself onto the platform of the train station. Now that I'm on solid ground, it's easier to maneuver around. With the gun raised, I slowly approach the train again before stopping abruptly at the sound of moaning from the bottom of the stairwell leading into the train station's lower level.

Out of instinct, I divert my aim in the direction of the noise. After a second of hesitation, I quickly glance at the men in the *Overwatch Convoy,* unaffected by the various noises surrounding them. I refocus on the stairwell and quietly start descending them with my gun in the air.

As I descend toward the middle of the staircase, I pause and bend down to get a better view of the station without fully exposing myself to whoever, or *whatever,* maybe down there. As I scan the musty room from right to left, I notice a man sitting in the booth near the center. The man moans as I position myself against the railing on the staircase for better shot alignment. Even from about twelve feet away, I can see he's looking at an explicit magazine that seems to be on the brim of falling apart in his left hand. I don't even *want to know* what he's doing with the other.

As I peer through the glass on the door separating the bottom of the stairwell I'm crouched near the center of the train station, I notice that the door to the booth itself is wide open. All I have to do is open *this* door without a sound, and he's mine. Without taking my eyes off the back of the *Locker's* head, I use my support hand to slowly fumble in front of me until I feel the door's metallic handle. I glance at the door's hinges, praying they don't creak as I pull it open, then back at the preoccupied man as the door creeps open.

Don't turn around. Don't turn around. Easy does it…

As the door is opened enough for me to pass through, I pull a spare magazine from its pouch on my belt and quietly prop it under the door to keep it from slamming shut. As the door leading into the stairwell remains open, I cautiously approach the man until I am right behind him. Amidst his "leisurely activity," I see his face turn white as he glances at me from the reflection emanating from the glass window in front of the booth. Before he can even stand, as best as he could anyways, given his pants were around his ankles, I drop the gun and place one hand over his mouth before wrapping my other arm around the man's neck. His inaudible words are muffled, but I let out a slight shriek as he finds enough space to bite down on my hand.

Ah, motherfucker!

I let go of his mouth and, instead, use both hands to tighten my grip on his throat and restrict his airflow. With every thrash, with every thrust, the man seems to be getting weaker at the knees until his body weight gives out from under him, and he falls unconscious. I quickly pick up the handgun from the floor and throw myself into a 180-degree spin as I align the iron sights with the door I had propped open, listening to any sounds that may follow. A second turns into a minute, and the continuous sounds of rain hitting the windows around the station reassure me that no one upstairs heard the commotion. *If they had, they'd be down here by now.*

"Alright, I'll be back for you soon. Don't go anywhere…" I whisper to the unconscious man as I take a set of zip ties from my bag and secure his wrists behind his back. Using my hands, I forcefully rip the guy's shirt off and tie it around his mouth using a knot he can't undo unless he's a magician. With the *Locker* temporarily out of commission, it's time to play the rest of my cards.

* * *

Standing motionless between two train cars, I slowly open the sliding door leading into the compartment of the *Overwatch Convoy*, where the men are fast asleep. As the opened door amplifies the sound of the rain and wind outside, some of the silhouettes in the darkness start to shutter from the noise. None of the men seem bothered enough to care, though, as they all choose to remain asleep even as I make my way into the convoy.

Now that I have a better view of the train car, I can count five guys in total. With the sliding door quietly being shut behind me, I holster the Glock and proceed to take out my knife. As I tower over to the first *Locker*, who's heavily snoring on one of the benches in the middle of the Convoy, he jolts awake as I cover his mouth with the palm of my hand. Unlike his half-naked associate downstairs, he barely has enough time to retaliate as I slide the knife into his jugular. There is *so* much blood, but I manage to maintain my strength as the man tries his mighty best to release his screams of agony into the open air, *to no avail*. As the man's body is quietly laid back down, *lifeless*, the only sound I hear is the sound of the blade retracting from his skin as I remove it.

Without wasting much time, I do the same to the next guy sleeping mere feet away. Then the next. With only two guys left, I reach the one lying on a makeshift cot held up by ropes attached to the overhead railings. The smell of blood and iron fills my nostrils as I bring the tainted knife up for another swing. Before I can bring the knife down, however, I hear the only other male left alive in the room grunt as he wakes from his slumber and charges me with a collapsible baton. There is not an *ounce* of hesitation in his body.

Instinctively, I swing my body around and wait for him to get close enough before using my forearm to block the swing of the man's baton. Even as a near miss, the pain associated with the sheer force from his swing suddenly coming to a complete stop seems to transpire throughout my whole body, but I use this momentum to twist the *Locker's* arm and slam him onto the floor. Before he can gather the wind that was just knocked out of him, I bend his arm until his bone is protruding from it. The scream he lets out bounces off the walls of the train as he unconsciously grabs his broken arm once I let it go.

The man attempting to stand up from his cot is put down with two suppressed shots fired in quick succession from the Glock that is quickly drawn from my belt. The dusty white ropes hoisting up the cot become stained with dark red ooze that came out of the deceased man's body as he slumps backward into an awkward position. I move my overgrown hair to the side to regain a full field of view and slowly turn to the incapacitated *Locker*. He's fumbling for the baton with his good hand and manages to grab it and swing it at my legs with little effort. With ease, I grab his hand mid-swing and yank the blunt weapon out of it before using as much force as I could muster to swing it at his jaw. His face falls to the ground, accompanied by a few teeth, and I stand over his body before repeatedly swinging the heat-treated baton onto the back of his now-idle head. By the time I am done, I notice that the baton is severely bent as it's effortlessly thrown onto the ground next to the ever-growing pool of blood gathering at my feet.

Well, that was dramatic…

The room is as quiet now as it was when I first stepped in. I glance around in the dark and take a mental note of everything now for the taking: firearms of various calibers, unopened MREs piled up underneath the benches, and a spotting scope to help with long-distance engagements. Not a bad haul. As I stand there in the dark, the blood in the convoy seemingly sticking to my pores, I remind myself that there's one more thing that needs to be done before anything else.

***

With little room to move, the now fully naked *Locker* jolts awake from the brief coma I had induced nearly half an hour earlier, but he only manages to move the same distance a tortoise would if it were faced with the same dilemma. His eyes widen as he scans the room to better assess what's happening. He catches me leaning against the desk in the booth we're in before his eyes become fixated on me. The hatred that fills them is something I haven't seen since I was last face-to-face with Graham over three months ago.

"Now that I've got your attention, let's begin…" I say aloud as I use both hands to propel myself to my feet. The man tugs at his restraints, which are firmly holding his forearms against the cushioned armrests on the chair he was jerking off in before I got here, but lets out a sigh of disappointment as he realizes that his futile attempt to change the circumstances of his situation had failed miserably. I grab a pair of wire strippers I had brought for occasions like this before bending both of my knees until my face is leveled with his. "I have a feeling that I already know what you're going to say, but I'll do you the courtesy of giving you a chance to die with dignity. Where is Graham's weapon cache?" I demand without showing any emotion.

"Y- you must be the one he always talks about…" the restrained male lets out alongside a half-assed laugh that only seems to agitate me. "I can see why you're always the topic of discussion in that place. You've got a set of balls the size of the Empire State!" the man shouts as he starts to laugh again.

"And if you expect to keep yours, I highly recommend you answer my question," I suggest as I stare into the man's eyes. It's as if I am looking into his soul for an answer, but I can't say for sure that he understands the gravity of the situation he is in. His response confirms that suspicion.

"We both know how this is going to go, *Miles,*" he says in a near whisper as he grips the edge of the armrest with his hands. I place my hands on my knees and use my weight to stand up tall as my eyes remain fixated on the vulnerable man in front of me.

"Yeah, I think we do, don't we?" I ask sarcastically before punching him as hard as I could in the nose. I know for a fact that it's broken judging by the sound and the stream of blood flowing out of both nostrils; the man releases both of his hands from the armrest in response to the pain. With the wire strippers in the opened position, I grab his hand and place them near the base of his pointing finger before squeezing the tool shut as hard as possible and pulling the blades outwards. The man's shouts are deafening as I forcefully strip the skin from his finger as slowly and methodically as I would for anyone else who calls themself a member of this sadistic organization. He closes his bloodied hand tight as I open the tool to remove the excess skin I had peeled from his finger.

"Is *this* how you thought it was going to go?" I holler out so the man can hear me over his own agonizing shouts. He lets out a few profanities as he flails about in his seat, no doubt a mix of both anger and an attempt to get his mind off the persisting pain in his hand, and tries his best to catch a steady breath. I don't even bother repeating the question as I smack his bloodied fist with great force and place the tool on the *Locker's* middle finger as his hand opens up again.

W- wait! Wait! Wait!" he pleads to deaf ears as I continue with my morally ambiguous method of torture. The tool's blades become lodged in his epidermis, causing me to yank harder to remove the skin. Blood is flying all over the place, but I can safely say I am not in the right state of mind to give it much thought. With two fingers down, I do my best to clean the tool in preparation for number three.

"I know better than anyone what losing a finger or two feels like. Now I guess you do, too," I say with a whole-hearted laugh as I grab his injured hand for a third time.

"No! No! It- it's in the elevator! He- He keeps it all in the *fucking elevator!*" the man shouts with more sound than I thought the human vocals were capable of producing. As if he didn't answer the question at all, I place the blades of the wire strippers onto his ring finger before pressing down tightly on them with the tool.

"And what about your boss's quarters? Huh? Where does that prick lay his head at night!? *Speak when being spoken to!*" I holler out as I grip the tool tighter and tighter with each passing second. The man's pleas for mercy go in one ear and out of the other as the pressure on his finger becomes nearly unbearable.

"Fuck, I don't know! *No one does!* I- I- I- I always see him on the fifth floor when I'm on patrols! The gym, but I don't know if-" he says as I rip the skin off his ring finger with one fell swoop. Under normal circumstances, I'd be concerned about the unwanted attention all of the screaming would cause beyond these walls, yet this was anything but a normal situation. I throw the tool as hard as I can at the window behind the *Locker's* head, shattering it in the process as I immediately lift the barrel of my Glock at the temple of the bleeding man before me.

"*Liar!*" I shout as I take a step forward. "Tell me the truth!" I holler as the end of the suppressor rests against the man's temple.

"I swear to God! I'm not lying! I swear! I swear… I swear…" the man says repeatedly as we both try to catch our breaths. He starts to cry as I gather my thoughts.

Along with all of the random shit lying around the interior of the booth is a small notebook. I pick it up and skimp through it, unintentionally leaving traces of fresh blood on the nearly perfect white sheets of paper as I do, before noticing what it was on them: *All of the Traders from my Network.* There are hand-drawn maps of their locations and various lines struck through the names of the people I used to consider trusted associates. Nearly all the traders, names I grew familiar with, are accompanied by ominous red lines that only signify one thing.

"You *killed them…*" I whisper as my mind fails to wrap around the news. As I continue to flip through the pages, there are a plethora of gruesome and detailed drawings depicting various mutilations, limb severances, and other heinous acts that I can't put words to. Every name had a photo to go along with it. It's like a morbid collection of horrible postcards from hell; amongst all of the horrors experienced today, this alone is almost too much to cope with. The hatred in my eyes as I pick my head up to stare at the man sitting in front of me feels as though I can set him on fire with just a glance.

"I didn't want to. B- but we only did it because-" he says before being cut off.

"Because you can't *live with yourself* knowing there are good people out there just trying to *stay alive*," I retaliate as I wrap my hand around his throat to prevent him from speaking again. "You savages burnt down *everything* I had given my life to build," I say as I forcefully push the man away from me. The chair the *Locker* was sitting on comes to a stop after rolling backward a couple of feet.

"Don't worry, though…" I say in a monotone voice that can only be described as emotionless. I grab the nearly empty gas can sitting directly outside of the booth and stand directly over the man, who is frantically flailing around in his seat in an attempt to get free of his restraints. The strong scent of gasoline fills the air as the cap is removed from the can and thrown onto the ground. "What goes around, comes around, I suppose…" I say before dousing the man with all the gasoline remaining in the can.

If he hadn't tried to get free before, he *definitely* is now, even as his desperate gasps for air remain futile. In the wake of his squirming, I grab his face and carelessly pour gasoline into his mouth before pushing him away and throwing the can behind him. I reach into my bag and pull out a set of matches that somehow managed to stay dry amidst the heavy rain outside.

"I'm going to burn all of them down to their roots. As for right now, I guess I'll have to start with you," I say as the match strikes the box and is thrown to the ground once ignited. The gust of heat accompanying the immediate flame causes me to instinctively step back as the fire quickly engulfs the man before me. His screams could only be described as that of a wounded animal squealing without vocal cords.

The flames quickly spread throughout the entire booth and, with the notebook in hand serving as a reminder of Graham's recent atrocities, I light another match before throwing it down on the trail of gasoline at the bottom of the stairwell, leading upstairs and directly into the middle of the convoy above. The flames and crackling sounds gradually become louder as the train is set alight. I nod with satisfaction and bend down to grab the green duffle bag containing the commodities I had stolen upstairs. Without so much as another thought, I hoist the bag over my shoulder and push through the turnstile, leading into the darkness outside and toward what I can only describe as the beginning of the end.

CHAPTER 18

RETRIBUTION

THE BLAZE COMING FROM THE *Overwatch Convoy* can be seen from another borough. It's fierce enough to illuminate the entire block and does so with little effort. As I duck down behind one of the corroded school buses in front of the *Consulate*, all of the commotion unraveling at the train station is causing the *Lockers* to run around chaotically in an attempt to assess what was going on. I hear the gate leading into the rear courtyard being dragged open as a small group of nearly half a dozen armed goons begin traversing toward the untamable inferno.

As my head peers around the bus to get a better view of the sentry positioned above the main entrance, who is frantically shouting into his radio on the balcony where the armory used to be months prior, I nearly jump out of my skin as the entire vehicle rocks back and forth; I can only imagine the infected inside are responding to the mayhem unraveling only a few hundred yards away. The sounds of groaning from within are heard as clearly as if there's no barricade between myself and whatever creatures lie idle inside.

Jesus, how many are in there?

I can't put a number on the amount of *Specs* they're keeping inside the bus, but I don't want to spend too much time pondering it. My focus remains on the chain securing the sliding door in front of the vehicle. As I place the commodity-filled duffle bag at my feet, I grab the bolt cutters still hanging off my bag and cautiously inch toward the front of the bus while the sentry above is distracted. With the *Locker's* back turned to me, I wrap a portion of the chain with the shirt I had previously ripped off his burning associate two blocks down to muffle the sound of my infiltration. The severed chain lets off a nearly inaudible sound as it's severed, and I use my elbow to prevent it from smacking against the side of the bus. *I can't give away my position now.* With the sliding door leading into the front of the bus slightly ajar, briefly exposing the silhouettes moving around in the darkness, I quietly take one step backward at a time and toward the side of the bus facing away from the *Consulate*.

Almost as if luck is my biggest adversary, the sound of the bolt cutters slamming into the side of the bus as I turn the corner forces the sentry standing overhead to divert his attention toward the front of the *Consulate*. Toward the buses nearly three dozen feet below him. Toward *me*. My heart is racing out of my chest, and as I hold my breath, it only seems to increase in speed. While leaning motionless against the bus, my peripherals pick up a stream of light that appears to be checking each corner around me.

Fuck. I can't move with that light ... wait, light!

With as little commotion as possible, I reach for the Streamlight in my bag. I cover a portion of the light with my hand, so as not to reveal my location to the threat looming overhead, and turn it on before aiming it through the poorly covered windows of the bus behind me. With the light flowing into the dark, cramped abyss, I get a slightly better look at the *Specs* within. *There are dozens of them.* In response to the illumination, the creatures in the bus begin frantically moving around. I switch off the light as quickly as it is turned on and turn my head towards the sentry's spotlight, which darts toward the front of the bus once the groaning inside grows ferociously as I peer around the rear to get a better view of the balcony.

Even from this distance, I can see the white leaving the *Locker's* face as the chaos unfolding around him only seems to be compounding with every passing second. The commotion inside the bus gradually dies once I turn the light off, but their agonizing moans still fill the humid air around me. I don't think the sentry notices the severed chain that was previously holding the sliding door shut, which is only confirmed once I see him turn toward the balcony window and lift his radio to shout out incomprehensible slurs to whoever was on the other end of the line. I kneel to grab the duffle bag before using the confusion and the cover of light rain to sprint toward the apartment overlooking the front of the *Consulate*.

* * *

Even as the hallways in the residential building seem to be soaking in the light radiating from the train station's inferno, I focus on catching my breath as the door to my apartment is hastily flung open. I throw the duffle to the ground closest to the window that the nearly eight-foot-long wooden dining table is propped up against and rummage through the contents inside until I find what I am looking for: *the flare gun.*

No turning back now…

I pry the flare gun open to ensure it's loaded before glancing at the bed sheet covering the table. As I place the flare gun down near the window, the sheet is yanked off to reveal the Falkor Petra lying idly on its bipod; its cold, free-floating barrel is facing the front of the *Consulate*. The table creaks as I lift myself on top of it and get in a prone position; I *half expect the weight to give out from under me as I do, but it holds sturdy*. The charging handle is pulled back slightly until I notice the faint glare of a .300 Winchester Magnum cartridge sitting in the chamber. The covers on the magnified optic are removed until I can get a clear picture of what's in front of me. Once ready, with the comb of the rifle's stock tucked comfortably beneath my shoulder, I take a few breaths before grabbing the flare gun and slowly aiming it near the front gate of my former home.

So much for drawing the line…

The sound of the flare igniting indoors is nearly deafening as the sound bounces off the walls of the confined space I'm in, but it soon passes as the burning propellant lands in the front courtyard of the *Consulate*. It's almost as if the train station's illumination is being overwritten for the first time by another object, and the *Spectrals* within the abandoned buses seem to take notice of that, as well.

Even with the windows covered, the light is bright enough to make every silhouette within the vehicle as clear to me as if there was no cover at all. It doesn't take long before the banging starts. Before the windows begin cracking. Before the windows begin shattering. Dozens of *Specs* pour onto the concrete below through various exit points created out of pure anger and desperation. Even as I lie on the other side of the bus, I can see multiple bodies pile onto one another as they fall from the open door at the front of the vehicle. As the once desolate streets become littered with ravenous beings, accompanied by their intolerable moaning, the *Lockers* seem to waste no time trying to control the ever-worsening situation.

"Who the fuck- The doghouse is loose! They're coming out of the doghouse! Fuckin' all of them!" I hear one of them shout on the balcony even as I lay nearly 300 yards away. "Kill the lights! Kill the lights!" the *Locker* shouts into the radio before positioning his handgun over the rail for stability as he starts firing at the crowd clawing at the gate. As the sudden flashes from his muzzle are made apparent, I adjust the rifle to face the *Locker* directly. With my sight lined up with his body, I quickly brush my overgrown hair to the side and position the reticle near his crotch before taking a deep breath and firing. Initially, the sound of glass breaking from the window behind him, which previously led into the armory, is the first thing I hear before the *Locker's* screams of pain fill the air.

Through the second-floor window, I briefly see the lights from the hallway illuminate the balcony as two *Lockers*, a female who looks no longer than twenty-five and a middle-aged male standing nearly double her size, rush into the now empty armory. I assume they're attempting to investigate the sentry's sudden agonizing hollers, but I don't give them the time to do so as my reticle aligns with the upper torso of the larger *Locker*.

Bang.

The man drops his rifle as quickly as he has entered the room, but he remains standing while he clutches the entry wound near his right lung. I'm almost impressed at how he could withstand the force of such a powerful rifle cartridge. The subsequent shot impacts directly in his other lung, forcing his body to go stiff and drop to the floor with a nearly inaudible thud from my perspective. The woman beside him doesn't move, presumably too stunned from what she just experienced, and slowly glances outside of the window as a round effortlessly pierces her neck. Unlike her associate, the shot instantly puts her out of commission.

That's two…

The chains holding the front gate to the *Consulate* violently break apart with the gate itself is flung open as nearly two dozen *Specs* ferociously throw themselves against it in an attempt to reach the flare; once in the front courtyard, a few of the infected reach for the withering flare, itself, while the remainder make their way toward the double doors out front. The mere sight of the carnage brings back flashbacks of the previous attacks on the *Consulate*. The difference, however, lies in the fact that this one will be successful; I am not leaving until they're all dead. I bring the reticle back up toward the screaming *Locker* rolling on the floor and stop once it's hovering over his forehead. I hold steady as I exhale and pull the trigger back with one clean stroke once my lungs are depleted of air.

Three.

As the seemingly fragile barrier is taken off its hinges, the *Specs* finally make their way into the *Consulate*. Just before the lights cut out, I scan each floor through their respective windows and see many of the occupants making a run for the stairwells, no doubt to fend off the threat piling into their home one body at a time. As a plethora of gunfire fills the air from within the building, I slide off the table and place the rifle on the table before putting the flare gun into my pack and slinging it. I also grab a Palmetto State Armory JAKL taken from the Overwatch Convoy and double-check the magazine is full of 5.56 caliber rounds before heading out of the apartment and into the cold abyss ahead.

****

The streets are filled with bodies, both living and otherwise, so I use the rain and darkness to my advantage as I run toward the East Courtyard entrance. As I approach the gate, which is held shut by a two-and-a-half-ton Humvee on the other side and blocked off by barbed wire above, I scan the windows with the rifle before placing it on the concrete below once I confirm the area is clear. I grab the bolt cutters and begin snipping the thin wire overhead before cautiously unraveling it until there is enough space for me to climb over.

Usually, I'd treat every rifle with as much love and care as anyone would a child, but with little time to waste, I throw it over the gate and hear it land with a muffled thud on the top of the humble. After scanning the windows once more to see if anyone heard the commotion, I prop myself over the gate using the front bumper of the Humvee as leverage. There is a short pain in my shoulder as I push myself over the top, but the adrenaline rushing through my body prevents me from acknowledging it any further. I grab the hand guard of the rifle before sliding off the vehicle and landing on the wet concrete of the East Courtyard.

With every step toward the rear entrance leading into the Cafeteria, I can't help but quickly glance at the spot where Corver and I had landed after barely escaping Graham's assassination attempt. Sometimes, you can't stop remembering the things you'd like to forget, but I use this horrid memory as a reminder of my objective. I stop at the edge of the building and peer around the corner slightly to get a better view of the rear courtyard. A handful of *Lockers* begin prepping their vehicles as the sounds of malicious groaning from around the *Consulate* grow substantially.

"Let's go! Let's go! Flank them from the front!" I hear one of them shout as they run towards the West gate to clear a path for the vehicles to exit the courtyard. I realign my focus on the Rear Cafeteria Entrance, which is locked from the inside, and grab the pry bar hanging on the pack as I position myself beside the door. I slip during my first attempt to open the door, yet catch my footing and reattempt to pry the door open. The chilling winds circling my body as I exert some effort onto the pry bar cause my teeth to clatter; however, my efforts prove worthwhile as the door flies open and slams against the metal railing beside me.

I drop onto the floor - *using the dumpster facing the rear courtyard as cover* - and grab the rifle before aiming it toward the stairwell in preparation for the *Lockers* to investigate the noise. Hoping the sound went unheard, I feel my stomach drop once muffled footsteps splashing in the small puddles nearly a dozen yards before me fill my ears. Deep breaths accompany the steam radiating from my body as I flick the safety selector on the rifle to *Semi* and slowly place my finger on the trigger.

"What the fuck was that noise?" I hear a male say. The approaching footsteps halt as another set becomes audible in the distance.

"Do you see that flame? Well, so can those on the International Space Station. Now move, or he'll have our asses!" a female shouts aloud. After a brief second of hesitation, the splashing of water transcends into the distance, indicating they're sprinting back toward the vehicles rumbling near the other side of the courtyard. I gradually lift my finger off the trigger while letting out a sigh of relief as my heart rate steadies.

"We need to clear out Section Three and Seventeen before this place comes down. Load up!" another *Locker* shouts before the roar of various engines fills the air, followed by tires spinning out in the puddles below as the group hastily exits the courtyard.

With the rifle resting on my chest, I remain on my back for what feels like an eternity while attentively listening to every sound around me. The cracking of the fire down the block. The rain, which is doing nothing to calm the inferno, is all around. The gunfire in the distance. The sporadic tire screeches on the streets. The feral moans echoing in the night sky. The place sounds like a war zone and is enough to drive anyone mad if they linger in it long enough. After regaining my composure following a few short breaths, I rise to my feet and slowly open the door leading to the rear of the Cafeteria.

* * *

Each footstep is met with a slush as I traverse the dark corridor leading into the Cafeteria. My clothes are soaked, but I push forward toward the commotion from within, nonetheless, as the barrel of the rifle remains pointed ahead. A ferocious banging is coming from the wooden doors at the other end of the Cafeteria. While cautiously peering around the corner, I briefly notice four *Lockers* struggling to secure the front entrance of the gigantic mess hall. Half of them are using their weight to push the large wooden tables in front of the doors, while the other half is propping their bodies against them to ensure they don't fall off their hinges.

"They're pushing in!" one of the *Lockers* shouts while pushing a table that looks heavier than him. The man slips on a yellow puddle, undoubtedly from the carton of Orange Juice resting sideways on the floor; I can only imagine it was spilled following the sudden chaos that ensued just minutes ago.

"You don't *fuckin' say!*" his companion hollers as the glass panels in the door begin to shatter due to the force of nearly a dozen *Specs* on the other side of them. None of them are looking my way. None of them know I'm here.

I clamp the end of the handguard with my pointing finger and thumb before positioning the palm of my hand against the doorframe for stability as I take a large breath. My forearm still hurts from the altercation in the *Overwatch Convoy*, so I try my best not to remain in this position for longer than I need to be. As I exhale, I hold my breath once my lungs are depleted of air and pull the trigger once my sights align with the lower leg of the *Locker* holding the door. He slumps backward, yelling as the doors begin to rattle uncontrollably. As the men try to assess what's going on, I fire at the *Locker* pushing the table as he attempts to grab the shotgun lying on the table.

Bang. Bang. Bang.

As the wall behind him is painted in an oozing red that is slowly dripping downwards in an ominous manner, the other *Locker* grabs the handgun resting in his holster and fires towards the rear of the Cafeteria. I push off the wall and retaliate by sending nearly half a dozen rounds in his direction. One of them seemingly hits him in the collarbone as he drops to his knee in an attempt to apply pressure to the wound. I don't hesitate as I fire two more rounds into his torso.

When the man falls to the ground, I swing the rifle toward one of the last humans standing in the room. As he stands with his back on the wooden doors behind him, his arms remain spread out to maximize how much coverage he has on the shuttering entrance. His eyes are filled with fear, not from what's behind the doors, but rather in front of him: *me*. The kid doesn't look any older than an undergrad at college.

"Sorry, kid…" I say under my breath as I position the weapon's sights at his thigh and pull the trigger. The pink mist that comes out of the exit wound is nearly immediate, and he falls onto the ground alongside his screaming companion. The doors are starting to give way, so I lower my rifle and make my way toward the stoves in the kitchen. I place the rifle upright on the side of the stove and start tampering with the hoses attached to the propane underneath. The smell that the gas lets off is disgusting, but I pay it no mind as I sever the lines for all six stoves. With that done, I rush to the half-opened metal gate that guards the pipes and windows from those who shouldn't have access.

Cmon… Cmon…

The windows facing the rear courtyard are lifted to invite a fresh, cold stream of air into the room. At a quick glance, I notice all cars have been withdrawn from the lot. With the sounds of various vehicles rumbling throughout the streets nearby, it's clear that the *Lockers* are trying to alleviate the situation. Without another second to gather my thoughts, the wooden doors fling open with enough force to startle me. The two incapacitated men on the ground, both of whom are clutching their legs as blood seeps in between their fingers, begin screaming even louder as the realization that their worst fears are about to come to fruition.

Without much delay, a group of Spectrals tear down the set of double doors separating the Cafeteria from the rest of the first floor. As the silhouettes of countless anomalies enter the once vibrant room, they nearly throw themselves onto the ground as they start dismembering the men one piece at a time. The sounds of gurgling from the men as their throats are ripped from their bodies bring me back to my senses. With the infected focused on their current prey, I turn away from the violent mutilation and make my way toward the staircase behind the Cafeteria.

Wasting no time, I grab the rifle and check the magazine as I run for the rear stairwell. The magazine appears to be half-full, so I reinsert it before grabbing the handrail and using it to propel myself upstairs. The lights being out throughout the building helps minimize the *Specs'* aggression, so I slow down after reaching the third floor of the *Consulate*. As I enter the hallway, I look around, half expecting to be met with sentries running around the floor; to my surprise, I am only met with silence as the commotion unfolding throughout the building seems to be on the ground floor.

Alright… please be here…

I place the rifle on the ground and quickly retract the pry bar from my bag as I glance at the elevator door. The Armory was said to be here, so it better be. *I can't take on a group of this size with half a rifle magazine, a Glock, and a revolver.* The bar is propped in between the two metal doors before being pushed with as much force as I can muster. It starts giving way, so I reposition myself to gain more traction on the ground before taking another go at it. The doors make a small gap, enough for me to place my hands through, and I use that opportunity to pull them apart. As they're opened just enough for me to fit in between with ease, I peer into the elevator shaft and notice that the elevator itself is one floor beneath me.

Looking back toward the shadow-ridden corridor once more, I confirm that the coast is clear before carefully lifting myself onto the roof of the elevator below. As my feet land on the surface below, the elevator seems to shake violently but stops within a few seconds as I catch my balance. I lift the elevator hatch before cautiously dropping my rifle into the elevator and following suit. As I land, I turn on my flashlight to get a better view of what's around.

Holy shit…

There are enough guns to outfit an entire battalion for months. Even in such an enclosed space, the amount of firepower this group has access to is both mesmerizing and terrifying. I place the flashlight in my mouth and begin peering around to see what to take. I had forgotten what it felt like to have this many resources, so it's as if I have been granted a gift from above. AR-15s, bolt-action hunting rifles in a variety of calibers, various handguns, and a few semi-automatic shotguns. Even some Pistol Caliber Carbines. My head starts spinning as I notice a familiar-looking gun: *my Kimber.* It has the same scratches it did when I initially lost it three months ago. Even with everything this handgun has witnessed in the past year alone, it seems to have been cleaned recently, judging by the smell of gun oil that fills my nose as I examine the handgun more closely.

I place the Kimber behind my belt before scrounging around to find more 1911-style magazines, then begin replenishing them with loose .45 ACP rounds once I do. The sound of the Kimber chambering a round warms my stomach with feelings of contentment. I glance around and pick up a Benelli M3 before loading it with some 12 gauge buckshot. I chamber a shell before inserting one more into the tube and sling it over my back before picking up the Palmetto State Armory JAKL from the ground; instinctively, I insert a fresh magazine into it before racking the charging handle. As I place a spare 5.56 magazine into my jacket pocket, I look toward the hatch and toss my rifle into the elevator shaft before jumping to climb out of the confined space.

As the elevator shakes slightly due to the commotion, the makeshift tables from within it start to rattle. I hear a metallic *thud* against the floor, causing me to instinctively glance down at what caused the noise. In doing so, I notice something that takes me a few seconds to digest: *a single M87 Hand Grenade*. The thought of such a volatile and destructive device landing carelessly on the floor of a poorly maintained elementary school elevator lingers in my mind longer than it should have. With the white glow emanating from the flashlight pointed at my feet, I release my grip on the hatch and bend my knees slightly to pick up the small yet hefty item. As it rolls around in the palm of my hand, I can't help but smirk before putting it into my other jacket pocket.

That's what I'm talking about... Now, let's get this done.

As I grab onto the ledge of the third floor and glance over, Kimber in hand, I quickly duck down as a trio of *Lockers* barge into the hallway from the rear stairwell where I had come from and begin sprinting toward the front of the *Consulate*. They pay no mind to the half-opened elevator shaft, but I'm not about to complain, considering I am still inside. Unable to comprehend the language they are speaking to one another, I wait for them to pass before pulling myself out of the elevator shaft.

As I crouch down, scanning the desolate halls as best as possible, given the darkness that has consumed them, I begin digging into my jacket pocket until I get a firm grip on the M87. Even in the dark, I can make out the silver pin keeping the device disarmed. Although slightly hesitant about the idea, I forcefully yank the pin out and extend my hand until the grenade is dangling directly above the aerial opening to the elevator. As my hand releases the device, I hear the spoon being flung from the grenade as it falls into the weapon-filled abyss below. Without as much as a second to think, I practically throw myself on the ground and hold my hands over my ears as I get into a fetal position.

The explosion is smaller than I had anticipated, but the severance of the elevator cables and the sound of the once cramped space falling three stories vibrate the entire building. I wait a second or two once the debris from the elevator shaft erupts through the slightly opened doors before getting up and grabbing the rifle near my feet. Once I've confirmed that the rifle is loaded, I open the door leading to the stairwell and start climbing, climbing toward uncertainty. One thing is certain, though: *whatever happens next will be forged in history forever.*

* * *

"Get me in touch with the Exterior Patrols…" I hear Graham command as I inch closer to the fifth-floor gym he's hiding in. The sounds of murmurs within the room indicate he has a lot of armed guards with him; seeing as though he is arguably the most influential person within the group, that is to be expected. As I position myself beside the thick wooden door, I hear one of Graham's men respond to him after a moment of slight hesitation.

"Sir, w- we've had no radio contact with the patrols since they converged onto the horde nearly fifteen minutes ago-" the *Locker* says before being interrupted.

"Then go secure this floor in preparation for an assault!" Graham declares as the various sounds of firearm manipulation echo throughout the hallway. "And Cyrus, find out where the *fuck* Luca is. I want him here, *now!*" he barks out with slight aggravation.

"Y- yes, sir," the *Locker* responds before charging toward the front entrance of the gym. I duck inside one of the open classrooms near the entrance and kneel behind the door just as the man in question bolts into the hallway. Even as the *Locker* sprints out of sight, holding a rifle that swings ferociously with every step, I am surprised at how scrawny he is, given the deep voice he had displayed just seconds ago. After glancing down the hall to ensure the coast is clear, I stand up and slowly approach the entrance to the gym. The chatter amongst the group from within seems to get louder as the mayhem around them continues to grow. I find myself shaking with fear as the thought of what lies ahead festers in my head. I take a few deep breaths while gripping the door handle with one hand and keep my rifle lifted with my other.

Inhale… Exhale… Inhale… Exhale…

As I yank the door open, everyone in the room glances in my direction; their guards are up, but they are still caught by surprise. Within milliseconds, I take a mental note of the six or seven guys within the room, and I don't give any of them a chance to retaliate as I begin discharging the rifle at whoever my closest target is.

Bang.

The walls within the room begin to illuminate as the flashes coming from the end of my muzzle paint the walls with the silhouettes of those standing in the gym; each subsequent round makes my ears ring more than the last. Within a moment's notice, one of the *Lockers* falls to the ground suddenly, as does the one closest to him. Various wooden crates are strewn throughout the room; I can only imagine these to be the excess resources forcefully procured from the innocent groups who were once considered friends. From the very people who had families here. To the people who *were* family. As everyone in the room raises their barrels in my direction, I dash behind one of the wooden crates just in time to hear the ricochets zip over my head.

"Yeah, did you think this was over, motherfucker?!" I shout over the gunfire. I can barely hear my own thoughts, so I'm not too sure Graham heard what I said; that is, until I hear him respond once the gunfire subsided.

"*Goddamn!* Now *that's* an entrance!" I hear Graham yell once the room is nearly silent. "*This* is the Miles I have been waiting to see-" he shouts before firing a shot at me as I peek over the crate for a better view of his location. "The one who had the *balls* to put his foot down-" he says before firing again, forcing me to keep my head down. "The *"legend"* who created an empire of weak-minded people. People who didn't have what it took to live up to their own name! *Thrivers?!* What a fuckin' joke!" he shouts before firing another shot at the wooden crate.

"Talk all you want, you piece of shit! You don't have enough people to stop what happens next!" I holler while inserting a new magazine into the rifle. As rounds seep into the thick wooden material around me, it's as if I'm getting more splinters by the second. Once the rifle's bolt is sent forward, I bring the weapon around the corner and begin firing blindly. I keep shooting until they start returning fire. Out of instinct, the rifle drops to the floor. The *Lockers* in the room are moving closer, and I glance around for an opportunity without picking up my head.

"Oh, we *both know* you aren't walking away from this one..." Graham says as he lets out a whistle. I can't see him, but I assume he's issuing an order for the others to flank me; the footsteps a dozen yards or so to my left pause briefly, then resume in a different direction after a second or two. I unsling the M3 and flick the safety off before shouldering the weapon.

"*Nobody* here is walking away," I mutter as I peek around the corner and fire at a Fire Extinguisher on the wall facing the rear courtyard. The explosion causes me to jolt backward slightly, but I catch my footing before peering over the other side of the crate and aiming at the head of one of the *Lockers*; with all the chemical foam in his eyes, he fails to notice me until it is too late.

Bang.

The recoil isn't as noticeable as the stump left behind after the *Locker's* head seemingly disappears within a split second of the trigger breaking. I use the momentum from the shotgun blast to kneel above the crate and gain a brief sight picture of Graham. He dives behind another crate near the rear stairwell as the shotgun is discharged. The buckshot makes various impact points on the wood, yet I'm not sure they perforated the material. I quickly duck back down as his bodyguards begin unleashing a hailstorm of bullets toward my location.

With the white particles still looming in the air and spreading throughout the room with each passing moment, I wait for a temporary ceasefire before bolting toward another crate propped up on a wooden pallet close to my attackers. Even with my hearing in disarray, I can tell that my footsteps are quiet as the powder beneath my feet absorbs most of the sound. With the mix of concealment and nearly inaudible movement, the *Lockers* are unaware I had moved my position; this is confirmed once they resume their assault on the wooden crate I was crouching behind merely seconds ago.

"Take notes, gents! We have a great teacher in our presence! I'll be honest, though, Miles… your clever little ideas… it's not going to be enough," Graham says before I raise the Benelli in his direction, causing him to duck behind the crate once more as I fire.

I transition my aim toward the last two *Lockers* and begin as their gazes turn toward me. Trying my best not to close my eyes as the shotgun is discharged, I miss a few rounds before a set of buckshot connects with the upper torso of one of the assailants. I turn the gun to the other *Locker* and fire before he gets an opportunity to react. The man falls to the ground as the all-so-familiar-looking pink mist fills the air behind him; even with such an adrenaline rush, there is a sharp pain radiating from my ear as a warm stream of blood immediately seeps down the left side of my head.

Ah… My ear! Motherfucker!

Still crouched, I jump over the crate and sprint to where the shooter is firing from behind. The *Locker* who shot me is struggling to breathe as one of the buckshots seems to have pierced his throat; I consider it an act of mercy as I bring the shotgun up to his temple and pull the trigger. The metallic taste of blood seems to replace every particle of air around me as his body lies there, motionless. My face is dripping with blood, but I look up, seemingly unfazed, in Graham's direction. With the shotgun out of ammunition, I throw it to the ground and remove the Kimber from my waist before flipping the safety off.

"I should've killed you when I met you!" I holler as I eject the magazine to double-check it's full.

"Yeah, you should have. Maybe your friends and your little girl-friend would still be alive-" Graham proclaims before I stand up and start walking in his direction. With both hands gripping the Kimber, I fire a round with each step I take. He lets out incomprehensible profanities with every shot that rings out. In my anger, I lost track of the number of rounds I had fired and am, instead, graciously met with the slide in the locked position: *out of ammo*.

Shit...

Standing nearly twenty feet away with no cover in sight, I grab one of the corpses on the floor and lift it in front of me as Graham pushes off of the crate he was previously using for protection. He turns his handgun to me, the chrome body of which is considerably noticeable even with the lack of light within the room, and begins firing; most of his shots impact his deceased comrade's body. The weight of the corpse, which seems to be compounding with each blow, forces my legs to give out from under me and fall backward as the body lands on top of me. As a result of such vulnerability, one of the rounds hits the side of my calve, causing me to wince in pain as Graham continues his advance. Within a few seconds of continuous gunfire, I hear the unmistakable *click* that is accompanied by a firearm failing to lock the slide to the rear once it is out of ammunition.

With this realization, I quickly eject the empty magazine from the Kimber, using gravity to let it fall to the ground next to me, as Graham does the same. While on the ground, I fumble into my pocket to grab a spare magazine with the weight of the *Locker's* body still pressing down on me before raising both the gun and the magazine over my head so I can gain more room for the reload. As the magazine is inserted and a round is chambered, I hear Graham release the slide of his handgun. With one fell swoop, we both swing our guns toward one another and let our shots ring out simultaneously.

Bang.

I don't know what happened. I don't know who fired first. Did I hit him? Hell, did he hit *me?* My heart is racing, and it isn't until I hear Graham's gun drop to the floor that I realize he's injured. He spits up blood, which spatters all over the ground in front of him as he stumbles backward before landing on the ground a few yards away. The round I fired had hit him in the head, but I can't tell where. I break my gaze and let out a shout as I do my best to push the remains of Graham's former subordinate off me; with blood and energy slowly depleting from my body, the corpse feels as though it has the same weight as a motorcycle. With the *Locker's* corpse rolling onto the floor beside me, I push myself to my feet and ignore the crimson vitality seeping from my leg and ear as I limp toward Graham; he continues to roll around on the ground while simultaneously beginning to choke on his own blood.

For the first time, I *finally* know what Graham looks like when genuinely alone and helpless. Even when isolated in his cell all those months ago, this bastard couldn't help but carry an arrogant demeanor that just spelled trouble; yet here, at this very moment, he *actually* looks afraid. As Graham breaks his gaze from me, he crawls toward the .357 Desert Eagle he had undoubtedly grown attached to. This was the weapon he had used to execute the girl on the roof a few days ago. As he inches closer to it, I can't help but imagine how his victims looked as if they were on the other side of that barrel.

"Go ahead… Grab it," I instruct in a suggestive yet slightly sarcastic tone. After casually tucking the Kimber behind my belt near my lower back, I grab the revolver from my faded black shoulder holster. He doesn't even seem to acknowledge my statement as he continues crawling toward the weapon without any deviation in his body language. Blood is trickling from his cheek, and a portion of his jaw is hanging. His odds of survival are already minimal, yet his incessant slithering on the ground leaves a red blood trail that only worsens his condition. As he begins to reach for the handgun, I align my sights with his fingers and pull the trigger. Three of his fingers are severed in one swift shot, which is accompanied by an ear-shattering screech soon after as Graham clutches his fingers with his other hand.

"*That*… was for me…" I say as I bring my hand up to reveal the stump where my fingers used to rest before Damien's interrogation, directly caused by the man lying before me. He continues to clutch his hand before slowly looking up at me. I kick out his leg and align the barrel of the revolver with Graham's knee before firing once again. The blood that expels from his wound lands all over the place as he rolls around on the ground to alleviate the pain.

"*That* was for David…" I whisper as the ringing in my ears continues. As he lays on his back, I step on his head slowly and bring the gun up to his stomach before firing another shot. The bullet seems to have expanded within his stomach, as no exit wound is visible once he rolls onto his stomach. His cries for help seem to be diminishing as the pain is compounded.

"*That* was for your brother. For Derrick…" I mutter as I pull the hammer back on the revolver. At this moment in time, he isn't even attempting to escape. His previously futile attempts to do so have only made the situation worse, so he lies still with his torso rising and falling with each breath he struggles to take. With his bloodied cheek resting along the dusty wooden floor, I bring the weapon up to the back of his head as he closes his eyes in submission.

"And *this*… this is for everyone else," I say with unwavering conviction. With my finger resting on the trigger, the thought of everyone he has directly or indirectly inflicted pain onto enters my head at supersonic speed as the sound of banging echoes from down the hall. Within seconds, the cracking of wood is soon replaced with the agonizing moans of countless *Specs* turning the corner and stumbling toward where all of the noise had been coming from: *toward the gym*. I stand there with the gun still pointed at my immobile adversary as an idea comes to mind.

"Y- y- you… w- will not make it out of h- here, Miles…" Graham says while glancing at me with his peripherals. Although he's not able to lift his head from the ground due to his weakened state, Graham lets off a devious smirk that is reflected in the dark puddle of blood pooling around him.

"Maybe. But neither will you," I say as the revolver's hammer is decocked. I limp toward the west wall of the gym facing the sidewalk and shoot the lock to the gate separating us from the windows. At such proximity, the bullet ricochets and forces me to wince; the door creaks open just as I turn around to see the *Specs* stumbling into the gym. With as much effort as he could find from within, Graham pushes himself onto his back and glares at the starving threats approaching him. While digging through my pack, I pull out the flare gun and slowly lift it until the sights are aligned with Graham.

Control…

Almost as if everything unfolds in slow motion, the flare impacts Graham with incredible force, engulfing him in flames as his clothing catches fire. The screams that follow sound inhumane, even for someone with Graham's stature, and the sudden illumination attracts the attention of every *Spectral* in the area. Without so much as a care in the world, the flesh-eating humanoids begin piling on top of the burning man, causing the size of the fire to grow with each body added to it. I can't begin to describe the sounds filling the air. The smell of decay and burning flesh is even worse than anything I had ever experienced.

Turning my head from the growing inferno, I shimmy between the heat pipes before slamming the metal door in front of me. With the lock having been destroyed, I know it won't remain locked. With the light from the fire stirring up some of the other *Spectrals* in the room, the ones who aren't participating in Graham's mutilation let out a wretched shriek as they begin shuffling toward me. Without much thought, I start unraveling the paracord bracelet around my wrist. I had always worn it, even in the military, because we were taught how it could always come in handy if the right opportunity presented itself. I guess this proves it. I insert one of the loose ends through the metal slot in the gate before yanking it and tying the other end tight. I create a knot strong enough to hold the door shut as the feeling of false safety temporarily grants me some satisfaction; I nearly slide down the wall as my back is brought up against it.

There's about two feet of space between me and the monsters propping themselves against the thin metal gate standing tall an arm's length ahead. This is the first time I've ever been face to face with a *Spec* for this long, so I can't help but notice something: *their eyes*. They're a nearly transparent, milky white resembling an authentic white pearl; although I had not noticed that before, they don't seem as lifeless as I had once expected. With the fireball near the middle of the gym becoming snuffed out due to the plethora of bodies piling on top of it, I get a better visual of the infected in front of me as their aggression gradually diminishes. There is no hatred or resentment in them, no anger or spite. They seem… *lost*, like a deer that turns to look at a hunter who stepped on a branch nearby. In any case, one thing is clear: *I need to get out of here.*

I place my bag against my leg and start rummaging through the contents inside; a thin stream of blood begins oozing from underneath the material of my dark cargo pants, creating tiny crimson dots on the wood floorboards below. I feel a spare cartridge for the flare gun and use the dwindling light to my advantage as I insert it into the weapon once it's opened. After tucking the flare gun behind the front of my belt, I take the Kimber and carefully place it in the bag; after glancing around the gloomy room, nodding as if taking pride in what was just accomplished over the past few minutes, I zip the bag shut and nearly strain my shoulder as I stand to put it on my back.

Glancing over to the window, I pry it open, instinctively letting out a grunt of pain while I do so, and peer out to look below. With the small amount of light from the rising sun above, it's easy to make out the carnage that has unfolded before me. The spent bullet casings are strewn around the concrete below. Corpses, unmoving and otherwise, litter the sidewalks. The engines of various vehicles idle on the sidewalks. Blood spattered along every crevice I could lay my eyes on. There is only one word that I can use to describe the immeasurable disarray plaguing the streets accurately: *War.*

I turn to face the rooftop above and notice it's within reach. If I can prop my body on the windowsill without plummeting five stories to my death, my chances of getting out of this are still marginal at best, considering the wear I feel on my body, but I have to try. I tighten the straps on my bag before extending an arm out of the window and propelling myself onto the edge of it. Doing my best to refrain from looking down, especially with the breeze hitting the back of my neck only heightening my paranoia, I grab onto one of the exposed bricks on the *Consulate's* outer wall and lift myself as much as possible. Before I know it, I'm standing straight up alongside the exterior wall of the building.

This is insane. This is crazy...

With my eyes glued to the ledge above, I try to leverage myself onto it before noticing it's *just* high enough to be out of reach, merely inches away. With the excessive gusts of wind around me, I take a few deep breaths before bending my knees and using all the force I can muster to jump toward the ledge above. Even with eight fingers and a substantial amount of sweat built up in my palms, I find myself letting out a relief-ridden chuckle as I grip the roof's edge. Not wanting to fumble and lose my grasp, I do my best to stabilize my body before attempting to pull myself up. As I reach around with my support hand, I hear the sound of groaning that my entire organization has grown to dread over the past year. I can't tell where it's coming from, but it doesn't take long to figure it out as a sharp pain erupts from my left hand.

Ah! What the fuck...

I quickly retract my hard as best as possible without letting go of my grip on the ledge before pulling myself up slightly and noticing the periodic jaw movement of a severed head resting just inches in front of me. A *familiar*-looking severed head: *It's Derrick.* His head, along with a few others that I can't positively identify, is lying on the rooftop with blood-stained ropes attached to his dark, unkempt hair. His ivory-shaded eyes are filled with the same sense of loss I had seen in the other *Spectral* just minutes ago. With the pain in my hand still at the forefront of my mind, I glance over to it and realize one of my worst fears was about to become a reality.

Oh, Christ...

Even as my grip is getting weaker every second, my eyes remain fixated on the various puncture marks on my left hand. Small yet infectious incisions caused by an excessive bite force are slowly spilling blood onto the roof above. The revelation causes a moment of hesitation, but I can't afford to wait any longer: *I need to get onto the roof.*

With all of the agonizing moans below me, both in the streets and within the putrid-smelling room I had just escaped from, I can't help but feel a warm blanket of relief cover my body from head to toe as I pull myself onto the rooftop. My feet start pushing my body away from the edge as I lie on my back, trying to catch a breath or two in the process. A moment of sorrow enters my mind as I grip my left hand tightly. With Graham dead, the realization that I had done the impossible, especially given the odds against me, overwhelms me. I begin to let out a few tears as my half-painful laugh fills the moist air above. Still, it doesn't *feel* like I achieved anything other than a temporary solution to a lifelong dilemma.

With my jacket soaking up all the water on the ground from the rain, which has since stopped, I lift my upper body with an audible grunting. Transitioning my gaze to Derrick, whose mouth is consistently opening and closing as nearly inaudible groans fill the air, I use my forearms to position myself in his direction. Even with the moisture overhead, my eyes begin to water as the thought of my closet friend being put on display, like some twisted Christmas ornament, floats around in my head. Seconds seemingly turn to minutes as I sit there staring at what remains of the man I once considered family.

Every ounce of being within my body pushes me to do what's right, but for the first time in a long time, I find myself struggling to maintain control of my emotions. Hesitation takes the wheel once I start reaching for my knife. My right hand is shaking ferociously as I do, and even with the blade hovering over the side of Derrick's head, I find myself desperately searching for support one final time.

"I'm so- I'm so sorry..." I whisper to Derrick, unsure if he can hear my words as they leave my shivering lips. With the knife shaking in the air, I use my bloodied support hand to stabilize the trembling in my other before forcefully bringing the blade down onto the side of Derrick's skull. The movement of his jaw seems to cease almost instantly as he lets out his final breath. "I'm sorry. I'm sorry. I'm sorry," I repeat over and over again as I place a hand on the top of his now motionless head. I can feel the tears running down my face as the words echo throughout the desolate rooftop.

Forgive me…

My breathing finally becomes more relaxed as a stream of cold air enters the atmosphere once I exhale. After a few minutes of sulking in the ambiance surrounding the ever-brightening horizon near the South, I place the palm of my hand onto the cold shingles below and lift myself onto my feet with one fell swoop. My legs start to tremble, yet I catch my balance as I glance at the beautiful sunrise ahead.

For the continuation of a good-

I jolt forward and stumble to my knees as a sharp pain emerges from my neck. Out of pure instinct, I try to take a breath, only to be met with a mouth full of blood as I do so. I slowly turn my head to glance behind me as I begin choking on the thick metallic substance flooding my throat. Even with my vision becoming more blurred with each failed attempt to breathe, I notice two silhouettes emerging from the entrance of the rooftop. The sound of footsteps splashing in the puddles below becomes louder with every step taken in my direction.

"We've gotta stop meeting like this, Miles!" a man shouts as his arms extend to his side in a hubris manner. My body slumps forward as I soon find myself on my stomach, crawling forward just as Graham had done minutes prior. In my weakened state, I still recognize the voice fostering a distinctive, authoritative tone accompanied by years of military experience.

"*Luca!*" I holler as loud as my blood-filled lungs would allow before hurling an abnormal amount of the crimson substance to my side. The thought of standing, or even sitting upright, is out of the realm of possibility; all I can do is use one hand to apply pressure to my wound as I continue to crawl toward the edge of the roof facing the rear courtyard with the other. Crawling toward what I had been prepared for over the past few weeks. Crawling towards my *death*.

"You see what I'm talking about, Cyrus?" Luca says to the man standing a few feet beside him. I reach the roof's edge and slump over until I can see the concrete below. My vision continues to pull in and out of clarity as I notice how vacant the rear courtyard is. No vehicles. No *Lockers*. Nothing other than a bleak and ominous darkness to accompany the pain and misery I'm feeling. While on my stomach, I reach toward the front of my belt as my other hand remains on my neck to stop the blood loss. *To no avail.* "Even *legends* can bleed…" Luca says as a plastic magazine hitting the floor echoes throughout the air.

Without looking, I can hear Luca fumbling with another magazine as he attempts to replenish his rifle. From my peripherals, I see Cyrus, the same scrawny guy who had run past me before my standoff with Graham in the gym, with a rifle of his own as he stands beside my former ally. Given the loss of feeling in my fingers, I grip the flare gun as tight as I can and slump over the edge of the roof a little more.

"They can die, too…" *Sandman* says as he inserts the magazine into his rifle and hits the slide release button. As he raises his rifle, I do the same with the flare gun before firing in the direction of the cafeteria windows. With as much violence as can be expected, given the proximity, the roof shakes ferociously as the flare ignites the propane radiating from within the kitchen five stories below on the other side of the building. The heat from the explosion is felt nearly instantaneously as the men before me begin to stumble once the entire cafeteria disintegrates within milliseconds.

As the two men do their best to catch their footing, I release the tension on my neck and push myself onto my back while retracting the 1911 from the small of my lower back. I do my best to align the iron sights as the handgun is raised in front of me. My eyes lock with *Sandman's* as a .45 ACP bullet pierces the upper portion of his head, killing him instantly. Without much time to react, I transition the weapon to Cyrus before gripping the gun with both hands; as I hastily stabilize the trembling in my hands accompanied by the excessive blood loss, I pull the trigger as the remaining *Locker* begins raising his rifle.

Bang. Silence.

Besides the crackling from the fire down below presenting itself to the entire borough, the silence that follows as Cyrus and *Sandman's* bodies fall idly to the ground is unsettling. A squirt of blood protruding from my neck causes me to instinctively drop the handgun and reapply pressure to the wound once more. In a futile attempt at survival, I know my chances of doing so are diminishing as the blood in my body is depleting one ounce at a time. Even with the thought of seeing my family again looming over my head like a fresh berry just out of reach, that is, anyone left to be considered family, I knew that Graham was right. For once, I'm afraid of the inevitable; my death is imminent, and nothing in the present moment can convince me otherwise.

I... I...

With my upper back propped against the small lip of the roof, I release my hand from my wound. Bloodied and wet, I finally understand what it feels like to be truly alone. As the feeling in my fingers withers away, my toes ultimately follow suit. After a few seconds, I can't move any of my limbs, but I realize I'm not afraid anymore; for the first time, I also know what it feels like to live.

It wasn't for nothing... I...

As my breathing becomes slower, I glance at the sky above until there's only one thing left to embrace—the only thing that lies ahead for me: *darkness.*

EPILOGUE

"KEEP UP, KID," I SAY to Vito, who is loosely following suit as he and I traverse the everlasting morbid streets of the Bronx. With our truck having blown its transmission during our commute down the Sawmill, we've been traveling on foot for the better part of an afternoon. Considering we haven't eaten in a few hours, we try to conserve our energy as best as possible by catching some breaks every half mile.

"I am…" Vito retaliates with a little bit of attitude. It's understandable, maybe even justifiable, given the fact that we're both in a state of mental anguish. With ammunition at a minimum and our food at critical portions, I can't help but feel a sense of relief that presents itself once we manage to lay our eyes on a familiar building: *The Consulate*. Vito and I nearly fall to our knees at the sight of our former home, but I almost vomit as I examine it further.

"Oh my God…" I mutter as smoke radiates from various parts of the building. As the sun hits each nook and cranny of the building, it becomes apparent that there's no one nearby. No one to greet us. No one to defend against intruders. Against *us*. I'm shell-shocked at the carnage that has unfolded before us. An immeasurable number of corpses litter the streets, and there are various armored vehicles strewn around the block, some of which are still humming as they remain idle in place as if what occurred was fresh. The damage to the structure, ranging from various bullet holes and scorch marks to blood spatter, is nothing short of appalling.

What the hell happened here?

"Here, take this… " Vito whispers to deaf ears. I can't break my gaze from the chaos ahead. The thought of the *Thrivers* who once lived here, people I called friends, is nearly too much to bear as their faces flood my memory. "Corver…" he says again as he tugs on my dirty flannel sweater.

"Huh, yeah… okay. Thanks, kid," I say as I grab the sawed-off double-barrel shotgun he had handed me. The weapon looks old, but it's still in excellent condition. I kneel and break open the action to discover the shells inside haven't been fired, so I shut the weapon before retracting both hammers and standing back on my two feet.

"You see these?" I ask sarcastically to a crouched Vito, who's stripping the rounds from a 9mm magazine he ejected from a handgun previously lying on the ground. He looks up at me as he places the small handful of bullets into his backpack. "These are called *heels*, and I want you to stay close to them as we go inside. Do you understand me?" I say as I gesture for him to stand.

"Okay," he says in a whisper.

I transition my body towards the *Consulate* and contort my shoulders slightly, primarily due to the cold but also the fear of what lies inside, before nodding and pushing forward. Forward toward an uncertain future, without so much as a glance at the distant past. I don't know what happened here. I don't know what will happen from this moment onward. The only thing I can be certain of is that we will never be the same after today. I can feel it… No matter what happens now, I know there's more to come. We will always take the extra step to ensure we do more than what the other guy thinks is possible. Vito and I are not going to survive. We've come too far to merely *get by*. No, we're going to *Thrive*.